DYING TO MEET YOU

ALSO BY SARINA BOWEN

The Five Year Lie

DYING TO MEET YOU

SARINA BOWEN

HARPER PERENNIAL

NEW YORK • LONDON • TORONTO • SYDNEY • NEW DELHI • AUCKLAND

HARPER PERENNIAL

HarperCollins books may be purchased for educational, business, or sales promotional use. For information, please email the Special Markets Department at SPsales@harpercollins.com.

FIRST EDITION

Designed by Jen Overstreet

Library of Congress Cataloging-in-Publication Data has been applied for.

ISBN 978-0-06-328064-9 (pbk.)
ISBN 978-0-06-344210-8 (simultaneous hardcover)

25 26 27 28 29 LBC 5 4 3 2 1

For my sons.
Thank you for sharing your location with me,
so I could think up the terrifying plot of this book.

1

THURSDAY

ROWAN

My favorite college professor used to say that the best thing about being an architect is that no two days are alike. "On Monday you're wearing a hard hat to inspect a building site, on Tuesday you're touring a client's newly acquired estate, and on Wednesday you're drafting at your desk."

He failed to mention that on Thursday you'll be frantically vacuuming mouse droppings off that desk.

"Enough already," I mutter, jabbing the vacuum's brush attachment at my keyboard. "This is disgusting."

Beatrice—who, in spite (or perhaps because) of her antique name, is my younger, hipper colleague—shuts off the vacuum and takes it from me without a word. I think she can tell how strung out I feel today. How close to the edge.

And our boss is arriving at any moment.

"We need bigger traps," I mutter. "I saw some at the hardware store."

Beatrice shakes her perfectly straightened blond hair. "Wouldn't help. These mice aren't large—they're just entitled. Here."

She hands me a packet of disinfectant wipes, which I tear open immediately. "But I want revenge."

"Babe, I want a martini and a ninety-minute massage. But we're getting a meeting with Hank instead." She grabs a wipe, nudges me out of the way, and disinfects my desk blotter more efficiently than I'd done it myself. "I think I heard the car outside. Go stall him?"

"Sure. Okay." I grab my clipboard and go, my heels clicking on the newly refinished hardwood floors as I leave our makeshift office and cross through the library.

The moment my contractors finished the mansion's structural renovation, Beatrice and I adopted this space on the first floor, which we plan to use for the remainder of the construction project. Both the library and the historic Wincott office—now *our* office—have hand-carved moldings and trompe l'oeil ceilings. Plus, we can seal off the library on days when the contractors are making a lot of noise on the property.

It's a heck of a lot nicer than the construction trailer we'd been using before.

As I stride past a gilded mirror in the corridor, I check my outfit. Blouse, heels, a pencil skirt. Makeup. At least I remembered to put in some effort this morning.

Hank Wincott—our boss—always looks like a million dollars, probably because his family has billions. The Wincotts are the oldest, most successful Maine family that I can name. They first staked their claim on Portland in 1805, when a shipbuilding ancestor built a modest brick home on this property. Then, in 1860, Amos Wincott—the architect of the family—expanded that home into the mansion that stands here today.

A century and a half later, my role is to burnish the Wincott legacy and preserve this property for a new generation of Mainers. I'm six months into a two-year contract as the architect of the project. It's a job I fought for, because I'm excellent with the details of restoration.

Client meetings, though? Not so much.

In the atrium, I pass the elaborate curving staircase, where dappled light filters down from a blue-and-gold skylight thirty-odd feet above my head. When I reach the foyer, I grasp the front door's oversize brass knob and twist it. The door is heavy, and I have to hold on tightly to prevent the salty Maine breeze from yanking it out of my hand.

It's a surprisingly warm day for early June, and the sunlight in my eyes is a shock after the mansion's shadowy interior. Once my vision adjusts, I see a shiny black Jaguar parked beside the house.

Hank Wincott leans against the passenger side, his phone to his ear. He tilts his strong jaw in greeting but lifts a finger in the universal sign for "just a minute." He's obviously finishing up a call with someone more important than me.

Honestly, I'm a little fuzzy on the details of how Hank spends his workdays. His older brother is the CEO of their global shipping corporation, while Hank is some kind of finance guy. He manages his family's investments and also runs the Wincott Charitable Foundation.

Twenty years ago, Hank and I were in the same class at the expensive private high school where I now send my daughter. He was a popular party boy. If Chatham Prep had been large enough to have a prom king, he would have been a shoo-in.

I was a nerd, so our social circles didn't overlap much. But everyone knew everyone at Chatham. The connection certainly helped me get this job—Hank said as much when he gave it to me.

I retreat back inside the house, making sure to leave the door unlocked. In the atrium, I lean against a hand-carved pilaster, lifting my gaze slowly upward, as the original architect had intended. Amos definitely had visitors' awe in mind when he designed this space. He wanted them to be wowed by the elaborate staircase, which coils, serpentlike, up to the second and third floors. The upper levels of the house form a gallery, with every upstairs room opening onto the U-shaped open corridors.

Tilting my head back at a severe angle, I can finally make out the details of the ornate stained-glass window shimmering from the top floor. It's 160 years old, and done up in a wave pattern of blues and golds with the Wincott family symbol in the center—a *W* styled like a trident.

Ocean imagery is everywhere in the mansion, because the Wincotts made their first fortune in shipbuilding. If I try hard enough, I can picture Portland's leading nineteenth-century citizens in their dinner jackets, climbing the staircase toward the smoking room upstairs.

It's all very beautiful. This commission is a big moment in my career. But it's not an easy job. Parts of the house are so ornate that I'm struggling to merge twenty-first-century design elements into the floor plan, and all those handmade fixtures are blowing up my budget.

Then there's the ghost. Some of our contractors think a woman haunts the place. They say they've heard her crying. I haven't. Not yet, anyway. But if I had to make a bet on which old mansion in Portland is haunted, I'd put my chips on this one.

A sudden breeze tells me that the front door has been opened again. "Rowan?"

"Right here," I call and step into the foyer.

He shuts the door and turns to me, all shiny shoes and gabardine wool and perfectly straight teeth. "Sorry I'm late."

"It's no problem," I say, giving him what I hope is an energetic smile and a firm handshake.

"How are you?" he asks as we cross into the atrium.

It's not a serious question. He doesn't want to hear that I'm barely holding it together. It's not his problem that I'm spiraling from a breakup. So I hold my smile. "I'm doing great."

"Glad to hear it." He glances around, as if checking for any new details since the last time he stopped by. The mansion is Hank's ancestral home, although he never lived here. The family decamped in the forties to a newer, grander compound in a more private location up the coast.

In the decades afterward, the property was used as a home for unwed mothers—with the charming name the Magdalene Home for Wayward Girls—until the home closed down in the late eighties.

Now we're in the process of converting it into a brand-new cultural institution: the Wincott Center for Maritime Heritage. It will be part museum and part educational center. The ground floor will serve as an event space and contain exhibits of maritime history. Upstairs will feature meeting rooms and offices. And out in back, I'm constructing a new-age lecture hall.

It's a good gig. A career-making commission. Except I'm horribly behind schedule and over budget.

"Hey there, Hank!" Beatrice sweeps into the atrium wearing a smile that's far less stilted than mine. She and our boss have worked together for years, and it shows. "Big shame about the game last night."

His eyes crinkle at the corners as he takes a performative glance at his watch. "Seven seconds. That's how long I was in the building before you decided to rub it in."

She spreads her graceful arms in mock disbelief. "If you don't want to talk about the Sox losing, maybe don't bet on the Sox?"

"Fine, fine." He pulls a handsome leather wallet out of his trouser pocket, plucks a crisp $10 bill out of it, and passes it to Beatrice. "Can we talk about the floor plan now? Or did I just come here to be humiliated?"

Beatrice pockets the cash. "I'll leave you to it. Find me afterward for an update on the construction schedule."

"Will do." He turns to me. "Now let's see this wall painting that's causing all the trouble."

"Of course. Follow me." I lead him up the grand staircase to the second floor. Given the lofty ceilings in this place, it's quite a climb. "I know you've earmarked the Blue Room for the director's office. But I need to show you what the conservators did in there. It's very impressive."

"It ought to be, after a two-month delay," he says.

I cringe. Privately.

Hank already knows how the conservators work—an inch at a time, with cotton balls and Q-tips. He should be grateful they rearranged their work schedule to prioritize the mansion as soon as we'd discovered additional hand-painted walls throughout the second story.

Hank is a charming man, but he's not a patient one.

On the second floor, we follow the curve of the gallery toward the front of the house. I step aside to let Hank enter the Blue Room first. Then I follow him, temporarily blinded by the glint of the afternoon sunshine off Casco Bay.

The room is empty and echoey, but it was once a guest bedroom with an elegant four-poster bed, hand-knotted rugs from Scotland, and curtains from France. Those furnishings were removed decades ago, but the scale of the room still gives a sense of grandeur. The ceiling height tells you straightaway that Amos Wincott had an ego. And the walls? Astonishing. They were painted by an artisan brought over from Italy.

Behind me, Hank whistles under his breath. "No wonder this took so long."

I turn around so I can admire the largest interior wall, unbroken by windows or a door. It took the conservators weeks of work to reveal several figures from Greek mythology. The centerpiece shows the sea god Poseidon, who turns up everywhere in the mansion. This particular scene depicts him with his wife, a mermaid-like nymph named Amphi-trite. She's coiled around her husband, her bare breast plumped against his chest. Their ardor is unmistakable.

"All the upstairs murals are horny," my favorite conservator pointed out last week. "There's really no other word for it."

I keep that observation to myself as Hank moves closer to squint at the brushstrokes. "Can't believe they were able to uncover this. No wonder they're so expensive."

"They do impressive work," I agree.

But it's a shame they needed to. For seventy years, this lush imagery has been hidden under a layer of cheap house paint. Sometime in the 1950s, one of Hank's uncles—Marcus Wincott—decided to cover the walls in a dull shade of beige.

Marcus had a different kind of Wincott ego. He was a religious man who probably thought that frolicking Greek gods were too scandalous for the pregnant girls who took refuge here.

So he'd painted over everything. He also broke some of the bedrooms into a rabbit warren of smaller rooms, forcing my demolition crew to painstakingly remove lots of slapdash drywall before the art restorers could even begin their work of rescuing the hidden paintings.

More than once I've stood here thinking: *The balls on these guys.*

"It's very ornate," Hank says now. "Organic. Colorful."

"Agreed," I say. And then I hold back my gasp as he reaches out and *runs his fingertips* across an 1860 masterwork.

Seriously, the balls on these guys.

"But it complicates the floor plan," Hank says. "That's the issue, right?"

"Right. Our plan had a wall right here." I indicate a spot that's in the center of another mural panel—this one depicting Poseidon's horses. "We can't unveil a rare work of art and then chop it in half."

He frowns, possibly wondering why we can't do exactly that. When you're as rich as Hank, you can usually do as you please. "The director needs this space. And he'll need to be separated from his assistant by a wall."

That's what I was afraid he'd say. "Can you tell me why it has to be *this* room? If we put the director's office in the next room . . ."

He's already shaking his head. "It's the ocean view. Donors are going to sit right here"—he indicates a place on the floor—"and look at this view. They'll contemplate the majesty of the ocean and our history upon it. And then they will open their wallets. The director needs to occupy the grandest space. It's all about posturing."

My heart sags. I don't care to live in a world that's all about posturing. Yet here we are.

Hank's phone rings. He checks the screen, and I expect him to silence the phone. Instead—without a word of apology—he takes the call. "Hey, Mack! What do you have for me?"

Great.

Giving Hank privacy, I leave the room and tap on the door of the neighboring one.

"Enter!" comes a female voice from inside the room I'm calling the West Room on my floor plan.

I open the door to reveal Zoya, the younger of our two conservators. She's artsy, with a septum piercing and an angular haircut that reminds me of an I. M. Pei building. She's standing on a ladder in overalls, dabbing a brush at the wall. When she sees me, she turns down the NPR broadcast on her Bluetooth speaker and climbs off the ladder.

"He's impressed with your work next door," I say in a low voice. "Just thought you'd want to know."

She gives me a sly smile. "Did he complain about the delay, though? Only a billionaire would be upset that his house has important works of art all over it."

"It came up," I whisper. "But I know you can only work so fast. Is Bert gone for the day?" They often start work early and leave by three.

She nods. "I should get out of here, too. But I was listening to an interesting interview." She grabs her tool tray off the ladder. "Look, I found Poseidon again." She points at . . . two horses? The larger one is nuzzling the smaller one.

"If you say so?"

Zoya grins. "Poseidon pursued Demeter, but she didn't want to be his next side piece. So she turned herself into a mare and ran. But Greek gods don't take no for an answer, and Poseidon changed himself into a stallion to chase her down. Later, she gives birth to the horse Arion." She shrugs. "Honestly, we're just lucky the painting isn't two horses fucking."

I snort.

She grabs a drop cloth off the floor and folds it with quick competency. "Bet you ten bucks I'll find Poseidon and Scylla next. Amos Wincott *loved* Poseidon. I know they were a seafaring family, and blah blah blah. But let's face it—Amos Wincott was a dude bro. The family symbol is basically a triple penis."

"Let's not put that in the promotional pamphlet." I head for the door.

"You know I would." She chuckles. "Why keep all the interesting shit a secret? I'd also want visitors to know that there's a sad female ghost wandering around here."

I stop and turn around. "Have you *seen* her?"

"Nah." Zoya shakes her head. "But I don't have to. The aura is intense. Especially around the third-floor gallery."

"Huh," I say, because I've never used *aura* in a sentence, and I don't know the polite response to that.

She shrugs. "The tile guys saw her, though. They say she was one of the pregnant girls who lived here. I don't know if that part's true but trust me—the lady ghost has the blues. There's some bad juju in these walls."

"I'll keep that in mind."

2

I return to Hank, who's still on his call. "I approve, man," he says, pacing the hardwood floorboards, his voice booming around the empty room. "Way to actionize the opportunity."

I gravitate toward the windows. As if a little sunlight could thaw the chill in my heart.

"Maybe we can sync up next week." Hank's gleaming loafers move into my peripheral vision. "I'm not sure there's a use case, but I'm willing to be convinced. I'll need more granularity."

And I'll need a drink if I have to listen to this much longer.

"Later, man." He finally disconnects. "Sorry, Rowan. Now where were we?"

"We were admiring the conservators' work on these wall paintings and trying to come up with a suitable floor plan."

He shrugs. "Find a spot for the assistant in here somewhere. You'll figure it out," he says, turning back to the painting. "Are the murals this elaborate in every room on this floor?"

"Probably," I say, because it sounds better than *I don't know because I left my crystal ball at home, and I'm having a terrible week*. And I smile, because I fought for this job.

"Does that imply more changes to the schedule, and the budget?"

"Possibly, but the surprises are almost over." *At least I pray they are.* "Spot tests of the third-floor walls haven't revealed any paintings. And the servants' quarters should be clear. So here's my latest budget summary." I hand him the folder I've been carrying around just for this purpose.

He takes it and begins to flip through the pages, his frown deepening. "Not loving these numbers. Why did the elevator cost go up?"

It takes me a second to react, because I'm not expecting him to be so intimately familiar with every line item in the budget. "We needed to make the elevator car six inches wider to comply with a local ordinance."

"And the custom carpentry? Aren't we done with that?"

"You'd think. But let me show you something." I walk out to the gallery and proceed up the staircase that leads to the third floor, with Hank on my heels. "Okay, stand here. Put your hand on the banister."

Hank is taller than me, and he has to bend a little just to reach it. "It's too low?"

"Six inches shorter than code. Which is a real pain in my backside, because these balusters"—I point at the wooden supports—"were hand-turned from walnut. And replacing them will not be cheap."

His jaw ticks, and my heart quavers. I've spent the week anxious about my personal life when I should have been worrying about job security instead.

Hank closes the folder and lifts steely blue eyes to mine. I feel a bone-deep certainty that he's about to replace me with someone who's willing to chop paintings in half and cut corners.

Then he hands my folder back. "Okay, well. It's better than someone going over the railing. Keep plugging. But find me some good news, okay? Before our Phase Two budget meeting?"

"I'll sure try," I croak. The meeting is only a week away.

Done with me, Hank turns and heads downstairs, his shoes tapping on the treads. I practically sag with relief when I hear Beatrice's voice echo from the atrium. Even though I'm the architect, and more senior than the project manager, Beatrice has worked for him for years.

The truth is that Beatrice is better at managing Hank. Better at flattering him and getting him to approve her ideas. It's a real skill.

There's no telling how much longer Hank will put up with overruns and delays. And I've been spending too much energy on the wrong things. Like my first real boyfriend in fifteen years. Who just dumped me.

I'm a hot mess.

Stalling, I find a few things to keep me busy on the second floor, at least until I see Hank walk out to his car ten minutes later. Then I head back to our office, where Beatrice has flung herself into her desk chair. "It's almost quitting time. Praise Jesus."

"Rough meeting?"

She frowns. "I've had worse. But it's been *months*, and Hank is still leaning on me for things his new assistant should be doing. Swear to God, he just asked me to order the right kind of ink for his fountain pen. That is *not* my job anymore. But he says the new girl can't find it." She rolls her sea-blue eyes.

Maybe I'm a traitor to the sisterhood for thinking this, but it's possible that Beatrice is just too pretty for Hank to take her seriously.

She told me that she's gunning for the directorship of the new Maritime Center—a major promotion—but I worry she's in for a rude awakening. Whenever Hank and I discuss that office upstairs, Hank always refers to the director as *him*. My hunch is that Hank pictures someone like himself for the directorship—a prominent Mainer with deep ties to the country club set.

But it's really none of my business.

"I'm going to need a drink after work," Beatrice says now. "Join me? For full disclosure, though, your calendar says *book club*."

"Oh right," I murmur. "That's tonight."

She gives me a plaintive look. "You suffered through that book, so you might as well enjoy the white wine and gossip. Don't sit home alone and mope about your ex."

"I'm going. Promise. And I don't mope. I *seethe*."

Beatrice has a beautiful laugh, like bells ringing. "Hey, I appreciate the difference. That guy was too old for you anyway. He was a bore."

Beatrice only met him once, and the age thing isn't really true. Tim is forty-five, but I'm almost forty myself. Anyway, I'm not ready to be rational about Tim. It's only been four days since he ended things. "You're not helping. Who wants to be dumped by a bore?"

She spins her chair around in a complete rotation. "I'm just saying, you can do better."

Can I, though? Tim's quiet personality was a feature, not a bug. He's a grownup, with a real job and good habits. We ate out together. We went running together. And when he accidentally left something in my bathroom, it was a pair of cuff links, not a bong, like my ex used to leave lying around.

My other ex, that is.

I thought dating a wearer of cuff links was a safe choice. But it wasn't. Monday night he dumped me via a callous text message, and by Tuesday night he'd started dating someone else.

Not that I'm supposed to know that.

"What are you up to tonight?" I ask Beatrice, changing the topic.

"A cocktail mixer for the symphony orchestra." She shrugs one tanned shoulder. "You're always welcome to join me."

"Sounds fun, but I've got book club." I'm happy to have the excuse. I love Beatrice dearly, but she and I don't have the same ideas about fun. She favors benefits and yacht parties. Wine tastings. Booze-soaked outings with Portland's most well-heeled people.

Beatrice is fantastic at networking, because she actually enjoys it. "That's the only way a scholarship kid can climb the ladder," she said once.

I'm less enthusiastic, especially after a long day. The one time I went out to a party with her, she declared me "the worst wingwoman ever" after I turned down a guy who wanted to buy me a drink. Never mind that he had a tan line on his left ring finger.

I don't care how successful he is, or how slick—I am not flirting with a married man. I barely remember how to flirt with a single one. And after my latest romantic disaster, I don't even mind very much.

"You have fun," I tell her. "I'll be discussing a celebrity memoir with my high school friends."

"You animal," she says with a laugh. Then she rises from her chair. "I have to leave for my meeting with the publicist. See you tomorrow?"

"The publicist? Is there a problem?" We've had complaints from the neighbors. They objected to the noise during our demolition phase, and they're worried about the impact of a museum—no matter how small—in the midst of the quiet residential neighborhood.

She shakes her head. "No problems. We're just discussing future messaging for the Maritime Center."

"Right. Got it."

We're still a year out from the center's first public programming. But

Beatrice is the kind of person who works ahead. Maybe she's grabbing the reins of the director's job before they can find someone else.

Not a bad strategy, really.

"Say hi to Natalie for me," she says. "Tell her I have a new nail color set aside for her. It was too pink for me."

"She'll be thrilled." My sixteen-year-old daughter loves Beatrice. They have the same expensive taste in beauty products, and they go to the same yoga class on Saturdays.

After Beatrice leaves, I do a lap of the second floor, shutting off the lights. Then, downstairs, I check the lock on the back door.

That done, I cross the atrium with hurried steps. It's my dirty little secret that I don't like to be alone in the mansion. The shadows are heavy and the space seems to echo.

I don't believe in ghosts, and yet I understand why some people think this place is haunted. All old houses make noises, but this one makes more than its fair share. Creaks and groans. Century-old beams stretch and shift, like weary bones, and the atrium seems to magnify them.

My last stop is in the parlor—the biggest, brightest room on the first floor. There's a carved marble fireplace imported from Italy and exquisite wall paintings of gods and goddesses, dolphins and ships.

To my eye, they're a little overwrought. That's my other dirty little secret—I don't love the house like Beatrice does. My feelings about the mansion are the kind you have about a formidable acquaintance—one you respect, but whose company you don't actually always enjoy.

This room is my favorite, though, with its high ceilings and French windows. The air smells of sunbaked varnish and perseverance. That's the allure of old buildings—their dignity and their wisdom. I like to imagine this room in 1860, when the wall paintings were new. There would have been imported carpets on the floor and elaborate silk curtains on the windows.

Nobody becomes an architect by accident. You have to have an appreciation for grand spaces. You have to acknowledge the miracle of hand-carved moldings.

Although sometimes when I stand quietly in these empty rooms, it's easier to evoke the Magdalene Home for Wayward Girls, circa 1965, than it is to picture the elegant mansion of 1860. I can almost hear the squeak of saddle shoes and the clank of the steam radiators that Marcus Wincott had installed to modernize the heating.

As I stare through the dust motes swirling toward the floorboards, I swear I can hear the murmur of the mealtime prayer from the dining room across the hall. The clatter of forks and the clink of teacups. The girls and their babies are almost more interesting to me than the Wincotts' grandiosity.

After all, I was once a freaked-out pregnant girl myself.

I pause at the doorway and listen once more. Like people, every building has its own voice. The creak of the beams expanding under the slate roof. The rush of Maine's coastal breezes buffeting the leaded-glass windows.

This home was built when Thomas Jefferson was president, and was expanded when Lincoln was president. Teddy Roosevelt slept here once in 1902, right upstairs.

And now another summer begins. This is the season when tourists swarm Portland. They're here to eat lobster rolls and walk past the old buildings. The Wincott Mansion has stood like a solemn doyenne on this block for almost two centuries, as Portland grew from a little fishing village to a bustling city.

She stands here, watching through leaded-glass eyes as people swirl around her sandstone skirts with their ever-changing desires. They come and go with the seasons and the tides. The mansion looks down at them with a benign smile and thinks: *Your petty dramas have nothing on me.*

3

CORALIE

When Mr. Wincott returns to the office, Coralie is taking a call from the caterer.

"He can have the goat-cheese cups," the caterer says. "But not the prosciutto and melon. There are no decent cantaloupes this time of year."

"Understood," she says, scribbling this down on a pink telephone message pad.

"No other changes to the hors d'oeuvres."

"Wonderful," she says, wondering how you spell *hors d'oeuvres*. She writes *appetizers*, because otherwise he'll mock her for her ignorance.

Unfortunately, she misses the next thing the caterer says, because she's watching Mr. Wincott stomp over to the coffeepot, which is empty.

Oh no.

"Everything else looks good. See you Tuesday," the caterer says.

"Yes. Thank you. Goodbye, now." She hangs up, her head pounding. This job is easier when she's not hungover.

Probably.

"No coffee?" he says in lieu of a greeting.

"I'll make some now," she says, hating the quaver in her voice. "You didn't say if you were coming back."

He slaps the empty carafe onto the counter with enough force that she winces. "Make it quick. I have a call in ten. Is the memo on my desk?"

"Yes, sir." She's just praying there aren't many errors in it. Not like last time. *That's sloppy work, Coralie. You're lucky I forgive you.* She hears that a lot.

This is her fifth month on the job, and she can tell that his frustration is building.

She grabs a fresh coffee filter and fits it into the basket in a pantomime of "hardworking girl making coffee."

"That skirt is too tight. You look like a sausage."

She opens the packet of coffee grounds and dumps them in without comment.

The skirt *is* too tight, and growing tighter, which is terrifying. She wishes he hadn't noticed.

"Great blouse, though," he says, his gaze dipping pointedly into her cleavage.

"Thank you, Mr. Wincott." It comes out sounding a little breathless. He'll like that, though, the same way he likes that she always addresses him formally.

She has to play to her strengths.

"Bring the coffee in when it's ready," he says.

Her eyes flick toward the private office. "Yessir. Of course."

He has a call in ten, she reminds herself. If the call is with his brother, he'll be snarly afterward.

She waits until he's on the phone, then she places a white cup and saucer on a tray, along with a matching creamer of milk and the sugar bowl. This is the best part of her job, really. Not serving the coffee—but handling the Wedgwood china it's served in. All the Wincott furnishings are so beautiful. She can pretend they're her own.

To the saucer, she adds a silver spoon from the collection in the drawer. The spoons have the luster of age, each one with an elaborate *W* engraved in the handle.

There are exactly sixteen of them. She'd slip one into her handbag if she thought she could get away with it.

She carries the tray through the open door to the inner office. He's behind his desk, the phone cord stretched out to where he leans back in his chair. "Mmm-hmm," he says, but his piercing gaze tracks her movement across the thick rug.

The darkest part of her heart enjoys the attention. The way his eyes linger as her hips sway. His expression is feral.

She knows it's wrong, but she slows down her journey instead of speeding it up, so the weight of his hungry eyes will last just a little longer.

She's a terrible assistant. They both know it. She's too slow. Too dumb.

He tells her so. Frequently.

But he wants her, and there's power in it. His gaze is hungry, his hands assertive. She encourages him, even though she knows she's playing with fire.

Today, though, she carries the tray to the opposite side of the desk, her body out of reach. His expression turns sulky as she backs away, a Mona Lisa smile on her lips.

Bad girl, he mouths.

They both know it's true.

4

ROWAN

"Natalie!" I call up the stairs an hour later. "Dinner!"

There's no answer, except for a low woof from Lick Jagger, our Belgian Malinois. She's always ready for dinner.

"Natalie!" I holler for the second time. But she doesn't hear me over the music that's blaring from her Bluetooth speaker. She carries that thing from room to room, like it would kill her to go without Taylor Swift for five minutes while she's spreading her cosmetics all over my bathroom.

Dinner is a pesto pasta salad with grilled chicken, halved cherry tomatoes, and cubes of fresh mozzarella. I'm so hungry that I want to stick my face in the bowl. "Natalie!" I practically scream.

No reaction.

With a sigh, I start the trek up the surprisingly steep staircase of our narrow 1909 two-story New Englander. Sure enough, Natalie has shut herself in *my* bathroom. And she must be on the phone, because she's shouting to a friend. "My. God! Do *not* call him a snack." She howls with laughter. "Don't be gross!"

I raise a fist to knock on the door, but something makes me hesitate.

"Yeah, I know. I'm *totally* sneaking out to meet him later."

Oh Jesus. I pound on the door. Angrily. "Natalie?"

Taytay stops singing, mid-note. "I gotta go," my daughter mutters. "Call you later."

There's a delay before the door opens, and when it does, I'm startled by the person looking back at me. In the first place, Natalie is five eight, so I actually have to tilt my chin to make eye contact.

In my mind, Natalie is eleven and wearing her Wonder Woman

T-shirt with cutoffs and sneakers. She's not this startlingly beautiful young woman with high cheekbones and poreless skin.

Natalie's wide, gray eyes are currently made up in a style that makes her look thirty, not sixteen. It isn't garish. The colors are muted and done with a level of skill and sophistication that I have never achieved in my lifetime and never will. Even if I were willing to watch ten thousand hours of TikTok makeup tutorials. Which I'm not.

She's wearing a very short denim skirt and a cropped blouse that shows off long limbs and endless tight, youthful skin. It's a humid June night, and I have no logical standing against this skimpy outfit that looks adorable on her.

Her scowl is her only unattractive feature. "God, Mom. *What?*"

I bite back my frustration, which is a thing I do a lot. "I was calling you for dinner, but now I'd *love* to hear who you plan on 'sneaking out' to see? Your words, not mine."

Her scowl deepens as her glance slides conveniently away. She grabs her ever-present phone off the vanity and shoves it into an impossibly hip little clutch purse I've never seen before. "Nobody," she grunts. "Just a boy. But it doesn't matter, because it's not even true. That was just smack talk for my friends."

"Oh."

It is, of course, the exact right thing to tell me. Who among us hasn't exaggerated to sound less pathetic? I do it hourly.

"What's for dinner?" she asks, sliding past me into the hall and heading for the stairs.

"Pesto pasta salad. It's already on the table."

"Omigod, I can't eat that. Too much garlic." She practically sprints down the stairs. "I'll eat something at Tessa's."

"But Nat!" I chase her down the stairs. "I cooked."

"I'll have some tomorrow," she says in the kitchen. "Can I borrow the car?"

"No," I say as a reflex. "Where are you even going?"

"To Tessa's, like I just said." She shrugs. "We're studying for the bio final. It's the worst one."

"Oh." I hesitate. "Then you might as well take the car." Natalie is a very new driver, and I'm still struggling with the idea it's legal for my sixteen-year-old to get behind the wheel of my Volvo and just drive away unsupervised.

But her best friend lives on the other side of town, and if I don't send her in the car, she's going to take her bike, which is possibly even more dangerous.

To her, anyway. If not to innocent bystanders.

"You sure?" she asks. "You said it's book club night."

Honestly, I'm surprised she remembered. It's a rare day when she actually listens to anything I say.

"I'm blowing off book club."

She gives me an arch look that teenage girls must practice in front of the mirror. "Got a better offer? Or are you just going to stay home and mope?"

"Just take the damn car."

She grins, and it's a little evil. "Bet you wouldn't have made pesto if Mr. Stupid was still in the picture."

"Well, now that you mention it."

She laughs, and I'm hit with a wave of tenderness for my daughter. Natalie didn't start referring to Tim as Mr. Stupid until he abruptly dumped me a few days ago. The loyalty is nice, even if it's new.

Before this week, she called him *that guy*, and not in a nice way. She'd ask, "Are you making dinner? Or are you going out with *that guy* again?"

I couldn't work out why she was so offended by his existence, when she can hardly be bothered to show her face when I'm at home. Before Tim, I'd had fewer than ten dates in fifteen years.

Our discussion is apparently over, because Natalie is lifting the car keys from the hook by the door and slipping her feet into . . .

"Wait. Those are my shoes." They're black Mary Janes with a sling-back heel.

She offers me a shrug of one smooth shoulder. "You said they pinch your feet. Bye!" The door slams.

I wait by the window, watching as she backs the Volvo onto our street at a rate of three feet per hour. Backing up frightens her, and it should.

Our street is narrow and littered with parked cars. I didn't realize the car was capable of moving so slowly, but eventually she makes it, and I have to watch her pull away. She flips on the turn signal at the corner like a good girl.

And my heart is a mixed-up mess, like it always is. Natalie amazes me. She's witty and clever and capable. She's also stubborn and frequently selfish, and half the time we talk, I leave the room wishing I could list her for sale on Etsy. With free shipping.

Once her taillights disappear, I serve myself a generous portion of pasta and carry it to the sofa. This is more or less where I've spent every evening of this week, drinking wine and feeling sorry for myself.

I probably should have gone to the damn book club tonight. But at last month's meeting, I'd giddily disclosed to my high school friends that I'd met someone. "His name is Tim, and he writes for the *Wall Street Journal*."

They'd promptly pulled out their phones to google his head shot as well as his bylines. "I don't know half the words in this article, but he's a DILF!" my friend Mindy had clucked.

"Wow, Rowan! It's always the quiet ones."

Here I sit four weeks later, feeling heartbroken.

Okay, not exactly heartbroken. But shocked. And angry and depressed.

Although *heartbroken* sounds more poetic.

Bottom line—I'm just not in the mood to go sit on the rooftop terrace of my friend's downtown condo and admit that I'm still the only single person in the bunch. I prefer to lick my wounds in private.

Too bad I'm already tired of the typical cures for the breakup blues. I'm sick of sulking on the couch, and I already ate all the ice cream. Or maybe that was Natalie. I hope so. After his brutal dismount from our relationship, Tim Kovak doesn't deserve to send me up a size in jeans.

I open my phone and read his breakup text again.

> **Tim:** Hope you get this before you leave. But I can't make it tonight. This thing isn't working for me anymore. And I wish you the best.

That was it. That was the whole message. I read it five times in a row, trying to make sense of it. That night, I ended up texting a screenshot to Beatrice.

Rowan: Did this guy just break up with me a half hour before our dinner reservation?

The fact that he wouldn't take my call was a pretty good indication.

Beatrice: Oh honey.

I spent the evening in a tailspin, at times cursing his name and other times redialing him to leave him voice messages. *I don't understand. Why won't you even talk to me? Did I do something wrong?*

No pickups. No explanations. Just radio silence.

It was baffling. So much so that I'd opened up the FriendFinder app to make sure he wasn't waiting for me at the restaurant we'd booked. Just in case the whole thing was a misunderstanding. But nope. His avatar was at his parents' place, where he'd been staying. That night, anyway.

Twenty-four hours later was another story.

And now I'm all worked up again. Just thinking about it makes my eyes feel hot and gritty. Ten weeks of dating followed by four nights of anguish, with nothing more to show for it than a few tears.

"I hate him," I say into the stillness of my home.

Lickie whines. She comes to sit at my feet, watching me with sorrowful brown eyes.

"You want a walk, don't you?"

Her tail swishes.

After taking her for a halfhearted walk around the block, I change into my pajamas upstairs and settle into bed with the TV remote. The dog is a comforting weight against my knee. But after a half hour of surfing Netflix, nothing sticks.

Muting the TV, I eye my phone the same way I'd contemplate the last cookie in the jar. There's nobody around to see how far I've fallen, so I grab the damn thing and wake it up.

Even so, I just hold it in my hand for a long beat, gazing at the lock screen photo I took last summer of Natalie in front of the palace of Versailles. I can see the whole photo, because I have no notifications. It's after eight p.m., and my work colleagues are occupied with their lives. I'm almost forty years old, and I barely have a life outside architecture and Natalie.

Being with Tim was a little like uncovering one of the murals in the mansion. Before I met him, I'd painted over my romantic life with the brushstrokes of a workaholic and single mom. I'd done this for so long that I'd forgotten anyone else was under there.

Then he showed up, and there was someone to meet for coffee. Or Thai food. And, eventually, slightly awkward sex.

I wasn't in love with him. The truth is I don't think I'm capable of really falling for someone. I was burned so badly in my twenties that I'm probably just numb inside.

Tim, though. He was a good man. And I could have sworn he had real feelings for me. It was the way he looked at me sometimes. With a banked fire behind his eyes.

Or so I'd thought, right up until the evening it all ended. His departure from my life was so abrupt that he'd left a watch—one of his collection—and a set of cuff links on my bedside table.

Who leaves his watch if he's not planning to be back?

It nags at me. The violence of it. Like he'd finally caught a whiff of my neediness, and couldn't get away from me fast enough. I spent the first twenty-four hours feeling ashamed that I'd misread the situation so terribly. I did a lot of looking back on our time together, wondering what I'd done to scare him.

Wondering whether I'd leaked desperation from every pore.

I poke my phone again, but instead of opening a text box, I tap on the FriendFinder app. It's a recent habit, since Natalie got her driver's license. That's how I reassure myself about her safety.

But the week before our breakup, Tim and I got separated while jogging together on a trail. I'd texted to ask where he was.

Rowan: Can you share your location?
Tim: Sure, if you tell me how.

He'd shared it, but then forgotten. And now I'm obsessed with peeking at his location. The night after our breakup, his avatar had appeared on Middle Street at Honey Paw, the bustling Asian fusion place he'd brought me on our first real dinner date.

I've always *loved* that restaurant, and when I'd suggested it, Tim had given me a quirky smile and said, "That's my favorite. And it's kind of a litmus test for me with people—to see whether they'll like it or not. I guess you pass the test."

Obviously, I failed some other test, because his avatar has shown up all over town this week.

Last night he went to a movie at the Nickelodeon. I'm not proud of immediately googling the lineup, trying to guess which film he'd seen. It's possible he's going all these places alone. But I doubt it.

How could I so badly misread the nature of our relationship? So badly misread *him*?

And here I am again, watching the spin as it tries to make contact.

Natalie's avatar appears first, glowing on Munjoy Hill, at Tessa's house. I wish the app could also tell me if they're really studying for the bio final, but technology only allows me to invade my daughter's privacy up to a point.

Then, inevitably, I tap Tim's name.

Once again, he's not at home. But he's not in a restaurant, either. He's driving, his icon gliding down Spring Street.

He stops at a light. I wait and watch like a stalker, although I feel no actual remorse.

When he zigzags onto Park, prickles rise at the back of my neck. What's he doing in my neighborhood?

Never mind that thousands of other people live on this end of the peninsula. His location brings on an irrational fantasy, where he pulls up in front of my house and knocks on the door. When I open it, he's standing there with flowers—peonies, my favorite.

I don't know what I was thinking, Rowan, he says. *I was an idiot to let you go. I care about you so much. I must have panicked.*

Ugh. I want to kick myself for even thinking it—and for opening this app in the first place. I need to stop. All it would take is a couple of taps on his icon. *Unfollow this user? Confirm.*

My finger hovers above the button, but then Tim turns onto Danforth.

I hold my breath, watching as he stops in a spot I know well—in front of the Wincott Mansion. There's no mistaking it.

I zoom in on the map, and it seems he's in *our* spot—where we used to sit together by the waterfront. My breath comes out in a whoosh.

"Timothy Kovak, you are an *asshole*."

What kind of guy hangs out in the empty parking lot of his ex-girlfriend's workplace? It's also the place where we shared our first serious conversation, our first kiss.

I drop my phone and climb out of bed, stunned. The dog follows me, expecting something. A snack. A game. A visitor. She wags her fluffy tail and waits.

But I don't know what to do with my outrage. So I walk downstairs, open the refrigerator, and stare inside.

Nothing stares back except for a tub of hummus and the rest of the pasta salad. The bottle of wine I'd been nursing this week is long gone.

I slam the door and pace into Natalie's former playroom. When I'd decided to leave my old architecture firm, I'd boxed up the dolls and the Legos, and I'd started tearing off the old wallpaper. I'd intended to turn this room into a home office for myself. But then I took the job with Hank and put the project on hold.

Now there's a dusty futon sofa in here, some sandpaper, and not much else. It's a little depressing.

Needing a project, I pick up the scraper and attack a stubborn blister of old paint on the windowsill. This holds my attention for all of about ten minutes, until I put down the scraper and pull out my phone again.

Tim is still sitting there in front of the mansion. "Can you believe this bullshit?" I demand of my empty house.

Lickie whines.

I return to my bedroom but nothing has changed. Tim's avatar is still parked by the mansion. My mind whirs through various scenarios. There's another woman in Tim's car. A new one. A younger one who also passed the litmus test at Honey Paw. Now they're on to stage two already, and—outrageously—it's happening three blocks from my house.

Three blocks . . .

My gaze snaps to the dog, who's staring up at me with doleful eyes. The words are out of my mouth before I can think better of it. "Lickie, want to go for a walk?"

5

I change my clothes and leash up the dog. She trots happily beside me as we set off down the sidewalk. At least I've made someone happy tonight. Lickie's tail is in constant motion as we make slow progress down the block. She stops to sniff the ground so often that it will take us fifteen minutes just to walk down Clark Street toward the water.

The salty ocean breeze tangles my hair, but it doesn't cool my churning thoughts.

On some level I appreciate that Tim showed me his stripes early on. Two or three months of dating is nothing, really. Just a blip. The whole thing would feel so much worse if he'd strung me along.

In hindsight, I should have realized we wouldn't go the distance.

Shame on me for thinking we could. I should have known he had one foot out the door. There were signs. Like the time I met his mother—but only by accident.

We'd been standing by the Whole Foods cheese counter, shopping for a spontaneous picnic. An attractive woman in her sixties had leaned between us, laying a hand on Tim's shoulder. "If I'd known you were here I would have sent you a shopping list."

I knew that Tim was staying with his parents. He'd come home to Maine to help his father after a surgery. And now he was staying on a few more months, deciding whether or not to make the relocation permanent.

Still, it took me a second to realize who this woman was. Tim must take after his father, because his mom was shorter, rounder, and frankly warmer than her son.

Tim had been startled to see her. He'd stumbled through an introduction. "Mom, this is my friend Rowan."

My friend. Okay, ouch.

His mother clearly wasn't fooled, though. "How lovely to meet you!" she'd said in a voice that sounded like she meant it. "I didn't know Tim was dating anyone new."

Ouch again. Here I was, congratulating myself for trusting my heart to a man for the first time in years. And Tim—who saw his parents every day—hadn't even mentioned me to his mother.

I liked her immediately, though. She had a quick smile and a warm laugh. Her shopping basket contained the same strawberries I'd chosen, as well as a bar of dark chocolate with salted almonds, and I'd filed that away as a little piece of intel I might need later.

Joke's on me. I won't be bringing dark chocolate to any Kovak family gatherings, will I?

Lickie stops to sniff a fire hydrant, just like a dog in a cartoon. That makes us both clichés. The bitter woman, pushing forty, surreptitiously walking the dog toward the guy who dumped her, hoping for a glimpse of the new girlfriend.

Just a glimpse, though. If I see him with a date, that will tell me everything I need to know. I swear I'll stop letting this man live rent-free in my head.

I meander onto Orange Street, where the view opens up to the Fore River, and Casco Bay beyond. Twilight is rapidly deepening, the river turning an inky gray-blue. In the distance, I can see the headlights of the cars snaking across the bridge. And the wind has kicked up, chasing the day's humidity out to sea.

This bit of Portland crouches on the edge of a tall bluff, the mansions facing the water. This whole end of town is full of nineteenth-century homes, but none of them approach the size and grandeur of the Wincott Mansion.

It's not until you make that final turn onto Bond that you can see the scale of the house. The square turret. The peaked rooflines. The stone railings on her porches.

That's not what draws my eye, though. Even in the waning light, it's easy to spot Tim's shiny black Tesla facing the darkening water.

Another gust of anger blows through me. We'd sat there together so many times. Since I wasn't ready to introduce Tim to my daughter, and

Tim is staying with his parents, we didn't have many private evenings together. On several chilly spring nights, when we weren't ready for the date to end, our best option was sitting in his car before he dropped me off at home.

Sitting here without me is just plain cruel.

Lickie stops to sniff a lamppost, and I pull out my phone and open the FriendFinder app one more time. I tap Tim's glowing icon, and his profile pops up, complete with the photo of his smiling face that I snapped one day at the farmers market.

Enough, Tim Kovak. I'm tired of thinking about you. We're done here.

Then I do what I should have done long before. *Unfollow this user?*

This time, I tap *yes* to confirm.

The new woman—whoever she is—can have him. Good luck to her. I mean that.

Mostly.

Lickie gives the leash a tug, and I follow her up the sidewalk, toward the mansion. She huffs softly as she pads off the concrete and into the grass.

The wind cuts through my sweater, and the distant honk of a boat's horn dies on the breeze. The darkened mansion hovers, as if she's watching me, her old windows like hooded eyes.

Twilight has deepened the brown sandstone into foreboding purple shadows. It will be a while before we reinstall outdoor lighting, but even after we do, the mansion will never look warm and inviting. It was designed to impress, not beckon.

Lickie squats by a shrub, and I start to feel self-conscious. Odds are good that Tim has spotted us by now. Unless he and his date are staring into each other's eyes.

These are my stomping grounds. Literally. And I have every right to be here. But stalking must not come naturally to me, because I feel more dread than anticipation as we draw nearer to his car.

Suddenly, Lickie strains at the leash and lets out a friendly bark. "Hey!" I yelp, jerking her back. "Bad dog."

Another bark has me squinting past the house, toward a clump of trees at the back of the property. But I don't see anything back there except the contractor's toolshed.

"Stop that," I grumble.

For one more long moment, I keep my eyes trained on Lickie, as if watching her tug at the leash is fascinating. We amble a few crucial paces farther, and then I finally glance casually at the passenger's side of Tim's car.

The light is dim, though. A more experienced stalker probably would have anticipated this. So when I can't quickly pick out a face on this side of the glass, I have to stare a little longer.

But it doesn't help. I don't see anyone there. The seat is empty. In fact, there's no motion at all inside the car.

My gaze sweeps the sidewalk across the street. Maybe they went for a walk. It's a nice night, after all. It begs the question—how much effort am I really willing to put into spying on Tim? One mile? Two?

We pass the car, and I look over my shoulder, in case Tim is in the car alone. Maybe I'm a fool, and he's sitting there returning emails. He likes working in his car. I called it his "office." It was our little joke.

There's no glow from a laptop screen, though. So I'm about to pass by when my attention snags on the driver's side door. I think it's open a couple of inches. Which is weird. I draw closer for a better look. Yup. Definitely ajar. Maybe he needed some air? And now I'm standing here like a loser, staring at the car.

"Lickie, come." I give the leash a gentle tug.

If Tim's alone in there, I'll say a casual hello. That's something a completely sane ex might do, right?

The closer I get, though, the less sense the scene makes. A shadow seems to lean against the driver's window. And it looks like Tim himself.

Something dark and oily drips from the open door and onto the pavement below.

"Tim?" My voice comes out sounding high and strained.

He doesn't answer.

The dog whines. She lunges forward, her nose dropping to the glistening liquid on the ground.

I'm close enough to grasp the door handle. "*Tim?*" When I move the door, he moves, too.

Lickie and I jerk backward as he rolls out of the car and tumbles mostly to the pavement, face-first.

A gasp punches from my chest when I look down. My mind isn't quite able to make sense of what my eyes just showed me. Blood. Everywhere. And as he rolled past me, I saw a whole lot more of it.

Also, his face. It wasn't right. At all.

I gasp out another breath. Shock makes me stupid. I stand there for one more beat, before slowly squatting down to grasp his shoulder. "Tim."

He feels solid under my hand. He feels like Tim. But I'm terrified as I roll him a few inches off the ground and get a look at his jaw and throat. *Splintered* is the word that leaps to mind.

I fall back onto my ass. There's blood on my shoes.

Lickie whines, her ears flat on her head.

"Oh my God."

Oh my God.

6

I sit on the mansion's front steps, swallowing bile and trying to answer questions.

The last fifteen minutes are already a blur. I remember screaming, and a jogger finding me hovering over Tim's body.

I'm not sure which one of us called 911. The jogger had been the one to check Tim's pulse. The poor man got sick after his fingers had come away covered with the gore.

The police came quickly, two cops in uniform who herded us away from Tim's body, ordering us to stay put in front of the mansion while they called for backup.

Now there's yellow police tape around the car, the scene illuminated by the garish headlights of multiple emergency vehicles.

An officer stands in front of me, holding a small notebook and a pen. She's not in uniform, and although she introduced herself, I recall nothing.

"Can you tell me your name?" she asks, and I get the feeling this isn't the first time she's asked it.

My eyes are still locked on Tim's prone form. Several people are leaning over him. Someone is taking pictures.

He's on the *ground*, blood everywhere. Shouldn't they pick him up?

"Your name?" the officer prompts again.

"Rowan Gallagher," I manage to gasp. But it feels like trying to communicate from underwater.

"Thank you," she says. "And your address?"

I stumble through her questions. My address on Spruce Street. My phone number. When she asks why I came out here tonight, I point to the dog at my feet.

Then she asks me what I saw. What I heard. And she asks me why I approached the car.

"I knew him," I babble. "I knew his car. I was going to say hello."

Her forehead furrows. "You knew him," she repeats. "How?"

"We used to date." My heart hammers against my chest. "He . . . He broke it off." My gaze snaps back to Tim. One of them is touching him. "Did he *kill* himself?" I wonder aloud. "That wound was from a gunshot, right?"

That doesn't really make sense. But nothing else does, either.

"Seems like it," she says softly. "Look, is there someone I should call for you?"

I close my eyes and consider the question. I decide that the answer is no. "I live just a few blocks away." Although it feels farther now.

"How about I walk you home?" she asks.

"Um, okay. Thank you."

————————

On the walk home, the cop—Detective Riley, according to her business card—asks me a couple more questions.

How long have I lived in Portland?

Forever, except during college.

How did I meet Tim?

He stopped me in a coffee shop. He'd seen my photo in the news.

How long had we dated?

Since April.

Had Tim ever seemed suicidal?

No way.

Did he own a gun?

I have no idea. If he did, he never mentioned it.

Could she stop by in the morning and ask me some more questions?

Of course.

"Take care of yourself," she says as I unlock my front door with shaking hands. "Lock your doors."

I turn to her, spooked. "Why?"

"Because that's what cops want everyone to do. Makes our jobs easier."

Inside the house, I collapse onto the couch. When I close my eyes, all I can see is the remains of Tim's throat. His neck. His jaw. Part of it was missing.

I'm freezing, but I don't want to get up.

Outside, it begins to rain, big drops smacking against my drafty windows.

He's going to get wet. He's just lying there on the ground, in the rain.

I must doze off, because suddenly there's a jingle and the slam of a door and a woof.

"Mom?"

I open my eyes and find Natalie standing over me. "Why is Lickie dragging her leash around the house?"

"Oh." I sit up suddenly and reach for the dog, who's sniffing my hands. "Sorry."

"Mama?" Her voice is high and strained. She hasn't called me *Mama* in a hundred years. "Are you okay? What's that on your shoes?"

I swallow. "You know Tim?"

"*That* guy?"

"He's dead."

Natalie gasps. "Omigod. How did *that* happen?"

"I wish I knew."

———————

My own child puts me to bed. That's never happened before. As she pulls up the quilt, I make her promise to double-check the locks before she goes to bed.

"I will, Mama," she says quietly. "Sleep tight."

I lie awake for hours. I'm exhausted, but my brain won't let me sleep. I keep thinking about the day I met Tim in the coffee shop on Congress Street.

"Excuse me. Are you Rowan Gallagher?" he asked. He gave me an easygoing smile that I'd soon consider to be one of his best features.

At the time I'd been startled. Handsome men don't usually stop me in coffee shops. "Yes? That's me."

After telling me his name, he held out a hand to shake. "I recognize you from that article in the *Press*. Interesting stuff. You have a cool job."

"Well, sometimes." My laugh was probably awkward. "The article covered one of the more exciting days."

He was referring to a find I'd made at the mansion—a cache of historic Wincott family documents. There was a valuable Bible along with a few other items in a box under some rotting floorboards.

It wasn't that big a deal, but it did make me feel like Nancy Drew.

Afterward, Hank Wincott had called a reporter to suggest that it would make a good story. Up to that point, all the news about the mansion had been negative. Neighbors didn't like the construction noise or our plan for a new parking lot.

The reporter liked the story idea, and I ended up smiling from the Local News section, holding the Wincott Bible. I thought it was silly.

But Tim asked interested questions, making me feel fascinating. "Sit with me?" he'd said, pulling out a chair as if my agreement was a foregone conclusion.

And I guess it was. I was flattered by his attention. Starved for it, really.

He was smooth, but in a comfortable way. Confident, but not cocky. I liked his smile. But more than that, I liked how carefully he listened when I spoke. He wanted to hear all about my work on the mansion. "It's like a Victorian ghost story," he'd said. "Finding ancient documents under the floorboards."

"They'd only been there since the eighties. But, sure, let's go with your version."

He'd laughed, and I'd admired the way his eyes crinkled warmly at the corners.

We talked for two hours. I lost track of time and was late for a Zoom call with our roofer. Beatrice was about ready to start phoning area hospitals asking if they had any unidentified accident victims.

"You never disappear like that. Is he hot? Is he your type?"

"He's cute," I'd said, skirting the truth. "Snappy dresser. Kind of preppy."

My type, though? Not really. But that was a selling point. He was quieter and nerdier than the kind of guy I used to go for.

I can admit it now—there was no electricity. No desperate cravings, as if I might die if I didn't see him again soon. But that was fine with me. I'd done heart-pounding desire before, and it hadn't ended well.

A slightly nerdy journalist in a crisply laundered shirt was more my speed now. Or so I'd imagined.

But then he broke up with me, and I hadn't seen it coming. That's what shakes me up the most—having seen something in our relationship that wasn't real. Trusting Tim required that I trust myself, too.

Look what a huge mistake that turned out to be.

My mind does confusing loops, trying to understand how the Tim-sized hole he'd blown through my life had somehow just gotten exponentially larger. Now he was dead, a giant hole blown into his jaw. I'm afraid to close my eyes.

Every time I do, I see blood.

7

FRIDAY

I must have fallen asleep, because suddenly it's morning. My phone alarm plays its nameless wake-up tune while I stagger out of bed.

Downstairs, I stand in the kitchen sipping coffee, watching Natalie run back and forth, gathering all her stuff and trying not to be late for school. I feel half alive.

"Are you going to be okay?" my daughter asks, hopping up and down as she tugs on a shoe.

"I'll be fine," I say sluggishly.

After one more worried glance, she leaves. I let the dog out to do her business in our little fenced-in backyard, then I drag myself into the bathroom for a shower.

My clothes from last night are on the bathroom floor. There's blood on my socks. With a shudder, I carry my clothes to the utility closet and heave them into the washer, adding a double pour of detergent. I know to put the water on the cold-water setting for blood stains, but I freeze for a moment when I imagine Tim's blood swirling down the drain.

Back in the bathroom, I lock the door. I've showered alone in this house thousands of times, but this is the first time I feel vulnerable. The shower is loud. Anyone could sneak in, and I'd never hear it. I've seen *Psycho*.

So it's a quick shower, which is just as well, because I think I remember the police detective saying that she'd come by at eight thirty. *If that's okay with you.*

As if I'd been in any shape to protest.

In the kitchen, I start more coffee and call Beatrice.

"Hey, girlie!" she whispers into her phone. "Good morning."

"Why are you whispering?" I ask, and then I realize there must be a man there with her. "Oh wow. Somebody had a fun night."

"What can I say? It was a good party. What's up with you?"

"Well . . ." I don't even know how to explain. "Last night I walked past the mansion. I saw Tim's car."

"*Your* Tim?"

"Is there another Tim?" I ask tiredly. "But Beatrice. He was . . ." I swallow. "He was dead. In the car."

"*What?*" she gasps. "Are you kidding me right now?"

"No. I think he killed himself."

There's silence on the line for a long moment. "Oh God, Rowan. I'm so sorry."

"It's okay," I say reflexively. "I called 911 and the police came and handled it. I have to talk to them again this morning."

"Yikes," she says again. "Want me to come over?"

"No, I'm all right."

I'm touched by the offer. Beatrice and I are friends at work, mostly because we both report to the same aggravating billionaire. But we're not the kind of friends who swing by to make tea for each other when things get rough. "I'll be late, though. The police tape is probably still up. I had meetings planned. Can you make excuses to the electrician? That was my nine o'clock."

"Of course. Anything."

"Thank you."

"Call me when you know what your day will look like, okay?" she says. "Or call me if you're not coming in."

"Okay. Yeah. I think I'm coming in." Aren't I? What are the rules? I've never found my ex-boyfriend dead before.

"All right," she says gently. "Don't be a stranger."

"Thanks. I mean it."

I end the call, then force down a cup of yogurt. When a knock sounds on the front door, Lickie gives a single woof of warning, and I give her the side-eye. What would Lickie actually do if someone broke a window and came into the house? This breed of dog has a strong bite. They're often used for police work. But ours is the most docile dog on the planet.

Plus, I trained her not to bark at visitors. Maybe that was a mistake.

Gathering myself, I open the door to find Detective Riley blinking back at me. Her hair is damp, as if she did a hasty job with the hair-dryer, too.

"You look almost as tired as I am. Don't they let you go home?"

"It depends." She gives me a droopy smile.

"Coffee?"

"I would *love* some."

I make myself busy pouring our mugs and offering her milk and sugar. I dust toast crumbs and Natalie's crumpled napkin off the table.

I feel strangely like I'm living in two universes—the one where I'm supposed to feel ashamed of my shitty housekeeping, and the one where Tim shot himself to death in his car last night.

We sit down. I take a bracing sip, and Detective Riley does the same across from me. "Do you mind if I record our conversation?" she asks, taking out her phone.

"Um . . ." I do kind of mind, because that feels invasive. But I don't want to get in the way of police work. "No, it's fine."

"Thank you. I've been tasked with the job of retracing the last days before Tim's death."

"Okay. I'll help however I can. But I hadn't talked to him in several days."

She nods easily. "Since he'd ended things between the two of you? Was it ugly?"

I swallow hard. "It was hurtful. But not ugly. He just cut me off. Didn't even give me a reason."

She rests her chin on her hand. "How did he tell you? Phone call? Text?"

"Text. Monday night. It was very abrupt. We'd had dinner plans." I pluck my phone off the table, open my texts, and show her Tim's.

She reads the screen and winces. "Okay, wow. That's curt. And you didn't respond?"

"I called him. I'm too old to break up by text."

She gives me a feeble smile. "And did he answer?"

I shake my head.

"That's rough," she says gently. "So when was the last time you saw him in person? Besides last night."

Last night. Tears threaten again. "Um, the Friday before that. We had dinner and then hung out in his car."

"And where did all that take place?"

"Dinner at David's Restaurant." I feel sweat gather under my arms. "And then we sat in front of the mansion, actually."

"The *same* mansion?" she clarifies.

"Yes. We used to park on the property a lot. I work there, so it was me who told him that it's no trouble to park there after hours."

She blinks. "All right. We'd wondered why his car was there. It's not public property."

"I'd wondered, too," I admit. "Because I'd assumed he'd only go there with me." I absolutely do *not* add that I'd noted his presence by way of an app, though. She doesn't need to know that.

"So you two parked there before?" she asks. "Did this happen a lot?"

"Maybe . . . six or seven times, if I had to guess. We dated through-out the spring. On chilly nights, we'd sometimes sit in his car after dinner. He was staying with his parents, and he'd never invited me over there. And I rarely invited him here." I indicate my kitchen. "I hadn't in-troduced my daughter to him yet. I assumed I would eventually, though."

"But did he ever visit your home?"

"A few times, yes."

"How many is a few?"

It's a struggle not to sound irritated at the personal question. "Three? Four?"

The first time Tim came over was when Natalie went on a class trip to Boston. It was understood that he would stay the night, and I'd been anxious beforehand. It was hard to show my almost-forty body—with its stretch marks—to someone new. I was out of practice.

After that, he came over twice more for sex.

Luckily, Detective Riley changes the subject. "Where did you two meet?"

I tell her the story about the news article and his coffee-shop introduction. "After we met, he emailed the next day and invited me out for dinner. We dated for a couple of months."

"Was it serious?"

"Obviously not to him," I point out.

"But what did you think?"

I struggle for words that don't sound egomaniacal. "I thought we had a long future of more of the same. He seemed really into it. More than me, if I'm honest. But I assumed we enjoyed each other's company enough to keep it up."

"You weren't in love with him?" she asks softly.

"Not yet. No." I shake my head. "But he was a great guy, and I really enjoyed dating him."

"And how did you feel when he ended it?"

"Angry," I admit. "And very embarrassed. It made me remember why I don't date."

She gives me a quiet smile. "Sing it, sister. So that was it? No further contact?"

"No. He didn't answer my calls. And maybe it's for the best. You shouldn't have to beg someone to pay attention." I tried that once fifteen years ago. It didn't go well.

Another wince from the detective. She's younger than I am. Early thirties, I guess. "I'm sorry."

I shake my head. "I'll be fine. I can't quite get my head around him dying. It doesn't seem real."

"Tell me about your job. Do you go to the mansion every day? Weekdays?"

"Almost every weekday for the last six months. Unless I have back-to-back off-site meetings. It's going to take another year and a half before the project is done."

She scribbles some notes. "Who's your employer? Or do you work for yourself?"

"I work for the Wincott Foundation, on a two-year contract."

Her pen pauses. "And how did that come about?"

"Well, I used to work for a big architectural firm. But I wanted out."

"How come?" she asks.

"Um . . ." It feels like a lifetime ago now. "I didn't like the power structure. The firm was owned by two brothers. I was the only female architect on the team, and they always tried to give me the least interesting work. Things like kitchen renovations, because I had 'a feel for the domestic.'"

She makes a sympathetic face.

"So I started to think about going off on my own. And when Hank Wincott started interviewing architects for the mansion, I went after that job hard. Hank and I went to high school together."

"That's a lucky leg up," she says, lifting her gaze to mine.

"Well, it didn't hurt. When I told him I wanted to leave my firm and go out on my own, Hank was willing to consider me for the project. He asked me to come on board as an employee until the mansion is finished. I liked the idea of having a steady paycheck for two more years, before I launch my own firm. And I'm on the Wincott Foundation's health insurance now."

More scribbling. Unlike Tim, she doesn't use Moleskines and fountain pens. Her notebook is a cheap spiral version. "Do you think there's any chance that Tim expected to run into you at the mansion last night?" she asks.

"No way. The hour was strange, and we weren't in contact."

Maybe I say this a little too forcefully, but I'm not going to tell her that I knew he was there. That will just make me sound crazy.

"Are you sure?" she presses. "He went to your place of work, which is only a few blocks from your home. He didn't live in this neighborhood, so it seems like a strange location to choose if he didn't want to see you."

I hold out both hands and shrug. "If I'd known how to read his mind, I wouldn't have been so surprised when he broke up with me."

"And you?" she asks. "Did you expect to run into him?"

"No." My pulse whooshes in my ears, and it's suddenly difficult to control the muscles in my face. "But there he was."

She watches me carefully. "And you're certain the two of you didn't have any more contact? No calls? No emails? No other apps?"

I shake my head, but my good-girl complex is burning me up inside. *No other apps?*

"Okay, please tell me everything about your walk to the mansion last night. Did you walk from here?"

"Yes."

"What time was it?"

I consider the question. "After eight. It was getting dark, but it wasn't dark just yet."

"What route did you walk?" She pushes her notebook toward me on the table. "Can you show me?"

As I draw the streets and an outline of the mansion, her eyes widen. "Lord, you have an eye."

"I'm an architect. Drawing is literally my job. This was my path . . ." I tap the pen on the page and give her a meticulous description of my route.

"Wonderful. Now, did you see anyone else nearby?"

"No. I mean—there are always a few people out walking dogs in the neighborhood. But I didn't pass anyone on the sidewalk near the mansion."

She nods thoughtfully. "And did you hear any strange sounds?"

"You mean like a gunshot? No."

"Anything," she says.

I shake my head. "It was as quiet as ever."

Her face is impassive, but her fingers worry the edge of the table. "When you saw his car, what did you notice about it?"

"At first nothing seemed weird. I approached from the passenger side"—I indicate my path with a tap on the paper—"and I did wonder if there was another person in the car with him . . ."

"Like a date?" she asks.

"Yeah." I take a breath. "That's exactly what I was thinking. But I didn't see anyone in that seat. Then, as I passed the car, I looked over my shoulder. I saw the driver's door was open, so I doubled back."

"It was open?" She sits up just a little bit straighter. "Like, how far?"

I use my hands to indicate a couple of inches. "It looked like maybe someone had forgotten to close it all the way. So I walked Lickie over, thinking I'd close it for him. Unless he was there in the car. And then I would have said hi."

"Tell me exactly what you saw."

I try, but it's rough going. I explain how the light was bad, and I didn't understand that I was looking at blood on the asphalt. "I got a bad feeling, but it just didn't seem real, until he rolled out of the car. His . . . *face*. I only saw it for a second." The coffee in my stomach turns into paint thinner. "I'd just never seen anything like that before."

"It's upsetting," she says quietly.

"Upsetting doesn't even cover it."

"Did you see the gun?" she asks.

I shake my head.

"It didn't roll out of the car with him?"

"Not that I noticed."

"Then you touched him," she prompts.

"Yes. I grabbed his shoulder. He felt solid, I thought. Like normal. And I had this weird idea that maybe he was okay. So I said his name and I rolled him toward me a little. And . . ."

Bile rises up in my throat. I gag and have to swallow it down.

Detective Riley gets up and finds a glass in my cupboard. She fills it with water and brings it to me.

I accept it wordlessly and drink some. It helps a little.

"Okay, what about the jogger?" she asks. "How much time passed between Tim rolling out onto the ground, and the jogger reaching you?"

"Um . . ." I try to think. "Not long at all. Less than a minute? I couldn't scream right away. But when I did, the jogger came pretty fast."

She asks me some more befuddling questions. Which direction did the jogger come from? Did the jogger say anything? Had I ever seen him before?

I don't remember much, and I feel like I'm failing a test. "Why are you so interested in the jogger?"

She folds her hands and goes quiet. As if she's trying to decide how much to share. "There was no gun found at the scene, Rowan. And we need to know where it went."

8

"No gun?" I ask stupidly.

Slowly, she shakes her head.

"So . . ." I say, and I feel like I'm trying to speak from underwater, "he didn't shoot himself?"

Another slow shake of her head. "Not unless someone removed the gun from the scene afterward."

"You're *sure*?"

"Very sure," she says firmly. "But why is that more shocking? You said yourself that you didn't think he was suicidal."

"Because he wasn't . . ." *Parked there for very long.* Even in my half-addled state, I quickly back away from this mistake. I'm not supposed to have any idea how recently he'd arrived there. "Because there was nobody else around. And it *seemed* like it had just happened. When I touched him."

"He was still warm?" she says softly.

"Yes," I quickly agree.

"Okay." She reaches across the table and gives my forearm a squeeze. "I need to ask if you can think of anyone who was angry at him. Did he have enemies?"

"If he did, I never heard about it."

"Did you meet any of his friends?"

My stomach drops. "No, I didn't. I got the impression that most of them are in New York."

And if that's wrong, he clearly wasn't interested in introducing me.

"All right. His LinkedIn profile says he was an investigative journalist. Did he talk about work with you?"

"Sometimes." I rub my eyes, as if it might help to remove the memory of his dead body. "But what he described sounded routine. He had a lot of phone calls with CEOs. Interviewing them about earnings reports. Or something. There were a lot of spreadsheets involved."

"Anyone specific?" she prodded.

"He talked about trying to pry quotes out of people. But he'd tell me in a comical way. And he never named names."

"Did he tell you what story he was working on now?"

"No clue. But you could find out. He took a lot of longhand notes. He liked Moleskine notebooks—the hardback kind. He had them in a few different colors. He kept them in a basket on his car's back seat. He liked working in his car, and I'd started referring to it as his office."

She frowns. Then she jots something down. "All right. Good tip. Did you notice the notebooks in his car?"

"Last night? Not a chance."

"How about his laptop or phone. Did you see those? Neither one was found in his car."

Another shake of my head. "All I saw was his dead body. And I wish I'd never seen that." Although the only person I have to blame is myself.

"I'm so sorry," she says patiently. "I have just a few more questions. Do you and your daughter live here alone? How old is she?"

"Natalie is sixteen. It's just the two of us, plus Lickie."

The dog raises her head when she hears her name, and her tail swishes a couple of times.

"What a good baby," the cop says in a soft voice, offering Lickie her hand. "Do you look out for your humans?"

Lickie gets up to give her a sniff, just in case she's holding a piece of bacon.

"My father gave her to us as a guard dog, but she only looks menacing. She's the most docile dog ever born."

Riley grins. "Well, sometimes a deterrent is all you need. Right, girl?"

Lickie accepts some head rubs.

"I need to ask you about other men in your life," Riley says. "Are you dating anyone else?"

"What? Why?"

She looks back at me with a tired expression. "We need to figure out who'd want Mr. Kovak dead. If someone in your life saw him as the competition, that person might have a motive to harm him."

Jesus. "You can cross that idea off your list. There aren't any other men in my life. There haven't been for years."

She raises an eyebrow. "Your daughter's father is . . . ?"

"Harrison Jones. We were never married, and I haven't seen him since Natalie was a toddler. That's when he went to prison."

She looks up from her notes. "For what?"

"Assault. It was a bar fight. He was abusing drugs at the time."

I fight the urge to squirm in my chair. I recognize the irony of telling her that no man from my past could have murdered Tim—and then saying in my next breath that my ex went to prison for assault.

"Okay," she says slowly. "And where did this take place?"

"Here in Portland."

"What was the fight about?" she asks. "Were you there?"

My stomach drops, like it does every time I think of that night. "There was a guy giving him a hard time, and Harrison basically lost his mind. He'd never been violent before, and it was the most terrifying night of my life."

"Where was he incarcerated?"

"Maine State Prison, originally. I lost track of his whereabouts more than a decade ago."

"Is he currently incarcerated?" she asks. I can almost see how badly she wants to whip out her phone and check.

"No. He got out a few years back." My neck heats again.

"And when did you last speak?" she asks.

"Um . . ." I try to think. "After he went away, he relinquished his parental rights and stopped speaking to me."

I don't tell her that my mother offered him a bribe—a couple of thousand dollars in his commissary account if he'd sign over his parental rights.

He sold us off really cheaply. I'll never forgive him.

"So, no contact?" she asks. "None at all?"

"None over the past decade, but he emailed once recently."

"Really, when?"

I pick up my phone again and type *Harrison* into my email app's search bar. "Um, May twenty-fifth." The subject line is *I'd like to talk to you about Natalie.* I pass her my phone.

She scans the message, her brown eyes serious. "It's friendly. He's asking about your daughter and asking for a phone call with you. Did you speak to him?"

I shake my head. "I have full parental rights. I don't have to give him visitation. He's an ex-con and a druggie, so I can blow off his emails."

"Understood." She taps her chin, thinking for a moment. "Do you own a gun?"

The change of topic surprises me. "Me? No. I've never even *held* a gun."

"Does anyone else keep a gun in this house?"

"*No,*" I say sharply. "Why are you asking me this?"

She glances up, her pen pausing on her pad. "I have to. If I didn't, I wouldn't be doing my job. Don't you want the police to be thorough and find his killer?"

"Of course I do."

She looks down at her notes again. "You said you've been inside Tim's car?"

"Absolutely. Many times."

"Which seats?" she asks. "The crime-scene techs will be collecting physical evidence. Looking for DNA."

"Um, the passenger seat. And once in the, uh, back seat." My face is the color of a tomato now, and a drop of sweat rolls down my back.

"For sex?" she asks.

"Well, no. Not, um, quite." That night, I'd felt like a hot young thing as Tim slipped a hand under my skirt. Now I regret everything.

"Did you leave anything in his car?" she asks.

"Besides my dignity?"

She doesn't laugh.

"No, I don't think so."

"I need to ask a favor. I'd like to take a set of elimination fingerprints. I brought a scanner." She reaches into her bag and pulls out a device the size of a cordless phone. "Is that okay? By excluding your fingerprints, it will help us figure out if the killer's fingerprints are in Tim's car."

"Okay, sure."

She pulls out a release form. After quickly skimming the legalese, I scribble my name at the bottom, because I feel I have no choice.

She taps some buttons on the scanner, and it beeps. "Okay, we'll do it one finger at a time. Please roll each finger from one side to the other. Like this." She demonstrates on my kitchen table.

I roll my index finger on the screen, and it beeps again.

"Great. Next one."

Inside, my good-girl complex is shrieking. I don't want my prints in some database forever. But I don't want to look guilty, either. So I keep rolling one finger at a time across the little screen.

"After the two of you broke up," Detective Riley says, "what did you tell your friends about it?"

"Um . . ." I roll my thumb. "I told my coworker that I was upset. And surprised."

"Did you tell her you were angry?"

Another drop of sweat rolls down my spine. "Well, yes. And embarrassed."

"How angry were you?" she asks.

My pulse kicks up another notch, and if I wasn't agitated before, I'm getting there now. "Look—I was angry enough to finish the Ben and Jerry's and sulk on the couch. But if you're implying I might *murder* a man who dumped me, that's outrageous."

The machine beeps after the final print, and I yank my hand back and cross my arms.

Detective Riley squints at the readout, then looks up at me again. "Rowan, I *have* to ask these questions. If something terrible happened to someone you love, you'd want the police to poke all the sore spots, wouldn't you?"

I let out a hot breath of air. "Of course I would. And I want you to find the guy who did this."

"We're going to," she says, pushing back in her chair. "I promise. You've been very helpful. But you can't go into work today, because the mansion property is a crime scene, and we'll probably need at least the weekend."

That hadn't occurred to me. "So we can't go into the mansion?"

"Not yet. We need to take a good look around, in case the perp dropped anything on the grounds. And when you do go back inside, please let us know if anything is missing. Off the top of your head, is there much worth stealing on the property?"

"Um . . ." I have to think it over. "That just depends what kind of thief you're dealing with. The stained glass is all valuable. There are several Tiffany pieces, but they're hard to fence and it would take special skill to remove them. There's some old furniture locked into rooms upstairs. But again—you'd have to know the market for a nineteenth-century dining chair."

She scribbles a note. "Anything else? Electronics?"

I shake my head. "I never leave my computer there. Beatrice—the project manager—does, I think?"

Another scribble.

"Take a look at the contractor's trailer. It should be locked, although tools are sometimes stolen from a job site."

"Will do," she says, rising to her feet. "More soon, okay?"

"Thank you," I say, elated that the interview is over. "Let me know if I can be of any more help."

"Oh, I will," she says. "And if you think of anything else that we should know about Tim, I want to hear from you right away."

She gives me another one of her cards, then opens my kitchen door to go. I'm already mentally collapsing onto the sofa. Before she departs, she turns to look at me one more time. "After we get Tim's phone data from the cell phone carrier, we might ask for access to your phone records to help us track his last weeks."

My heart seizes, and I feel my expression harden.

She just stands there. Watching me.

"Okay," I manage.

She gives me a smile and finally departs. At the sound of the door closing, I let my eyes fall shut, but my heart won't stop hammering.

That damn app. If I give her my data, she'll know I was following him.

If I don't give her my data, I'll look guilty.

And I wish I'd never met Tim Kovak.

9

SUNDAY

I spend the weekend acting like the breakup was still fresh—huddled on the sofa with the dog, or crying in the shower. I keep thinking about Tim's last moments, facing down the barrel of a gun.

Did he *know* it was the end? It's comforting to think that maybe it happened so fast he didn't have time to be afraid. I hope so.

Meanwhile, Natalie sticks close, skipping her Saturday yoga class "to study for exams." But her main occupation seems to be sending me worried looks from the other end of the sofa.

Sunday afternoon I try to resurrect myself. I invite my father for dinner, and I roast a chicken so my daughter will stop looking so worried.

When my dad arrives, he rattles the doorknob, because it's locked. As I cross the living room to let him in, I realize how stiff my muscles are. I'm still walking around with a heightened sense of fear—as if a murderer might be hiding behind the boxwood shrubs beside my front porch.

I open the door and find my father standing there with a small bouquet in a little galvanized pail. Three pink peonies—my favorite flower.

"*Dad*," I gasp. "That was so nice of you." I don't think he's ever brought me flowers before in my life.

"They're not from me, honey." He thrusts the flowers at me. "I just found them sitting here on the porch."

I take the pail and turn it in my hands, but I don't see a card.

"Who are those from?" Natalie asks as I carry the flowers into the living room, my dad on my heels.

"I don't know," I manage.

"Some friend who's worried about you," my father suggests. "Aren't we all these days."

He could be right. It's just that peonies are my favorite, and not many people know that.

Tim did. A couple of weeks ago, we'd walked past a florist on Congress Street, and I'd pointed at the pink peonies in the window. "See those? I used to paint still lifes of peonies. I love how round they are."

"You paint?" he asked.

"I dabbled."

"Were you any good?"

"Not even a little," I told him, just to watch him grin. "So now I stick to drawing floor plans."

A week later, he surprised me with a bouquet of peonies. Much like the ones my father found on the front porch.

Fighting the irrational suspicion that the flowers were sent to me by a ghost, I put them on the coffee table and avoid looking directly at them all day.

———————

Monday arrives, as it has no other choice. But I'm still a wreck. When I approach the mansion on foot, I find two police cars, a lot of yellow police tape, two different news vans, and about a dozen gawkers standing on the sidewalk.

It's a circus. The very worst kind.

My eyes dart fearfully toward the parking lot and the place where Tim died. The spot has been cordoned off, but otherwise there's no obvious clue as to what happened there. The rain has washed away the blood, but I know I'll still see it when I close my eyes.

Trembling, I duck past the police tape and walk up to the porch. A uniformed officer with an acne problem stands guard outside the carved door. "Hi. I'm Rowan Gallagher," I tell him. "I work here."

He opens the door, puts two fingers in his mouth, and whistles. "Riley! You got a customer."

The detective appears in the doorway. "Come in, Rowan. Let's walk through together. I just need you to tell me if anything is missing from your office."

"Why? Was the lock broken?"

She purses her lips. "There's no evidence of forced entry. And the contractors I've spoken to haven't reported anything missing. But Tim's electronics were stolen from his car. We're trying to make sure that's all that was taken."

"Okay. Sure." I trail her as she struts through the atrium like she owns the place. I'm getting the feeling she spent a lot of time here this weekend.

She leads me toward the library. "They *did* tell me that the house is haunted."

"And did you find that helpful?"

"Not particularly." She moves aside when we reach the door to the library, allowing me to enter first.

Inside, I give the room a wary scan. It's exactly as we left it. The walnut bookshelves are mostly bare, except for our collection of fabric samples, plus some lighting catalogs and paint decks I'd brought from home. "Everything looks fine. Let me just check the inner office."

When I do, it also looks untouched. There aren't even any new mouse droppings on my desk. "Doesn't seem like anyone's been in here."

"Glad to hear it. You're clear to come and go as usual now. But before I leave, can you just look over this list of contractors your colleague gave us on Friday? Can you think of any other person or outfit who worked here in the past month?"

I take the list, which is in Beatrice's handwriting. It's thorough, because Beatrice is not a slacker. The general contractor, HVAC guys, the electricians, the art conservators, the interior designer . . . It's a lot. "This looks comprehensive."

"Good." She takes the list back. "Thank you for your time. We'll be leaving now, but I'll still need to keep the parking area cordoned off until my boss gives me the word."

"Okay," I say numbly.

Then she leaves me alone in the mansion, just a few yards from where my ex-boyfriend died.

After flipping on the desk lamp, I take a seat in my ergonomic chair. I drop my computer bag into my lap and unzip it, feeling like I'm performing a pantomime of my former life. This is how the workday is supposed to begin. The motions are correct.

The problem is that I've forgotten how to be this person, and after I open the laptop, I stare at the login screen for a moment, until the desk lamp suddenly flickers. My gaze jumps to the green glass shade, just as it steadies again.

The last time the lights flickered, one of the conservators made a comment about ghosts, and I'd found it charming.

I don't anymore.

————————

A couple of hours later, I'm up in the Blue Room, measuring the paintings I'd discussed with Hank just days before. I still can't seem to focus, and it takes me three tries before I successfully write down the proportions in my notebook.

Rationally, I know that whoever killed Tim isn't coming for me next, but I don't feel safe here, even in the daylight. I've already checked the FriendFinder app several times today, just to see Natalie's icon securely at school. As if knowing her whereabouts would keep her safe.

Tim's avatar is gone, of course, and I wonder absurdly if he might still be alive if I hadn't unfollowed him.

Leaving the room, I wander out onto the second-floor gallery. The conservators are working in the next room, and I give the door a knock. Nobody answers, and after another tap, I push the door open.

Zoya and Bert are standing on separate scaffolds, both of them dabbing the walls with cotton balls. And both are wearing headphones.

Bert jerks when he sees me, and Zoya picks up on the motion and whirls, whipping off her headphones.

"Sorry, guys," I say, my voice rusty from disuse. "Didn't mean to startle you."

Zoya puts a hand to her chest. "Not your fault. We're just jumpy."

I don't have to ask why. We're all jumpy. Beatrice spent her morning ordering new security cameras that will cover every exterior inch of the property. That's in addition to the new keypads on the doors.

"I have a very aggravating question for you two. Don't"—I almost say "shoot the messenger" before I realize the callousness of that cliché—"be too annoyed."

"Well, let's hear it," Bert says. "Do I need to climb down for this?"

I shake my head. "Regarding the murals in the Blue Room, would it be possible, in your opinion, to move a panel?"

His gaze sharpens. "Why the hell would you want to?"

"I don't," I admit. "But I may need to consider it. If the door to the room could be closer to the corner, it would save my floor plan."

"Do I have this right?" Zoya asks. "You want to move a hundred-fifty-year-old mural to make your floor plan a little sleeker?"

"*Easy*," Bert says. "I'm sure Rowan would prefer to leave the walls where they are." He removes his cap and gives his graying head a shake. "You could make it work. We'd use a very fine saw to remove that panel and relocate it. Then we'd essentially caulk it back into place in its new home. There'd be some risk to the artwork. The plaster could crumble. But it probably won't."

"Okay. Thanks. I'll view it as a last resort."

"The *very* last," Zoya growls. "The artist arranged those scenes the way he wanted them."

"Understood."

I walk toward the door. "Should I close this after myself?"

"No, wait." Zoya hops down off the platform. "There's something I need to show you in the smaller sitting room."

My stomach drops. "Please don't tell me there's another mural in there." Another delay might get me fired.

"Not exactly," she says. "Just look."

I follow her next door to a small room facing the back of the house. It was originally the ladies' sitting room—somewhere the women could gather while the men were smoking or playing billiards. The wallpaper we'd removed from this room wasn't in good condition, and there was nothing interesting beneath it.

Or so I believed.

Zoya marches past the lovely empty walls and opens a closet door. "I found more of the beige paint in here, and I wondered why they needed it."

"Inside the closet?"

Her nod is grim. "I did some patch tests with my solvents. Look." She points indignantly down at the interior wall near the floor. "It's a cry for help."

I wave her out of the closet so I can get a look. And what I find there sends a shudder down my spine. Scrawled on the wall in a shaky hand are the words: *Help me. I want out.*

"That's awful," I mutter.

"Right?"

"Can you tell when this was written?"

"Well, it's pigment based, probably with xylene and toluene as binding agents."

I straighten up. "In English?"

"Sharpie marker," she says. "They were introduced in the mid-sixties."

"Oh." I glance down at the desperate scrawl again. At that time, the house was being used as a girls' home. I can appreciate the sentiment of the message, because this week has shaken me to the core. But the message could be decades old, and it's not a problem I'm meant to solve. "That's dark."

"Someone painted over it," Zoya sniffs, "to shut her up."

"I realize that," I say softly. "But we don't know who wrote it. Is there more marker under there?"

"Not sure," she says. "I'm going to spot-check a few more areas, though."

"Okay," I say heavily.

"I also took some photos. I'll send them to you."

"Okay," I repeat. "Thank you for showing me."

She shuts the closet door carefully and pauses. "You know, when people are trying to figure out why an old house feels creepy, they ask if anyone died there. But that's the wrong question. What they should really be asking is did anyone *suffer* there. It leaves a darker mark."

Once again, I don't have the vocabulary to respond to that.

"You should let Hank Wincott know," she presses.

"That's a good idea," I lie. It's one thing to be fascinated by an old family Bible pulled from the floorboards, but Hank won't give a damn about some graffiti in the closet. "Thank you for showing me. Let me know if you find anything else."

"Oh, I definitely will."

We head back to the room where she and Bert are working, and she climbs back onto her platform. "Can I put some music on the speaker?" she asks Bert. "Not too keen on leaving my headphones on today."

"Sure, honey," he says. "But you don't have to worry, ZeeZee. I'd fight the killer off with my palette knife."

She gives him a tender smile, and I leave the room just as one of Bach's cello suites begins. I close the door and go back to the Blue Room to take another photo of the wall section I'm thinking of moving.

But then a glance out the window makes me do a double take. Hank's car is out there. *Hell.* Did I forget a meeting? I'm not sure he can get inside, unless Beatrice already texted him the new passcode.

I leave the room again and pull up short in the gallery. Hank's voice echoes from downstairs, and it's angry.

"You realize this fucks *everything* up. I can't make an announcement while there are police cars outside."

What announcement? I pause beside a painter's ladder to listen.

Beatrice replies, but her words are harder to make out. ". . . get past this. When the news cycle changes, people will stop hearing your name in the same breath as a murder. It's going to be okay."

"Did I *ask* for your opinion?" His voice is so sharp that I have to draw a slow breath. And then Beatrice replies in a voice too low to hear.

"I can *count*, Bea," he snarls. "But the cops should be done by now. Can't they get the hell off our lawn?"

Yikes. The second-floor gallery has shockingly good acoustics. The Wincott family must have had a fun time eavesdropping on one another, because I can make out almost every word.

"I'll ask the cops for an update," Beatrice says. "But a man *died* out there, Hank. Do you want to be the rich guy who's getting in the cops' faces?"

"No, I want *you* to do that."

I don't think I've ever witnessed Hank losing his temper before. Not even in high school. He was more the kind to charm his way out of a situation. But today he's worked himself into a real lather.

"You want a job at the mansion? Then *lock this down*. Park a damn excavator in front of the police tape if you have to. The goddamn *show is over*. Get *off my fucking lawn* and get my name out of your fucking headline!"

I'm practically trembling on her behalf, so when she answers in a voice like ice chips, I'm surprised. "Hank. Do not, *for one second*, pretend like you're the only one who cares about protecting the family. That's insulting, especially when you rarely make it through a day without asking me to cover your ass. I said I'm on it. That means *I'm on it*."

Whoa. There can't be many people who aren't afraid to push back at Hank Wincott.

"Fine," he grunts. There's an extended silence, as if they're both taking a minute to get their tempers under control. "What other fires need putting out?" he asks. "How's our architect holding up? Any problems there?"

Once again, I stop breathing.

There's a pause before Beatrice answers. "Honestly? She's kind of a mess. But give her a few days. We'll be back on schedule."

"As if," he grumbles. "I need you to deliver a message to her—no speaking to the press. Absolute blackout. We don't want her describing the murder scene on TV."

Gosh, you think?

"No problem, Hank."

"She's too straightforward, you know? Probably isn't any good at spin."

I want to be offended by this, but he's right. Spin is not my specialty.

"We'll have a conversation," Beatrice says firmly. "She's not a sharer, though. Can you really see Rowan holding court on Channel Four?"

"No. But if she's stressed out and distracted . . ."

"Okay. You've been heard. I already told you we'll have a conversation."

"Thank you." There's a tense silence. "What else? Anyone scared? Any issues with the contractors?"

"Lots of whispering. This is worse than the damn ghost stories. But so far everyone has shown up for work. I called the electrician this morning and ordered him to get the new exterior lighting done yesterday. And the security company got here an hour after I rang them. So that's something."

A sudden bang startles me. I practically jump out of my skin until I spot the source at my feet—a metal paint scraper that's somehow leapt off the ladder. I must have bumped it.

Below me, the voices stop. If Hank and Beatrice leave the library, they'll spot me. Heart pounding, I ease back into the Blue Room.

A moment later, I hear their voices start again, at a murmur this time. I can still feel the tension between them.

I lean against the window and give Poseidon a sulky eye. He's the part of the mural that's causing all the trouble. If I move him to the other side of the door, the symmetry will be ruined.

My head pounds, and I can't remember why I should care about a single thing in this building. The whole place is tainted now.

I want to walk out the front door and never come back.

10

CORALIE

When Mr. Wincott returns from his lunch, she's in an awkward position on her hands and knees in front of an open filing cabinet. At least the coffee is ready, and the files he'd asked her to clean up are in order.

Mostly.

He aims an appreciative gaze at her backside as she scrambles to her feet. "Don't stand up on my account," he says darkly. "I liked that view just fine."

"How was your meeting, sir?"

"Dreadful." He shucks off his suit jacket on his way to his office. "But then I had a nice lunch with a generous donor and his fat checkbook. Things are looking up."

When he smiles to himself, she relaxes. "Coffee?"

He shakes his head. "Is the payroll waiting for me?"

"Of course." The file is right on his desk alongside the foundation's checkbook. And his luxurious fountain pen with the Wincott trident etched into its gold surface.

She's not going to screw anything up today. He'll have to find someone else to complain about.

Coralie follows him dutifully into the office and waits while he tests his Montblanc on the blotter. Then he signs all seven of the checks the accountant dropped off earlier.

It's a small organization, as Mr. Wincott likes to say. But we make great change in people's lives.

She'd been hoping hers could be added to the list of lives changed. That's why she'd taken this job.

And it looks like she was right, but not in the way she ever intended.

After signing the last check, he hands back the folder so she can send off the checks. "It's month end," he says expectantly.

Well, shit. Seems she forgot something after all. "Yes, sir," she says quickly. "One moment." She trots to a cupboard on his office wall and locates three more white envelopes and three stamps. She delivers them promptly.

He unlocks his bottom desk drawer and pulls out another checkbook—a special one. She's only seen glimpses of it, but it's drawn on an island bank she's never heard of.

The last girl who had this job told her about these, too. Three more checks to three more people. You won't be asked to address the envelopes or mail them. And don't watch while he signs them. It makes him cranky.

She carries the payroll folder back to her own desk to give him some privacy.

Her hands are shaking a little bit, and her eyes feel achy in their sockets. That's never a good sign. Whenever she feels like this, she knows a migraine is coming on. Sometimes they last for days.

"Coralie?" he calls two minutes later.

She smooths her skirt and walks back into the office. The envelopes and the special checkbook are already gone. "Yes, sir?" He loves it when she calls him *sir*.

"What did you get up to while I was gone? Anything fun?" He's in a playful mood.

She rearranges her face into a smile. "Depends what you mean by fun. If you're excited by alphabetizing folders, then I had a blast."

His laugh is indulgent and meant to be seductive. "Bring us two glasses," he says. "And ice if you wish."

"Of course, Mr. Wincott." She goes back to the outer office and opens another cabinet over the coffee bar.

He keeps the scotch glasses up here, the last girl had said. "They're fragile, so be careful. I chipped one once and I thought he was going to fire me," she told Coralie. "Listen—if he's in a certain mood, he'll tell you to bring two of them. But please understand—you don't have to. You can just bring a single glass. It sends a message. Because if you take that drink? His hand is up your skirt two minutes later."

It's not even a difficult choice. She's already played with fire, and she's already been burned. That's why she retrieves two of the hand-cut crystal glasses before closing the cabinet.

She might as well. There's nothing to lose now.

By the time she sets the glasses on his desk, two ice cubes in hers, he's already pulling the top off the bottle that he keeps in another desk drawer.

She knows how much the scotch costs. You could get a pair of designer shoes for the price of that bottle. And when the scent of it reaches her nose, she tastes revulsion on the back of her tongue.

He pours her two fingers. That's two more than she'd like, but you can't always have exactly what you want.

She lifts her glass to touch his. "Cin cin, as my grandmother used to say."

"Was she Italian?"

She tosses her hair in a way that shows off her throat. He loves her throat. "I don't really know." Not everyone is like the Wincotts, who can trace their history back for ten generations.

"Bottoms up," he says, winking.

The first sip of whiskey burns going down. But she already knows, from a couple of months' experience with Mr. Wincott, that this unpleasantness will mellow on the tongue. A few more sips and she'll forget to be shocked.

She needs this paycheck. And that's not even all she needs from him.

"Get the door, will you?" he says.

"Yes, sir." She locks the door and returns to hover near his desk.

He grasps her hip and guides her into his lap, his hand on her knee, his touch a little rough.

"That's a good girl," he says. "I like this skirt. Very pretty." He strokes her leg.

"Thank you."

"Now drink your whiskey."

She takes another sip, but just a small one. She knows she shouldn't drink at all right now.

He takes the glass out of her hand anyway. "I have a little present for you," he says silkily. "For a job well done this week."

"*Oh*," she says softly. The truth is that his presents are incredible. Last month he gave her a silver necklace from Tiffany's. In the robin's-egg blue box and everything.

It's so nice that she hasn't worn it yet. Before bed each night, she takes it out just to look at it.

"There was a Coach store in the New York airport." His fingers trail up her thigh. "Made me think of you."

"So nice," she says breathily.

"I'll show you in a little while. After you fix the invitation list I asked you to type. Some of the addresses are missing zip codes."

Oh God. Again? "I'm so sorry, Mr. Wincott. I'll fix it."

"That's sloppy work, Coralie. But I forgive you. On your knees now," he says.

"Yes, Mr. Wincott." She begins to slide off his lap.

He makes an eager noise, but she knows to take her time. To build the anticipation. With stubborn slowness, she slides down to the floor, past the bulge in his wool gabardine, until her knees hit the rug.

Looking up at him, she licks her lips suggestively. She's better at this than typing. Much better. Sometimes a girl needs to play to her strengths.

He reaches for his belt.

Coralie allows her gaze to soften. She retreats inside herself. It's a useful trick she learned in childhood. Had to. Whenever her stepfather took a belt to her, she would send herself to a private room in her mind. She knows how to be here on her knees, yet not really present.

She puts her forearms on his knees, her mind already drifting. His groan sounds far off. She can barely feel his hand in her hair, and when he puts his other hand possessively on her throat, it doesn't really register.

"Straight from the devil, aren't you?" he murmurs. "Choke on it, girlie. That's it. The best little sinner in town."

At peace, somewhere else, she can hardly hear him.

11

ROWAN

"Rowan?"

I look up from my computer, where I'd been searching for news updates on Tim's murder. "Yes?"

"Didn't you say you were going to get coffee?" Beatrice prompts from her desk across the room.

"Oh. Sorry." I did say that, but then I'd forgotten. Now I push my chair back.

"Or I could go," she says. "It's no problem. But you said you could use a break."

"I'm going," I insist. My finger hovers on the lid of my laptop. *Senseless Murder at the Wincott Mansion. No Suspects Yet.* The article speculates that he was killed for his "valuables." Which must mean his wallet and his computer.

I close my laptop, unease swamping me again.

"Survivor's guilt," my father said last night, as we were washing the dishes together. "That's normal."

He's a shrink, always quick with a diagnosis. But he has a point. I'd been so angry at Tim. I'm struggling with the idea that I was thinking mean thoughts about him—probably during the minutes that he'd died.

"Rowan?" Beatrice prods gently.

I rise from my seat. "Should we have half caf? It's almost three."

She's about to answer when the lights flicker again.

My eyes fly to the fixture on my desk, which blinks one more time before steadying. "You know what? At this point I actually *hope* the mansion is haunted. It would explain a few things."

Beatrice makes a grumpy noise and stands up. She hates it when anyone mentions ghosts. She feels it's undignified. "I'll walk with you. I haven't been outside all day."

In other words, I seem like someone who needs babysitting. "Sure. But it's my turn to buy."

"Sweet. Let's hustle." She heads for the door. "Don't forget that you have a call with the glazier at four."

"Right. Thank you." I trail her into the library. It's not really her job to keep my calendar. She's not my personal assistant. But there's no denying that I'm operating at 50 percent capacity today. "After that call, I have to head out. The funeral starts at five thirty."

She looks over her shoulder. "You want company for that, too?"

Yes. Desperately. "No, I'm okay."

I don't mention that I still have Tim's watch and cufflinks, too. It feels tawdry, but I need to return them to his family. I follow her into the corridor.

"Back door," Beatrice says, just as I turn reflexively toward the front.

"Oh. Shit." I reverse course immediately. "Good call." I'd forgotten about the police tape in front and the gawkers.

Beatrice leads the way toward the back, which means descending a few steps into the grim, cavernous galley. There are no Greek gods on the walls in here. This was a room where servants worked.

My plan for this space will divide it into a sleek catering kitchen and a passageway toward the Orangerie, which is what I'm calling the new glassed-in gathering space at the back of the mansion.

There was once a real orangerie on the property. I found a reference to it in the old plans for the house, and Hank was charmed by my idea to reference it in the new design.

Of course he was. Growing citrus fruit out of season was the way the elite of New England used to show off their wealth. Before there were Amex Black Cards or private jets.

Beatrice stops at the exit. "Remember the new code for the door?"

"Um . . ." It takes me a second. "Eighteen-sixty-one." It's the first year that Amos Wincott lived in his new home.

"Then press pound."

"Got it."

We slip outside together, and I look carefully around the backyard. We seem to be alone, but I'm too shaky for surprises.

Beatrice seems less afraid, or at least she's the better actor. She heads straight into the yard, avoiding even a glance toward the parking lot, where there might still be traces of blood on the ground.

I follow her in silence. The grass is tatty back here, owing to all the contractors' activity. We approach the tool trailer. It blocks the back portion of the yard, and my footsteps slow as we approach its shadow.

Beatrice turns to look over her shoulder. "You okay?"

"Yes," I say shakily. But then I remember Lickie's reaction to the trailer on the night I'd found Tim, how she'd tugged on the leash. My feet grind to a halt.

"Rowan?" Beatrice asks, stopping to look at me.

"I just remembered something. From that night."

She gapes at me. "Really? Something you saw?"

"No. But I wonder if Lickie did. She practically pulled me off my feet when I was in view of the tool trailer. I forgot until just now."

Beatrice swivels, taking in our surroundings. It would be so easy for someone to hide behind the trailer or the dumpster. We'd never see them from this angle.

"You think someone was lurking back here?" she asks me.

"Maybe?" I say queasily. "Impossible to say now. And I guess it could have been anyone."

"Or a squirrel."

I give her a weak smile. "True."

Beatrice makes a point of checking behind the trailer as she passes it.

Before I follow her, I pause and look back at the mansion, which looms over us, darkening the property with her angular shadow. *What happened? Why did Tim have to die? And why here?*

The mansion offers no answers.

We head toward Orange Street, approaching the only grave on the property. It's an elaborate headstone carved with an angel cradling a baby. MARCUS WINCOTT: 1925–1997.

My skin prickles with awareness when we pass the grave.

I hurry after Beatrice through a stand of mature trees. Last week I thought this part of the property was majestic. Today it seems like another place for someone to hide.

We finally reach the sidewalk and turn wordlessly to the north. The coffee shop is three blocks away. "You sleeping any better?" Beatrice asks eventually.

"Somewhat," I lie. "Coffee will help."

But it's hard to imagine ever sleeping well again.

———————

The coffee shop is quiet when we step inside, but my head echoes loudly with memories of Tim.

The burly, tattooed barista waves me over. "Omigod, *hiiii!* I'm *so* sorry. I just can't *believe* it. When I saw his photo on the news? I was shocked. Never had a regular get murdered before."

And now I wish I'd let Beatrice do the coffee run alone. My sluggish brain can't figure out what to say to this near stranger. "I'm sorry, too. It's shocking."

"You must be out of your mind." He runs a hand through his curly hair and visibly shivers. "It's just fucked up, you know? The police had better solve this."

I nod, fighting the urge to spit my coffee order at him so I can leave.

"He was just so *nice.* And you guys were, like, my little afternoon fairy tale."

That's what you think. But I'm not going to stand here and argue the point.

"I mean, that first time? When he came in and showed me your picture?" He clutches his hand to his chest. "It was the most romantic thing."

"Sorry? What?"

His eyes widen comically. "Wait, he didn't come clean about that? Oh, it was fricking adorable." He laughs. "So, yeah. Before you guys had a coffee together at table six?" He points vaguely in the direction of the windows. "He came in, like, the day before, with your picture on his phone. He says, 'I met this great lady in here a year ago. We talked for hours, but I was just passing through. Now I'm back, and I never forgot her. Does she still come in here?'"

I stare at him. "He did *what?*"

"I know, right?" The guy nods his shaggy head, all wrapped up in his anecdote. "I told him you usually turned up in the afternoon, and he smiled. It was the most romantic thing I ever heard. He never forgot you."

"Okay, look," Beatrice says crisply. "You're upsetting my friend. Any chance we could get two half-caf coffees to go?"

The barista—Davey, according to his name tag—swipes at his eyes. Then he seems to gather himself. "Sure. Sorry. So sorry for your loss." He grabs two paper cups off the stack.

I pull a twenty out of my wallet, dumbfounded by what he said. I never met Tim until he introduced himself that day in April, and so we sure as hell never had the conversation the barista described.

Beatrice doctors our coffees, and I cash out, dropping a five into the tip jar. Then she tows me outside. "Okay, what the fuck? Did you *really* meet Tim a year ago?"

"No!" My heart spasms in time with our footsteps. "That story made no sense."

Beatrice marches me down Danforth. "So . . . Tim lied?"

"Maybe? I just can't picture it."

"You're a catch, Rowan. But it's hard to imagine him haunting the neighborhood, trying to figure out where you like to buy your coffee and quizzing baristas just because he liked your picture in the paper. If it's true, that makes him a creep."

"*If* it's true," I echo. I try to picture Tim scoping out the neighborhood, trying to craft a spontaneous meeting. There aren't many coffee shops on the West End. He wouldn't have to ask more than a couple of baristas *Does she come in here?*

Still. That's oddball behavior. I can't imagine he'd do that.

"What if our man Davey is just confused?" Beatrice wonders. "Baristas meet a lot of people. Maybe it was some other dude who told him the story about meeting a girl and then losing track of her."

"Maybe," I say slowly. "That's a pretty good theory. Tim wouldn't have bothered."

"And it's not like you can ask him," Beatrice points out, striding onward.

"Nope," I say with a dull finality. "Could you slow down, though? These shoes are killing me." They're the ones I'd reclaimed from Natalie, and they do pinch my toes, damn it.

"Sure, sorry," Beatrice says. "That story just put me on edge."

It would have done the same for me, but I was already there.

———————

Five o'clock comes before I'm ready. Beatrice leaves first. "Take care of yourself tonight," she says gently.

"I will," I promise. "Thank you."

Her footsteps echo as she retreats from the room, and I put my face in my hands.

It's time to pull myself together and go to Tim's funeral. But I'm so full of dread. I don't know what I'll find to say to his parents. Not after what I saw.

I stand up and button my blazer. It's either leave or sit here ten yards from where it happened.

After grabbing my handbag, I switch off the desk lamp, plunging the library into gloomy shadows. This room made me uncomfortable *before* Tim's death, so I don't waste time as I propel myself out of the office suite and through the atrium. The echo makes it sound as if ghosts are on my heels.

When I reach the door, I pause for a moment and put my hand on the lion's head that's artfully carved in walnut above the brass mail slot. Sometimes tourists poke open the mail slot to get a peek inside.

Not two weeks ago I'd told Tim all about this door. How the craftsmen used four different kinds of wood, to prevent warping. How it was one of the only things in the house that actually came from Maine. The sandstone cladding came from Connecticut, but almost everything else was shipped from Europe—marble from Italy. Rugs from France.

"All that trouble just to show off," Tim said.

I shiver, remembering exactly how he smiled at me after he said it. Like we were in on the same secret.

I hear a creak, and the hair stands up on the back of my neck. I turn around sharply. But there's nothing behind me.

Get moving, Gallagher. I grasp the iron handle and open the door. The new security system gives a low beep, and I immediately realize my error. The news trucks are finally gone, but the gawkers aren't. A handful of people linger on the other side of the boxwood hedge, scanning the police tape that's still blocking off the gravel parking lot. They look up at me as I step outside.

Dropping my chin, I close the door and test the new lock to be sure that it holds. Then, without making any eye contact, I cross the porch and hurry down the steps.

Tim's car is gone now, thank God. There's literally nothing to see. I've never understood why death and violence always draw a crowd, but until Thursday night, I don't think I understood that someone close to me could be murdered. I'd felt immune.

I don't anymore.

The funeral home is on State Street, so I walk inland. The wind kicks up, and a seagull flies past overhead, casting a mournful cry.

I take a different route than we took earlier, just so I can avoid passing the coffee shop. So there's no chance of running into Davey the barista.

His story bothers me. The day Tim had introduced himself used to be a happy memory. I just don't buy the idea that he staked me out beforehand. Tim didn't have a creepy vibe at all.

Beatrice called him a bore, but it was more accurate to say that he was a little old-fashioned. He read a lot of books and favored older music. He had old-school manners, too, like pulling out my chair at restaurants and texting in full sentences. With punctuation.

That's what I'd liked best about him. I've already had a lifetime's worth of bad-boy antics. (See: Natalie's father.) The whole reason I dated Tim was that he seemed settled. Rational.

And I still believe that. The barista's story just doesn't add up.

It's getting close to five thirty, so I pick up my pace to the funeral home. It's a stately old mansion in the Federal style with five Ionic columns lined up on the porch. They're painted in a crisp white. Mourners in tasteful clothing stream past them toward the entrance.

I recognize no one.

On the porch, one of the heavy paneled doors is propped open. Inside, I see a large foyer, decorated to look tasteful, but solemn. My shoes sink into the thick carpet. The wooden furniture gleams. Bach plays softly on the sound system.

There must be a style guide somewhere for funeral homes. Architecture for Bereavement: Sad people require classical lines, heavy moldings, gently creaking floors. Nothing too rococo—that's gauche. But nothing too sunny. Danish modern or mid-century furnishings are disrespectful to the dead.

Even as I'm having this slightly unhinged thought, it occurs to me that Tim would find it funny. He liked my nerdy observations about architecture. At least, he said he did.

The parade of people in front of me slowly filters through a set of double doors. Beyond, I get a glimpse of a big room heaving with people.

I'm just about to step inside when I hear, "Mom, wait!"

I spin around, surprised to see Natalie hurrying toward me. For one terrible moment, I assume that something is wrong. But then I notice her outfit—black jeans plus a black blouse from my closet.

"Am I dressed okay for a funeral?" she asks.

"Of course," I sputter. "But I didn't expect to see you here." I hadn't even told her where it was.

"Don't you want me to come?" She looks stricken. "I was trying to be supportive."

"Oh, I *do*." My voice almost breaks. "Sorry." I reach out and hug her, which she allows. "Thank you. But are you sure?" I glance at the crowded room full of somber faces. "Don't you have an exam tomorrow?"

She gives me a look that implies I'm insane. "It's only Spanish. Let's get seats. If there are any."

The regular chairs are taken, so we end up on a bench against the paneled back wall. This suits me fine. I don't need a direct line of sight to the coffin at the front of the room.

"Do you know anyone here?" Natalie whispers.

I shake my head. "Your grandmother had a rule—always go to the funeral. Even if it makes you uncomfortable. Even if you're not sure it matters."

"But I didn't go to hers," Natalie points out.

"You were five. She would have understood."

Natalie takes the program out of my hands. It's just a folded page that reads: *Timothy Everett Kovak, February 1, 1979–June 6, 2024.*

"He was an Aquarius. Clever. Self-reliant." Natalie gives me a sideways glance. "But also moody and unpredictable."

"Is that so?" I knew Tim well enough to be sure that he would have rolled his eyes at any mention of astrology, and yet I hadn't known his middle name.

At the front of the room, a man with an acoustic guitar slung around his neck sets himself on a stool and begins to play. The song is Kamakawiwo'ole's version of "Over the Rainbow."

Natalie puts down the program and listens.

The guitar notes wash over the room like a gentle rain. Voices go quiet. When the guitarist begins to sing, goose bumps rise on my arms.

After the first verse, I notice two older men taking the podium—a pastor and a rabbi. Tim had told me that his mother was Jewish, but not religious, and his father a "lapsed Catholic."

It's so easy to hear his voice in my head. He's still in there.

Just as the song comes to a close, a woman opens the door and slips into the crowded room. Since I'm so near the door, she hovers at my elbow for a moment until I scoot a few inches closer to Natalie, making room on the bench.

"Thank you," she whispers, claiming the seat.

I sneak a glance at her. She looks familiar, but it's not the time or place to ask how I might know her.

The service begins with a greeting from the rabbi and a few words about Tim. It's nice, but disorienting. I feel as though I'm hearing about a stranger.

Probably because I am.

12

NATALIE

Among the beautiful pictures
That hang on Memory's wall.
Is one of a dim old forest,
That seemeth best of all.

Chills rise on Natalie's back as she listens to the rabbi read a poem. She can't seem to take her eyes off the coffin at the front of the room. It's a closed casket. It would have to be, wouldn't it?

The thought makes her shiver.

She hadn't lied. Well, not exactly. She's here to support her mom, but she's also curious. Although she hadn't counted on the strangeness of sitting in the same room with his body.

Do they still put makeup on corpses that were shot in the face?

What does it say about her that she thinks about these things?

But even without the bullet hole in his head, this ritual would be eerie. A shell of a person, lying in a box—and all these people sitting politely in front of him.

Moving only her eyes, she surveys the mourners in the room. Friends of the dead man, carefully dressed. Rows and rows of them, with sad expressions on all their faces.

She needed to see this for herself. As if she might understand him a little better—this jerk who made her mother cry. And her mom is *not* a crier.

Natalie can't say the same for the woman who came at the last minute and perched on the end of the bench. Her eyes are red, and there's a nervous energy radiating from her body. Natalie can feel it from two seats away.

She sneaks another glance down the bench. The woman is older than her mom and skinny. Like, *bony*. Her hands are clasped together, the grip so tight that Natalie almost expects to hear the bones snap. She looks like she's climbing out of her skin.

A relative, maybe. There's a strong resemblance between her and the dead guy. Her hair is mousier, but she has the same cold blue eyes.

It's a little creepy. But so was Tim, and Natalie would know. Her mom thinks Natalie never met Tim. But they did meet. Twice.

The first time was on a Saturday morning after she'd stayed the night at Tessa's. She came home early, because Tessa decided to go to the boys' lacrosse game in Augusta, and Natalie didn't want to waste half a Saturday on it. Lacrosse players are so full of themselves.

But when she'd popped through the front door of her house, *he* was there. Just sitting in the center of the sofa like he owned the place. Scrolling through his phone. She'd dropped her backpack and kind of stared at him for a second.

Then she noticed the sound of the shower running upstairs, and when she realized the implication, a wave of distaste ran through her body. At least Tim was fully dressed, thank God.

She was swallowing her shock and getting ready to grudgingly introduce herself when she noticed what he was doing.

He was easing her mother's phone onto the coffee table and picking up his own.

It was her *mom's* phone he'd been scrolling.

Her mouth fell open in shock. Skipping right past the introductions, she'd snapped at him, "What were you *doing*?"

"Just looking at our photos together," he'd said easily. Like she was the crazy one. "I take it you're Natalie?" He'd given her a friendly smile.

Her face went hot, and anger rose like a wave.

That's also when the shower shut off upstairs.

She did *not* want her mom to arrive downstairs, hair still wet, trying to pretend this wasn't weird.

Later, Natalie would feel dumb about running, but she didn't stop to think. She grabbed her backpack off the floor and walked back out the front door again. She sat at the coffee shop for two whole hours until her mom started texting with nagging questions, and so she knew the guy was gone.

When she got home again, there was no evidence he'd ever been there. No extra coffee mug on the counter. Nothing. Mom had erased him from the house. But not from Natalie's mind. She couldn't stop thinking about the way he'd casually set her mom's phone down. As if that wasn't creepy as fuck.

Then her mother didn't mention it. And if Tim had told her mom about their awkward encounter, her mother would have brought it up for sure. Probably in the car, where her mom usually broke out the most awkward conversations, using that faked casual voice. *It's time for a friendly chat with my teenager.*

But nope. No chat. Tim hadn't said a thing about meeting Natalie.

Natalie wasn't sure what to do about all of it. Wasn't she supposed to warn her mother? Because if *Natalie* was dating a guy who looked through her phone, she'd want someone to tell her.

But God, Natalie did not want to be the one to break the news to her mom. *Hey, Mom, your first boyfriend in my entire life is a controlling creep. Sorry.*

Days passed and still the meeting with Tim never came up. This seemed to prove Natalie's point. If Tim were a good man, he'd have mentioned it. *So, I met your psycho daughter and I think she got the wrong idea about me.*

Or something.

Natalie didn't know what to do, so she asked two friends. Tessa said she should just tell her mother everything. The other one said not to worry, because the trash usually takes itself out.

It didn't. But then it did, and her mother started crying in the bathroom.

Natalie waited a whole day after the breakup before asking what happened with Tim. Her mother had said that he'd ended things. "But it's fine," she'd said with her puffy red eyes. "It wasn't serious."

Natalie expected to feel relief, but instead she felt more rage. Because her mother was feeling rejected by a *loser.*

She still hasn't told her mother about the phone, because it doesn't matter anymore, right? And she didn't tell her about the second time she and Tim met. Same reason.

Instead, she did that thing where you rehearse what you'll say if you ever run into the guy again. *Hey, dude. You made my mother stress-eat the Ben & Jerry's. I hope your dick falls off.*

Mom didn't mention him again, but Natalie could tell she wasn't over it. Her mom started using that FriendFinder app in an unhealthy way—watching Tim live his bougie life, ordering oysters at Eventide or whatever.

Her mom thinks Natalie doesn't know how often she opens that app. That's why Natalie sometimes leaves her phone at Tessa's when they go out.

Except now they're here together at Tim's *funeral*, and Natalie is all mixed-up inside. She knows that she had a small part in the way things ended for them, but God, he wasn't supposed to *die*.

It's not her fault, though. It's really not.

A wasplike buzz emanates from her crossbody bag, sending a zing up her spine. A new message on her phone. Possibly from *him*. Her other secret.

There are different kinds of secrets. There are the kind that hurt like a hole in your stomach. Tim was one of those. But there are also secrets that sparkle.

Her fingers itch to unzip the bag and peer at her phone. But no way. Not at a funeral, and not with her mother sitting pressed up against her on the bench.

It can wait. It *should* wait. Even when she reads his messages immediately, she makes herself wait to answer them. She needs to play it cool.

There's someone new at the podium now—a friend of Tim's. He's telling stories from their childhood. "Tim was a nerd, but a nerd who still liked to get into trouble. He had a deeply curious mind, and he used it to prank the teachers at our middle school."

There's a misty chuckle.

"One time he noticed that our science teacher often stared into a desk drawer during class. Tim decided that the teacher didn't really know anything about science, and he was hiding his lecture notes in there so nobody would be the wiser."

The crowd chuckles again, including Natalie, who's mostly just relieved that he's trying to be funny.

"So Tim planned a sting operation. We hung back in the classroom when the teacher stepped out at lunchtime. That drawer was unlocked, and we opened it. But there were no notes inside. Instead, we found our very first *Playboy* magazine."

There's a sudden burst of loud laughter. Like a thunderclap.

"We learned some *very* exciting science that day."

The room practically shakes.

"But, wait, there's more. The teacher came back into the room when we were still there, paging through the magazine. We got caught red-handed."

"Oh jeez," Natalie whispers, and her mother gives her a gentle smile.

"I was about to pee myself. I was picturing the phone call home to my mother. 'Your son read a dirty magazine.' But Tim coolly handed it over, saying that he didn't suppose the teacher wanted to take this up with the principal, did he?"

More laughter.

But, see? Natalie privately scoffs. Tim was a slippery fuck. Who blackmails their middle school teacher?

"This is probably the first time Tim's parents are hearing this story. The teacher did the smart thing and let us off the hook. And he never looked into that drawer again. So that's my experience of being friends with Tim—he was thoughtful, and yet always pushed the limit. I will miss him for the rest of my life."

Natalie's mom makes a sad face.

This is the weirdest mother-daughter outing ever.

The service closes with another song. The hot guy with the guitar begins strumming gently, and the tune turns into "What a Wonderful World" by Louis Armstrong.

Natalie is fine until he starts singing about green trees and roses. He has a good voice, and she can feel it resonate behind her breastbone. Sadness starts to creep through her chest, making her eyes hot.

The pallbearers line up beside the coffin. There are about a million roses on top. The men bend down and slowly lift it onto their shoulders. With grief on their faces, they carry it out the side door.

Tim departs from his funeral, feet-first. Everyone in the room is openly weeping. Natalie is not made of stone. Tim was only a little older than her mom.

And maybe he really *was* only looking at their selfies on her mom's phone. Maybe.

The singer really rocks the chorus. And when he gets to that line about babies crying, Natalie's throat closes up, and she has to concentrate really hard on not crying.

Mom pulls a tissue out of her purse and dabs at her own eyes.

The woman on the other side of Mom is in rough shape, sobbing so hard her whole body is shaking. Yet it's almost completely silent. She has a paper napkin pressed to both eyes at once, and the thing is already shredded.

Digging into her purse, her mother finds a tissue and passes it to the sobbing woman.

She takes it with a jerky nod. Then she suddenly jumps to her feet. Whirling around, she pushes the door open and bolts from the room. Natalie gets a narrow glimpse of her literally running through the foyer before the door closes again.

Meanwhile, everyone else begins to stand up and follow the casket out the double doors at the opposite end of the room.

Natalie does the math. She and her mom are in back. They'll be stuck here for hours.

The guitar player keeps strumming for several more minutes, until he eventually gives up. The line moves so slowly that she can barely see outside. There's a lawn. Some people—probably Tim's family—have formed a receiving line.

Natalie will be legal to drink before they ever make it to the front of this line. "Do we have to stay?"

"Well, I do," her mother says.

"Okay," she grumbles. "Whatever."

Mom gives her a soft, patient look that she knows she doesn't deserve.

Because she's a liar, and her mom can never find out.

13

ROWAN

Natalie is fidgety as we creep toward the lawn. And I get it. This line is atrocious. Even after we make it outside, there are still a hundred people in front of us, chatting in low, respectful voices.

A gleaming hearse waits nearby, the casket inside. There's an ocean of flowers covering its lid.

"My feet are killing me," I whisper in a feeble attempt to commiserate with my daughter.

"It's those shoes," she points out. "You should just give them to me."

I snort. "Fine. But you can't have that blouse. It's dry-clean only." And black is too severe on her anyway.

She glances down at it and looks annoyed. "Can we get take-out sushi tonight?"

"Heck yes. We deserve *all* the sushi."

"Cool." She takes a step back from me and pulls her phone out of her bag, but only a few inches. She peeps at the screen and then zips her bag shut again.

She's on that thing so much I'm honestly surprised she didn't whip it out during the service.

The line moves forward, and we're suddenly in front of a display of framed remembrances of Tim. There are photos, articles, and awards.

"So this is him," Natalie says under her breath, bending close for a look at the pictures. "He looks, um . . ." She grasps for something nice to say. "Smart."

"He was," I quietly agree. Someone has done an impressive job commemorating his life. There are birthday party photos, with an apple-cheeked Tim blowing out four candles on a cake. There's a photo of

Tim as a schoolboy. Maybe he's six or seven, but he's already wearing a button-down shirt. No cuff links yet, though.

I peer at the earliest photo. A pair of smiling adults are cradling a newborn, although you can't really see his face. Then I see something in the picture's background that startles me.

"What?" Natalie asks. "You're holding up the line."

"Look," I whisper, pointing at the photo. "The banner. What does that say?"

Natalie leans in and squints. "'Adoption Day! Welcome Home . . .' The rest is cropped out."

We move forward. "He never told me he was adopted," I whisper.

"Oh," my daughter says with a shrug.

The line moves again, and now we're in front of a bunch of newspaper clippings. His articles, I guess.

"And I had no idea he'd been a finalist for a Pulitzer Prize," I murmur. "For investigative reporting." I had no idea about a lot of things.

Natalie nudges me. "Who's that? She keeps looking at us."

Following her gaze, I see Detective Riley standing at the edge of the crowd. She nods in greeting.

I give her a wave, maybe a beat too late. "She's a police officer. The one investigating what happened to Tim."

Natalie's eyes grow huge. "She's looking for the killer *here*? Right now?"

"Maybe," I whisper, as we move forward another two paces. "I really don't know."

Natalie glances at Detective Riley again. "I guess that makes sense. Most people are killed by someone they know. That's what they taught us in health class."

"Shh."

She gives me an evil look, because nobody likes to be shushed by her mother. But nobody wants to hear this kind of speculation at a funeral, either. I'm painfully aware of the cliché—*it's usually the boyfriend*. Or girlfriend, I guess. That's why it's a health class topic.

Detective Riley implied the same thing at my kitchen table. *I have to ask, Rowan.*

Every cliché has truth in it. The pastor called Tim's death a *senseless tragedy*, yet it must have made sense to someone.

We finally approach Tim's family at the end of the receiving line. I eye Tim's mother as she greets the couple in front of us. Her warm eyes are red-rimmed and far more exhausted than they'd been that night at Whole Foods. And his father—a slender man with fairer hair—looks as white as a sheet.

Buried in my pocketbook are Tim's cuff links and watch. I've placed everything in a little cotton pouch, because it seemed more discreet than simply handing them over. *He left these on my bedside table. Draw your own conclusions.*

But this moment isn't right for returning Tim's things to his parents. Not with Natalie at my side.

The couple ahead of us gives the Kovaks a last hug and then moves on. Suddenly I'm eye to eye with Tim's mom.

"Rowan," Mrs. Kovak says softly. "Hello again."

I'm surprised she remembers my name. "I'm so sorry for your loss. I just wanted to pay my respects. This is my daughter, Natalie."

Her eyes take in Natalie, and then she tries and fails to smile. "It's lovely of you both to come. The police told us that you found him. That must have been terrifying."

"It was," I agree quietly. "But I'll be okay. I'm just so sorry."

"We'd *just* been speaking about you," she says, shaking her head. "I'd been asking Tim when he was going to bring you around for dinner."

"Oh." I don't know how to respond. She must not know that we'd broken up.

"He spoke of you a little," she says with a sad smile. "After we met at the grocery. I'm a very nosy mother, I guess. He said you're an architect."

"Right," I whisper. "He was a good listener. In happier times, I appreciated how interested he was in my work. I'm just so sorry for your loss."

"We should have had the chance to get to know each other better," she says with a sniff.

I don't know what to say to that. But Mr. Kovak bails me out with a "Thank you for coming."

I take that as my cue to go, and so does Natalie, who puts her hand on my arm.

"Finally," she whispers as soon as we're out of earshot.

We walk toward the edge of the lawn, and I look around to get my bearings. My gaze snags on Detective Riley. She's standing on the sidewalk, pad and pen in hand, watching the guests.

She nods again when I spot her.

The memory of our conversation passes over me like a dark cloud. *Did you expect to run into him?*

I told her no to protect myself, but the lie is eating a hole in my psyche. I wish they'd just arrest someone already and put me out of my misery. I haven't been this fearful in years. Not since I was twenty-four years old and watching the police handcuff Natalie's father. They'd pushed him into the back of a police cruiser and upended my life.

Different circumstances, of course, but that night changed me forever. And I know Tim's death will, too.

We pick up sushi on the way home, as promised.

I lose my appetite when we find a stranger standing on our front walk. It's a woman in her thirties. Pretty, with intense brown eyes.

"Ms. Gallagher?" she says. "Can I have a word? My name is Jules. I'm an investigative journalist."

"I'm sorry," I say, not caring how abrupt it sounds. "No comment."

She doesn't move, and her intense eyes narrow. "I worked with Tim. I was at the funeral. I want to ask you a few questions."

We're basically at a standoff. She's still blocking the path, but I could follow Natalie's example and step around her onto the grass.

I'd promised Beatrice that I'd never talk to the press. But I hadn't realized how difficult it is to be rude to someone asking for help. "I'm sorry, but I can't talk to a reporter. You should know, though, that I wouldn't be much help. I didn't know him that well."

"But you could just talk to me on background. That means—"

"I know what it means," I say crisply. "I can't help you. I'm sorry. And this is private property."

I walk past her and into the house. All I need in this world is some sushi and a decent night's sleep. What I *don't* need is another chance to describe how Tim had broken up with me a few days before he died.

I lock the door carefully and then peek through the peephole. Apparently, the reporter's given up—she's climbing into a blue SUV.

Good.

We eat our take-out dinner, but I barely taste it. "I'm going to put on my pjs and get in bed with a few episodes of . . . something. And you're going to walk the dog and study Spanish?"

Natalie rolls her eyes. "Of course I am. Big fun here tonight, yeah?"

"Yup." I don't care about big fun. All I want is to roll back to a time when nobody was dead.

I clean up from our meal and head upstairs to change and climb into bed. After propping my laptop on my knees, I decide to check my email before navigating Netflix. Big mistake. There's a new message from Natalie's father, Harrison. The subject line reads: **We have to talk about Natalie.**

He's wrong. On the day of a funeral, I absolutely do not have to talk to anyone. Least of all my ex-con ex-boyfriend.

I close the tab and open up a search window. *Tim Kovak adoption*, I type. There are no results. *Tim Kovak Magdalene Home*. No hits.

The first conversation Tim and I ever had was about the Wincott Mansion, and my discovery of family documents relating to the maternity home. Many of those babies would have been adopted in the Portland area.

But if he had a personal connection to the place, he never said so.

14

TUESDAY

I start the workday with a meeting at the lighting consultant's office. We spend our time discussing the conversion of the mansion's handmade nineteenth-century gasoliers to energy-saving electric lights, and I learn a lot. This is why I became an architect—to surround myself with beauty and function.

Afterward, I check my messages on the way to the car. Natalie has texted to say her Spanish exam went well, and that she's off to study for tomorrow's English test.

I'm looking forward to a peaceful date with a sandwich and my CAD software when I return to the mansion. I text Beatrice to ask what she wants from the deli. But her answer makes my stomach clench:

Beatrice: Forget the deli, just come back.
Beatrice: There are two cops here to talk to you.

Oh God. I dash off a quick response, saying I'm on my way.

The drive is less than ten minutes, but that's plenty of time to panic. I keep thinking back to the lie I told Detective Riley. Does she know?

Why else would they want to interview me again?

I park on a side street and slip onto the property from the back. Crossing the lonely stretch between the hedgerow and the tool trailer makes me twitchy. I can't stop wondering if there was a murderer hiding back there the night I discovered Tim. And if he watched me approach Tim's car.

Hurrying toward the house, my gaze shifts automatically to the crime scene. I do a double take. The police tape is still fluttering in the offshore breeze, but there's now a six-foot construction fence standing between the sidewalk and the parking area. It wasn't there this morning.

I enter the mansion through the back door and almost shriek as Beatrice steps out of the shadows. "I told the cops you were out at a meeting," she hisses. "But they insisted that you'd want to speak to them."

"Do you think they arrested someone?"

Beatrice gives her head a quick shake. "We would have seen it on TV. And two detectives at your desk? That means they're feeling desperate. They asked me a bunch more questions, too. Where was I that night? Did I see anything?"

"Sorry about that," I whisper, because Beatrice looks strung out. The Wincotts hate bad publicity, and Beatrice hates anything the Wincotts hate.

She lets out a harsh breath. "You don't *have* to talk to them, you know. They can't just turn up on the property every time they have a thought. The family are losing their minds."

The family. Sometimes Beatrice sounds like she's starring in a Godfather movie. "I know I don't. But let's just get this over with."

As we walk through the library, I feel dread. Detective Riley glances around our office, her face its usual unreadable mask.

With her is an older, scowling man, who's scrutinizing the woodwork on a nineteenth-century cabinet. "Detective Fry," he introduces himself after I greet them. "Pleased to meet you, Rowan."

"Pleased" doesn't seem like the right word, given the expression on his face. I recognize him from the TV press conference.

"We have a few more questions for you," Riley says. "Is this a good time?"

My stomach rolls. "Sure. Have a seat." I gesture toward our two extra chairs.

The cops glance at each other. "Is there someplace more private we could talk?" Fry asks.

"Not really," I say. "This room is the only one with furniture. The rest of the mansion is a construction site. I don't have a lot to share, so it's best if we just talk here."

Riley shrugs. "Okay." Her partner sits down beside her. "We won't take up much of your time. First of all, we did some digging into your ex. George Harrison Jones is no longer incarcerated. He was working in Bar Harbor until last month. His whereabouts are now unknown."

"Oh." That's unsettling.

"Any contact from him?" she asks.

"Another email. Last night."

"What did he want?"

I shake my head. "I didn't open it."

"If he pops up anywhere, I'd want to know right away." She passes me another copy of her business card.

"Sure."

She flips a page in her notebook. "Regarding the night of Tim Kovak's death, we've learned that his wallet, laptop, and phone are all missing."

"I read that in the paper."

"Can you describe his wallet?" Fry asks. He has a pen poised above a legal pad.

"It's . . ." I have to think. "A bright color. It's that kind they make out of upcycled billboards. Maybe it's blue and green? I can't picture it exactly."

He nods. "How about his laptop?"

"A gray MacBook."

He writes that down. "Any distinguishing features?"

"Um . . . Yes. There was a sticker on the cover for the *Wall Street Journal*."

Across the room Beatrice gives a soft snort. She's hovering, obviously eavesdropping.

"The computer is missing, as I mentioned," Riley says. "But we were able to access his iCloud drive. It has recent backups from both the computer and the phone. And there were some of your photos on his device. Can I show them to you?"

"Photos of me?" I can't keep the surprise out of my voice. "We didn't take many." I took a total of two selfies with him, because he didn't seem that into it.

Probably because he'd already decided to bail on me.

"The pictures aren't *of* you," she says. "Well, most of them. But the metadata indicates that they were transferred from your device to his."

"That doesn't make any sense. Pictures of what?"

She unlocks an iPad and passes it to me. "Can you verify that you took these shots?"

The first two are selfies—the only ones I'd taken of the two of us. But when I swipe to the third photo, I'm astonished. It's a shot I took of the interior of the Wincott Mansion. As I swipe through the photos, I find a few more shots, from every floor of the house.

And then I swipe again, and my heart practically stops. It's the Wincott family Bible that I found under the floorboards. The one that was featured in the press. "He had *this*? Why?"

Riley stares back at me silently.

I keep flipping. Another shot of the Bible. Then photos of the other book we found under the floorboards—the ledger of babies born at the mansion.

The back of my neck prickles.

"Can you tell me what this is?" Riley asks.

"It's—" My voice cracks. "It's a ledger found right here in this room. It recorded the birth dates of babies born in this building."

"He had *that*?" Beatrice gasps.

Fry gives her a dirty look. Beatrice returns it, and then strides over to me, peering at the screen as I zoom in on the ledger pages.

Each entry lists a birth date, the sex and weight of the child, and a name—first initial followed by a surname. *4 April 1951—Baby girl—7 pounds, 4 ounces—to Miss M. Wattford.*

He has every photo I took. There are eight in total—some interior pages, the front and back covers, and an undated list I'd found in the back of the book, which had included four names.

"What was *up* with that guy?" Beatrice murmurs.

That's my question exactly. *What the hell, Tim?*

"He shouldn't have had any of this," I say quietly.

"Can you confirm—did you take those photos?" Riley asks.

"Yes, I did. I took them in March when I found these items here in the building. I sent them to Hank Wincott so he could see what I'd found."

"Did you share them with Tim?" she asks.

"No! I mean, I *showed* them to him. He asked about my find, because he saw it in the news. But I didn't *give* him the photos. They aren't really mine to share."

"Then how did he get them?" she asks coolly.

"I don't know." My voice rises with stress. "Maybe I set my phone down and walked out of the room. Or maybe he figured out my passcode. It wouldn't have been that hard."

"Can you guess why he wanted them?" she presses.

"*No*," I say sharply.

"Let's do this," Fry says. "You give us permission to clone your cell phone data, and we'll look into it on our end."

"What do you mean?" My voice sounds high and thin and panicky. "A clone?"

He pulls a piece of paper from his legal pad. "If you sign this, we can ask your mobile carrier to share all your data with us. You'll still have your phone. We'll just be able to see the data on it."

To say that I'm alarmed would be an understatement. "What kind of data?"

He shrugs. "Whatever's there. Photos and texts. Calls you made. Apps you use. Stuff like that."

Holy shit. "I don't see how that helps you figure out why Tim took those photos. And I'm not handing over my entire life to strangers for no good reason."

"Think about it," Riley says, her face placid. "Can I show you a couple of unrelated photos from the scene?" My face must go pale because she says, "They're not of the victim, Rowan. Just items found in his car."

I exhale. "Okay. Sure."

She takes the iPad back, taps the screen a few times, and passes it to me. "Are these Tim's?"

The photo shows a pair of wireless earbuds in a sporty steel charging case. I point to the screen. "He had his initials engraved on it. Yes, they're his."

She flips to another photo. "This?"

It's the basket where he kept his Moleskine journals. "That sat on the back seat, and he kept his notebooks in there."

"Hmm," she said. "But there were no notebooks in the car. So this thief liked notebooks, and not earbuds?"

She seems to be waiting for me to weigh in, but all I can do is shrug. My mind is churning through scenarios where the cops look at my phone and find out I was basically stalking Tim for the last few days of his life.

"How about these? Are they familiar?" Riley flips to a new photo—two paper receipts side by side. "From the glove box."

I have to enlarge the screen to read them. One is from Portland Grounds. "That's the coffee shop where we met. It's a few blocks away from here." I point in a northerly direction. "We went there a lot."

"Did you go there on June fifth?"

"Is that the date on it?" I squint at the receipt again and find the date, which is, in fact, June fifth. "Maybe? I go there almost every day. It's my usual spot. But we were broken up by then. And if Tim went there, he didn't tell me."

"Do you find that weird?" she asks. "That he went to your coffee shop?"

"No? Maybe?" I rub my forehead, and the barista's strange story echoes in my brain. "I don't know what you want me to say. Tim and I went there together, and then we stopped. But I don't own the place. He clearly did whatever he wanted to."

"How about the other one," she prods.

I zoom in on the other receipt, and I probably don't do a very good job of hiding my flinch. "Docksiders. We never went there together. I don't go there anymore."

"Why not?"

"That's where I . . ." *Met the man who derailed my entire life.* "That's where I worked in college. I met my daughter's father there. I smelled like fried clams for an entire summer, and it's not somewhere I like to go anymore."

Riley smiles for the first time since she sat down. "Noted. When's the last time you saw your daughter's father?"

I blink. "We covered this before. I last saw him when Natalie was a toddler."

"Any contact with him since you and I spoke on Friday?"

I shake my head, bewildered, because she asked me this a few minutes ago. "I told you. He sent me another email, but I didn't respond."

"What did he want?"

"Why?" I demand.

She says nothing. Just holds her pen over her little pad and waits.

"The subject line said he wanted to talk about Natalie. I didn't."

She nods. "All right. Now tell us again why you went to the mansion on the night of June sixth?"

"To walk the *dog*. We've been through this, too."

"And did you know Tim would be there in the parking lot?" Riley asks.

"No," I say without hesitation. But my heart is beating wildly.

"He shared his location with you," she says evenly. "On his phone. Didn't he?"

My heart might explode. "Yeah? He shared his location one time, so I could find him on a jogging path."

"And did you use it to find him after that?" she asks.

I'm sweating through my blouse.

"*Rowan*," Beatrice's voice is sharp. Hearing it is like waking from a bad dream. "I need a minute please. It's about the drywall order."

There is no drywall order.

"One moment." I push back my chair and walk over to Beatrice's desk on the other side of the room.

"Look," she says, pointing at her screen. There's a random email on it.

But then she rests her hand on a notebook, and I see what she's written there:

"I don't like your tone. I don't like what you're implying."
  "If you're out of reasonable questions, this interview is over."

Beneath that:

They need a warrant if they want your phone!
  And if you want to get rid of them, just say you want a lawyer.

It's all very good advice. More crucially, the visit to Beatrice's desk has given me a moment to regroup.

"Is this okay?" Beatrice asks, waving toward the email on her screen.

"It's fine. We'll make it work."

"Cool." She tosses her hair in a way that makes her look vacuous. As if.

I take my seat again. "Sorry. What were we talking about?"

Riley gives me a *look*. "Tim shared his location with you. That means you could have known exactly where he was on the night when he was killed. If you just give us your phone data, we can clear this right up."

"That won't clear *anything* up. Neither me nor my phone knows who killed him."

"We could just get a warrant," Fry says. "But that makes you look . . ."

"Like someone who values her privacy," I say through gritted teeth. "Get a warrant if you want to waste your time. And if you don't have any more reasonable questions, then we're done here."

They exchange glances while I try not to hyperventilate.

"Just a couple more pictures to show you," Riley says. "Are any of these items yours? His family doesn't recognize them."

Fear has gripped me from the inside out. I'm desperate for them to leave, but I sure can't show it. Trying to regulate my breathing, I lean on the desk and look down at Riley's iPad.

There's a photo of a single pearl earring, with no backing. "Nope. That won't be mine. I have pearl earrings, but I haven't worn them in ages." They make me feel old.

"One more," she says quietly, flipping to another picture.

And it's a struggle not to gasp when she shows me a silver medallion. It *can't* be. I lean in close to see the detail, using my fingers to zoom in. Steel bands tighten around my chest as I stare down at the familiar figure sculpted against an oval background.

"It's a saint," Riley says, misinterpreting my silence. "We're not sure which one. It was in the glove box. Do you recognize it?"

I shake my head. I don't trust my voice right now, and my mind barely registers that I'm lying to the cops for the second time.

But I'm too afraid to say it out loud.

15

I'm reeling. And it's hard for me to focus on the rest of Detective Riley's questions. I'm about to ask her to repeat herself when my phone buzzes with a text.

"One moment." I glance at the screen and find a message from a contractor who needs to meet with me about the HVAC system.

Stalling, I craft a reply to him, and it calms me down a little. After hitting send, I meet Detective Riley's gaze. "Excuse me. Duty calls."

"Of course," she says in a soothing voice.

It's not lost on me how much her demeanor changed when I pushed back on her demands. She knows she can't push me too far, or I'll just stop talking to her altogether.

"I know this is all very upsetting," she says placidly. "We'll go now. But please understand that we need to gather every speck of information about Tim's last days. *Somebody* knows what really happened. We need to find that person."

"Of course you do," I manage. "But I'm as baffled as anyone."

Detective Fry gets to his feet. "We really appreciate you taking the time to speak to us. If you think of anything at all that could be helpful, you'll call?"

"Right. I have your card."

"You've been helpful, too, Miss Chambers," Riley says to Beatrice.

"I can't see how," Beatrice says tightly. "I'll show you out." She crosses to the office door and holds it open. It's not subtle. I kind of love her for it.

But the cops are unhurried as they file past her, and I can almost see Beatrice fighting the urge to shove them through the corridor.

Trying not to look ruffled, I trail them into the foyer. Fry stops to glance around, his shrewd gaze sweeping over the crystal chandelier and following the curve of the staircase upward toward the gallery. "Wild to think that this was someone's home."

Riley nods in agreement. "It's a magnificent building."

"Magnificent. And so cozy." Fry snorts.

When I glance at Beatrice, her face is full of rage.

Fry moves toward the door but doesn't open it. He runs a hand over the carvings in the oak. It's almost a caress.

I want to yank the door open and kick him through it.

Then, finally, the two cops leave, tossing meaningless pleasantries our way until Beatrice finally closes the door behind them. She leans back on the door and closes her eyes. "What the hell was that?" Her eyes spring open. "We have to talk."

She marches past me, heading back to the office. I follow and immediately collapse into my chair. Beatrice takes the seat that Detective Riley vacated only minutes ago.

"Buddy, are you okay?" Beatrice asks.

Not even close. It's just hitting me that I lied to the cops a second time. But what the hell was my daughter's medallion doing in that car?

Beatrice stares at me, waiting for an answer.

"Honestly, I'm tired of that question," I mutter. "Not that it's off base."

"Hey, I get it." She folds her hands in her lap. "But that was really intense."

Intense doesn't even begin to cover it. I grab my phone and open the FriendFinder app to check on Natalie. It's a relief to see her avatar at the high school where she's supposed to be, but I won't be able to take a full breath until I figure out if that really was her medallion in Tim's car.

"Why did Tim have those photos?" Beatrice asks. "Did he *steal* them from you?"

A queasy feeling washes through me. "He must have? I have no idea why."

"Yikes." She blows out a breath. "Hank would lose his ever-loving mind if he knew the cops were asking about stolen photos of the family's records on a dead guy's phone."

I feel bleak. "Do we have to tell him about it?"

She makes a thoughtful face. "Why do you *think* Tim took them? If you had to guess."

"There's no reasonable excuse. But he liked hearing about the history of the house. That's all I can figure."

But then there's the fact of his adoption . . .

"What kind of questions did he ask you about the mansion?" she presses.

"Architecture questions. How gasoliers work. Where slate roof tiles come from." None of it was very suspicious. "Why the servants' entrances are always a few steps up or down from the other rooms in the house." That's because the servants' wing had four stories to the mansion's three. Apparently, commoners don't need high ceilings. "He was a little obsessed."

"But you don't know why?"

I shake my head.

Beatrice rolls her neck in an uncharacteristic show of stress. "First that weird story in the coffee shop. And now this."

"I know," I say lamely. "But if he betrayed my trust, I don't know if we'll ever understand why."

She frowns. "Why do you think the police are so obsessed with your phone?"

I pick up the incriminating device and turn it over in my hands, so that I don't have to look her in the eyes. "They're right about one thing," I say in a voice that's almost too low to hear. "I did check Tim's location the week after he dumped me. More than a few times. I was just trying to understand what happened."

When I lift my chin, Beatrice wears an expression of shocked disbelief. "You followed him everywhere he went?"

"No." I give my head a firm shake. "I didn't watch him every minute of the day. I wasn't that bad. But the night after he broke it off, I saw him on the map. He'd gone out to dinner at his favorite first-date place. I was upset."

She blinks. "And then?"

I shrug, even as my face is reddening. "I looked the next three nights, too."

"So you saw him parked at the mansion on the night he died? You walked the dog here on purpose?"

I nod guiltily.

"*Rowan*," she whispers. "Don't tell another *soul* what you just told me. And don't let them bully you into giving up your data."

"Oh, I won't. Because it's even worse than that—I unfollowed him on the way to his car. I knew keeping track of him was unhealthy. I was going to stop." I swallow hard. "But the timing would look suspicious. I must have tapped the unfollow button right around the time when he died."

The color drains from her face. "Jesus fucking Christ."

This is exactly why I wasn't forthcoming to the police. "But I didn't hurt him!"

She leans forward, her gaze pinning me to my seat. "Of *course* you didn't. And his death is not your fault. But that looks *bad*, Rowan. You need to be more careful."

"I'm trying." The image of Natalie's medallion swims through my vision, and I'm more frightened than I can admit.

She rubs her temples. "So he took those photos, but you don't know when or why."

Again, I shake my head. "I barely remember our conversation about them. He didn't seem particularly fixated." *Or that's what he wanted me to think.* "Hank's going to fire me if he hears about this, right? It's bad."

"We're not telling the family," she says in a hushed voice. "This stays between us. Hank would get angry, even though this will all blow over. As soon as they catch the guy, we can all move on."

"Thank you," I say stiffly.

"But listen." She keeps her voice low, but her tone vibrates with intensity. "You need a lawyer. Tim's death is all over the news, and those cops must be under a lot of pressure to make an arrest. I'm going to give you the names of a couple litigators that Hank has used." She crosses the office and sits in front of her computer. Her manicure clicks rapidly on the keyboard. "I'm not joking. Put these numbers in your pocket."

"Okay. But they can't seriously pin this on me. I've never fired a gun. I don't *own* a gun."

"Don't be naïve." She's scribbling something on a card. "You're a white woman who's never been in trouble. That helps. But a white man is dead, and they need a killer. You need a professional in your corner." She brings me the card. "Put this in your wallet. If you get another request for an interview, call one of these two."

"Thanks," I say, tucking the card away.

Beatrice collapses into a chair. "Is it five o'clock yet? It must be."

The clock says two thirty. I need to see Natalie. "Seriously, I don't think I can work right now. I'm too stressed out."

She eyes me from her seat. "What if we knocked off early? We need a mental-health day. Nobody needs to know."

"Good idea." I give her a weak smile and rise from my chair. "Girl pact?"

"Always," she says.

———————

"Natalie?" I call out the moment I get home.

Silence.

She's still at school, then. Or out with a friend.

Lick Jagger follows as I run through the house and up the narrow stairway to Natalie's room. I push open the door and survey the wreckage. Clothes and shoes everywhere.

She'd kill me for searching her room like a cop, so I start with the visible surfaces—the tops of the desk, nightstand, and dresser.

No medallion anywhere.

She could be wearing it right now—that's what I'm hoping. Aside from some books boxed up in our basement, this is the only thing she has of her father's. It isn't fancy, though. It's the sort of thing they sell in Catholic church shops—Saint someone or other, depicted in silver with a palm frond over one arm and a lollipop-shaped religious artifact in the opposite hand.

There's a jewelry box on top of her dresser, and I look there next. Under the lid is a mess of beaded friendship bracelets and clunky baubles from her dangly-earring phase.

No medallion, though. Hell.

Feeling frantic, I get down on my knees and begin poking through her desk drawers, looking for a flash of silver.

There's no abyss as deep as a teenage girl's bedroom, and panic begins to claw at my throat. Her desk drawers reveal nothing except a vast collection of cute office supplies.

She must be wearing it. She has to be.

I'm making myself ill trying to think up reasons it could have ended up in Tim's car—without Natalie herself being in Tim's car.

Unless Tim took it. I can't think of why he'd do that. But neither can I imagine why he'd take photos off my phone.

Taking a deep breath, I try to recall if Natalie was wearing the medallion the night Tim was killed. I remember our argument outside my bathroom. Pesto pasta. A warm night. She was wearing a cute little white top.

If I try hard enough, I can picture the medallion around her neck. But I've seen it there a thousand times before, so I don't know if it's an actual memory or just an easily conjured desire.

So where is it? I get up and rifle through the dresser drawers. But I come up empty. Leaving Natalie's room, I head for my own. Lickie whines when I pass by. She can't understand why I'm home midday and not showing her some love.

But a terrible thought has occurred to me. Natalie loves to help herself to my jewelry without asking . . . I'm weak with relief when I find two pearl earrings inside my jewelry box.

"Okay," I tell the dog. "Okay. There could be two identical medallions in the world, right?"

Lickie wags her tail.

"All right. Let's go for a walk, then."

She's out the bedroom door and down the stairs before I can finish the sentence.

Outside, I scan the street for Natalie. While Lickie sniffs a tree, I take out my phone and debate texting her. I'm not sure what to ask. If Tim searched her room and took the medallion while I was in the shower, that's one conversation. But if she'd been in Tim's car herself . . .

Shivering, I open the FriendFinder app and check her location. But her avatar doesn't pop up on the map. Beside her name it says: **No location found.**

I send a text.

Rowan: Call me. I need to speak to you.

I wait a polite thirty seconds or so, but when I call her, it goes right to voicemail.

There was a murder not four blocks from here, and my daughter can't answer her phone when I call?

I march Lickie around the block and then try her phone again.

No answer.

16

CORALIE

"Mr. Wincott's office, this is Coralie speaking . . ." She has to stop in the middle of the sentence and swallow the extra saliva in her mouth. Sudden nausea is a new and unwelcome sensation in her life. "How may I help you?"

"I need to speak with him," the caller snaps without identifying himself.

She takes a steadying breath and a sip of water. The fact that Mr. Wincott's older brother has to wait is just a side benefit. The man is *such* an asshole. He always rings in this way—overbearing and in a big hurry.

"One moment," she says eventually. "Let me see if he can be interrupted."

"It's important."

She rolls her eyes as she puts the call on hold. Then she scrubs a hand across her face before pressing another button on her phone. The door to the inner office isn't very thick, so she hears the answering chime inside. "It's Mr. Wincott, sir," she says. "He says it's important."

"That's *just* what I need," he grumbles through the open line. "Fine. I'll take it."

She releases the button and watches as the light on her phone goes from blinking to solid.

The other Mr. Wincott calls maybe twice a week. She's never met him, but he's always a dick. Her boss is always grouchy after those calls.

That's usually when the bottle of scotch comes out. Among other things.

Coralie finds her handbag and freshens her makeup. Her face is sallow, and her eyes are tired. The boss has a thing for red lipstick. She doesn't need him asking questions. She's not ready. She may not ever be ready.

Mr. Wincott's voice is raised now, one question coming through quite clearly. "Would you just let me handle it, you arrogant fuck?"

Such a charming family.

She pops a Tic Tac, because they seem to help, and bends over her work. She's labeling and alphabetizing a heap of donor files. If she misspells anyone's name, he'll berate her for it.

Her concentration is so intense that she startles when he comes storming out of the inner office.

She braces herself for a barked order, but it doesn't come. Instead, she watches as he marches out of the room and makes a left into the corridor, his footsteps receding as he leaves the premises.

Okay. Well. Maybe he'll return in a better mood. In the meantime, she can file these away without his looming presence. She picks up the stack of finished folders and hurries into his office.

The first file drawer she'll need is behind his desk. She files ALLEN in the "A" drawer and moves on down the stack. She's kneeling in front of the "G" cabinet when she notices the bottom drawer of the boss's desk has been left ajar.

Hot diggity. This is the chance she's been waiting for.

She goes still for a moment, listening. When she's satisfied that no one is coming, she places her stack of files on the floor near the open file cabinet. Her cover, if she needs it.

Then she turns and crouches behind his desk. She can't see the doorway from here, but she'll be able to hear him coming. She hastily opens the desk drawer all the way and starts sifting through the contents.

It only takes a second to find the extra checkbook—the secret one. But the check register is blank. He hasn't been recording the recipients, and the carbon copies have been torn out.

Shit.

But hang on. When she squints at the next check's carbon, she can make out the name and amount. It's faint, but the heavy pen he uses makes an impression.

Elizabeth Jones. $700.00.

Not a bad payday, Elizabeth. Not bad at all.

She hears footsteps and freezes, her heart jumping into her mouth. Slowly, she releases her grip on the checkbook and prepares to back away.

But then a vacuum cleaner starts up, and her eyelids slide shut with relief.

That was close. She can't listen for him anymore, not with someone vacuuming the corridor. Still, a few more seconds seems worth the risk.

She quickly reaches into the drawer again, opening the checkbook. She tears that blank check and its carbon out of the book—for inspection later. She's returning the checkbook to the drawer when she notices his elegant handwriting on the tab of a file folder. *Address Labels.*

Hmm.

She lifts the folder to peer inside. There's a page of typed-up labels in three columns, and a few of the labels are missing. Each column has the same address—the first column is Elizabeth in Westbrook, the second is for a woman in York, the third to one in Biddeford.

Three women. None of them employees of the foundation. Fascinating.

Working fast, she nabs one label for each woman and sticks them onto the back of the stolen check. Then she tidies up the drawer and closes it.

She gets off the floor and straightens her skirt. It's a looser style than she'd usually wear. Getting dressed is trickier than it used to be.

She folds the check and the carbon into thirds and tuck them into her shoe. Then she picks up her stack of folders and hastily finishes her filing.

As she works, the pilfered check itches against her foot, and she can't shake the feeling that Mr. Wincott will somehow know what she's done.

BECAUSE YOU'RE A STUPID BITCH, CORALIE.

The voice in her head startles her, and she has to take a deep breath.

She glances around the office and then out the window. Often, she has the prickly sensation of being watched.

You never know where the eyes are. Some days it feels like they're everywhere.

17

NATALIE

Her mother would kill her for riding her bike with no helmet, but she doesn't want to flatten her hair. Besides, her mom would kill her *twice* if she knew where Natalie was going.

She takes it slow, sticking to the streets with bike lanes, even if it means she's going to be a few minutes late. Being late is not a problem anyway. She doesn't want to seem too eager.

It's not a long trip, and soon she's one turn away from the bakery café. The meeting spot was her idea. It feels like a safe choice. Casual.

The whole plan is rock solid. So why does she feel like throwing up?

Pausing at the last light, she takes a deep breath and pulls out her phone to check her Instagram. When she sees a new message from him, her heart veers sideways.

He's going to cancel. She just knew it. She's half disgusted, half relieved. But no. The message says,

I'm at a table in back. Hope you like cookies, but I didn't want to guess what you drink.

A surge of anxiety swirls through her belly. She stashes the phone, turns the last corner, and approaches the shop. There's a bike rack right outside, and she takes her time parking, giving herself the option to bail. She could turn around right now and go home.

But of course, she doesn't. She throws back her shoulders and opens the door.

And, yup, when she flicks her eyes toward the back wall, she sees him. He looks just like the videos she found on Instagram. Longish hair down to his shoulders and a slim mustache. It looks cool, though, not trashy. More Keanu than Snape.

His band posts promo clips on social media. Playing in a bar. Playing at a wedding. Playing on a party boat in the bay.

She'd left a comment on a recent video. *Looks like fun.*

She'd basically dared him to notice her, and it worked.

The very next day he requested a connection. Her account is private, so she let the request sit there while she wrestled with herself. In the end, her curiosity outweighed her anger.

She'd answered him, and they'd started talking. Just a little at first. And then multiple times a day. That was a couple of weeks ago. Now she's a nervous wreck.

Stalling, she heads for the counter, where she orders an iced hibiscus peach tea with lime and mint.

"Two ninety-five," the cashier requests.

At the last minute, she decides the order sounds too childish. "Wait. Sorry. Can I have a cappuccino instead?"

The cashier gives her a withering look and rings it up again.

She drops a dollar into the tip jar and scrolls her phone while she waits, fighting the urge to finger-comb her hair or check her outfit. This morning she changed her clothes, like seven times. She wants to look good, but also doesn't want to look like she's trying to impress him.

It's a fine line. She'd settled on faded jeans and a Post Malone T-shirt. No makeup.

Way before she's ready, the barista hands over her drink, and now she's out of reasons to stand here.

Deep breaths, her mother would say. Though she'd hyperventilate if she knew where Natalie was right now.

That man against the back wall is her father. After all this time.

She turns with forced nonchalance and carries her coffee across the room. He's spotted her and stands up as she approaches. Even though her knees feel squishy, she forces herself to look him in the eye.

That means lifting her chin. He's taller than she'd imagined. That shouldn't be so startling, but it is. And now she's there at the table and doesn't know what to do next.

She's *not* going to hug him. And shaking hands would be weird. "Hi." That's all she's got as she puts her coffee on the table and sits down.

"Hi," he says, flashing her a quick smile before dropping back into his seat. He steeples his hands in front of his mouth and blows out a heavy breath. "I wasn't sure you'd actually come."

"I almost didn't." It comes out sounding a little mean.

All those years wondering why he couldn't even be bothered to send her a birthday card. All those times people asked, *What's the deal with your father?* Not knowing what to say. There's no good way to tell a friend your father is in prison for beating someone almost to death.

"Yeah, okay. I can understand," he says softly.

"Can you?" Years of anger seem to be spilling out. And that's not what she planned.

His expression falls. "Yeah, honey, I can."

Honey.

He looks down at the table. "You don't owe me anything. I'm just glad to see your face. All I've got to say for myself—and it's not much—is that when you were small, I didn't have a lot to offer."

And now? She's too chicken to ask it aloud, and sips her coffee instead. It's so hot that it burns the roof of her mouth.

Across the table, he picks up his drink, too. The sticker on the cup says hibiscus peach iced tea with lime and mint.

Her eyes get weirdly hot. *My father.* She tries those words out in her head. They're words she never says aloud. Not if she can help it. But now they're just sitting here together. Like any father and daughter in a coffee shop.

He nudges a plate toward her. It has four cookies on it, two different kinds. "So I need to know—are you a chocolate person?"

"Well, sure," she says quickly. "Who isn't?" She chooses a chocolate crinkle cookie, breaking it in half. He picks up the other half.

They bite. They chew.

I look a little like him, she realizes. It's his nose and the shape of his face. His voice is lower than she expected it to be. But his hands are the same shape as hers, she realizes.

This is weird.

"Your mom is okay with this?" he asks suddenly.

She almost laughs and gives herself away but then manages to stick to the lie she'd rehearsed ahead of time. "She's not happy about it."

His face falls. "I suppose not. But please tell her that I need to speak to her. It's about some health stuff you guys need to know about my half of the gene pool."

Oh shit.

She must look surprised, because he frowns. "Nothing to panic over. It's just that you're not a little girl anymore, and my side of the family has some particular issues with substance abuse. My mother was an addict. I had my own issues. And a lot of that stuff is genetic, Natty."

Natty. She hasn't let her mother call her that in years. But it rolls off his tongue like he thinks of her as Natty in his head.

"You don't have to worry about me," she says. "I don't do drugs. *Ever.*"

Drugs are, after all, for losers.

"That helps," he says quietly. "My singular wish is that you can avoid some of the things I went through. It's why I'd like to talk to your mom."

Her stomach gives a nervous lurch, because it hadn't occurred to her that he'd ask that. And she's not about to relay the message. "I'll ask her."

"All right." Another super-quick smile. "I'm sure you hear this all the time, but you look so much like her. Maybe you got more of her genes than mine."

"Does it work that way?"

He shrugs. "Didn't do that well in science class. Ask your mom. She was the smart one in our relationship."

"She's still smart," Natalie says, and it comes out sounding defensive.

He smiles down at the cookie plate. "I don't doubt it. How's she doing?"

She hesitates. "I don't think I should talk about her. She wouldn't like it."

"Yeah, fair. And I don't want you to think I'm pumping you for information. I don't want either of you to feel uncomfortable that I'm back in town."

"Then why are you?"

"Opportunities. There are more jobs here, not that mine is special."

This is a safe line of conversation. "Where do you work?"

"In the kitchen of a touristy restaurant on the waterfront. The same place I met your mom. She was the waitress . . ."

"And you played in the band on Thursday nights."

He blinks. "She told you that story?"

"Sure," she says with a shrug that's as casual as she can manage. "That's about all, though. She never talks about you."

He flinches, but it's true. Her mother avoids the topic the way you avoid something that hurts. It was such a long time ago, too. He must have put a real dent into her.

But Natalie overhears things. She's heard her mother tell friends that he'd signed away his parental rights. *Just wrote us off like a bad check.*

"What do you do at the restaurant?" she asks just to fill the awkward silence.

"Most nights I work the grill. It's a sweaty job, but the owner is a good guy. Willing to hire someone with a record. Some nights I fill in as the manager, because people keep quitting on him. And you know my other hobby. My band plays here and there around the coast. Mostly in Portland."

That's how she'd found him. One day she searched his name and there he was, named on the band's Instagram account. "Is it the same band you used to play with?"

"Heck no." He puts down his tea. "Those guys were heavy into drugs, and they pretty much self-destructed. But the new guys don't do anything harder than light beer, so they're good company for me. I need to make new friends."

"Sure," she chirps. "Like that's so easy."

His grin is surprised. "You're snarky. The last time I saw you, all you could say was *Dada* and *Mama* and *book*."

"Book?" she asks, studying her coffee cup. But the more interesting word is *Dada*. She can't remember what it was like to have someone in her life called *Dada*.

"You loved books. We carried them with us anywhere we went. You had these little books made out of cardboard—the kind that babies can't tear. But you chewed on them sometimes."

It's like hearing a story about someone else's life.

"Every night we'd read you a few stories before we put you down to sleep. Then your mom and I would tiptoe around, because it was a small apartment, and we were afraid to wake you up."

"What kind of stories?" she hears herself ask.

"You liked that monkey—he got into a lot of trouble."

There's suddenly a lump in her throat. "Curious George?"

"That's the guy." He gives her a sad smile. "Still a big fan, I bet? A little Curious George—a little Post Malone?"

She startles herself by laughing.

"No? What are the cool kids into these days?" He puts a hand over his heart. "If you say Taylor Swift, I can handle it. I swear."

She laughs *again*. "Don't throw shade on TayTay. Mom got us concert tickets last summer. It was a really good time. But we had to drive all the way to Foxboro, and we didn't get home until five a.m."

"Aw, you went to a concert with your mom?" His smile is pure delight. It's a little shocking how happy he looks right now. She had no idea what to expect.

"You think I had a choice? She was paying for those tickets."

They both smile, but then his expression grows serious. "I hope she calls me. It's not on you if she doesn't, but I'd like a chance to apologize to her."

Oh boy. "She's got a lot on her plate right now. There's a lot happening at work."

"You mean that dead guy?" He rubs his jaw.

"You heard about that?"

"It was on the news." His gray eyes lift to hers. "They said the mansion's architect found the body in front of the building. That was her, wasn't it?"

"Well, yeah." The back of her neck tingles, because her mother would hate this conversation. Also, she doesn't remember that detail on the news. Didn't they say "an employee" found him?

"Is she okay?" he asks quietly. "That's pretty dark. I've been thinking about her."

"She'll be okay. She's tough." She's one of the strongest people Natalie knows. Not that she's ever paid her mother that kind of compliment.

His jaw flexes, and it makes him seem harder. Less familiar. "I know I wasn't there for your mother when she needed me. But I'm here now, and I'm in a better place." He raises those gray eyes to hers, and they're steely. "I'd do anything for you two. You probably don't believe me, but it's true."

That just sounds like an excuse—too little, too late—and she hates herself a little for not calling him on it.

"When can I hear your band?" she asks instead.

18

ROWAN

Over the next two hours, I edge toward a total breakdown. Natalie's phone doesn't reappear on the map.

Without my digital tethers, I feel helpless. I realize phones sometimes run out of batteries or accidentally get dropped off the pier. There could be a perfectly rational explanation.

On the other hand, there's a murderer loose in Portland, and my daughter might have been in my dead ex's car.

So I'm apoplectic.

That phone is practically glued to my daughter's hand. Why has it suddenly gone dark?

With the school directory in hand, I do what I can. I call the mother of her friend Tessa, who connects me with Tessa herself.

But Tessa tells me she has no idea where Natalie is. "She was going to hang out with some kids, I think," she says casually.

"Which kids?"

"Dunno, she didn't say."

I don't believe a word of it. Those girls tell each other everything.

Then, as I'm clutching my phone in a clammy hand and picturing my daughter's dead body, her avatar suddenly reappears on the map. She's on the move—heading down Fore Street in the direction of our home.

I want to faint with relief. Right after I shake her.

Unable to contain myself, I'm actually waiting by the kitchen door when she rides up the driveway. I hear her lock up her bike. Then she opens the door and gets blown down by the hurricane that is me.

"Where have you *been*?" I demand before she's even made it all the way into the kitchen. "I've been trying to call you for hours."

She jerks to a halt, her expression guilty. But just as quickly it turns to indignation. "Hello to you, too."

"*Natalie.*" My hands are white-knuckling the back rail of a dining chair. "Where were you?"

"At a coffee shop!" she screeches, looking close to tears. "With a *guy*. I had a cup of coffee and a cookie. He had iced tea. Does that answer all your questions?"

It takes a lot of self-control not to ask which boy. I would only alienate her, and I still need answers. "Look. I found a dead body last week. And the killer is still out there somewhere. Don't pretend like this is just a normal Tuesday. Why was your phone off?"

Her mouth drops open. "Do you hear yourself? Aren't you the one who's always telling me to put my phone down for once?" She drops her backpack in the center of the kitchen floor.

"Answer the question. Where were you? Tessa didn't even know."

"You called Tessa?" she squeaks.

I don't bother answering because I'm too busy watching her peel off her jean jacket. There's no chain around her neck, no medallion.

"What is your *problem* with me?" she practically shrieks.

I take a slow breath and study my child. There's a budding pimple on her chin, the only blemish on her impossibly young face. She has big, gray eyes so much like her father's.

I take another breath and try to de-escalate the situation. "I need to ask you a question. Where is your medallion? The one that was your daddy's?"

I haven't referred to him as "daddy" in over a decade.

Her jaw drops again, and her face reddens. "Why would you ask me that?"

"Do you still have it? I looked in your room and couldn't find it."

"You looked in my *room*?"

I've probably made things worse, but I need to be honest with her. "Where is it?" I ask softly. "Please."

Her eyes dart away from mine. "If I show you, will you tell me why you care so much?"

"Probably." It comes out sounding bitchier than necessary.

"Why are you like this?" she hisses, kneeling to open her backpack. She unzips a tiny exterior pocket and draws out the familiar chain with the medallion on it.

I let out my breath for the first time in hours.

"Seriously, *what* is your deal?"

I'm so relieved that I can't even speak. I take the medallion in hand and squint down at it. I wasn't wrong—it's the same weirdly rendered saint that the detectives showed me. He's molded against an oval background, holding a religious object in one hand and a palm frond on the other arm.

It's right here. It's been with her all the time.

19

NATALIE

Natalie's heart pounds with both indignation and unspoken guilt. For a second there, she was sure she'd been busted—possibly tattled on by Tessa or just really unlucky.

But her mom doesn't seem to know where she's been. She's staring at the medallion Natalie has worn for much of her life. It's precious to her. She only took it off this morning so her father wouldn't see it, wouldn't know how tightly she's held on to it. Even now, it takes great stores of restraint not to snatch it from her mother's hand.

They *never* talk about her father. And her mother—who comments on everything Natalie says or does—never mentions the medallion. As if it's invisible. As if there's no gaping hole in her life where her father should be.

"What the hell, Mom?" she asks shakily. "Why the sudden interest in Saint Raymond?"

"Raymond? Is that a joke?"

Natalie shakes her head. "No, that's who this saint is supposed to be. I looked it up on a website that sells Catholic stuff." She holds out her hand, reaching for the medallion. When her mother passes it back, her fingers close around the silver.

When she was younger, she used to pretend it had magical powers. She'd press it between her hands and pray for her father to appear. Because that seemed like the right thing to do with a magical medallion, even if she isn't sure that saints are real.

Her mother slides into a dining chair and points at another one, indicating that Natalie should sit, too. "I have to tell you something."

A chill races up Natalie's back. She sits, bracing herself. Maybe her mother *does* know her secret.

"Today the police interviewed me again about Tim's death. They showed me a bunch of pictures of things they found in his car. And one of them was a medallion just like that."

Natalie's heart actually skips a beat. "Seriously?"

Her mother nods, and Natalie notices the dark smudges under her eyes, the exhaustion in her expression.

Natalie's anger cools by a few degrees. "And you thought it was *mine*?"

"I guess? I didn't know what to think. Have you ever seen another medallion like that one?"

"No," she admits. "Raymond is not a very common saint."

"Saint *Raymond*." Her mother smiles suddenly. "Trust Harrison to run with an off-brand saint. So tell me—what is our man Raymond the saint of?"

Natalie fingers the chain. "Believe it or not, Raymond is the patron saint of prisoners and the falsely accused."

Her mother's eyebrows jerk. "*Prisoners?* How prophetic."

Natalie has thought the same thing many times. And since the topic of her father is on the table for once, she has questions. "Where did this come from, anyway? Is, uh, Harrison religious?"

Her mom shakes her head. "But maybe his mother was. The medallion was hers, I think. I never met her. She died the year you were born."

"Oh."

"She wasn't a well person. And your father didn't hear about her passing until months later. A friend of hers mailed him her driver's license and that medallion. That's all he had left of her."

Natalie looks down at the medallion in her hand. "And you gave it to me?"

"Didn't have much choice," her mother says. "When you were five, you found it in my dresser drawer, and I said it was your daddy's. You put it on, and you didn't want to take it off."

Natalie can't even look her mother in the eye right now. She's afraid her mom will be able to read her treachery off her face. "So what you're saying is that it's basically cursed."

Her mother lets out a sudden laugh. "I don't believe in curses. Your father made a whole string of poor choices. He sealed his own fate."

It's hard to argue with that, which makes Natalie's stomach sink. "Isn't it weird, though? That Tim had a Saint Raymond, too?"

"Maybe?" Her mother shrugs. "I'm not Catholic. I don't know how it works. I never saw him wearing it. The cop said they found it somewhere in his car."

That weirdo. "It couldn't have a thing to do with me."

Even as she says this, she feels a prickle of unease. Tim might have seen the medallion around her neck. He had two opportunities.

But so what? Why would he have cared?

"Can I borrow your phone?" her mother asks. "I want to google Saint Raymond."

Maybe the coincidence bothers her, too.

"I'll do it." Natalie opens a browser and searches for the saint. "Saint Raymond Nonnatus . . . imprisoned for preaching the gospel. He converted some of his prison guards to Christianity. He's also the patron saint of childbirth, midwives, children, and pregnant women. His intercession is often sought for safe deliveries and for protecting infants . . ."

Her mother leans forward. "Really?"

She turns the screen so her mother can see, but she averts her eyes. "I think Nonnatus is Latin for *not born*," her mom says.

Natalie looks at the screen again. She scrolls down. "Yeah. It says he was cut from the womb of his dead mother." *Gross.* Suddenly, she's sick to death of discussing this. "Can we get BaoBao for dinner?"

Her mother massages her own forehead. "Maybe. If you make me one promise."

Oh God. "What kind of promise?"

"You'll leave your phone on all the time. Just until the murderer is caught."

"Okay," she says quickly. "Whatever."

Her mother pulls out her own phone. "You want the chicken salad?"

"And the pork and cabbage dumplings." She scoops her backpack up off the floor and makes her escape.

"You're welcome!" her mother calls after her.

20

ROWAN

Our order isn't ready, so I wait outside our neighborhood dumpling house and check my email. I glance up when Lickie makes a warning noise.

I'm instantly on my guard, but the person approaching us isn't scary at all. She's very pretty, with wide-set eyes and kickass ankle boots. "Excuse me, Rowan?"

It takes me a second to place her, but then I realize where I've seen her before—on my front walk. She's the reporter who said she knew Tim.

I shove my phone into my pocket and choke up on Lickie's leash. "I'm sorry. I still can't talk to you." I turn to go, willing to abandon our dinner to avoid this conversation.

"Wait," she says. "I know you can't talk, but can you listen for a minute? I have information that concerns you."

"I doubt that," I say, even as my spine tingles.

She leans against the building, eyeing me intently. "Look, I know the police have interviewed you multiple times. You're still a person of interest in the case."

I feel sick. "How do you know that?"

"By palling around with the local reporters." She shrugs. "Sometimes they have friends in the police department. Sometimes they overhear things. And if you're a flirty, female reporter from out of town, sometimes you hear things, too."

God. "The police and I don't have much more to say to each other," I say stiffly. "It sounds like you already know more than I do."

"You're right about that," she says quietly. Then she looks up and down the street, as if to make sure we can't be overheard. "But you're involved in this thing whether you want to be or not. I think Kovak was killed for a story he was working on. And I'm a journalist, too, Rowan. That's horrifying to me."

"But why are you so sure?" A selfish part of me hopes she's right, though. Because if that's true, his death has nothing to do with me or my family.

"All his notebooks were taken from his car. The police can't find them."

"Yes, that's weird." But it's also flimsy evidence.

Her gaze doesn't leave mine. "Here's the thing—before he died, Tim asked me to run a whole bunch of background checks. He and I sometimes traded favors like that, because he was very skilled at money stuff, and I'm better at criminal stuff."

"And?" I can already tell that I won't like whatever she says next.

"Let me show you some names," she says in a low voice. "You can tell me if they're familiar." She reaches into her pocket for her phone and opens the Notes app.

"I thought I was listening, not answering questions."

"Just look," she whispers. "It won't kill you."

"Isn't that what Tim thought, too?" Still, I can't resist a glance at the list. There are a few names, all women. None are familiar, though. "Sorry. I don't know any of these people."

"Okay. How about these?" She taps something on her phone and hands it back.

I read another list of four names—first initial and surname. "Shit," I whisper as a wave of fear buzzes through me. Because these names *are* familiar.

"What?"

"These names were all in a photograph that Tim stole off my phone." From the handwritten birth ledger. "Did he tell you I was his source when he gave you the names?"

She shakes her head slowly. "Lucky guess on my part."

"Not to speak ill of the dead . . ." I take a shaky breath. "But I might have been more of a research project than a girlfriend to him."

Her expression turns empathetic. "I'm thinking you might be right. Because that first list of names I showed you? All those women worked for Marcus Wincott during the sixties and seventies. Tim wanted to interview them."

My stomach drops. "Marcus Wincott ran the Portland Magdalene home. At the mansion."

"Right," she says quietly. "And Tim told me he was chasing a big story."

"About the home? Or the Wincott family?"

"He didn't say, probably because we're competitors. He thought I might scoop him." She flashes me a quick smile. "Since he died, I've been running every name I just showed you. I don't have a lot to go on, but I'm convinced that he made someone very angry."

"Look." I rub my forehead where an ache is blooming. "It's not that I'm not curious. And I know Tim was smart. But he never mentioned any of this, and it's a pretty huge lie of omission. Whatever you're digging for, I can't help you. I work for the Wincott family, and I'd like to keep my job."

"Right. But how much do you really know about that boss of yours? Did you know he wants to run for Senate?"

It's probably very clear by the expression on my face that I didn't know that.

"Everyone's expecting Oliver Bean to announce his retirement before the year is out. That will give Hank almost a whole year to mount a campaign."

"What are you implying?" My mind whirls. "That Tim found something dodgy about Hank Wincott's"—what was their relationship?— "Uncle? Great-uncle? And Hank is so fired up about his future campaign that he'd shoot Tim *in the face*?"

"I'm not saying he pulled the trigger." She glances around again. "And I don't know what Tim dug up. Not yet, anyway. But somebody wanted him dead, Rowan. Someone shot him and then took his computer, his phone, and all his notebooks. *Somebody* did it."

I feel cold all over.

"I'm still digging into all these names, but the last four are a problem." She taps on her phone, where the second set of names is still showing. "Without a first name, it's a big haystack with too many needles."

The door of the restaurant opens, and a harried server in a black apron comes out with a paper bag. "Gallagher?"

"That's me." I show him the order screen on my phone, and he hands over the bag. "Thank you." I wait until he disappears inside again before I turn to the reporter. "Did you actually follow me here? That's creepy. It's almost as creepy as, say, Tim dating me just to get information off my phone."

She winces. "That's bad behavior, and honestly, I'm surprised. I always knew him as a stand-up guy. Maybe it was complicated."

It's still complicated. "I don't think I can help you. I don't know anything, and I'm not allowed to talk to journalists. I need to go feed my kid."

Lickie noses the bag of food hopefully.

"Wait," the reporter hisses. "This was personal for him."

Something keeps me from striding away. "You mean . . . the mansion?"

"He was born there," she says, her eyes flicking up the street.

I grip the bag tightly, afraid I'll drop it. The second I'd learned Tim was adopted, I'd wondered about it. "He told you that?"

"His mother did." She swallows. "I was over there after the funeral, offering to help clean out his place in New York. During our conversation, she mentioned he died outside the building where he was born."

I have chills. "Did she know he was investigating . . . something?"

She shakes her head. "And I haven't told her. But I did tell the police."

For once I'm relieved to hear that the police are involved. "And what did they say?"

"Not much." Her mouth twists. "It's quicker to focus on his ex-girlfriend, right? Especially when my theory sounds crazy—a man got himself killed looking for his birth parents."

"Because it *is* crazy," I point out. "People find their birth parents all the time. What's the worst that could happen if Tim's bio family was discovered? Someone is a little embarrassed?"

"That's what I need to know," she says. "And you're the only one I can think of with access to the Wincotts' archives. I need you to find the record of his birth—in that ledger you found. I need to see the page from 1979."

For a moment I only stare at her. "You're asking me to look up something that might have gotten Tim killed. Do I have that right?"

Her smile turns wry. "You get the photo of the page. I'll be the one digging up the dirt, Rowan. It's what I do."

"But why would I *do* that? I'd be risking my job for something that doesn't have a thing to do with me." And it never did. Not even from the first day Tim claimed to be so fascinated with me.

"Because the police would love to pin this on you."

"They can't," I insist, even as an icy spike of fear hits my breastbone. "I didn't have anything to do with his death."

She shrugs. "A conviction would be a long shot, I admit. But even an arrest would put you all over the news. Might be hard to find jobs after that."

"You're just as manipulative as Tim." I push off the wall, feeling shaky.

"Just get me his birth mother's name," she says. "I'll find her on the sly. It's the right thing to do, Rowan. Tim deserves justice, and I'm going to get it for him." She thrusts a sticky note in my direction.

I take it from her. It says *Jules*, no last name. The phone number has a New York prefix.

This woman is so "sketch," as my daughter would say. I take the sticky note anyway and tuck it into my pocket. "I don't know if I can help you."

"But you'll think about it?" she asks.

I'll probably think of nothing else.

21

Wednesday morning is rainy and dark. When my alarm goes off, I give serious thought to calling in sick just to curl up under the comforter and doze. But my job is the only thing in my life that's still roughly on track, and I need to keep it that way.

I get up and drive Natalie to another final exam before heading to work. I park in the gravel lot, as far away from the spot where Tim died as I can physically be without ramming the car into a tree.

My shoes are wet by the time I hurry onto the mansion's porch. After shaking off my umbrella, I glance over both shoulders while I key in the new security code. Thankfully, I get it right on the first try. When the light turns green, I push the big door open.

Without morning sunlight shining down through the skylight, the foyer is gloomy.

If this were 1860, I would have been greeted at the front door by the housekeeper. And honestly, I could use a friendly smile as I remove my raincoat and carry it into the reception room to hang it on the coatrack.

Back then, I would've placed my calling card on the housekeeper's silver tray, and she would've whisked it off for the judgment of the lady of the house, leaving me to ponder my significance amid the room's splendor.

Today, I trudge alone into the atrium, listening for signs of life in the mansion. Beatrice has a meeting somewhere off-site, but nobody else seems to be around, either. I don't hear the conservators' music playing upstairs. The quiet is so deep it presses down on my eardrums.

My heart thumps as I slip past the staircase, heading for the library. I practically jump out of my skin when I hear a noise. Sweat prickles my back as I peer around the doorjamb. There's nobody in the library. I creep forward, changing the angle of my body to gain a narrow view of the inner office.

Hank Wincott sits there, his foot propped up on a folding chair as he scrolls through his phone.

"Morning," I practically gasp. "Didn't see your car outside."

He glances over in my direction, then does a double take. "Morning. Did I startle you? I'm sorry." He makes a sympathetic grimace. "I walked here, which I now regret, because the rain has picked up, yeah?" He rises to peer through the windows. "It's coming down in sheets."

I walk slowly toward my desk, taking a moment to pull oxygen into my lungs, fighting off my irritation. He owns the damn house. He can come and go as he pleases. Still, I'm not used to sharing the space with him.

Besides, I probably look damp and frizzy, while Hank looks like he just stepped out of *GQ*. Today he's wearing a charcoal suit and a crisp blue shirt.

"Did I forget a meeting?" I ask, setting down my laptop bag.

"No." He gives me a patient smile. "I just wanted a word with you." He takes his seat again in one of our visitor's chairs. "First of all, I should have come by earlier to say that I'm sorry for your loss."

Oh. I drop into my chair. "Thank you. I appreciate that. Tim and I weren't close when he died, but it's still been a shock."

He turns appraising blue eyes on me. "Had you known him long?"

I pause for a second before answering. The question might be totally innocent, but after last night's ambush by the journalist, I don't trust it. "I only met him this spring. But the violence of his death is still a shock."

"Of course it is," he says easily. "And the police haven't made any arrests." He glances around the office. "Must be nerve-racking to show up here every day."

"I've had better weeks," I say gamely.

He drums his fingers on the surface of my desk. "Look, I have a favor to ask. But you should feel no pressure."

That sounds ominous, and a tingle climbs up my spine. "All right. I'm listening."

He plucks a Blackwing pencil from my desk, balancing it between his fingers. Then he flicks his gaze in my direction. "Next Tuesday is the Portland Historical Commission's annual fundraising dinner."

"Mmm-hmm?" I don't know where he's going with this.

It takes a second for him to continue, because his phone chimes loudly with a text.

I expect him to read it, as he always does when we're in the middle of a conversation. Instead, he says, "Rowan, I was hoping you'd accompany me for the evening."

"To the dinner?" I ask stupidly. I never was one of the cool kids in high school, and I'm a little confused. Did Hank Wincott just *ask me out?*

"As my date for the evening," he says with a smile so quick that I might have dreamt it. "And also, as the best person to answer what are sure to be a lot of pesky questions about what we're doing to the mansion and to the neighborhood. A lot of the people from the Landmarks Review Board will be at this dinner."

"Oh! Of course!" I say a little too brightly. "You're right—it's a great opportunity to talk up the project. Excellent idea." I'm babbling now, but I'm just so relieved that I misinterpreted the invitation. "I'm sure I can be there. It's no trouble."

"Excellent. I'll ask the new girl to forward you the invitation, and you can double-check your calendar."

"I'll do that." I take a breath and try to calm down. "Anything else?"

He rises from the chair and walks the perimeter of the room past the mostly empty bookshelves. "We're having another budget meeting on Friday, yes? For the Orangerie?"

"Absolutely. I'll have the whole budget annotated by then."

He nods absently and stops in front of a grandiose fireplace that hasn't seen a real fire in decades. "Remind me—what's your plan for this room?"

"Rare books," I answer immediately, like the first-row student I've always been. "Ships' plans, ledgers, and records. Plus, the plans for this house and Amos Wincott's marine designs." Hank's ancestor dabbled in cabin design for luxury craft.

"Right. Of course." He runs his hand along the walnut wainscoting. "Did you know Amos was a second son? Like me." Hank turns to give me a wry smile, and it reminds me how stupidly attractive he is. "The

Wincott family is thick with second sons. That's why Amos became an architect. His brother inherited the shipyard and the shipping contracts. He had to find something else to build."

"Lucky Amos." I shrug. "Architecture is more fun than shipping."

"You would say that." Hank throws another smile in my direction and then tilts his handsome face up to inspect the elaborate ceiling. "Although he wasn't very good at his job, was he?"

For the second time in two minutes, I'm caught off guard. "What do you mean? This house is the most significant example of Italianate design in New England."

Hank lowers his well-defined chin and gives me an amused glance. "If that's the way you want to play it, sure. But we both know that Amos wasn't a visionary. And I'm sure you've noticed that he just ripped his designs straight out of the fashionable parts of Europe."

He isn't wrong. Although I'm surprised that Hank acknowledges this. "You could say that he was *honoring* those traditions. As your professional cheerleader for this building, you won't hear me say otherwise. There's craftsmanship here that isn't replicable. That's exactly what I'll be telling the Landmarks Review Board, by the way. They won't know what hit them."

His smile widens, but before he can reply, his phone chimes again. Then mine does the same damn thing. Unable to resist the lure this time, he retrieves his phone from his pocket.

I take the opportunity to do the same and find a text from Beatrice.

Beatrice: Did you see the news? They found the gun!
Beatrice: This could all be over soon.

"They found the gun," Hank says as we both tap on our screens. The news story loads mercifully fast.

A caller to the PPD tip line sent authorities to search a dumpster in the same west side neighborhood where the murder took place. Police say they've recovered a pistol that was recently fired, as well as personal effects of the deceased.

The forensic investigation is ongoing, but the gun appears to match the make and serial number of a weapon owned by the victim.

I sit back in my chair, startled. Tim had a gun?

A suspect was seen by the tipster tossing the gun into the dumpster. The suspect was described as a white man wearing a dark hoodie sweatshirt and a baseball cap. He is reportedly about six feet tall. Anyone with knowledge or footage of the perpetrator disposing of the gun is encouraged to call the tip line. Police are searching for any other witnesses who may have seen the perpetrator in action.

"A white man in a sweatshirt?" Hank says. "That's half of New England."

"Maybe they'll find more. Fingerprints, or a hair, or whatever else police can get from a gun." From a gun that's been sitting in a dumpster? *Sure, Rowan. Way to sound sharp.*

"His own gun. Do journalists usually carry a weapon?"

"I wouldn't think so," I say as another wave of exhaustion hits me. "But maybe I'm just naïve."

Hank picks up his briefcase. "I think I'll head to the office and make some calls. Maybe I can find someone who's willing to share more of the details."

"Keep us posted," I say mildly. As if I'll be able to think about anything else today.

"Hang in there, Rowan. And I'll have my girl send you the details on that dinner."

My girl. Yikes. "Thanks. See you Friday."

He leaves, and I pick up my phone and read every word of the article about the gun. Two more times.

22

The rain continues to spatter against the windows, and I work alone in the office with my CAD software and my regrets. Until I nearly fall out of my chair when I hear a shout from upstairs.

Rushing to the second floor, I find Zoya on her scaffolding. I brace myself to hear another anecdote about a ghost, but she's excited about something else.

"I found it! Poseidon seducing Scylla! This painter was so fucking predictable."

I move closer to the new image that she's working on. The edges are still blurred by beige paint, but I can see a misbehaving Poseidon in a clinch with a young nymph.

"That's Scylla." Zoya points a Q-tip at the nymph. "And that's Poseidon's *wife*." She points at a neighboring figure—a goddess staring at the lovers with obvious contempt. "This house! It's so dark, yet so horny." Zoya dabs at the paint. "It's a good thing you guys pay well."

"Agreed."

———————

At five o'clock, I pack my laptop and leave the library, flicking off the lights as I go. The atrium is still gloomy without the blues and golds coming from the upper window.

Outside, I grab my umbrella off the porch and set off under a steel-gray sky. The gawkers are gone now, and so is the yellow police tape.

As I walk to my car, I crank my head around for an oblique view of the row of dumpsters on the property. The police searched them immediately after Tim died, so I'm assuming the gun was found somewhere else.

In the neighborhood, the article had said. But where?

I climb into the car and start the engine. But my phone rings before I put it in gear. The display says **Portland PD.**

My stomach dives. But Beatrice would be proud of me, because I don't answer the call.

The detective leaves me a voice message, though, and I hit play the moment the notification appears.

Hi, Rowan. This is Detective Riley of the Portland PD. Just calling to let you know that we're still pursuing electronic data from your phone. If you're ready to share it with us, please call me back. You seem like a good person who landed in the wrong place at the wrong time.

Gosh, you think?

. . . And I know we can work together to figure out what happened on the night of Tim's death. An authorized download of your cell phone data would be a good-faith gesture on your part . . .

It's just more of the same pressure, but it fills me with dread. I play back the message again, just to make sure I've heard it correctly.

We're still pursuing the data . . . she's said. That means they don't have it yet.

Does she know I lied? Or is it just a hunch? When I'm lying awake at four a.m., I always think back to the night of Tim's murder, and I picture myself telling the truth right from the start. *I was so confused by the breakup that I spent a few days watching Tim move around Portland on my phone.*

There's really no way to say that so I don't sound like a hardcore stalker. Which I was. But I'm *not* a killer. And telling the truth now will only make things worse. The police will waste even more time on me.

Still, it's selfish logic. Beatrice was right when she said that I can't afford to be under suspicion of murder.

It's just too late to change my story now.

Before I set down the phone, I check for a message from Natalie. But there's nothing. Not even a text to say how her pre-calc exam went today.

Maybe I even deserve it.

I toss the phone aside and put the car in gear. The drive through the neighborhood takes only a few minutes. There are blooming rhododendrons in most of the yards, their leaves slick with rain. When my sodden porch comes into view, I look upward and see two rectangles of light in Natalie's room.

And I feel instantly calmer. So long as Natalie is safe, then nothing else matters.

———————

My daughter's mood is upbeat when we sit down to dinner. She eats the salmon I've made and does the dishes without being asked.

I'm basking in the glow of her helpful demeanor when she hangs up the dish towel and asks to borrow the car. "Just for a couple of hours," she says.

"Where are you going?"

"Tessa's. Tomorrow's exam is a big one," she says, not meeting my eyes. "American Government."

Seriously? I haven't heard more than a few words about this class all semester. And I strongly suspect that "studying with Tessa" has more to do with gossip than memorizing the Bill of Rights.

But you have to pick your battles, so I give her the keys and remind her only twice to drive safely.

According to my favorite app, Natalie arrives at Tessa's house without delay. But even so, I find myself wandering around at loose ends, too much on my mind. The rain has stopped, and I need exercise. After changing into running clothes and lacing up my shoes, I look down at Lickie, who's been giving me hopeful glances.

"I'm going to run a few miles. You up for it?"

She thumps her tail and jumps off the couch.

I'm not convinced that Lickie would save me from a murderer, but having her at my side makes me feel less alone.

Outside, I stretch as I decide where to run. Not the Western Promenade—that's where Tim and I used to run. Lickie and I set off in the other direction, through the city and toward the back cove.

There's a breeze coming off the water as I curve around the peninsula, but my heart is thumping, and I'm sweating through my running shirt.

I love Portland. I don't want to be afraid of this place. What I wouldn't give to rewind my life ten days or so, when my biggest problem was an unexpected breakup.

By the time the light fades, I'm running toward the waterfront, where Commercial Street is humming with tourists. I need this. I need to see people whose lives aren't a dumpster fire. I hear the sound of a bartender shaking up someone's cocktail, and a woman's laughter.

I don't exactly fit in with the waterfront vibe tonight—I'm sweaty and panting like a bear—but nobody even looks my way. They're too busy eating lobster rolls and drinking craft beer at the dockside bars. That's the draw of Portland. It's a working harbor, with trawlers coming into port every morning and fresh fish for sale. But it's still cute and historical.

We're a little smug about it, to be honest. We understand why the tourists like it here, but we roll our eyes at them just the same.

As I approach Docksiders Bar and Grill, I feel a flicker of unwelcome nostalgia. This place is where I met Harrison when I was a nineteen-year-old fool.

"We were all nineteen-year-old fools," my therapist once said. Which is probably true, but it doesn't make my memories any rosier.

To make things even worse, strains of "Beast of Burden" by the Stones come filtering out of the building. The song is another powerful trigger for thoughts of Harrison.

When I first met him, he was the scowling cook on the other side of the pass-through, nagging me to garnish every basket before it left the kitchen. "Hey—new girl. *Gallagher.*" He always used my last name, like an army drill sergeant. "Parsley. Lemon. Tartar sauce. *Every* time. And when your orders are up, you need to grab them in ninety seconds or less."

I was a little afraid of him. The hours were long, and the smell of fried clams clung to me no matter how often I washed my hair.

On the plus side, Cal—the owner—was a great guy. The tourists were generous with their tips, and there was live music most nights of the week.

The music made the job feel a little less like military duty and a little more like a party. My fourth night working at Docksiders the featured band was called Most Definitely. I thought it was a stupid name, but they sounded great.

My eyes were drawn to the bass player, and then got stuck there as he added his deep, soulful voice to the chorus. There was something familiar about him, but also something darkly appealing.

Then it finally dawned on me that the same man who swayed to the beat as if the bass were part of his body was my kitchen nemesis. And that I was staring at him with my tongue practically hanging out.

Flustered, I forgot the order I'd just taken from table ten. So I had to go back and ask again. The rest of the night went pretty much the same way, because I kept watching Harrison play when I should have been doing my job.

To this day I don't understand it. Harrison wasn't my type. In fact, I didn't even have a type. I was too naïve to have refined my taste in men. But if you'd asked me what kind of guy I wanted to date, I would have pointed at one of the clean-cut boys from Chatham Prep. Someone like Hank Wincott. Or one of his nerdier friends, anyway.

But every Thursday after that—as I ferried steaming plates of fried fish and lobster rolls back and forth across the restaurant—my eyes always seemed to land on Harrison and stay there. It's a miracle I didn't drop half my orders, the way I used to drink him in. I liked the way he closed his eyes in the depths of a song, his forearms flexing deliciously as he played, his hips swaying.

Some of their songs required backup vocals, and those were my favorites. "Beast of Burden" quickly became my favorite song, because I could hear Harrison's deep-voiced harmonies on the chorus. I got goose bumps every time.

It's not like I had the guts to talk to him, though. So my crush would have died a quick death if he hadn't approached me one night after my shift. I stepped outside to drain my water bottle before heading home and found him standing on the dock. "Hey, Gallagher—cigarette?" he'd said, peeling his lithe body off the shiplap wall and offering me the pack.

"I don't smoke," I'd answered primly. Because I never was cool.

"Huh," he'd said. "I'd better quit then." He crushed the pack in his hands, as my jaw dropped. Then he hurled the pack toward the nearest wastebasket. It sailed right in, too. "Want a beer? I feel like we should get to know each other. We spend a lot of time staring at each other."

I was too surprised to speak—stunned that he called me out for my wandering eyes, and doing so in a way that made him sound culpable, too. It was bold, but also kind.

He took my silence as a yes and reached into a little Igloo cooler at his feet, pulling a Corona out of it. He offered it, much like he'd offered the cigarettes. I hesitated, and he wiggled the bottle in my direction. "Don't make me give up alcohol, too."

With a laugh, I'd taken the dripping bottle from his hand. The truth was that I hated beer. I'd spent the first year of college clutching Solo cups at parties, taking only an occasional sip.

But that night the cold, bitter liquid felt different going down. It tasted like victory. The air smelled salty and brand-new, as I stood there talking with Harrison about nothing and everything. My architecture program. The Roman Colosseum. Music. His favorite bands—most of which I'd never heard.

I don't know how long we lingered. Everyone else had trickled out and gone home by the time Harrison asked me out for dinner on my next night off. "We can stare at each other in a different restaurant," he said, while I blushed furiously.

"That sounds like fun," I stammered.

By which I meant *that sounds terrifying.* I didn't know how to be with this man I'd been crushing on for weeks. Harrison asking me out on a dinner date felt about as likely as Mick Jagger rolling up to play a gig in our bar.

That's how we got started. Because of a damn song, and my inability to stop undressing him with my eyes.

The song in question gets louder as I reach the front of the restaurant, and louder still when the door opens to belch out three drunk party boys with backward baseball caps.

I hear the song's chorus. The vocalist sounds different, of course, but he's getting the job done. Every other detail is shockingly the same. The steady beat of the drum and the low thump of the bass vibrating inside my chest. The scent of fried fish and lemon.

The baseball-hat guys are moving slowly and the sidewalk is narrow, so I have to stop and wait for them to gather up their smack talk and their laughter and cross the street. I'm stuck here just long enough to notice the pinned-up flyer for tonight's band. They're called Enough Already. Another terrible name, and it makes me smile.

My expression freezes as I study the black-and-white photo of the band. Three guys standing shoulder to shoulder, two of them smiling. They look like brothers. But the third guy . . .

He's aged, of course, but not as much as I have, damn it. Harrison stares coolly out from that photo, a bass clutched in his hand.

I can't believe it. And I mean that literally. This feels like a bad dream, one that I'd better figure out how to wake up from. Grabbing the old bronze door handle is a reflex, and within seconds I'm walking Lickie into the dimly lit space. All the action is in back, where there's a stage and patio seating. Up front is the hostess stand and a bar area that's only popular during cold weather.

A bored college girl looks up and greets me. "Table for one? With the dog, it has to be outside."

"No, I-I won't be staying," I stammer, neatly circling her and heading toward the back. The song grows louder, and the scent of fried clams and bad decisions is cloying.

It's only a few more paces until I can see the stage. The bassist is in profile, but it doesn't matter. I'd know him anywhere. He strums with a frown that's both serious and cool at the same time. Long hair in motion, body swaying in time to the music, his skin tinted by the red-orange stage lighting.

I'm caught in a time loop. I'm nineteen and I've forgotten tartar sauce for table twenty-two, because Harrison is up there playing "Beast of

Burden," and after my shift he's going to kiss me so thoroughly in my car that my panties will be damp before the engine warms up.

Then he looks up—like he can feel time warping, too. He lifts his chin and finds me on the first try.

For some awful reason I expect him to smile, just like the old times. Instead, the spell breaks as his gaze shifts to a table in the middle of the restaurant. Table sixteen.

When I see who's sitting there, my heart stops.

23

NATALIE

With her back to the door, and the thrum of the bassline thumping in her chest like a second heartbeat, Natalie watches her father play the hell out of an old song. He makes it look effortless. As if his hands just know what to do.

Live music on a weeknight and the breeze off the water. For once, she's living her *real* life and not just prepping for it, the way high school always feels.

Tessa sits opposite her, finishing off the last of their French fries, humming along with the band and slurping on a Coke that the waitress keeps refilling.

Until her friend's eyes suddenly widen. "Omigod, don't panic," Tessa says. "But you are in so much trouble right now."

Oh shit.

Natalie swivels in her chair, but it really isn't necessary. There's only one person in the world who'd give a damn that Natalie's sitting in a perfectly respectable tourist trap splitting fries and Cokes with a friend.

Her mother stands at the edge of the seating area. She's in running gear, her hand clenched around the dog's leash, her eyes full of rage.

Natalie's heart collapses inside her chest.

With Lickie in tow, her mother threads between the tables like an angry hornet on a mission. Natalie is already pushing back her chair. Maybe it's not too late to avoid a scene.

But her mom is already at the table, leaning over and hissing into Natalie's ear. "You're out of here. I'm paying your tab at the bar. Then you're going home, young lady."

Young lady. Ugh.

Natalie drops her gaze. But she can feel Tessa's worry. And people are staring. Shame heats her face as she weaves between the tables, her chin practically tucked against her chest.

So humiliating.

Her mother stops to make fake-friendly chitchat with a gray-haired man behind the bar as she pays the tab with her smartwatch. But her shoulders are up around her ears, and Natalie knows the yelling is going to begin the second they're out of here.

The song ends, and Natalie looks over her shoulder to see her father hastily shed his instrument and hop off the stage, gaze fixed on Natalie and her mom.

"We'll take a short break," the lead singer says. "Back in ten!"

Her mother glances at the stage, and her jaw hardens. "Time to go." She grabs Natalie by the elbow and turns for the door.

"Wait!" her father says. "Rowan. Now hold on."

"I will not *hold on*," her mother snarls. "We're leaving."

"*Hey!* I thought this was okay with you," he says.

"Nothing about this is okay," her mother snaps.

Natalie wants to die. "Mom. I told him you said it was okay."

"Really? Because you want to spend the *entire* summer grounded? Go outside. I will deal with *you* in a minute."

Having no other choice, Natalie goes.

"God, I'm sorry," Tessa says out on the sidewalk. "She is *super* pissed."

Natalie says nothing. She's never seen her mother so angry.

"You could say you didn't know he was here," her friend whispers.

"It wouldn't work," she mumbles. Her parents met here. This place is part of their origin story.

Natalie didn't *want* to lie. Her mother forced her hand by ignoring him. This seriously isn't her fault.

"Rowan, wait!" comes her father's angry voice from inside. "If you'd only answer my messages . . ."

"It was two emails!" her mother shouts back. "I don't owe you a damn thing. Stay away from us."

Natalie's heart is in free fall as her mother appears on the sidewalk. "Where's the car?" she asks tightly.

Natalie points toward the lot across the street. With Lickie's leash in her hand, her mother hurries in that direction.

Natalie lingers on the sidewalk, just in case her father follows her outside to say goodbye.

He doesn't.

Shaking with anger, she finally follows her mother to the car. "You could have just answered his emails."

Her mother halts midstep and turns. "That's rich coming from a liar," she growls. "Give me the keys."

Her mother has never called her a liar before. It stings. And in front of a friend? Close to tears, she opens her bag and fumbles for the keys. "We have to take Tessa home."

"Just get in the damn car. Both of you."

"Um, I could just Uber," Tessa says.

"Both of you, in the car."

Natalie walks around to the passenger side. "Do you even have your license on you?"

Her mother just glares.

"You can have the front seat," Natalie tells her friend, "otherwise Lickie is going to be all over you."

"The back is fine," Tessa mumbles, opening the door.

Natalie dies a little more inside. She gets into the passenger seat and pointedly looks out the window as her mother pilots the car—illegally, without her license—out of the parking lot.

The drive to Tessa's is mercifully short, and her friend is able to escape the car a few minutes later.

Natalie opens her own door, too, which makes her mother snap: "Where do you think you're going?"

"I just have to get something out of the mailbox," Natalie says in a small voice before she quickly leaves the car.

"Omigod' I'm so sorry," Tessa whispers as Natalie pulls her phone out of her friend's mailbox. "Call me later."

Natalie gives her a faint nod and braces for a fight as she gets back into the car.

"You left your *phone* in her mailbox," her mother says slowly. "Do you do that a lot?"

She looks out the window. "Sometimes," she mumbles.

Her mother actually puts her head on the steering wheel and lets out a shaky breath. "Of all the stupid things."

"Hey! I wouldn't bother if you weren't *stalking* me!" It feels good to clap back. For a second, anyway. Because there are prisoners on parole who have more freedom than she does.

"I don't even know what to say to you right now. Your father is not a stable person! And you *knew* I would never give you my permission to see him. How long has this gone on? When did he come back to Portland?"

"You don't even *know* him anymore!" Natalie shrieks. "If you just answer his messages, I wouldn't have to sneak around!"

They're still parked in Tessa's driveway, but her mother makes no move to leave. "I asked you a question. How long has he been in the area?"

She turns to stare out at Tessa's suburban street. It's a nicer neighborhood than theirs. Less interesting, but nice. Tessa has a big TV room in the basement with its own little bar area stocked with sodas. And Tessa's mother doesn't *hover*.

"I don't know when he came back, exactly," she says dully. "I've only met him once before this. We talk on Instagram, though."

"Instagram," her mother says, as if the word tastes bad. "Did he approach you?"

"No," she says quickly. "It was me. I searched his name. I found his new band. I left a comment. And then he messaged me."

Her mother is silent for a long moment. Finally, she takes a shaky breath and puts the car in reverse.

They roll down Tessa's quiet street, and Natalie is hollow inside. Like every happy thought has been drained from her soul. She'd been waiting for Harrison to show up for her entire life. Then he finally did.

And now her mother is furious.

"What else have you lied about?" she asks as they approach the peninsula again.

"Nothing."

"I'm *so* disappointed in you, Natalie. You want to be a grown-up and borrow the car. But then you go and pull this."

Anger rises inside her like a fire. "I didn't *pull* anything. There's nothing wrong with wanting to see my father! I'm the only one at Chatham who doesn't have one."

This is, of course, an exaggeration. But not by much.

Her mother brakes at a stop sign and gives her the side-eye. "Look, I'm sorry you don't have the right kind of father. But you have to be rational about this. He went to prison for beating a man almost to death. He might even be mentally ill, like his mother."

"So you're saying it's genetic?" Natalie demands. "Do you hear yourself right now? I have half his genes."

Her mother puts the car in park and leans back against the headrest. "God, Natalie. No. I don't mean that at all. There's nothing wrong with you. It's just that Harrison had a really rough childhood, and it affected his ability to cope. Some of the things that went wrong in his life probably aren't all his fault, but that doesn't mean he's a good influence."

"He's still family," she points out. "You don't write family off unless you have to."

"I *did* have to."

"Just keep telling yourself that. You just want to make him go away. Never mind that he asked me to tell you he has something we need to know. Something about his medical history."

Her mother seems to sag against the seat. "*Oh.*"

"Yeah. *Oh.* But if you're too afraid to even call or email him, I guess we don't need to know what it is, yeah? We'll just wing it."

"That's low," her mother says quietly. "My most important job as your only parent is to keep you out of harm's way. And that's what I've been trying to do for fifteen years."

Anguished, Natalie asks a question that's been weighing on her mind. "Tell me this—did he ever hurt us? Like, physically? Were you afraid of him, you know, before?"

Her mother sighs. "No, he was never physically threatening until the night he tried to kill a man with a metal bar stool."

Natalie can't stop herself from flinching.

"There's a *reason* I don't want you anywhere near him."

Natalie turns to stare out the car window and says nothing.

Eventually, her mother puts the car in gear and drives home. After they pull into the garage, her mother says, "Now hand me your phone."

"Why?"

"You're not getting it back for a week."

"A *week*? That's outrageous."

"Child abuse, for sure. You'll think twice next time you break a promise to me. We had a deal—you'd keep your phone on until the killer was caught."

It *was* on. Natalie knows better than to make this argument. Instead, she closes her eyes and wishes she were anywhere else. An hour ago she'd been eating fries and watching her friend sway to the music. An hour ago she'd had a secret, and she'd also had a cool dad.

Now she's facing a week without her phone and an exam she hasn't studied for. Everything is bleak.

"I'm still waiting for that phone," her mother says as she cuts the engine.

Natalie almost throws it out the window. Her finger is literally on the window's button.

She puts the phone in the cupholder instead. Then she marches into the house, races upstairs to her bedroom, and slams the door.

24

ROWAN

After dealing with the dog and locking the house, I retreat upstairs, my heart galloping as I lock my bedroom door.

Harrison is here in Portland, playing "Beast of Burden" at Docksiders. I'm still shaking.

I flop back on my bed and stare at the ceiling. Natalie's anguish cuts deep. I had no idea how much she cared about knowing her father. And yet Harrison's return to Portland scares me in ways that I can't share with her.

After finding my phone, I open Instagram and guess the password for the account I made months ago for my architecture portfolio.

And then—just like Natalie did—I type in Harrison's name and find the band's Instagram account. I flip back through the pictures until I find the first posts with Harrison.

May. He's been in Portland for more than a month.

And I'm the fool who told the cops that we hadn't heard from him in fifteen years. I told them *repeatedly*.

This is bad.

I blow out a shaky breath and picture Natalie sitting in the bar, clapping along with the band, five paces from the man who blew up both our lives.

I find Detective Riley's card and compose a text.

> Rowan: This is Rowan Gallagher. Tonight I learned that Natalie's father is back in Portland, and my daughter has been in touch with him. I didn't know.

After sending it, I drop the phone and go down to the kitchen to pour myself a glass of wine. A tall one. When I pass Natalie's bedroom door, I can hear her speaking to someone in a low voice. She must be using her laptop to talk to Tessa. Maybe taking her phone doesn't even matter.

Do any of my parenting decisions matter?

In my room again, I pick up my phone to find that Detective Riley has already responded to my text.

> **Riley:** Thank you for telling me. Can you do me a favor and click on this link? I need to know if you think this footage is Harrison.

Oh God. It's suddenly hard to catch my breath, and I tug my sports bra away from my chest.

If the footage is of Harrison throwing a gun into a dumpster, I don't know what I'll tell my child.

When the link appears, I click, and a video loads. It shows the fishbowl view that's common to doorbell cameras. But there's no dumpster in view. It's a house. *Our* house.

A man walks up the short path from the sidewalk to the front door. He has a guitar case strapped onto his back.

I feel sick.

The picture isn't great, and our little front porch casts gloomy shadows over him as he steps up to our door and knocks. My heart is in my mouth as I picture Natalie opening the door and letting him inside.

But that's not what happens. Nobody comes. He knocks twice more and then gives up, turning around to retreat down the walkway, his gait so familiar that it socks me in the chest. The set of his shoulders, and the loping, confident stride. I used to light up inside whenever I saw him coming toward me. He'd give me a slow smile. *How's it going, Gallagher?*

Now he's back, at the worst possible time, and I feel more crushed than afraid. *What have you done, Harrison?*

I slide off the bed and cross to the bedroom window, staring down at the darkened street. As if he might be out there right now.

After yanking the curtains shut, I go back to my texts with Riley.

Rowan: Where did you get this?
  Riley: Your neighbor's doorbell camera. Do you recognize him?
          Is it Harrison?

I tap out the word *yes*, but I hesitate before sending it. What will she do if I confirm this? The police found a receipt from Docksiders in Tim's car.

Seriously? Could Harrison have killed him?

My phone rings in my hand, and I jump. It's Riley, of course. I answer with "When was this video taken?"

"I can't provide that information," she says coolly.

"Why not?"

"This is an ongoing murder investigation."

Jesus Christ. Like I don't know that?

"How did you learn he was in town?" she asks. "You said you found out tonight?"

"By accident. I was walking past the restaurant where we worked when I was in college. I heard the band, and I saw his face on a flyer. I went inside and found my daughter with a friend at a table."

She gives a low whistle. "And you had no idea they were in contact?"

"Look, have you ever raised a teenager?"

"No," she says, her voice softening. "I haven't had the pleasure. Did she tell you when they first made contact?"

"The date? No. I can try to ask, but she's really mad at me. I took her phone away for lying to me about her whereabouts."

"Okay, but I need that information. Either you get it, or I'll have to interview her myself."

Oh no you don't. "We need a cooling-off period, but I'll ask her tomorrow. Were you even going to tell me that he came to my house?"

"My responsibility is to the deceased, Rowan. It's my job to ask more questions than I answer."

Like that's not infuriating.

"Listen," she says. "I did some research on Harrison's first offense. The bar fight."

My stomach bottoms out, the same way it does every time I think about that night.

"You never mentioned they were fighting over *you*."

"They weren't," I argue. "It wasn't like some TV love triangle."

"Then tell me how it was."

The steel band around my chest tightens again. I hate remembering. Hate talking about the night that took my relationship from doomed to eviscerated.

"It was date night, I guess. We weren't doing that well as a couple. We had a toddler who didn't like to sleep in her own bed, and he had just lost his job. So we spent money we didn't have on a babysitter, and we went out to a comedy show."

"At the Parker House. That's in the police report."

Why do I have to tell this awful story if it's all in the report? "Harrison was really . . . off that night. Sort of hard to reach. I knew something was wrong, but I didn't know how to fix it."

"Like, mentally off?"

"Yes. I thought he was depressed. But he also kept asking me questions that didn't make sense. And that made me livid, because it meant he'd probably taken drugs."

"He did that a lot?"

"Well, yes and no. Not when I met him. He said he occasionally did some Ecstasy when he partied with his friends, but after Natalie was born, he started smoking pot. He was careful to smoke only outdoors, but it annoyed me because we had money issues. He told me it helped him feel less anxious."

I remember yelling at him that getting another goddamn job would make *me* less anxious.

"Anyway—that night he was acting so weird that I thought he was on something new. I was afraid, and I was angry that he'd get high on our big night out together. So I picked a fight. I told him I was pissed off, and we might as well go home if he was going to act like a zombie."

"And he got mad?" she asks.

"No, that's the weird thing. He hardly reacted at all. Like he was checked out. Until this stranger butted in and said, 'Hey dude, your lady is trying to tell you something.' And finally Harrison sort of woke up and asked the guy, 'Who are you talking to?' Which sounds like a smart-ass thing to say, but Harrison really meant it."

"Weird."

"It was. Then Harrison asked, 'Who sent you?' and the guy starts laughing. He calls Harrison a freak and a bunch of other names. Harrison flipped out. He started screaming questions at the guy. The whole bar kind of stops to watch. The bouncer steps in and tries to grab him. And Harrison *freaks*."

"Meaning . . . ?"

"Punching. Kicking. Like the devil possessed him. And this is a man I'd never seen violent in my life. The guy's friends pulled him back, but Harrison grabbed a bar stool. It was heavy. Made of steel, I think. And he charged the guy."

I shiver. I'd never been so scared, and I'll never forget the sound of that man's head hitting the concrete floor.

"The question is—do you think Harrison was capable of murdering Tim Kovak?"

Air rushes out of my lungs. "I just don't see why he would."

"Can't you? Tim had what he once lost."

"He didn't really."

"But Harrison is sometimes capable of great violence, and he has a history of drug use, correct?"

"Yes," I say softly.

"Did you speak with him tonight? How did he seem to you?"

"We only spoke for a second. I sent my daughter outside and then told him not to come around. He seemed . . ." I close my eyes and picture his gray eyes. I hadn't expected them to still look kind. I thought I'd see a monster. "He seemed a little angry, but also embarrassed. He said Natalie told him that she'd cleared their meetings with me. He fell for it."

"Did he sound mad at your daughter? At you?"

"A little? At me. He said 'If you're never going to answer any of my messages . . .' But I cut him off. I said I had a lot on my plate and told him not to bother us anymore."

"What was his response?"

"He just looked sad. And then he asked me not to be too hard on her."

"Hmm," the cop says. "We have a man with a violent past who wants to get back in touch with his family. And your recent ex turns up dead. It doesn't seem like a coincidence."

"Maybe." I sure hope it is a coincidence, though. "What are you going to do now?"

"I'm sorry. I can't share that information. But I'll be in touch if we learn anything or have any more questions. You've been very helpful, Rowan. You did the right thing by letting me know."

If only I was sure it was true.

25

THURSDAY

Thursday crawls in on its hands and knees. My head aches, but I get up early to make banana pancakes and thick-cut bacon.

My kitchen is the nicest room in the house, with its warm wooden floors and cozy dining table. When Natalie was a kindergartner, I redesigned the space for the two of us. This was our refuge.

But now it feels as though our sanctuary is being invaded.

Whenever people ask me about Harrison, I say "I was young and dumb." As if falling for a felon is just a thing teenagers do. But the truth is we had several good years together, starting with that first summer at Docksiders. I was so obsessed with him. And when fall came, and I had to return to school, I cried in his arms when he said goodbye to me.

"You're something else, Gallagher," he'd whispered to me. "I'm going to miss the hell out of you."

I didn't believe him. I thought he'd move on and find another nerdy girl to worship him.

But then he didn't. I went back to school, and we spent the next eight months on the phone together or texting. Or sneaking away to be together on the weekends. I used to borrow my roommate's car to meet Harrison halfway between Ithaca and Maine. There's a little motel off 190 in Massachusetts that became our hookup spot.

Our second summer together in Portland went by in a flash. But then we were facing a new kind of separation—my semester abroad in Rome. And since architecture is a five-year program, I'd have another year in Ithaca after that.

I couldn't bear the idea, so I was looking for architecture programs in New England when Harrison made a startling offer. "What if I found an apartment in Ithaca while you're in Italy? I can't afford to fly to Rome, but I don't want us to be apart forever. I can find a job in upstate New York while you're gone."

It had never occurred to me that he'd leave Maine for me. "But what about your band?"

"That's a hobby, baby. You're my whole life. I'd follow you anywhere."

Then he did. He got a job in an Ithaca café. When I came back from Italy, I moved in with him. We had a cramped little one-bedroom with creaky floors, but I loved everything about it. Coming home to Harrison felt like winning the lottery.

My parents were appalled. *He's not good enough for you* was my mother's constant chorus. *He's not the kind of man you marry.*

But I believed in us. I had faith in Harrison. Then he destroyed what we had, just like my mother said he would. Now he's back, knocking on our door.

I'll follow you anywhere, he once said.

I shiver.

The electric griddle beeps to tell me it's hot. I pour the first pancakes and then call up the stairs to wake Natalie.

The hot breakfast is an olive branch. I have a little speech ready when she stumbles into the kitchen. She gives me a wary glance as I set her plate on the table.

"Listen," I begin. "I reacted very strongly last night to a man I haven't seen in fifteen years. Seeing him was a shock, but I feel calmer now."

She yanks her chair out and sits down. "You acted like a stone-cold bitch."

I have to take a slow breath and swallow down the retort that's rising in my throat. *I'm the adult in the room*, I remind myself.

"I'm trying to get my head around this. For your sake. So maybe help me out, here?"

She sulks all the way through her gourmet breakfast and feeds bacon to Lickie even after I ask her to stop. But at least she answers the handful of questions I have for her.

"Do you know where he lives, exactly?"

"No clue."

"But it's in Portland?"

"I think so. Or close by."

"Where does he work?"

"At Docksiders. In the kitchen."

My heart spasms again. He's been right down the hill—full time? Part of me doesn't believe it. Like I should have sensed a disturbance in the Force.

We stumble through a couple more questions. Then Natalie says, "Don't forget, you're supposed to contact him. He said it was important."

"Yes. I'll do that when I'm ready."

She gives me a dark look. Then she gets up from the table—leaving her sticky plate as if the dirty-dish fairies were swinging by later to pick it up—and leaves for her American Government exam.

After cleaning up, I call Detective Riley, and I'm grateful when she doesn't answer. Voicemail is so much easier. "Good morning. Natalie doesn't know where her father is staying. He didn't tell her. She says he works in the kitchen at Docksiders most nights and plays occasional gigs wherever the band can get a slot. The band members are new people—not the same ones he had when I met him. Um . . ." I try to remember what else Natalie told me. "The first time they met in person was on Tuesday. They were supposed to meet last week, but the gig he was playing was twenty-one and up, and he had to tell her not to come. She says she didn't ask him how long he's been in town, but to her ear it didn't sound like very long. Whatever that means. And that's all we know. Sorry we couldn't be more helpful."

I hang up before the system cuts me off, tuck away my phone, and get ready for work.

As I leave, I notice the peonies on the coffee table. Harrison knew they were my favorite. He sent them to me once when we were long distance. My dorm room wasn't stocked with vases, so I had to put the flowers in a Brita water jug. I cried over them.

My mother was right all those years ago. We were doomed as a couple from the start. At twenty, though, I didn't care. I lived for his calls and his visits. I paid for Skype so I could see his face on my computer screen.

That warm smile. The soft look in his eyes when he glanced at me. The deep sound of his laughter when I said something witty. No man had ever made me feel like a treasure.

Just like an actual drug, it was both intoxicating and dangerous. Natalie and I both paid the price.

———————

Beatrice is at her desk when I arrive in the office. "How are you?" she asks. "You look tired. Isn't it my turn to run out for coffee?" She smiles. "I feel a cappuccino coming on."

"I wouldn't turn it down."

She departs, and I settle down to work. It doesn't provide its usual welcome distraction, though. I've got too many questions on my mind. I wonder if Detective Riley is going to question Harrison.

And then there's Jules the journalist. Her phone number is still in my pocketbook, while the fact of Tim's adoption—and his connection to this house—is still rattling around in my head like loose change.

My life is either full of strange coincidences or liars.

I open my inbox to find Harrison's message from earlier this week. *We have to talk about Natalie.*

Reluctantly, I open it. If he really has medical information concerning Natalie, of course I need to hear that. But if it's just a ploy for sympathy, or an excuse to toy with my daughter's affections, then he's underestimated me.

Hi Rowan,

I understand why you don't want contact with me. But Natalie wants to meet me and I've been stalling her until you weighed in. I want to hear any concerns you have.

And it's important that we talk—just once. I have some medical information that affects Natalie as she grows older. It has to do with my history with substances, and how to protect her going forward.

Please write back or call.

Love for you both,
H

Love? *Please.*

The message makes me grind my teeth, mostly because it's so above-board. He tried to tell me he'd been in contact with Natalie.

Damn this message. Damn everything.

He also leaves a number, and I save it to my contacts before drafting a reply.

I will, of course, hear you out about the medical information. But not right this minute. There is too much turmoil in our lives. Natalie lied to me about seeing you, and that's unusual. We need some time to work on what happened before I can consider letting her see you again.

Please respect my wishes and steer clear for now.
R.

I read it back and feel like chucking my computer across the room. I sound uptight and sanctimonious—especially the point about Natalie usually telling the truth.

That's just wishful thinking, isn't it?

But I shouldn't care what Harrison thinks, should I? So I press send.

Beatrice arrives a half hour later with two coffees in a cardboard holder, plus the day's mail.

I pop out of my chair to unburden her.

She puts a cup of coffee on my desk, while I sort through several slippery catalogs for lighting and hardware. I also find a manila envelope addressed to me at the mansion's address in blocky writing. I slit open the envelope with my thumb and extract a single sheet of paper.

There are only four words hand-lettered in Sharpie marker. HE HAD TO DIE

Beatrice gasps. "Oh God. Don't *touch* it!"

I drop it like a hot potato onto the floor.

After Beatrice calls the police, it takes twenty minutes for Detective Fry to arrive.

He collects both the envelope and its contents and carefully bags them. Then he asks us a dozen questions.

How often do we get the mail?

Every workday, because the mailman drops it through the front door.

Did both of us touch the envelope?

Probably.

"Do you happen to have a sample of your ex's handwriting?" Fry asks me.

"Why?" Beatrice demands. "A dead man didn't write that."

My head throbs. "He means my other ex. Natalie's father is back in town."

"*Oh*," Beatrice says softly.

I think about it for a second. "No, I can't think of anything I kept that he wrote. Except . . ." I feel the first hint of relief since opening the envelope. "He never made many written notes. Harrison is severely dyslexic."

"Huh," says the cop with a frown. "All right. You'll tell us if anything else turns up?"

"Of course," Beatrice says.

Then Fry takes his leave, wearing a grim expression. Although I think the scowl is standard on that model.

"Unhelpful as usual," Beatrice grumbles after she shows him out.

"This is a damn disaster. I was still holding out hope that the killing was just a robbery gone wrong."

I put my head in my hands. "So was I."

"Is Natalie's dad really back? How do you know?"

I drain my coffee. "Now *there's* a story."

26

NATALIE

Natalie reads the latest news story a second time just to make sure she didn't misunderstand.

> The PPD has revealed the location of the dumpster where the weapon was found—behind Mick's Rock Café on Congress Street. Police are still searching for anyone who witnessed the disposal of a gun on or after the night of June 6.

Mick's Rock Café is an over-twenty-one venue on the west side of town. That's where her father had played on the night of Tim's murder. She knows this firsthand, because she tried to get into the club that night, even after he told her she couldn't attend.

It didn't work. The bouncer turned her away at the door, and she'd gone back to Tessa's house.

The gun was found behind *Mick's*?

She feels sick. Although a hundred people must have seen her dad on that stage with his bass. He wouldn't be able to play a gig and shoot a guy at the same time.

Except bands take breaks, and the club is on the same side of town as the mansion.

She rubs her bare arms, which are suddenly cold in the school library's air-conditioning. There's only fifteen minutes until she has to take her next exam.

Any other week, she would have been outside in the sunshine with her friends. Tessa is out there with a handful of other kids from her class. The problem is they all know what happened last night, judging by the stares she received first thing this morning when her eyes were still gritty from crying.

"Are you *okay*?" Tessa had asked.

"Fine. Why wouldn't I be?" she'd lied. Because you can't show fear. Not even to your best friend.

The dumbest part is that she'd brought Tessa along for the express purpose of telling people about their trip to hear her dad's band. It was supposed to be Natalie's only badass moment, like, *ever*. Because nobody else's dad looks like Harrison or plays the bass.

If her mom hadn't shown up last night, everything would be fine. Great even.

It's just so mortifying. And this morning, when she'd snuck into her mom's bedroom to dig her phone out from her mother's bedside table, she'd found a two-word message from her father. *I'm sorry.*

She doesn't even know why he's apologizing when she's the one who lied. Unless he's an even bigger liar. Or a murderer.

It hurts to think about.

She opens the library's research portal and types in her father's full name, adding *Portland Maine arrest* to the query.

It's been a while since she tried this. When she googled him at home, all the articles about her dad were trapped behind paywalls. But the school library has paid access, and now she can actually read the details of her father's crime.

The first story she finds is super short. *Massachusetts Man Assaulted at the Parker House Bar. Local Man Arrested.* There are barely two paragraphs about the fight and her father's arrest.

She tries again, incorporating the victim's name into her search, and finds a more extensive story. She hadn't known that the man her father assaulted was a stranger.

That's somehow even more disturbing. And the victim's wife's statement is downright horrifying: *That man was completely out of control. He was terrifying, and I've never been so scared in my life.*

Natalie has to look away from the computer screen.

When she was little, she used to ask what happened to her father. She knew he existed, because there was a single picture of Natalie in his arms in the family photo album.

Her mother's answers to her questions about him changed as Natalie aged. At first she'd explained, "He made some bad choices, and he had to leave us."

When Natalie was in fifth grade, she expanded. "He was taking drugs. And I guess he couldn't stop. It's called a substance use disorder. When you were just a year old, he got high and got into a bar fight. The other guy got hurt really badly, so your father had to go to jail."

A bar fight sounds like an argument that got out of hand. A few punches thrown. But now she knows that the victim—Barry Peterson—suffered a brain injury and spent several months in a rehab unit.

Steeling herself, she rereads Barry Peterson's wife's account of the fight. *He kept screaming at Barry.* Don't look at her. Don't (expletive) look at her. Don't you (expletive) dare. *I thought he was going to kill Barry, and then me, too.*

She looks away again. Her pencil case is spilled open on the desk, and she straightens it and zips it shut. As if to organize the chaos in her heart.

The problem is that she'd *liked* him. At the coffee shop and at the bar he'd seemed kind. And interesting. And a little tentative—like he cared, but he was still just winging it and hoping for the best. Which is how she feels pretty much all the time. He felt *familiar.*

But the Harrison in these newspaper articles is someone she never wants to meet. He went to jail, and he stayed there a long time.

That doesn't happen to people who keep their worst urges locked down.

She closes the browser tab and searches *Tim Kovak murder* as she's done before. But now she's reading with fresh eyes. She tries to imagine her father enraged and shooting Tim in the face.

It doesn't make any sense. Then again, she can't make sense of *anyone* shooting someone in the face.

Tim stares back at her from the photo accompanying the article. He stands on the deck of a boat with the ocean behind him. He's smiling faintly. It's the sort of picture that's meant to make you think *Now there's a nice guy.*

But nice guys don't search through your phone.

"Natalie?" the librarian says. "Don't you have somewhere you have to be?"

She kills the browser window and leaps to her feet. Her exam starts in two minutes. "Right. I'm going."

Hurrying down to the classroom, she'll spend the next two hours writing about the Bill of Rights and the three branches of government.

It will take another twenty hours for her to hear that the police have arrested her father and taken him to the Cumberland County Jail.

27

FRIDAY

ROWAN

I'm finishing up my shower when I hear Natalie wail. Before I can even process the sound, I'm slapping at the faucet and grabbing my towel. I trip over the bath mat and career out the door.

"Natalie?"

She crouches on her bed, curled around her laptop, tears streaming down her face.

"What's happened?"

Face crumpling, she shows me her computer screen. *Area Man Arrested in Connection with Mansion Murder.* Bile creeps up my throat as I squint at the page to find his name.

She scrolls down, and Harrison's mug shot appears.

Oh God.

Perching on the bed, I skim the article, trying to take in facts with a muddled brain. Harrison was arrested "on a warrant for a probation violation," but they're "questioning him in connection with the murder of Tim Kovak."

If he's innocent, I feel sick. If he did it, I'll feel sicker.

"I'm not going," my daughter sobs.

"What?"

"My last exam. Call me in sick."

"Let me get dressed," I say, trying to wrap my head around Harrison's arrest.

Numbly, I move through the rituals of the day, pulling on socks and trying to figure out what you're supposed to do when your daughter's father is arrested. There's no playbook for this.

I walk downstairs—out of earshot—and call the biology teacher. "Mr.

Blinkman, I know the timing is terrible," I say, my voice shaking. "But we're having a family emergency. I need to keep Natalie at home today."

One of the blessings of sending your child to an outrageously priced prep school is having the teacher's phone number handy. The downside is the curious tone in his voice.

"I'm so sorry to hear that," he says. "I hope everything is going to be okay?"

"I sure hope so. Can she email you this weekend about a retake?"

"Of course she can. Please remind her that the honor code forbids her to talk to her friends about how the test went."

"Absolutely. I'll make sure of it."

After hanging up, I towel off my hair and try to think. Could Harrison really have done this? Two days ago, I'd told Natalie that her father might be a dangerous man. But I didn't want to be right. I feel no relief that he's been arrested.

After another deep breath, I get off the couch and climb the stairs again. At the top, Natalie's closed bedroom door feels like the Berlin wall.

I rap lightly with a knuckle. "Natalie? The bio teacher is giving you an extension."

"Who *cares*." The door suddenly flies open. "Did *you* do this? Did you tell the cops you think he's guilty?"

"No." But I'm quailing inside. "The detectives knew he was in town before I did."

She squints at me with bloodshot eyes. "Did you tell them there's *no way* he did this? Because there's just no way!"

I'm not sure which one of us she's trying to convince.

"He'll get a lawyer," I say quietly. "And if he didn't do it, they won't find him guilty."

"*God*, Mom. That's so naïve." Fresh tears stream down her cheeks. "He needs a *good* lawyer."

"Sweetheart, this is not your problem to solve."

"That's *bullshit*," she rages. "You're all, *He's not a good person*. But do you know who wasn't a good person? Tim fricking Kovak! Did you know that?"

My blood stops circulating. "What are you talking about?"

Natalie spins and hurls herself onto her unmade bed. "Your stupid boyfriend looked through your phone! I saw him."

A chill climbs up my spine. "*When*, Natalie? *When* did you see this?"

She rolls over and pins me with a glare. "One Saturday morning. I came home from Tessa's and found him scrolling through your phone in the living room. You were in the shower."

I feel sick. "You never told me."

"*Right*." The word is dripping with disgust. "Like I wanted to be in the middle of that problem. I just turned around and left. But *Mom*—that's what an abuser does."

Natalie is red-faced and sneering, and there's snot running out of her nose. But she has never been more beautiful to me, raging about the injustices done to me by my not-quite boyfriend.

"I'm sorry," I say quietly. "You shouldn't have to try to protect me like that."

"He was acting strange, Mom. He just put the phone down so casually. Like he wasn't doing anything wrong."

"Thank you for telling me. I'm sorry you felt like you couldn't before."

She flops back on the bed. "They think Dad killed Tim, but Tim was obviously doing some shady shit. And now Dad is in jail. I need to see my phone. What if he tried to message me?"

"I'll get it. You can check." It's a relief to turn away and fetch it from my drawer, where I'd stashed it yesterday. Maybe it will provide her a small comfort.

It only takes her a moment to unlock the screen and check her notifications.

"He called me! There's a voicemail."

A moment later I hear my ex's voice.

"Natty, hi."

Natty. I feel an unwelcome tug behind my breastbone.

"This isn't a call I ever wanted to make. But if you were thinking about worrying about me, please don't. I didn't do . . . whatever they think I did. That means I'm going to land on my feet eventually. But it might take a while. Your mother doesn't want to hear from me right now, and I get it. But please let her know that I still have important things to say to her. And please know that I love you very much. Always have."

The message ends with an abrupt *click*.

My eyes get hot, and I dig my fingernails into my palms.

Natalie cries, and when I sit down and grab her into a hug, she lets me. "I'm sorry, baby. It'll turn out okay."

"Really?" she sobs. "That's what you're going with? If you were sitting in jail, you'd want me to just shake it off? What if it was me in jail?"

The idea makes me feel cold despite Natalie's octopus grip on my cotton sweater.

"Mama, we have to *do* something. What if Tim got himself killed by some psycho, and they pin it on Dad?"

"I'm not sure what we can do to help right now," I say quietly.

She straightens, eyes lifting. "You could go to the jail and make sure he has a lawyer."

Oh baby. "I'm sure he does."

"You can still check. If you don't, I will. I'll go there myself. The jail is biking distance."

"Natalie . . ."

"What?" She shrugs. "You may not care what happens to him. But that doesn't mean I can't."

Shit. "Look, there's someone I could call who might know why he was arrested, and how it all works."

Her eyes burn with hope. "Will you? Today?"

"On my walk to work," I say, regretting it already. "I'll make the call."

"Awesome. Go!" She waves me toward the stairs. "If you hear something, you'll call me?"

I stand and pretend not to notice her hands are clutching the phone she's not supposed to have. "I'll text you later. It might take her some time to get the answers, though, okay?"

"Okay." She gives me a miserable little smile.

I'm out the door ten minutes later, my phone in one hand and the sticky note with Jules's number in the other. I don't want to owe this woman a favor, but I promised Natalie, so I make the call.

She picks up immediately. "Hello?"

"Hi," I say tightly. "This is Rowan Gallagher. Did you see . . ."

"Yes. They arrested your ex-boyfriend, right?"

That shuts me up for a second. "How do you know he's my ex?"

"Found his name on an old lease when I ran a background check on you."

I stop walking. "On me? Was I on Tim's list of names, too?"

"No," she says curtly. "But you're a person of interest in a murder investigation, and I needed all the facts. Didn't take you for the kind of girl who liked bad boys, either. Harrison's file was a fun read."

I have to take a deep breath. "My ex and I don't really speak. But even given his history, it's a stretch to think that he'd kill Tim. It doesn't really make sense."

"Maybe it does, maybe it doesn't. Why are you calling me?"

"Because my daughter is losing her mind, and I thought you might know something. What do they have on him, and what does it mean?"

I can almost hear her wheels turning. Should she help me or not? "They picked him up on a probation violation. That's what they call a parole violation in Maine."

"Yeah, I can read the newspaper, too. But what does that *mean*?"

"It means they can hold him over the weekend while they're waiting for a probation hearing. And it also means they don't have enough to charge him with murder. The actual violation is probably something stupid—like he drank a beer, or missed a date with his probation officer."

"And then what happens?"

"A judge will hold a hearing—Monday or Tuesday—to decide if the breech is serious enough to send him back to prison. Jails are crowded and expensive, so the state will have to convince the judge that it's too risky to leave him on the streets. Could go either way, depending on how skilled his lawyer is. The prosecutor is probably hoping to find better grounds for a murder charge—and lock him up for good—before the judge decides."

Natalie will be inconsolable.

"Find me Tim's page in that ledger," she says. "Unless your ex has a thing for killing journalists, I think there's something else going on.

Tim started digging into the Magdalene Home, and then died in front of it? That's what keeps me up at night."

"I'll think about it," I say tightly. "Thank you for the information."

"Feel free to repay in kind," she says before I end the call.

Refocusing on my surroundings, I realize I've made it all the way to the mansion. From where I'm standing, it's only a few paces to the spot where Tim died.

I make myself look over at the parking lot—to that place where his blood seeped into the earth.

Who pulled the trigger, Tim? I silently ask.

The only answer is the distant screech of a seagull.

The mansion rises above me in all its hulking glory, and it takes all my strength to go inside.

28

As I hang my trench coat in the reception room, I hear Beatrice talking with a couple of people in the parlor. I'm late for my first meeting of the day.

Conversation stops when I step into the doorway, and three faces turn in my direction.

Along with Beatrice, there's Lillian, the sixtyish designer, wearing a Chanel suit and red lipstick. She openly gapes at me. Then there's Matt, the young furniture restorer.

Given their matching stares of curiosity, they must be current on the local news.

"Sorry I'm late," I say, my cheeks flaming. "What did I miss?"

Lillian frowns at the easel she's set up by the windows. Like she can't remember what it's for. "Upholstery," she says eventually. "We were discussing the original upholstery."

Matt says something about armchairs, and Beatrice sends me a searching look. *Are you okay?* she mouths.

I give her a quick nod and look away. Nothing to see here. Just your average morning when you get the news of your ex's arrest for murdering your other ex.

"I want to come back to the conversation couches," Lillian says. "The original parlor had two of them centered in the space. And they were spectacular."

"Oh yes!" gushes the restorer. "We couldn't live without the conversation couches."

I'll bet you can, says my uncharitable mood.

"They're very unique," Beatrice says carefully. "But the parlor requires a flexible floor plan. None of the furniture can be wider than the door frames, since we'll need to remove pieces for larger events."

I sneak a look at the easel and discover that Lillian's plan calls for two couches, both large and donut-shaped.

Lillian purses her lips. "What are the dimensions of the doors?"

Everyone turns to me, and it takes me a beat to reach for my laptop. "One moment. I think they're thirty-three inches."

With my computer balanced on a folding chair, I find the precise measurements, and Beatrice and the decorator begin to argue about whether or not a conversation sofa could be constructed as a sectional on wheels.

This morning, I'm finding it hard to care. We're almost literally rearranging the deck chairs on the *Titanic* right now.

"What if we widened the doorway?" Lillian offers. "Problem solved."

"That would be structurally inadvisable," I say, finally tuning in.

Matt says, "Then is it time to take a look at the dining chairs?"

"They're in storage in the servants' quarters," Beatrice says. "Follow me. And Rowan? We'll need the diningroom dimensions."

"Of course."

With my computer under my arm, I follow them out of the parlor and toward the back of the house. Beatrice opens a door that leads to a double stairway—the choice is five steps down to the left or seven steps up to the right.

We climb, and the half flight brings us to a new corridor of servants' rooms.

Beatrice unlocks a door, and I'm the last in line as we file inside. The room is filled with stacks of old furniture, much of which dates to the mid-nineteenth century, and with four of us vying for space, it feels claustrophobic.

The first time I saw these rooms, they still held metal bunkbeds—four beds to a room for the girls of the Portland Magdalene Home.

I think the Home's directors were hoping for a summer-camp feel, but the close quarters resembled a prison. Metal beds and lockers. Cheap bedside tables. Everything was depressingly spartan.

Now I look at the room with different eyes. Did Tim's birth mother ever stay here? Did she give birth upstairs in the West Room—the one with the paintings of horses on the wall? That's where we'd found a baby scale, high-beam lights, and an obstetrical bed with stirrups still pointing toward the painted ceiling.

I have to wonder why Tim didn't simply tell me about the deeply personal connection he had to this place. Was he ashamed? Or maybe he thought he was protecting me from something dangerous.

But that doesn't track, either. What secret could've gotten him killed? The Wincott who ran the home has been dead for over twenty years. I know because I googled it at four in the morning the other night.

Matt stands by a stack of chairs, lifting one chair after another to study the bottoms of their seats. This is a thing furniture people do. The manufacturer's marks are always on the underside of the chairs.

"This is a French piece, mid-nineteenth century. You see this dark spot?" His tone is scandalized.

I peer at the cross pieces under the seat. "Sure?"

"Chewing gum," he says distastefully. "That's a tragedy."

I'd agree with him, except my definition of a tragedy has shifted since last week.

I join Lillian at another grouping of furniture. "These are battered," she says, examining a side chair. "How does a chair get scarred like this?" She runs her fingertips over the chewed-up outer edge of the piece.

I lean down and peer more closely. The scars are deep, the finish and some of the wood grain scratched away, as if something abrasive was dragged repeatedly against the edge. The abuse seems purposeful. When I examine the opposite side of the chair, I find more of the same thing. "It's symmetric."

"*Both* sides?" Lillian raises her eyebrows. "Even my sister's cats couldn't do that kind of damage. But maybe teenagers are worse. You know the house was used for a maternity home?"

"I'm familiar."

———————

The morning drags on, punctuated by texts from Natalie.

Natalie: Did you hear anything about Dad?

Rowan: Heard some technical stuff about his arrest. We'll talk tonight. Did you write to your bio teacher about the retake?

No response.

When the designer and the furniture guy finally leave, Beatrice corners me and asks her favorite question. "Are you okay? You look exhausted."

"I'm fine. Natalie is a mess, though."

She cringes. "That poor kid."

"Yeah," I agree. "I can't imagine what's in her head right now."

"Do you think he really did it?" Beatrice whispers. "Because if he did . . ."

She doesn't finish the sentence, but we both know what she means—I ought to feel grateful that he's off the streets again.

"I don't know what to think. I can't picture him killing a man for dating me."

"Are you sure?" she asks warily. "Men are so . . ." She sighs. "He wouldn't be the first one, you know? Abusers never change their stripes. The best you can do is get away."

I've heard this many times, including from both my parents. "Listen— has Hank said anything about my connection to Harrison? Do you think he knows?"

Hank is so hung up on optics that I'm bracing myself for more of the anger he showed to Beatrice earlier in the week. And I'm due in the man's office in an hour.

"Well . . ." Beatrice frowns. "I didn't mention it to him. And I won't. And he's pretty pumped up to see some progress from the police." She makes a thoughtful face. "But Rowan—he's likely to find out. He knows a lot of people in city hall."

God. "And how do you think he'll react?"

"I'm not sure," she says slowly. "The family name means a lot to him.

He won't be too thrilled if your private drama brought a murder to his doorstep."

"*My* drama? All I did was date a guy who asked me out in a coffee shop."

Beatrice winces. "I know, I'm sorry. That came out wrong. But you asked me what Hank would think."

I guess I did. "So you're saying Hank might need someone to blame, and I could be the convenient target."

"For a minute, anyway," she says. "But he'll get over it. He chose you for this job for a reason. Because you're one of them. Part of the inner circle."

"One of . . . Sorry?"

"The Chatham Prep crew. And then an Ivy League degree. From an old Portland family. The Wincotts care about two things—pedigree and loyalty, in that order."

I blink. "That's a pretty generous interpretation of my place in the world."

She gives me a funny little smile. "When your résumé came in, I put it right on top of the pile. Because I know how Hank works. It worked out fine. But I'm going to have to campaign twice as hard to get the director's job here." She pats the desk. "It will be hard enough to get them to accept a woman in the role. And yet if my degree said Princeton on it, or if my last name was Wincott, it would be an easier sell."

I don't even know what to say to that, because she probably has a point.

"So don't let him rattle you," she says. "If Hank has another tantrum, you'll remind him that nothing on the news is your fault. And that if he wants his mansion finished on schedule, he should get over himself."

"Okay," I agree. As if I'd ever speak to Hank that way.

She smiles suddenly. "I can tell you don't believe me, and I love you for it. But this *will* blow over."

"Sure hope so."

She picks up her purse to head to her next meeting. And on her way out, she gives me a squeeze on the shoulder. "Hey—make sure Natalie comes to yoga tomorrow? I'll buy the poor kid a donut after class."

This is why Beatrice and Natalie are friends. They can both eat donuts and still wear spandex. "I'm sure she'll appreciate it."

———————

By noon, I'm hurrying to Hank's office, a little sweaty, the walk longer than I'd bargained for. At a traffic light, I pull out my phone to see how late I'm going to be.

I find a text from Beatrice.

Beatrice: Call me. Change of plans.

I call immediately. "What's happened?"

"Hank took a meeting somewhere else, last minute. He's not in his office. He wanted me to tell you that he'll have to reschedule for next week."

My heart plummets. "Did he say why?"

Her brief silence makes me uncomfortable. "He didn't. But he sounded like he was in a mood."

The light changes, and I cross the street on autopilot, the phone still pressed to my ear. "Any reason he didn't call me directly?"

Another beat of silence. "I really couldn't say."

Can't or won't? Pressing Beatrice for details won't solve anything, and this isn't her fault, so I say, "Okay, thank you for telling me."

"Don't panic, Rowan. This could be unrelated to the arrest."

And yet I don't think it is. "I'm going to drop off my budget at his office. And then maybe get some lunch. See you later?"

We hang up, and I find myself in front of another building designed by Amos Wincott. Old copper letters spelling WINCOTT are arranged in the pediment at the roofline.

Amos built this one a decade after the mansion. It doesn't have the same ornate splendor, but it's still very attractive, rising to four stories, with a brick facade. The Wincotts have been counting their money inside this Congress Street address for a hundred and fifty years.

Beatrice is probably right about the way that Hank sees the world differently from most people. How strange it must have been to grow up seeing your name splashed across office buildings, university libraries, and monuments all over Maine. Even the private school Hank and I attended has a Wincott Terrace on the campus.

I push through the revolving door and enter the lobby. An elderly security guard in a blue suit with gold buttons blinks at me from behind a desk.

"I'm here to leave a file for Hank Wincott," I tell him. "Isn't that the fourth floor?" A few months have passed since I last visited Hank here at the office. He usually comes to the mansion.

The old man nods, and I walk over to the elevator and press the brass button.

When the car arrives, I step inside and fish the file folder out of my bag. Maybe if I leave my carefully annotated budget revision at his office, we can Zoom this meeting next week, and I won't have to return here.

I get off the elevator on the fourth floor and proceed to the C-suite. On my first visit, Hank explained how the entire Wincott shipping empire had been housed in these offices before the corporation relocated to the mid-Atlantic in the eighties.

Now the Wincott Foundation is the major tenant, with Hank occupying the best office suite in the building. As I step inside, I realize two things, and they're both startling.

First, this office is nearly identical to the library in the mansion. The dimensions of the room are a little different, but the paneling, the fixtures, and the ornate ceiling are just the same. As if Amos Wincott only had one idea in his entire life.

It's a little eerie.

The second striking thing is Hank's assistant, who's seated behind a mahogany desk. She's in her mid-twenties and ravishingly beautiful, with straightened blond hair, perfect red lipstick, and beautiful shoulders. Like a ballerina.

Hank Wincott has a *type*. The dataset may be small, but I've noticed that he surrounds himself with beautiful young women. Beatrice fits the same mold.

"Oh, Rowan," she says softly. I guess she's not quite Beatrice's twin, because this one lacks my friend's confidence. "I'm sorry to say that Hank has left for the day. He was supposed to call you."

I open my mouth to say hello, and then I realize I've forgotten her name. It's something delicate and a little unusual. Hank always calls her *the new girl*.

So now I'm just as bad as him, because I can't remember it.

"Um, I heard about the meeting. Beatrice just called me on my walk over here."

Her quick smile is apologetic. "I'm so sorry you came all this way."

"It's fine. I thought I'd just leave my report for him. So he'll get it on Monday."

"Oh sure." She rises from her chair as I hand over the folder. "I'll just put it on his desk."

As she turns toward the door to the inner office, I'm struck by an idea. A risky one, but I might never get another chance like this. "Actually . . ."

She turns.

"While I'm here, I thought maybe I could sneak a peek at the mansion archives? I'm preparing a presentation for Hank about our lighting restoration, and there are some relevant documents in Hank's office. Could I see those, please?"

She frowns, and I brace myself for her refusal. "They're in a file box, I think? Let's see if I can find them." She's already crossing through to the inner office. "Let's just look in the cabinet. If you could follow me."

I trail her inside. Again, it's just like the library's setup—except a little larger, and with a killer view. Casco Bay sparkles in the June sunlight. It's almost blinding.

Everything else, though, is weirdly familiar. Last time I was here, the mansion was still in the demo phase, and Beatrice and I weren't working in the library yet. That's why I hadn't noted all the similarities. The same cabinet drawers. The same leaded-glass windows. The same brass hardware on every file drawer.

Hank was right—Amos Wincott was a hack. Not only did he knock off the European countryside. He plagiarized *himself*.

Hank's assistant drops my report on his enormous desk—a mahogany monstrosity by the window. It's exactly the piece of furniture you'd buy if you wanted to show the world how rich you are, and how large your penis is.

On the other side of the room is a meeting table for six. Hank's assistant crosses to the cabinets on the adjacent wall and opens a couple of them tentatively.

"This is it, I think?" She lifts out a familiar archival box.

"Yes ma'am." My heart beats a little faster as she sets it on the table.

"Since he's not around, you can work right here. Just poke me if you need the copy machine, but you'd need to check with him before removing anything from the premises."

"Oh, that won't be necessary. I just want to refresh my memory on a few details of the original plans. Maybe I'll take a photo or two with my phone?" I'm babbling. Espionage doesn't come naturally to me.

Or so I used to think.

"I'll be right outside," she says. "Let me know if I can bring you anything to drink."

"Thanks so much!" I say with too much enthusiasm.

The moment she's gone, I lift the top off the box and peer inside. Hank and I pored over this stuff together before I began the renovation. There's a set of old blueprints from when they'd upgraded the plumbing in the 1920s. Other documents are as old as the mansion itself—bills of sale for original fixtures and furnishings. Letters between the architect and the painter.

I pull out an archival album and find many of the documents carefully stored in acid-free sleeves. This isn't what I came for, but I briefly page through the album in case there are cameras watching me. Knowing Hank, it's entirely possible.

For show, I unfurl the old blueprints and spread them out on the table. The remaining items in the box include a set of old photographs of the facade, as well as a few 1940s postcards featuring the mansion.

What I don't find, however, is a small leather book full of babies' birth details.

I poke around the blueprints for a few minutes, idly taking photographs, trying to decide where Hank might have put the journal. Time's wasting, so I hold my breath and quietly open several cabinet doors, looking for the old book.

And—bingo—I find the small metal strongbox behind door number three.

It was me who'd plucked this from its hiding place in the mansion on that winter day back in March. I'd been lurking in the library, watching the contractor pull up the rotting floorboards so I could assess damage. A glint of steel caught my eye. "Wait! Stop!" I said to the men wielding crowbars. "There's something under there."

I knelt on the joist and extracted the box. After carrying it to my desk, I had a Nancy Drew moment. Inside the box I'd found the Wincott family Bible and the leather journal.

Old books hidden under the floorboards would make anyone's spine tingle. This is why people like old houses. It's not just the handcrafted details. It's the history.

Not *my* history, though. And since Hank wasn't around that day, I'd carefully taken some photographs of these treasures and sent them along.

Later, without my knowledge, Tim had helped himself to those photos. And now I might finally learn why.

I open the lockbox and pull out the journal. Fresh goose bumps rise on my arms as I open the cover. It's an old-school, leather-bound volume with ruled pages. And someone's crisp handwriting trails down each page. Given the location of the lockbox in the mansion's office, and the history of the Home for Wayward Girls, I have to assume that the handwriting belonged to Marcus Wincott.

The first pages are from the 1950s, and I've already photographed them. Only the bare facts are recorded, but it's still a poignant record of the babies' births.

4 April 1951—Baby girl—7 pounds, 4 ounces—to Miss M. Wattford
7 June 1951—Baby girl—6 pounds, 9 ounces—to Miss L. J. McManus
11 June 1951—Baby boy dead-born—to Miss J. Connelly

Poor Miss J. Connelly.

With occasional nervous glances toward the door, I continue to flip through the book and the pages that I didn't photograph the first time. The pace of births increases over time. There's a baby or two born every month during the 1960s. Hospital births were the norm then, but I'm pretty sure that these babies were born in the mansion.

And now I'm going to figure out if Tim Kovak was one of them.

By the late seventies, births tapered off to five or six a year. I'd like to think that this is because the world was changing. Maybe unmarried women didn't feel quite so much pressure to hide themselves away at the Magdalene Home.

I'm biased, though. I got pregnant in college. That first week after I missed my period, I already knew. But I didn't take a test for three more weeks, because I was nervous about telling Harrison.

But then I gathered my courage, made a batch of cookies, and peed on a stick while they cooled. When the + showed up, I wasn't even surprised.

Harrison came home at four thirty, tired from a shift at his low-paying coffee shop job. Before I could lose my nerve, I sat him down and handed him a cookie. "I don't know how to tell you this, but . . ." I showed him the test.

The look on his face. I'll never forget it. Not anger. Not even shock. Just wonder. "Wow, baby. That's amazing. Don't look so scared. It's gonna be great."

"Do you promise?" I begged.

"Oh, I promise," he said.

There's a reason I have trust issues.

I continue to page through the ledger, watching other girls' stories flying past as I search for Tim's birth in early 1979.

And suddenly there he is.

1 February 1979—Baby boy—7 pounds, 7 ounces—to Miss L. Peoples.

An Aquarius, Natalie said. The irrelevant detail swims into my mind. I'm not a fan of astrology. It makes no sense that all the babies born on a cold February day in 1979 should have similar personalities.

But I have the chills even so. We're all born under a sign, regardless of the position of the stars. Some of us are born into a family like the Wincotts and end up running the world. While some of us are born to Miss L. Peoples and are quietly adopted by another family.

Surely more than one baby boy was born in Portland, Maine, on that date. But I'm willing to bet that this baby boy was Tim. Why else would he care so much about the ledger?

I pull out my phone and take a photo of Tim's page. And then I flip through to the end of the book. The ledger's last record is from 1989. Then nothing. Marcus Wincott spent a few more years running the foundation before he retired. Then he lived on in the mansion for a few years until his death.

The building sat empty after that, a mansion only for the mice.

And possibly a ghost.

"Did you find what you needed?"

My chin snaps upward at the sound of the assistant's voice, and I spot her in the doorway. "Yup! Almost done!" She turns away, even as my heart gallops.

I've overstayed my welcome. Quickly, I close the book and place it back into the lockbox. After tucking it in place in the cabinet, I carefully stack the rest of the materials into the archival box.

I'm all smiles when I emerge from Hank's office, twenty minutes or so after I'd entered it.

"Did you find what you were looking for?" Hank's assistant asks.

"I absolutely did. You've been very helpful. Have a great weekend."

She checks her watch. "It's not long now."

After snagging an outdoor table at a nearby café, I pull out my phone and begin composing a text to Jules the journalist.

Rowan: I think I found her.

But then I hesitate before sending it. Who is Jules, really? All I know about her is that she used to work with Tim. She didn't even give me a business card—just a sticky note with her first name.

Is that weird? Or am I paranoid?

I switch to a browser and google *Jules journalist Wall Street Journal.* Nothing.

She gave me so little to go on, possibly by design. On a whim, I google *Jules journalist Timothy Kovak.* And then the results load, and I let out a little gasp of rage that makes the hipsters at the next table look up from their falafel.

The first result is a wedding notice from 2006. For Jules and Tim.

They were *married.* And I am the worst judge of character who ever lived.

For a minute all I can do is seethe, and shuffle through all the clues I missed. Like when she'd mentioned Tim's mother. *I was over there offering to help clean out his place in New York.*

Wait. Did he even *have* his own place in New York? What if they were still married when I dated him? For a long moment I sit here, dumbstruck, wondering why I never learn.

Nobody can be trusted. Not Tim, and certainly not Jules. She played her hand so well. *As a journalist, I'm appalled at his death.* A journalist who was *married* to Tim.

The worst part is that I remember asking Tim if he'd ever been married. He'd said no.

I pick up my phone again and delete the text I'd been writing to Jules. If she wants the name of Tim's birth mother so bad, she can find it herself.

29

CORALIE

Coralie sits in Marcy's Diner, waiting for someone who probably won't show. The woman she's expecting had sounded really cagey on the phone.

Coming here was probably foolish. Mr. Wincott is away at a meeting, and she's supposed to stick close to her desk and answer the phone. If he finds out she's gone, he'll be awful. But this is the only time and place that Ms. Elizabeth Jones would halfheartedly agree to meet her.

She scans the menu as her stomach growls. *Breakfast all day*, it boasts, and the scent of bacon hangs in the air.

Lately, her appetite is an insatiable beast. It's a good thing the two-egg breakfast is only $3.99, and it comes with bacon and coffee.

She glances around the restaurant again, just in case she missed Elizabeth Jones during her first survey of the place. But none of the customers look like Mr. Wincott's type.

A harried waitress skids to a stop in front of her. "Do you know what you want?"

She places her order. "But could you, um, make the coffee decaf?"

"Sure, honey."

A girl has to eat, even if she's been stood up. Her food arrives almost immediately, which is a special trick of diners.

She picks up her fork and digs in. The first bite makes her even hungrier than she was before. She scoops some of the eggs onto a butter-drenched triangle of toast. It won't help her clothes fit any better, but she can't seem to care right now.

The plate is nearly empty by the time the waitress stops by again. "You need more decaf?"

"No, thank you."

"You're Coralie, then?" She slides into the opposite side of the booth. "I'm Elizabeth."

Coralie is caught off guard. This waitress isn't as pretty as she expected, and her polyester uniform doesn't do her any favors. At first glance, she's not Mr. Wincott's type, but there are hints of a curvy body behind her apron.

"Thank you for meeting me," Coralie says quietly.

"You said you found my name in a personnel file?" She has frown lines on her forehead.

"Right. But first I found it in his checkbook. The secret one. He left the drawer open."

Her eyes widen. Elizabeth wears contact lenses that are several shades too bright. They make her eyes look otherworldly. "Can't believe he's getting sloppy in his old age. And I'm not supposed to talk about"—she clears her throat—"any of it."

I'll bet.

"How many special month-end checks does he write these days?" Elizabeth asks.

"Three," Coralie whispers.

She sniffs. "I'm surprised it isn't more. Are you going to make it four?"

"That's kind of why I asked you to meet me. I seem to be in a bit of trouble." Coralie glances down toward her expanding waistline. "I need advice."

"And you thought I'd help you?" Her eyes narrow.

"No. But I had to ask." Coralie gives this stranger what she hopes is a plaintive smile. "I'm afraid of him. He's so scary when he's mad." She shivers for effect. "And I haven't told him yet. I'm afraid of what he'll say."

The other woman leans back and frowns. "Let me guess—you were already down on your luck when you got this job. You don't have any family to speak of. You're on your own."

"Well, yeah." It's a little eerie how accurate that is. "How did you know?"

Elizabeth makes a clicking sound with her tongue. "That's who he goes for. Can't say I'm too surprised that he's still up to his old tricks."

Her heart quails. "What should I do? The last girl tried to warn me about him, but I didn't listen. And now look at me. Maybe I should just stop showing up and get an easier job. But then, in a few months, when it's time . . ." She slips a hand in front of her stomach. "I don't know what I'll do. How did you get him to step up for you?"

Elizabeth looks over both her shoulders before leaning closer. "First of all, do *not* quit your job."

Coralie's heart begins to thump with expectation. This is why she wanted to meet Elizabeth. She needs to know exactly how to play this.

"He'll try to tell you it isn't his, and that you can't prove it. But none of that matters. All you need to say is that you'll go straight to his brother if he doesn't provide."

Coralie swallows hard, and it's not an act. "But his brother is a bigger dick than he is."

"Yes and no. He's tired of his little brother's bullshit. Why do you think they fight whenever he calls? Little brother is a liability. And big brother controls the cash flow."

"Okay. I think I understand."

"It's just a bluff, anyway. You and your boss will come to an agreement." She nods sagely. "Brace yourself, though—he'll make you work for him until the day you pop. You'll get another little present—a gold ring, like a wedding band—and he'll make you wear it so the staff will think you convinced your boyfriend to marry you."

"*Oh.* What a sneaky fucker."

The woman laughs. "That he is. And the ring isn't even the strangest part. He has the hots for pregnant girls."

"Wait, really?" she squeaks. That can't be normal. Coralie already feels puffy and unattractive, and it's still early.

"Oh yeah." She rolls her eyes. "You watch—he'll get even handsier. Your boobs. Your belly. He'll want you all the time. I don't miss that at *all.*"

Coralie shivers again, and it's 100 percent genuine. *God, rich men are weird*. All the other dudes she knows would run screaming from a pregnant girl.

"And look, the most important rule of all is—don't tell a soul who the father is. Not your best friend. Not your mom. If you already told someone, go back and tell them you made a mistake. I'm not kidding." Her strangely blue eyes look suddenly tired.

"Nobody knows. Except you."

"Good. Because that family loves their secrets. And if they think you're telling tales out of school . . ." Her mouth goes tight. "It won't go well." She looks at her watch. "I said too much already. I have to go pick up my kid from school."

"Oh, sweet," she says just to be polite. "How old is your little guy?"

"Not so little anymore. He's almost ten." She smirks. "Yeah, I was eighteen when he got me pregnant. He likes 'em young." She slides out of the booth. "We never had this conversation, you hear? I'll deny every word."

"Right. I know. Thank you."

"Hang in there, girlie. You got this." She removes her apron, hangs it on a hook near the door, and leaves the restaurant.

Coralie watches her through the window until she moves out of range on Free Street. Then she tries to put herself in Elizabeth's shoes—working here and picking up a child after school. It's like a foreign country she never thought of visiting.

She closes her eyes and tries to form a mental picture of her child. A little girl, maybe.

But she only sees darkness.

30

SATURDAY

NATALIE

Natalie finds it impossible to get up on the first official morning of summer vacation. She doesn't feel like going to yoga. Her eyes are gritty from crying.

"Look alive," her mother nags from the doorway. "I made coffee, and I made you a yogurt parfait. You have a half hour to eat it and get dressed."

"Maybe I won't go," she mumbles.

Her mother makes a sound of irritation, because the yoga membership isn't free. She's heard this lecture several times before. *I told you Saturday mornings were a bad idea, but you swore you'd go.*

Whatever. She's too mad to care. Her mother didn't learn much yesterday about her father's situation. Unless she's holding back the truth. That's Natalie's real fear.

"You know . . . Beatrice said something about donuts after yoga."

Natalie doesn't budge. She just lies there like a lump, wondering how far her mother will push her on this terrible day.

Not far, as it turns out. With an almost inaudible sigh, her mother gives up and retreats from the doorway.

Except now Natalie's thinking about donuts.

And she doesn't want her yoga membership canceled.

She gets up and puts on some leggings and a Lululemon top. Pops her hair into a knot and descends the stairs on silent feet.

In the kitchen, her mother is seated at the table with her laptop. Natalie approaches silently. The Google search screen says *Lisa Peoples.*

"What are you doing?"

Her mother jerks around, startled.

"Who is Lisa Peoples?" Natalie asks.

"Nobody. A dead end." She closes the tab.

"A dead end for what?" She sits down on the chair beside her mother's and pulls the yogurt parfait closer.

There are strawberries and blueberries in it. Her mom clearly feels guilty about something.

Natalie picks up her spoon, knowing she ought to say thank you. But she doesn't. "What are you doing?" she asks.

Her mother frowns. "You remember how I found out that Tim was adopted?"

"A hundred percent. Was he adopted from the mansion? That Home for Wayward Girls?"

What a screwed-up name that is, anyway. So old-fashioned. But even if the words have changed, the idea never will. Boys who have sex are studs. Girls who have sex are sluts or whores. Everybody knows it.

"He was born there," her mother says quietly. "I didn't know. But one of the pictures he took off my phone? It was a photo of the mansion's birth record."

"Well, *that's* not creepy."

Her mother's smile is just a twitch of her lips. "It is . . . odd. But I keep coming back to his interest in the mansion. I'm not the only one who thinks it's weird."

"Show me these pictures," Natalie demands through a mouthful of yogurt. If there's a good reason Tim got killed, they can't just sleep on it. Her father is sitting in *jail* right now.

Her mother hesitates for a second, then clicks through some photos on her computer.

Natalie spots Tim's entry right away. He's the only Aquarius on the page. "The birth date matches. So who is L. Peoples?"

"Nobody, apparently. I googled it and got nothing. Then I started guessing what the *L* was for, and it didn't help. Laura, Lydia, Lisa. There's nothing in Maine. Maybe she's dead."

Natalie sags in the chair. "What would you do if you found her?"

"I don't know. Tell the police, I guess?"

"You should show them that name. Right *now*. They need to know there might be another reason someone killed him."

"Honey," her mother says softly. "I'm curious, too. But they already know Tim took the photos off my phone. And think about what you're saying—if somebody really killed Tim for this, do I want to be the next one they go after?"

Natalie shoves another bite of fruit in her mouth to avoid saying what she really thinks. *So you're afraid to do anything? Dad is just going to rot in there?*

"Neither of us created this problem," her mother says. "It's not our problem to solve."

She pushes the yogurt away, mostly uneaten. She's lost her appetite. "I'm going to be late for yoga."

———————

"Surrender yourself to the intention you set for yourself today. Surrender and breathe."

The yoga teacher loves to talk about inner peace during the final resting pose, but it seems to have the opposite effect. Natalie's mind is already galloping into complications.

Like that bio exam she still hasn't taken. And the fact that you can't visit somebody in the Cumberland County Jail without being eighteen or having your custodial parent's permission. She checked.

After the class says *om* together, Beatrice rolls up her mat and smiles at Natalie. "You'll get a donut with me, right?"

She only hesitates for a half a second. It sounds like something the adults in her life dreamt up to pacify her. *Poor kid's dad is in prison again? A donut will fix it.*

On the other hand, they are some seriously good donuts. And Beatrice never lectures her, which is nice.

"Sure. I'd love one."

There's a long line at the Holy Donut, and now that summer is here, the lines will only get worse. "I could get a job here," Natalie muses aloud. "Although . . . maybe a discount on donuts is a bad idea."

Beatrice tips her head back and laughs. "It would be a terrible idea for me personally. And it's not just the calories. Hot oil is bad for your face.

I spent a summer working the fryer at a Burger King. I had the worst skin of my life."

"Good tip." Although it's difficult to imagine Beatrice with teen acne. She always looks perfect. Today she looks like Yoga Barbie.

Beatrice gives her a sideways glance. "How are you holding up, anyway? I'm sorry about your dad."

Ugh. "How did you know about that, anyway?"

"I've known your mother awhile. And Harrison is an unusual name. But most people won't be able to put it together. I'll bet most people don't know."

She's wrong, though. Natalie is getting a weird vibe from her friends, which makes everything worse.

"My mother won't talk to him," she grumbles as the line moves a little. "She says he's not a good person. The thing is, I wanted to make up my own mind about him. And now I won't ever have a chance."

Beatrice is quiet for a second. "Look, I never met my own dad. He thought he was too good for us, and it was a long time until I even knew his name. My mom never got over that rejection. She ran off the rails and died when I was a little girl."

Well, now Natalie feels like an idiot. Someone always has it worse.

"But look," Beatrice says. "I wasted a *lot* of time wondering why my dad never had anything to do with me. I thought maybe I wasn't a good enough little girl. I used to see all the dads around school. I thought if I was cuter or smarter, my dad would be proud to carry me on his shoulders, too."

Natalie's throat feels suddenly, horribly tight. "Get out of my brain."

She expects Beatrice to laugh, but she doesn't. Her eyes redden instead. "Listen, girlie, and listen good. I wasted so much time on those thoughts. Please don't make this mistake, okay? Because I'm telling you, Natalie . . ." There's no avoiding her big blue eyes. "You're already the best there is. The *very* best."

She is *not* going to cry in line at Holy Donuts. But it's tempting.

"And if that's not enough to make that man show up in your life until now? That's a *him* problem, not a *you* problem."

Natalie has to pull in a long, slow breath. Thankfully, the line moves again, giving her something else to focus on. She lifts her eyes to the menu and tries to think through the merits of strawberry glazed versus lemon blueberry.

Beatrice touches her lightly on the back. "If you can't decide, we could go halfsies."

"Let's," she says with a sniff.

31

ROWAN

Why am I doing this?

I ask myself that several times on the short drive to the county jail. And I ask it again as I coast slowly through the crowded parking lot, looking for the last spot.

When I finally get out of the car, I see entire families trooping together to the doors.

How depressing.

Trudging toward the entrance, I size up the jail. It's a low, two-story building that sprawls like a high school. Same institutional bulk. Same half-assed brick facade, with some clunky stone cladding that needs a good wash.

There must be architects who focus exclusively on jail design. Now there's a weird specialty.

Following the signs for the visitors' area, I have my first shiver of déjà vu. Fifteen years ago, I walked through this same corridor and passed through these same metal detectors, only to be told that Harrison wouldn't see me.

Distraught, I'd questioned the man at the desk. His response was brisk but kind. *It happens, ma'am. Sometimes they don't want you to see 'em like this.*

Harrison never did let me visit. He only saw my parents. And only to sign away his rights to his child.

Now I'm back in the same spot, showing my driver's license and answering security questions. Submitting my wallet for inspection.

I'm glad Natalie isn't here to see this. The gray walls. The scuffed doors. The hornets' buzz of locked doors open electronically as I'm led deeper into the building.

The visitors' room reminds me of high school—it's like a cafeteria with long tables and plastic chairs. But these tables have a wooden divider in the center, separating the inmates from the visitors.

There are rules posted everywhere. NO CONTRABAND. BRIEF TOUCHING ONLY. STAY ON YOUR OWN SIDE OF THE TABLE.

"Have a seat, ma'am," I'm told. I pick a deserted table and sink into a chair.

Before Harrison's first arrest, I thought our little team was just going through a rough patch, and that our love would go the distance.

Now I'm sitting here in this grungy room, waiting to speak to the potentially violent stranger I once loved more than anyone.

A door on the back wall buzzes open, and every head turns. Two guards enter first, and the one with a gray buzz cut speaks. "Good afternoon. Remember the rules—brief contact only. Stay on your side of the table. Passing contraband to a prisoner is a punishable crime."

He steps aside and the prisoners begin to file in. My stomach lurches.

"Daddy!" shouts a little voice from somewhere behind me. My throat closes up.

If Harrison hadn't cut me off after his arrest, that might have been us—visiting Daddy on the weekends in prison.

A dozen men—and they're all men—file into the room, but Harrison isn't among them. Then the door swings shut again. *For the love of God. Again?*

I'm shoving my chair away from the table when the door suddenly opens to admit one more man. And there he is. He's unshaven, and he's wearing orange prison garb, but it's Harrison, looking not all that different from the young man I used to know.

My stomach gives an unwelcome little flutter.

Harrison glances immediately in my direction, drawn to me like a magnet. I take a gulp of air as he heads my way, unsmiling.

All around me, families lean across tables and embrace, voices rising as everyone begins talking at once.

My face is stony, though, as he arrives across the table. "Hi," he says.

"Hi," I manage. "Take a seat."

He pulls out the chair opposite me and sits down. He folds his hands on the table, his long fingers so familiar that it makes me ache.

"Thank you," he says quietly. "I didn't think you'd come."

"Natalie wanted me to."

He nods jerkily. "You know . . ." He looks me dead in the eyes. "I've always pictured how it would be when I finally got to talk to you again. I figured we'd run into each other at a café. You're sketching something for work at a table. I'm having a good hair day . . ."

A stunned laugh bursts from my chest.

His lips twitch. "You look great, Rowan. Although I know you're not here for the compliments." He sighs. "They only give us thirty minutes, so I have to talk fast. Unless you have anything you want to say first?"

I'm too startled to do anything but shake my head.

"Fine. The reason I came back to Portland was to ask if I could be in Natalie's life. I started with you. Got nowhere. Then she commented on one of the band's Instagram photos, so I messaged her. Had no idea that she was going behind your back."

"I got that," I manage.

He nods. "Anyway, I'm sorry. I'm very unclear on why I got arrested on a bullshit violation, but we'll get to that in a second. I've got something to tell you about Natalie that can't wait. You have to keep her from smoking weed."

I play that back in my head. "Um, what?"

"Weed. Marijuana. Grass . . ."

"I know what weed is," I say icily. "But what has that got to do with Natalie?" *Please God don't let him tell me my daughter does drugs.*

He leans forward in his chair and studies me with a level gaze. "When she was born, I started lighting up. I had a lot of anxiety. New baby with a woman too good for me. Terrible job prospects. I smoked because it kept me level. After you and I moved back to Maine, I never did any other drugs."

"Okay . . ." I try to take that in. "Really? Never?"

He shakes his head. "Just weed, but I made it a habit. I didn't realize it at the time, but I'd begun to have bad reactions to it. Hallucinations.

That night in the bar, when I ruined our lives? I was hallucinating. Thought that guy was some kind of demon."

My head jerks back. "What?"

"Yeah, I didn't get it, either. Went to prison. Started feeling more like myself. There wasn't a lot of weed in prison back then. The smoke is too easy to smell. They tend to go for the hard stuff in there. Never wanted anything to do with the hard stuff, so I steered clear."

"I'm confused as to where this is going."

He gives me a sad smile. "Bear with me a second. A few years in, weed becomes legal in Maine, and edibles start making the rounds. I trade a guy for some. To break up the monotony. And—bam—I'm right back to major paranoia and seeing things. I hurt another guy. My sentence is extended."

My chest hurts. "Because of *weed*?"

"Well, weed and stupidity. The only good thing that came out of it is that I went to a court-mandated substance abuse class—they teach one inside. I told the substance abuse counselor my strange story, and he listened. Then the next week he brings me an article about a syndrome called cannabis psychosis. It's a real thing that happens to a tiny percent of the population."

Cannabis psychosis. I have chills.

"But hey—some guys are just lucky." He spreads his hands like it's a joke.

"God, I had no idea."

"I know. Me neither. And I'm okay now." He shrugs. "I'm sure you probably think I'm some kind of major druggie, but getting off weed wasn't even very tricky for me, once I understood what it was doing to my brain. Weed isn't as chemically addictive as some other drugs. The guys who get hooked on opioids have a harder time. But Rowan—my reaction might be hereditary. And marijuana is legal in Maine. Natalie can't *ever* try it."

"Oh." *Oh*.

"I was going to explain it all. To both of you. But I only sat down with her once. I brought it up. Said I had some health things she needed to hear. Especially about drugs, and she cuts me off. She's all, like, 'I'd never do drugs.'"

In those four words, he captures her flippant teenage tone so perfectly that my throat tightens again.

His gaze dips. "Rowan, she's *so* beautiful." His eyes are suddenly red. "God, I thought I'd die when she walked into that coffee shop. Couldn't believe it. She looks just like you. I thought I'd get more time to tell her exactly what happened to me." He inhales sharply. "*Promise* me you'll make her understand. No cannabis. No CBD oil or anything. We just don't know."

"Okay, okay."

He pinches the bridge of his nose and blows out a breath. And my eyes are hot, too.

"Thought I could get to know her," he says. "I chose the coffee shop, because it was a nice, public place. And Docksiders. I tried to guess what you might be okay with."

"I didn't know," I say, my throat closing up. "She thought I'd say no. And I might have. Guess we'll never find out."

He flashes me a sad smile. "Don't know when I'm getting out of here. Could be Monday—but only if the judge throws out the violation."

"What did you, uh, allegedly do?"

He looks down at his hands. "Housing is difficult for me. I don't have much cash, and nobody wants to rent to a felon. I answered a Craigslist ad for a room in a house with a few other guys. One of them is also a felon."

I blink. "And . . . ?"

"And one of the conditions of my probation is that I don't live with felons. That's standard. But of course, I didn't ask these guys, because I was better off not knowing."

"Oh. Shit."

He swallows. "It's an obvious ruse to get me into custody, though. They keep asking me questions about the night your boyfriend got shot. I didn't ever get near the guy, okay? In case you need to hear me say it. It wasn't me. They also asked me to write out a violent statement with a marker."

My pulse accelerates. "Four words? Like—he had to die?"

Harrison stares. "That's right. How'd you know?"

"That note was addressed to me."

"Jesus Christ." He puts his hands on his head. He glances up at me, expression panicked. "Are you all right? Did Natalie see it?"

I give my head a slow shake. "It came to the mansion."

He takes a deep breath. "Shit. Well, that explains why they handed me a sheet of paper and a marker. And that went about like you'd expect—you've seen my handwriting."

Harrison is severely dyslexic and never got any support for it at school. He avoids writing at all costs and used to illustrate our grocery list instead of using words. Cute little apples. A perfect stick of butter. A pig for bacon. I don't know who killed Tim Kovak, but I'm damn sure that Harrison didn't write that note.

"I heard about the murder on the news," he says. "I'm so sorry for your loss. Sounds like he was a stand-up guy. I sent you those peonies because I didn't know what else to say."

"Um, thank you . . ." I gulp. "Yeah, it's . . . We don't know why he died. But you should know that the police have a video of you knocking on our front door. I never knew you came to the house."

"Course I did. I tried." He runs a hand through the scruff on his chin, and my hand actually twitches with the memory of doing that same thing myself. Touching him used to be second nature to me.

"I wrote you a couple emails, but you didn't answer. And I went to that mansion where you work . . ."

"You did?"

He nods, frowning. "Knocked on the door a few weeks ago. Blond chick told me you were out. I left a message, but I don't think she wrote it down."

My mouth goes dry. "But how did you know where to find me?"

He tilts his head, and the gesture is so familiar I feel it behind my breastbone. "When I googled you, I found a news article about you working on that place. And your name is in the front yard, hon. On a sign."

"Oh right." I let out a short, hysterical laugh. "I forgot." ROWAN GAL-

LAGHER, ARCHITECT. I put it right next to the contractor's sign. Hoped people would remember my name for jobs down the road.

"So, yeah, I picked a hell of a night to knock on your front door."

"It was *that* night? The night Tim died?"

He nods. "I was on a break between sets."

"Wait. At Mick's Rock Café?" My heart starts thudding even harder.

"The police are all over that. Plus, they keep asking me why I turned off my phone that night. But I always turn it off on gig nights. You don't need it vibrating or whatever in the middle of a set. They still think it's suspicious. They keep asking who else I saw on my break. When exactly did I leave, and when did I come back? We took an hour between sets. They also find that suspicious."

"An *hour*," I whisper. "Shit."

He sighs.

"Do you have a lawyer?"

"Sure. You know—a public defender. He says if they charge me, the police will have to share whatever they've got. Then we can try to find proof that I couldn't be the one responsible. I'm just hoping they figure it out themselves first."

My hand finds its way into my bag, and my fingers close around the card Beatrice gave me. "This is a good lawyer. Maybe you need more help." I offer it across the barrier, and Harrison reaches for it.

"Ma'am," a nearby guard says abruptly, "you can't give him anything."

Harrison drops his hand. "Honey, the truth is I can't afford it anyway. Thank you for the thought."

Honey.

I tuck the card back into my bag. "What if I called her for you? Just to ask how much it is. Natalie would want me to."

He props his chin on a hand and gives me a gentle look. "Can we just talk about Natalie instead? I've probably only got a few minutes left. What does she like? What does she do for fun?"

"Um . . ." My mind whirls at the sudden change in topic. "She's smart, but not too smart to spend a ridiculous amount of time in the bathroom, working on makeup techniques and chatting with her friends on the phone. Ice cream is her favorite treat. She gets straight As, but if you ask her about her college plans, she runs out of the room. She uses a lot of words that I don't understand. Last week she told me my outfit was 'drip,' and she meant it as a compliment."

His sudden smile breaks my heart.

"She is shockingly competent. She can find anything on Google. She went through a poetry phase last year, and some of it was breathtaking. She makes really good bruschetta. But she doesn't ever rinse a dish if she can just leave it in the sink. And her dirty socks are just everywhere. All over the house."

His grin slips a little, and I can't imagine having to ask someone else what my own daughter is like.

And now my throat is closing up again. "Is there anything you want me to tell her for you?"

He drops his head. "God, I can't imagine there's anything I have to say that she needs to hear. But I have a favor to ask. I wouldn't, I swear. But there's nobody else . . ."

We lock eyes for a second, and my heart quavers. "What?" I rasp.

"I have a cat, and my three roommates are mostly strangers to me. I'm worried they'll forget to feed her. Could you, uh, go to my place and grab her? The animal rescue is in Westbrook. They would take her back. She's a good girl. And if the hearing doesn't go my way, I'll go back to prison . . ."

I swallow hard. "Okay. I'll see what I can do. I need your address." I pull out my phone and make a note, while he rattles off an address.

"The cat's name is Zoe. There's a soft-sided pet carrier in my room. If Rick answers the door—he's the nicest one—maybe you could also grab my bass. It's the only valuable thing I own, and I also keep my most important stuff in the case. Like my bankbook."

I look up from my phone. "All right. Natalie can hold on to it for you."

"And if I don't get out of here next week?" He looks away. "Just . . . don't let Natalie come to see me. Not here. If she wants to write me a letter—great. But I don't want her anywhere near this place."

"Okay," I say quickly. "Sure."

He rubs his forehead like it pains him. "Tell her I'm fine, okay? And I'm so sorry."

My eyes feel hot again. "I'll tell her. I promise."

32

NATALIE

With the help of the FriendFinder app, Natalie locates her mother in the tiny park on Exchange Street. She's sitting on a bench, holding a cup from Bard Coffee and talking to a stranger in a denim skirt and big owl-shaped glasses.

Natalie walks up to their bench and drops her yoga bag onto the bricks.

Her mother does a double take. "*Natalie.* What are you doing here?"

"Surprise, Mom. Your favorite app works both ways."

"Oh." Her mother looks so startled. Almost guilty. "Is anything wrong?"

Except literally everything? Natalie gives her head a shake. "Who's your friend?"

The woman on the bench smiles.

Her mother takes a breath and says, "Natalie, this is Martha Bean, a criminal lawyer. I was just asking her a few questions to see if she's able to help with Harrison's case."

No way! "Can you get him out of there?"

"Impossible to say at this point." Martha Bean rises from the bench. "But my son's karate lesson ends in"—she checks her watch—"three minutes. Feel free to email me tonight if you want me to step in. I could visit him tomorrow. My job doesn't respect weekends."

"Thank you." Her mother stands and shakes the lawyer's hand.

Natalie waits to speak until the lawyer walks away. But just barely. "What's going on? Are you hiring her for dad?"

Her mother sinks back down onto the bench. "Sit. We have some things to discuss."

Natalie sits, her heart racing.

"I went to see him this morning. At the prison."

"You *did*?" She's so surprised, she forgets to bury her enthusiasm. "Is he okay?"

Her mother's lips form a straight line, like she's not sure how to answer. "He told me to tell you he's fine, and that he's sorry."

Natalie suddenly has trouble swallowing. "But did he seem okay? Why did you go? Is something wrong that you're not telling me?"

A shake of her head. "No, I swear. I went because I wanted to hear the health stuff he'd mentioned. But also." Her mother swallows hard, too. "Because he is your family whether I like it or not. And I thought it was only fair to look him in the eye and ask him what happened."

"You mean, to Tim?" Natalie nabs the cup out of her mother's hand and finishes the coffee in one gulp.

"Right." She sighs. "He says he doesn't have a clue. He never met Tim."

"And you believe him, right?" The question sounds desperate to her own ears, but there's no helping it.

"I think so," her mother says softly. "Which is why I called the lawyer. She's willing to represent him at the hearing on Tuesday. It's not cheap, though."

"I'll pay," Natalie says quickly. "I'll get a summer job."

Her mother's eyes redden. "He wouldn't want you to do that."

"Doesn't it matter what *I* want? We can't let him go to jail for something he didn't do."

Her mom gives Natalie's knee a brief squeeze. "I'll hire the lawyer to attend his hearing, okay? One step at a time. If they actually charge him for murder, though, we'll have to regroup. That's a much bigger deal and a really expensive defense. And I'm told the police wouldn't charge him unless . . ."

"Unless they can prove it," Natalie whispers. An idea so terrifying that she hasn't really allowed herself to think it. Not really.

"In the meantime, we have an errand to run. Come on." Her mother stands up. "We'll need the car."

33

ROWAN

My daughter sneaks glances at me most of the way to Harrison's place. I can tell she's dying of curiosity but doesn't want to push me on why I'm suddenly Team Harrison. I don't think I could explain myself, even if I tried.

I've already sent the lawyer a text—hiring her to represent Harrison at his hearing on Tuesday. And now we're going to get his cat.

We turn onto a seedy residential street, and Natalie reads the house numbers. "There. It's that one." She points at a colonial that badly needs a coat of paint. "It isn't *too* bad."

She's a glass-half-full girl when it comes to Harrison, and it's painful to recognize how invested she is in his reappearance. I've been telling myself for all these years that she didn't care so much about her lack of a dad.

With a heavy heart, I park and then carefully lock the car after we get out. Natalie is already bounding up to the saggy porch and knocking on the door.

For a minute or two, I think nobody is coming, but then a young man answers the door. He's got bedhead and a Taylor Swift T-shirt on.

"Nice shirt," Natalie says.

"Thanks?"

"You wouldn't be Rick, would you?" I ask.

He licks chapped lips. "Depends who's asking."

"We're here about Harrison's things. He sent us."

The young man frowns. "You too? It's like Grand Central Station here. First the police with a warrant. That was fun. And then another woman came by yesterday. Needed access to his room to get her things, she said. Swear to God I didn't know Harrison even had friends."

"Another woman?" It comes out sounding wrong. Like I'm jealous. But I really don't want my daughter walking into a room strewn with condom wrappers.

He shrugs. "I didn't ask her name. But then she made it weird by staying in his room for a while, and I wondered what she was doing in there. I finally knocked, and she walked out a minute later, but she wasn't carrying anything."

I don't need this much information. "Okay, look. We're here for a couple of things at Harrison's request. Starting with the cat."

His expression brightens. "Oh shit! Be a real favor to me if you took her. Haven't seen her all day. And you don't look like pet thieves."

"We're not. This is Harrison's daughter." I lay a hand on Natalie's shoulder.

His first reaction is astonishment. Then he laughs. "Dude! I can totally see it. You play the bass, too?" He does a pantomime of someone shredding on the guitar.

Natalie smiles in spite of this idiot's red eyes and lack of hygiene, and then shakes her head.

"Bummer. Okay, what did you all need? Just the cat?"

"And his bass, for safekeeping."

"Sure. His room is back here." He leads us into a dark, little rabbit warren of a house. I'm mentally knocking down all the interior walls as we go, wondering if it's even possible to get decent light in this place, or if I should mentally bulldoze it instead.

But Harrison's room, when we reach it, is as neat as a monk's cell. He has so few belongings that if the police searched this place, there's no way to tell. There are two milk crates full of books. Music. Philosophy. Poetry. There's a mattress on the floor, but it's tidily made up. A reading lamp. A phone charger. And his bass leaning in the corner.

"Not very homey, is it?" Natalie asks, sounding despondent.

"Well . . ." It's so much like his room from that first summer I met him that it's almost eerie. This is the room of a man who's starting over. "I've seen worse. Your father never cared much for material things. Not a bad quality."

Natalie is already onto the next disaster. She crosses to a pet-bowl tray on the floor. "Oh *no*. Her bowls are empty." I hear a note of panic in my daughter's voice.

"Cats are very resourceful. She's probably been sipping from leaky faucets and dining on mice in the basement."

That's probably why Harrison has a cat in the first place. He's resourceful, too.

"Here, kitty," Natalie says softly. "Here, Zoe!" She checks behind Harrison's books and even the bass. She opens a door and finds a narrow closet. "Do cats like closets?"

"Sometimes."

"This one seems too small to hide her."

"Search around," I suggest. "Ask the guy to help you. I'll get the bass."

"Okay."

When I try to pick up the bass, though, several things slip out and onto the floor. The instrument case is unzipped. So I squat and tuck a checkbook and a savings account book back inside.

As their covers slide together, they reveal a photograph—a standard 4" x 6" print.

The photo is a selfie of me and Natalie, and it's recent. From only last winter. We're drinking Duckfat milkshakes and wearing gloves, like the diehard Mainers we are.

I can't decide if finding it here seems sweet or creepy. Maybe a little of both.

I push everything back into the case and zip it shut. Then I carry the bass and the cat carrier out of the room, and go looking for my daughter. She's made her way into a grungy kitchen with Rick. They're peering into a corner cabinet—the kind with a hinged, two-panel door.

"Come here, kitty. Please?" Natalie extends a hand.

Oh lord. We are going to be here until I'm fifty.

Natalie drops her voice. "I'll be your best friend. I'll buy you some stinky cat food." She clicks her tongue.

Miraculously, a black-and-white furry face appears. The cat takes a tentative sniff of Natalie's fingers. And then she bumps her face against Natalie's wrist.

"Come on. I'll find you some food, I swear."

The cat steps daintily down from the cabinet and winds like a serpent around Natalie's ankles.

"Slowly," I whisper. "Try to pick her up." I unzip the carrier.

Natalie closes her arms around the cat. "I'll just hold her. She'll be less afraid."

I say a silent prayer for the interior of my car.

A minute later, after loading the car with a few cat things and thanking Rick for his halfhearted help, we're ready to leave. I put the bass in back and gesture to the cat carrier. "She has to go in here. We can't drive around with a cat on the loose."

Reluctantly, Natalie scoops her inside. There's a plaintive meow as she quickly zips it shut. "It's just for a little bit," she tells the cat. "We have to buy you some supplies."

"*Natalie.* I told you . . ."

"We can't rehome his cat, Mom! He'll get out after the hearing, anyway. The new lawyer will help."

I let out a low moan of despair. I don't want a cat. I don't want my ex's cat. "What will Lickie think?"

"Lickie is a good girl," Natalie says. "And also a wimp. The cat'll swat her once, and that's all it will take to train Lickie."

If only Natalie were as easy. I start the car and point it toward Petco.

34

SUNDAY

ROWAN

Sunday morning I wake up in a daze. When I open my bedroom door, I almost trip over Lickie, who's lying in my path.

It's unusual behavior, and it puts me on high alert as I tiptoe down the hall. But five seconds later, I understand. Zoe the cat is sitting at the bottom of the staircase, glaring up at us with contemptuous green eyes.

Lickie whines.

"It's okay, girl. You're bigger than she is, and this is your turf. Lean into your own power."

Lickie is uncertain.

We all traipse to the kitchen together, where I get the coffee started and let Lickie out. Then I pick up the phone to see if the lawyer got back to me and instead find an email from Detective Fry.

Rowan, I hope this message finds you well. The Portland PD requests that you sign the following form authorizing the release of your phone's data to help further our investigation. Messages between you and the deceased can help us build a case. Details that might seem inconsequential to you could help us paint a picture of his final days.

It is vital that you assist us before 5 p.m. today, or we will be forced to ask a judge for a court order. Ignoring this request will naturally cause us to wonder who you might be protecting by withholding it.

Detective Captain Fry
Portland Police Department

I close the email, feeling queasy. And then I open it again and click on the attachment. The document is a nightmare, giving them access to everything on my phone, including photos, videos, plus all apps and messages.

They probably know I visited Harrison yesterday. And now Fry probably thinks I'm helping him get away with murder.

My hand shakes as I reach for a coffee mug. When my phone pings a second later, I assume it's the police, pressuring me again.

But this time it's the litigator.

On my way to see Harrison at the jail.

I wonder if hiring her was a mistake. I've made myself look even more guilty. And her hourly rate is sky high on the weekends. This lawyer was on Beatrice's list of Wincott family favorites, so of course she's expensive.

But I'm doing this for Natalie. And if Harrison breaks my daughter's heart, I might actually become the murderer that Fry thinks I am.

Full of nervous energy, I scrub the kitchen sink, and then all three bathrooms. Then I vacuum, even though Natalie is still in bed. She's supposed to be pounding the pavement for a summer job, so I don't even feel guilty about the noise.

When eleven o'clock comes, I've stress-cleaned most of the house. The lawyer calls shortly afterward, putting me out of my misery.

"Hello?" I answer quickly.

"Rowan, I've been to see him."

"Was he okay with it?" I made no attempt to warn Harrison that I was sending him a litigator.

"Mostly. He asked me my rates. I wasn't going to deflect. But I told him you'd hired me just for the hearing tomorrow. He says he wants to pay you back in full."

"Fine. He and I will speak about it later."

"I'll be calling his employer today, getting a statement in support of his recent work history. And I'll be emphasizing at the hearing that his living arrangement was a minor, unintentional infraction. He was acting in good faith. There was no contraband found on his person or in the room he rents. His drug test is also clean."

Clean.

I close my eyes and picture Harrison sitting across the table from me yesterday, making me laugh even in the grimmest circumstances. He told me straight up that he wasn't on drugs.

And it was true.

"Does any of that matter, though?" I ask. "Aren't the cops going to argue that he's a suspect in a murder investigation?"

"They can try. It will be my job to convince the judge that the two cases aren't related, and that a little bit of half-assed circumstantial evidence isn't enough to imprison a man. The judge knows it's wildly expensive to keep an inmate for no reason. He also knows how badly the police need a suspect. But if the police had any real evidence of Harrison's guilt, they'd have charged him already."

"Is there any way to know what the cops found?"

"Not directly," she admits. "But Harrison provided a lot of detail about what questions they've asked him. It seems like his biggest problem is his timeline on the night of the murder, and the fact that he was playing the same club where they found the gun."

My stomach drops. "Yeah, that's a hell of a coincidence."

"Yes and no. The club is on the same side of town as the Wincott Mansion. During the break, he walked south and knocked on your door. The police can time-stamp that from the video. And your house is on the way to the mansion. Plus, his cell phone was powered down the whole time, which the police seem to think is suspicious."

"Not everyone is glued to their phone twenty-four hours a day." Then again, I probably haven't powered down my phone in months.

"He says he always turns his phone off during a gig. But they're going to argue that he could easily have been at the scene of the crime."

I think that through. "So . . . he knocks on my door, and nobody answers. Then he decides to kill Tim. And somehow, he knows exactly where Tim is without using a phone or any other communication. He walks over there and kills him, before going back to play the band's next set? That isn't a very convincing storyline."

"Agreed, unless he had a second phone, which he denies. Then there's that note, which he couldn't have written. If they bring murder charges, we'd find a teacher to testify about his dyslexia. I'd also want to dig into the gun a little bit. The police have said where it was dumped, but not when. The club and the sidewalks around it were busy that night. Lots of people around, and they're still looking to corroborate the gun dump. It's much more likely that the perp threw it in there the next day, which is why nobody but the tipster saw it. Hell—the tipster could have thrown it in himself."

"Oh shit."

"That's just one of the lines of inquiry I'd try to explore. Did you know Tim had a gun?"

"Nope. Never saw it."

She hums. "I wonder whether he always carried it in the vehicle, or if he had it the night of his death for a specific reason. Did you ever open the glove box in Tim's car?"

"Never had a reason to."

She's silent for a second. "The police are looking at you as well, right? They'd have to be."

"Well, yeah. I was the one who found him. And we had just broken up."

"Recently?"

"A few days before."

Another silence. "Look, if they actually charge Harrison with murder, I can't help both of you."

"Why not?"

"Because you're not married. And as Harrison's lawyer, my job will be to remove suspicion from him any way I can."

It takes me a second and then it dawns on me with hideous clarity. "So . . . casting suspicion on me would be your plan?" I let out a nervous laugh.

"You don't make a great murder suspect." There's a smile in her voice. "But I only need reasonable doubt. And the police will think now that you two are working together."

Shit. "So . . . I'll have to hire an additional lawyer for myself?"

"Only if I represent Harrison for Mr. Kovak's murder. But that probably won't be necessary."

"Because you don't think Harrison did it."

"Listen carefully," she says. "It's not my job to decide if he did or didn't. It's my job to make sure that he has a strong defense, and that he can't be convicted on circumstantial bullshit. And it looks to me like they don't have a strong case."

"Okay."

"But, since you asked, I don't see him as a dangerous man. Which is why I'm about to make a suggestion you might not like."

35

NATALIE

Her mother doesn't notice as Natalie hovers at the top of the stairs, eavesdropping on the call with the lawyer.

Who cares if it's sneaky, childish behavior? It's the only way she'll hear the truth.

She knows in her gut that her dad didn't kill that guy.

And her dad isn't stupid, or her mother never would have fallen for him.

So if he isn't stupid, he wouldn't bother killing her mom's boyfriend, even if he *was* jealous. Murderers usually get caught. Why screw up the life you're working so hard to put back together?

This is the logic upon which she's built the sandcastle of her heart. So the lawyer had better be good at her job.

"I don't understand," her mother is saying. "He could go anywhere. Why would he have to stay here?"

Stay here? Natalie listens so hard that she might actually sprain something. Because it sounds like the lawyer is suggesting that her father move in here—to their house—if he's released.

When her mother speaks again, she sounds aggrieved. "What did he say when you floated this idea past him?"

Natalie can't hear the lawyer's response, and it's killing her.

"But I haven't shared a house with him in fifteen years. We're not a couple."

More unforgiving silence.

"Does he have a backup plan?" her mom asks hopefully. The answer she gets makes her flinch. "There's no girlfriend he could ask?"

There must not be, because her mother grips the muscle in her shoulder—the one that's always bothering her. "I know housing is tight in Portland, but it's still a big ask. What happens if he can't provide an address to the judge?"

Another pause.

"I just don't know what to say."

"Say yes," Natalie says from the stairs, and her mother whips around, startled. "We can put him in your so-called office." Natalie points toward her old playroom, with its peeling paint and the terrible old wallpaper. "Nobody uses that room."

"Can I call you back?" her mother asks with a sigh. "Thank you." Then she gives Natalie a glare. "Are you listening in on my phone call? That's not cool."

"You're in the middle of the living room. And how else will I ever learn anything about him? You pretended for *years* like he doesn't exist. You didn't answer his messages, even when he had something important to say. And now I'm supposed to believe you'll level with me if I don't listen in?"

Her mother's expression softens. "I'll tell you everything I know, Natty. But that's almost nothing."

"Why did the lawyer ask you if he could stay here?"

Her mother flops back against the couch like she's exhausted. "Because they'll make it a condition of his release that he can provide a home address. And he can't go back to that room he was renting, because a felon lives at that address, and it's against the terms of his parole."

"*Oh.* And you can't rent a new apartment from a jail cell."

"Right. He needs somewhere to go until he can find a new situation. But you shouldn't pretend that inviting him into this house wouldn't be a big deal."

It *is* a big deal, but that's why Natalie needs it to happen. "We have the room. And it's only temporary."

Her mother actually rolls her eyes. "It's not like the cat, honey."

"No, it's easier than the cat, because he'd probably show more gratitude. And Lickie won't be afraid of him."

Her mother snorts.

"Mom, either you believe he's innocent, and deserving of help, or you don't. Which is it?"

"It's not that simple!" She throws her hands in the air. "He let us down once before, baby. In the worst way. I can't just pretend like that never happened."

"Mama," she says, hating the tremble in her voice. "You talked to him. Did he really seem like a psycho who will turn on us? *Really?*"

She considers the question. "No, not really. But baby—my record for trusting people is not good. *He's* the reason I don't take chances anymore."

Natalie moves down the stairs and perches on the back of the couch. "What if he just needs a break, and we could give it to him?"

Her mother stares up at the ceiling. "We don't even have a first-floor shower."

"*Mom.*" There's fury rising in her heart. "It's *literally* your job to create spaces where families can 'flourish and grow.'" She uses air quotes. "That was on the website you started to make. Did you even mean it?"

"That's marketing!"

"So no, then?" She jumps off the back of the sofa and heads for the stairs. She can't sit here and listen to this. "Way to be generous. Thanks for nothing."

36

MONDAY

CORALIE

She spent the whole weekend rehearsing her speech and worrying what he'd say.

And throwing up from stress. And craving a drink.

You wouldn't think those last two things go together, but you'd be wrong.

Now she's standing in the doorway to his office, her heart fluttering. She's got to rip the bandage off or lose her mind. "Mr. Wincott, I have to speak to you."

He looks up from the document he's reading, the frown line in his forehead accentuated by irritation.

She takes a deep breath and forces a smile. "We have to talk. I have some news. Good news."

His frown lines deepen. "Spit it out, then."

She walks in and closes the door behind herself. It seems to take a long time to close the distance between them. But she makes herself walk right up beside his chair. Then she puts a palm on her tummy. "I've been to the doctor. I'm sure this will be a shock, but we're having a baby together. And I just know you're going to be a wonderful father."

His jaw hardens immediately. "That's ridiculous. I can't even have children."

"Clearly you can," she says as softly as possible. "There's no one else it could be."

"Well, you'll never manage to prove it." It's almost word for word what she'd expected him to say.

She takes a fortifying breath. "Is that what you also said to Elizabeth? And Mary Ann, and Theresa?"

His head snaps back. He rises from his chair so fast that she can't get out of the way. Her limbs are too startled to move.

One step forward and he slaps her face. Hard.

Her shocked hand flies up to her stinging cheek. *Do not cry.*

He surprises her by laughing. "You conniving little bitch. Got into my desk, did you? You pick the lock?"

Terror crawls down her spine. "No," she breathes. She ought to turn and run, but something makes her stand her ground. "You left it open and just walked away. That's sloppy work, Mr. Wincott. But I forgive you."

The *look* on his face. Pure shock.

"You're a sinner, too, aren't you? I think that's why you like me. Because we're just the same."

His eyes darken, and for a split second she thinks she's made a horrible miscalculation.

But then something unexpected happens. He leans in and takes her mouth in a punishing kiss, jamming his tongue in her mouth so suddenly that it scrapes past her teeth. One of his hands snarls into her hair, and the other one clamps to her ass.

It's so shocking that it unsteadies her. Arms flailing out to the sides, she finds nothing to hold on to except for him.

When she grips him, he makes a noise. A worked-up moan. His hands are everywhere now. On her sensitive, swollen breasts. On her ass and then her belly.

And God help her, but she likes the strangely broken sound of his moan. Like he can't stop himself.

She feels the balance of power tip a little in her favor.

37

ROWAN

Martha Bean estimated that Harrison's hearing would occur between ten a.m. and noon. But now it's twelve thirty, and the only texts I've received are frantic ones from Natalie.

Natalie: What happened? Is it bad that they haven't texted to say that he's out?

I suspect that it's not a good sign, but I reply with:

Rowan: I have no idea. I'm sorry.

My phone rings, and my heart does a somersault as the incoming call notification resolves onto the screen.

It's not the lawyer, though. It's Hank. And even though I'm distracted, I can't afford to blow him off. "This is Rowan Gallagher," I say in the calmest voice I can. "Hank?"

"Hey there, Rowan," he says. And unless I'm crazy, his voice is a little cool. "Sorry about our meeting on Friday. I got your file, and I'll read it tonight."

"It's no problem. Would you like to reschedule?"

"How about this Friday? I'll move some things around. I know you need to line up your suppliers."

"Thank you," I say, wondering at how smoothly he made it sound like he was doing me a favor.

"I heard you needed a peek at the old floor plans. Is there some hiccup I should know about?"

My heart spasms. "Nope. I was just having deep thoughts about the original placement of the lighting fixtures. Thought I'd take one more look while I was there."

Am I crazy? Or is there a tense silence? "All right. Glad to hear it. We'll do the budget meeting on Friday at twelve thirty. And I'll be seeing you tomorrow, as well."

"Tomorrow." I draw a blank. "Tuesday?"

Another weird pause. "The Historical Commission dinner."

The dinner. Oh shit! "Of course!" I say quickly. "My brain was on meetings. I'll see you tomorrow night."

"Excellent," he says. "Now I'd better run."

"Absolutely. Me too."

The call ends, and my muscles go limp. It's a good thing the lawyer didn't call when I was talking with Hank. That would've been a great way to pause a conversation with my boss. *I've got to run and pick up a murder suspect from jail.*

"Was that Hank?" Beatrice asks from her desk, where she's clicking away on her laptop. "What did he want?"

"He rescheduled my budget meeting for Friday." I scrub my forehead with one hand. "And he reminded me that he and I are going to some Historical Commission thing tomorrow night."

Beatrice stops typing and turns to me with a grin. "Wait, are you his *date* for the dinner?"

I answer carefully. "Only for work purposes. He thought I could help him fend off pointed questions about the new construction plans out back."

"Uh-huh." Her grin widens. "Hank never has just one angle, though. What are you wearing?"

"Um . . ." My mind blanks. Not only do I have no idea, but her reaction is a little strange. I've always thought Beatrice might have a thing for Hank. I wonder if she secretly hates that he invited me to this thing, and not her.

"It's kind of dressy," she says, turning back to her laptop. "I went last year. The doyennes of Portland like any excuse to get fancy."

"Oh *great*."

She laughs. But luckily, she begins typing again.

I sneak another look at my phone but there's no news. Which means I have too much time to think.

Back when I was twenty-one and deeply in love with Harrison, I would never have believed that at almost forty, I'd be waiting for a call about his release from jail.

My faith in him had been unshakable. When I got unexpectedly pregnant, I proudly told everyone in my life that we were expecting a child.

My college friends looked at me like I'd suddenly sprouted an extra head, but my mother's reaction was even worse. She cried and begged. "You don't have to do this! I'll help you."

Help me do what? This is what I want.

We'd fought. Bitterly. Luckily, my mother changed her tune after Natalie was born. She and my father helped me a lot. But I'll never forget her disappointment. Or how glad she was that graduation robes were baggy, so I wouldn't look so pregnant in the pictures.

My phone buzzes, and I read the screen.

Martha: We won. He's released but with electronic monitoring stipulated. Restricted to home and work only. We'll discuss details and next steps tonight. Can you meet him at your place in 15? He's got a ride there.

I'm stunned by how much relief I feel right now. For Natalie, of course. I send Martha Bean an affirmative reply, and then wait ten minutes to text my daughter:

Rowan: Natty—it worked. He's out. Can you go to the hardware and make keys for him?
Natalie: YES. OMG.
Rowan: Do it now. He needs a set.
Natalie: I'm going!

That done, I grab my keys and my phone and try to slip out while Beatrice is on the phone with the decorator. Unfortunately, she hangs up just as I rise to leave.

"Rowan? Should we get some lunch?"

"I can't. I . . ." This is awkward. But since Natalie has no filter, Beatrice is going to find out anyway. "They released Harrison from jail, and I have to run home and let him in."

Her eyes widen. "To your *house*?"

"Just for a few days."

"Is that safe?"

Something hardens inside me when I gaze back at her perfectly made-up face. "Do you really think I'd risk my life—or my child's—if I thought it wasn't?"

"Of course not, but . . ." Her expression fills with distress. "It's bad optics, Rowan. Even if they had to let him go, he's probably still a suspect."

"Optics," I say coolly. That's one of Hank's favorite words. "He's my daughter's father. I don't have the luxury of thinking about optics just now, okay?"

She looks away, as if she clearly has more to say on the subject but has opted not to. "I guess not."

"Gotta run. I'll be back within the hour." Without another glance in her direction, I leave.

———

As I hurry up the street toward my house, I see an Audi idling at the curb. Both doors open at the same time. Harrison gets out of the passenger side, and a gray-haired man exits the driver's door.

It's Cal, the owner of Docksiders and my first boss. He comes around the car, and Harrison offers him a hand to shake.

Cal pulls him into a hug, instead. "Anytime, buddy," he says. "You'll get past this."

Harrison's face is a little red as he steps back. "I still appreciate it."

They both turn as I approach, and Cal breaks into a grin. "Rowan! You still look nineteen."

"You're a liar," I say without breaking stride. "But I'll take the compliment. Business okay?"

"It's my busy season! Always strapped for help. Want to pick up a couple shifts this weekend?" He grins.

"I was a *terrible* waitress."

He hugs me, and maybe it's my imagination, but he smells a little like fried clams. "You kids behave, now. See you tonight, Harry."

Harrison salutes. "I'll be there."

A moment later it's just the two of us standing there on the sidewalk. Awkwardness sets in immediately. "Okay, well." I gesture toward the house. "I sent Natalie to the hardware to make you a set of keys."

"Thank you," he says. "Not just for the keys, Ro. For everything. I promise I'll get out of your way as soon as I can. You sure as hell didn't have to do this."

No, I did not. Honestly, I'm having a few regrets now that he's standing here in front of me with solemn eyes. I can't stop cataloging all the familiar things about him. Like the tilt of his chin as he studies me. The way he stands. The set of his shoulders.

"You're welcome," I say stiffly. "Now let me show you the room. It isn't fancy."

"Like I care."

"Where's all your stuff?" I say as we head up the walk.

"Still in Parkside. Cal and his wife are going to drive over there tomorrow and fetch things for me. I'm not supposed to go anywhere but here and Docksiders. I'm taking every shift he'll give me, Ro. I'll stay out of your way."

Maybe so, but this will be a lot of togetherness I hadn't counted on. I unlock the door and head inside, Harrison following.

"Wow, cool house," he says in a soft voice. "When was it built?"

Before I can answer, a black-and-white streak shoots across my feet and winds around Harrison's ankles.

He makes a soft sound of surprise and squats down. "Hey! Look who's here!" He lifts his handsome chin to smile at me. "You kept her?"

"Natalie did," I admit. "She insisted. Our dog needs therapy now, but whatever."

He gives a startled laugh and strokes the cat's chin, clicking his tongue. "Who's a good girl?"

The cat flings herself at his feet, rolling onto her back like a drunk sorority girl at a house party. He scoops her up and rubs her head admiringly, and for a split second I'm jealous of a cat. Then I collect myself and cross the living room toward the old playroom.

"I'm sorry this space isn't really ready for you, but I didn't want to get Natalie's hopes up."

"Yeah, it doesn't matter. I don't mind camping rough." He follows me with the cat in his arms.

"You can open up the futon. I'll find you some bedding. Sorry about the walls. I'd decided to remove the wallpaper and scrape the paint—and then quit halfway through. The silver lining is that I hauled all of Natalie's old toys out of here first."

"Is this supposed to be your office?"

"Someday. Now let me give you the rest of the tour." I step around him, feeling self-conscious. It's wild being in such close quarters after all this time.

Will I ever get used to this? If Harrison stays out of jail and stays in Natalie's life, will I ever feel blasé about seeing him?

I move through the living room with him on my heels. "Kitchen. Laundry. That door leads to our ugly old basement. And here's the half bath." I point. "You'll have to venture upstairs to shower. You can use whichever bathroom you want. The one covered in cosmetics is Natalie's."

His smile is so familiar that I have to look away. "Let me just grab you some towels."

Before I get very far, he reaches out and grabs my hand. "Hey."

I turn slowly around again, confused.

"Thank you for sending me that lawyer. She's a badass."

"I'm glad," I say, my throat tight.

"You don't understand—I didn't know how much I needed her. Then she dragged Cal in. I wouldn't have asked. But he told the judge . . ." Harrison swallows suddenly. "He said some nice things I don't hear very often. And the lawyer argued for me, which nobody ever does, you know? It meant a lot. It made all the difference."

"Oh," I say brilliantly. We just stare at each other for a second. And he's still holding my hand.

He drops it when the front door swings open and Natalie comes inside, Lickie at her heels. "I got keys!"

She stops and stares at her father, who's still got a cat draped over one arm. I can practically see hearts in her eyes.

This was a terrible idea.

But it's too late now. I hurry upstairs for the towels and the bedding. I need to get back to work. It's suddenly very crowded here.

38

NATALIE

Natalie's mother shoots out of the house so fast she practically leaves contrails behind.

Her father stands there in the living room—his arms full of the linens that were thrust at him—looking a little lost.

Natalie doesn't mind. She can ask more questions this way. She perches on the back of the sofa. "Do you need to unpack?"

"Nothing to unpack," he says. "I guess that makes it easier. But I could use a shower."

"Okay. Then we'll have lunch," Natalie says. "I'll see if there's anything good in the refrigerator."

"All right."

She buzzes around the kitchen while she waits for him, opening and closing the refrigerator, puzzling over what to make. She's aiming for competence, but not like she's trying too hard.

He joins her ten minutes later, hitching his hip against the counter. "What's your go-to?"

"Honestly, I'm not feeling it." The contents of the refrigerator aren't promising. "Looks like it might be a grilled-cheese day. I'd say salads, but we're out of lettuce. We could go out?"

Slowly, he shakes his head. "I can't do that. I'm supposed to stay on the property if I'm not at work."

She tries and fails to keep the shock off her face. "Wait. Do you have one of those . . . ?" She points at her ankle. She's only seen those things on television.

His expression turns grim. "I will. Tomorrow, I think. I don't know the rules yet, but I don't wanna break them while I'm waiting to hear."

"Okay. Fair. That's gonna be a drag."

"You're telling me." He rubs his forehead. "I don't know how I'm supposed to find an apartment to rent when I can't go look at them. Your mother is a saint for letting me stay here."

"Grilled cheese it is then." She pulls the cheese slices out of the drawer and gives the refrigerator a last look.

"Got a can of garbanzo beans somewhere?" he asks, looking over her shoulder. "I could make a chopped salad with that cucumber and that pepper and some feta cheese. To go with your sandwich."

"Uh, sure?" She goes over to the pantry, finds a can, and hands it to him.

He pulls the cucumber out of the refrigerator, correctly guesses the locations of both the peeler and a cutting board, and sets himself up on the far side of the counter. "Can't get enough vegetables. That's the worst thing about prison food. Nothing fresh. Nothing goes crunch."

Natalie absorbs this grim detail like a champ. Or she tries to. "What was it like?" she blurts a minute later. "Um, I mean, in jail?"

He's quiet, and she wonders if he isn't going to answer. "It's mostly just very humiliating. You're like a head of livestock, going where they want you to, when they want you to. Lots of picky rules. And no privacy."

Kind of like living with Mom.

"And then you adjust to it, and that's almost more unsettling. Like you forget how to think for yourself, and you have to fight off the impulse to just wait to be told what to do."

Her heart sags. "Sounds grim."

"It is pretty grim. It doesn't help that I was always surrounded by people who are even more hopeless than me. Like they never had a chance to be anything but a problem."

"Ouch."

"Yeah. To cope, I had to work on having a really rich interior life. I listened to a lot of talk radio. Then I tried my hand at drawing a graphic novel."

"Really? What about?"

"It's not finished," he cautions. "It's science fiction. About a cyborg who doesn't know he's a cyborg, until a glitch clues him in. It's a book about being in prison, honestly. But you're supposed to write about what you know."

He peels the cucumber in several quick strokes and then reaches for a knife in the block and begins to chop. "Before I go to work, I'll order some groceries. Do you know what store delivers?"

"Hannaford," she says. "Maybe Whole Foods, too?"

"All right."

Natalie sets up the griddle and starts in on two grilled-cheeses. She's careful not to burn them, because that would be so embarrassing.

A few minutes later they're sitting down to a better lunch than Natalie would ever have made on her own. "This is nice," she says uselessly.

He cocks his head to the side and smiles at her. "Happy to have lunch with you while I can. I'll only be here a few days. And I'm going to be working a lot and staying out of your mother's way. She seems really stressed."

"Oh, she is. That guy was bad news even before he died on her."

He frowns. "Bad news how?"

"Do you want to hear my theory of how he got killed?"

The corners of his mouth twitch. "It sounds like you want to tell it to me."

"Well, it's weird, right? He dies in front of that house, and they took all his stuff from his car. Like a robbery. But they also took his notebooks. He was a journalist. I think he was working on a story about the mansion. He was adopted from there, I think. It used to be a home for unwed women."

"I knew that," he says. "My mother worked there when I was little."

"She . . . What? Seriously?" Natalie puts down her sandwich.

"Yeah, that's what she told me once."

"Doing what job?"

"Could have been anything. She worked a lot of jobs when I was young. Hotel maid. Waitress." He shrugs. "This will sound weird to you, because you and your mom are close. But my mother was kind of a mystery to me. Things were okay when I was little—back when my dad was still paying child support. But then our lives got hard, and she just kind of gave up. Did drugs. Stayed out all night."

"Oh." *He had an unhappy childhood*, her mother had said.

He shrugs again. "Not everyone is built to be a survivor. And she didn't have help. Her parents kicked her out when she got pregnant with me. I used to be mad at her. But then I had some bad luck myself, and now I understand her a little better."

Natalie nods. But her mind is churning on something else. "Can I show you something?" She doesn't wait for an answer. She bolts from the table and runs upstairs, where her backpack was abandoned the minute school got out last week and not touched since. She digs out the saint medallion. Runs back downstairs.

"Here," she says a minute later, dropping it into his hand. "Remember this?"

"Wow. Yeah." He turns it over in his palm. "This was hers. You've had it all this time?"

"Uh-huh." She doesn't mention that she used to wear it almost every day. "Do you know where she got it?"

He looks up at her with gray eyes that are so much like her own. "I'm sorry, but I don't. Why do you need to know?"

"Because he had one, too. The dead guy. They found it in his car."

"That's really odd, Natty," he says quietly. "What does your mother think?"

"She thinks he was after the name of his birth mother before he died. That he was trying to write a story about the Wincotts, and he basically used Mom to learn stuff."

He puts down his fork. "That's a dick move."

"Well, yeah." She grabs her sandwich again, because gossip is hungry work. "She found the last name of Tim's birth mother. And she tried googling her, but she doesn't seem to exist."

"Hmm." He watches her chew with a soft expression. "Maybe she was a cyborg who didn't know she was a cyborg."

Natalie laughs suddenly and almost coughs with her mouth full. *Smooth.* "When do I get to see this graphic novel?"

"Probably never," he says, picking up a sandwich half. "But if I ever finish it, you can have the first copy."

———————

After lunch, they do the dishes together. Then her father disappears into his room to make some calls. "I have to figure out the housing situation," he says.

It's tempting to sit on the sofa and wait for him to reappear. Like a lonely puppy. But Natalie goes upstairs instead.

She flops down on her bed and opens her phone to find messages from Tessa.

Tessa: Well????? Is it weird? Is it cool?

It's both, but for once she doesn't feel like dissecting it. And she's supposed to be looking for a summer job. Her mother will ask if she applied anywhere.

She opens her laptop and halfheartedly googles a few touristy shops on the waterfront. Her mother says that's her best shot—stores that need seasonal help.

After a few minutes, she finds herself googling Saint Raymond instead. The results are mostly from Catholic websites.

L. Peoples, she tries next. Nothing.

Laura Peoples. Lisa Peoples. Lucy Peoples. It turns out that Peoples is a terrible search term, and pretty unusual for a name.

Did you mean Peebles? asks Google.

So that's what she tries next: *L Peebles Portland Maine.*

The screen lights up with possibilities. She clicks the link for Facebook, because this woman is old. Sixty at least.

Facebook gives her several L. Peebles results. Lily? Lisa? They're both too young.

She almost scrolls past Laura, because her avatar is a picture of a sunset, which isn't helpful. But she clicks on the link, just in case, and scrolls through her feed. It consists mostly of uplifting memes. *Be kind.*

Everyone is fighting a battle that you can't see. I only drink wine on days ending in Y. And so on.

She's about to give up when she finds an interesting photo. Someone's tagged Laura in a group shot of four women outside a stone church. They're working at what looks like a bake sale. And holy shit. One of the women is familiar.

Natalie doesn't know her, but she knows exactly where she's seen her before.

39

ROWAN

I walk up my street after work and see a delivery man unloading grocery bags onto my front porch.

I didn't order any groceries, so I hurry toward him. Before I get there, the front door opens and Natalie steps outside. "I'm supposed to give you this." She hands him a tip.

"Hey, thanks," the guy says. "Here's your receipt."

Natalie carries a grocery bag into the house, leaving the door open.

I grab another bag before I step through the door. "Natalie! For the love of all that's holy, could you please keep the doors shut and locked?"

"Sorry," she says, trotting out of the kitchen. "Dad shopped."

"I see that." I set down my work stuff, haul the rest of the bags inside, and make sure the door is shut and locked. Then I double-check the lock. "He went to work?"

"Yup. At four."

I practically sag with relief. I'm too tired to sit across from him at the dinner table and pretend not to feel awkward.

"But Mom—I found something." She's bouncing on her toes.

"Is it a job?"

She rolls her eyes. "No. Tessa and I are job hunting tomorrow after I take my bio exam. But seriously. I have things to show you right after I put the groceries away. I told Dad I would take care of it."

"Sure. But give me five minutes."

I run upstairs to change, trying not to feel shaky about the way Natalie's bubbling over with enthusiasm after a few hours with her dad.

After putting on jean shorts and an old T-shirt, I find a sticky note on the bathroom mirror, with a drawing of a roasted chicken and a steaming bowl of . . . mashed potatoes?

I forget to breathe for a second, because I'm back in our Ithaca apartment, finding another note just like this, telling me what's for dinner.

He's signed it "H," as if I wouldn't know who it was from.

Feeling slightly off-kilter in my own house, I pad downstairs to the kitchen. I open the refrigerator to find it full of food.

"There's also a salad he made earlier." Natalie points at a covered bowl containing a chopped Greek salad.

Hmm. Am I too petty to eat the groceries that Harrison sourced?

Natalie takes the lid off a paper carton of mashed potatoes and the smell of warm butter wafts through the kitchen.

Not too petty, then. I get out two plates. I pour myself a glass of wine and carry my dinner to the table.

Just as we're sitting down, the sound of a motorcycle hums down the street, grows louder, and cuts out completely in our driveway.

"Oh, that's Dad's bike," Natalie says. "That guy Rick said he was going to drive it over here. I'll get the keys from him."

I take a gulp of wine and say nothing. But of course Harrison still rides a damn motorcycle. I hope it's not the same one, because then at least I won't have to eye it in my driveway and remember the time he bent me over the damn thing and lifted my skirt.

Natalie returns a moment later and slides a key ring onto one of the hooks by the door.

"Okay, check out what I found." She plunks herself into her chair in front of me. "This is going to blow your mind." She unlocks her phone and shows me a photo of a woman.

Her face is familiar, but it takes me a minute to remember why. "Oh God. The funeral!" It's that woman who sat beside me—the sobbing one. The same woman who ran out the back door when it was over.

"Yeah. She cried so hard."

"Who is she?"

Natalie's smile is smug. "Her name is Laura Peebles. P-e-e-b-l-e-s. I found her on Facebook."

"*Peebles*," I repeat, as my stomach bottoms out. "So it was misspelled. Holy shit."

"Holy shit," Natalie repeats, and then laughs.

It's taking me a second to get my head around it. "So she knew Tim. Or at least knew *of* him."

"Yeah, but remember—she ran out without talking to anyone? Maybe nobody else in his family was in on the secret."

My head spins. "What am I supposed to do with this information?"

"We have to talk to her," Natalie says immediately. "If Tim got himself unalived by digging up dirt about the Home for Wayward Girls, then this woman probably knows something about that. She was *there*, Mom. She's at the center of it all."

"She is," I agree slowly. "But we should stay out of it. I should probably just tell the police. Or Tim's wife."

"Tim's . . . *what?*"

"His ex, I think. He lied to me about ever having a wife."

"Ick, Mom," Natalie says, her expression appalled. "Why would she want to talk to you?"

"Because she wants information. She wants to know why he died."

"So do we," Natalie argues. "You could visit Laura Peebles and give her that watch you're carrying around in your purse."

"Okay, what were you doing in my purse?"

"Getting your wallet, like you asked me to the other day." She rolls her eyes.

Hell.

"I could go with you," Natalie says. "I found her address in Westbrook."

"Nobody is going anywhere."

Natalie gives me a frown. "There's one more thing. I was telling Dad about Tim and the Home for Wayward Girls. And Dad knew about it already. He said his mother worked there when he was little."

My fork stops halfway to my mouth. "Really?"

"Really."

"Doing what?"

She shakes her head. "He has no idea."

———————

Harrison's restaurant shift will probably last until midnight, even on a weeknight, but I make sure to take myself up to my room earlier than that. Just in case.

I settle in with a book, but within moments my phone buzzes with a text.

It's from Jules Kovak.

> Jules: Any luck with the name?

I exhale sharply and then craft a reply.

> Rowan: You want a name from me but you won't even tell me yours? Out of business cards, my ass.

She doesn't respond for a minute, and I have the small satisfaction of having stunned her.

She finally sends a response:

> Jules: We've been divorced for over a decade. Didn't seem relevant.

I roll my eyes like my daughter would.

> Rowan: Why should I trust you? That's not the only thing you held back, is it?
> Jules: Like what?
> Rowan: You showed me the names of people who are connected to the mansion. But you left some off, didn't you?
> Jules: I left a lot of them off. Tim gave me a long list.
> Rowan: Were any of them Betsy Jones?
> Jules: There is, in fact, a Jones on the list. But I couldn't identify her. And then when they arrested Harrison, I realized that he's also a Jones, so I looked again. But Harrison's mother is dead. Nowhere to go with that lead.
> Rowan: Still sneaky AF.

I'm so tired of being the last one to know anything.

My phone rings in my hand. It's her, and I don't pick up. She texts a moment later.

> Jules: Rowan, please. I'm not trying to manipulate you. I just want to nail Tim's killer. You never get over your first love, right? I heard yours moved into your house today.

Anger flashes through me. She knows too much and says too little. I want to pass along the information Natalie found today. But I don't trust her to use it in a way that gets the cops off Harrison's back. And mine.

Still, I have questions.

> Rowan: Did you search Harrison's room while he was in prison?
> Jules: No. Why would I? And that sounds illegal. Did someone search his room?

I try another question.

> Rowan: What did Harrison's mother do for the Wincotts? When did she work for them?
> Jules: Tell you what. You find Tim's birth in that ledger, and I'll give you everything I have on Betsy Jones.

I put my phone down in disgust and shut off my lamp. But my head is too full of conspiracy theories to sleep.

Maybe Jules has some other angle.

Maybe Tim had a fat life insurance policy.

Natalie had better not bike out to Westbrook and knock on that lady's door.

Hell, she might actually do that.

Reluctantly, I pick up my phone again. There's someone else who'd be interested in Mrs. Peebles.

I text Detective Riley.

Rowan: I found something of interest regarding Tim and the Wincott Mansion. Call me if you want to hear it.

My phone rings a second later. "That was fast."

"You're a very important witness, Rowan. The whole investigation keeps circling back to you."

"It doesn't," I insist. "But I'm tired of hearing that, so I did a little digging. Did you know that Tim was born at the mansion?"

"I can't share information we may have uncovered during an ongoing investigation."

I roll my eyes again. "So you *do* know. His mother probably told you. This was news to me until recently. But now I think I found the name of his birth mother, and I'm pretty sure she was at his funeral."

There's a deep silence on the line. That's how I know I've shocked her. "Are you going to share the name?"

It almost pains me to be helpful to someone so aggravating. But I definitely need her help. "It's Laura Peebles. With a *b*. She has a Facebook profile, and I think she lives out in Westbrook."

Riley is quiet for another moment before she asks, "And how did you come by this information?"

"I found it in the handwritten birth ledger—the same one Tim had photos of from my phone. I went back to the original document and found the relevant page. The names don't match up exactly, but I think it's her."

She curses under her breath.

"Everything okay over there?"

"She won't open the door for me," she says. "We found her name in Tim's phone data, so we knocked on her door. But she's afraid of cops and won't talk to me. What do you know about her?"

"Just that she's grieving. She was a mess at the funeral. I handed her all the tissues I had. But she left the service the moment it was over, instead of greeting the family."

"Maybe she'd talk to you," Riley says slowly. "If you think this will change the direction of the investigation, maybe you can help me out."

"How?"

"We'll take a ride out there. You'll knock on the door by yourself. If she recognizes you from the funeral, you can talk to her a little and ask her to invite me in."

I don't see how that would ever work. But I'm mulling it over, because I think Jules is right about why Tim died, and I need the police to see that—and leave me and Harrison alone. "What if she won't let me in?" I ask.

"Then we tried," she says. "How's tomorrow afternoon? Two o'clock?"

"I can't get away until four. And you don't even know if she'll be home."

"I'll drive by first to see if there's a car in front of the house."

She's left me almost no room to argue. "Fine. I have one of Tim's watches. I'll bring it for her. That might get me in the door."

"I'll be in front of the mansion at four." She hangs up.

I roll over and try to get comfortable. But I haven't been truly comfortable since Tim died. Too many regrets.

If only I hadn't sat down with him in the coffee shop.

If only I hadn't followed his avatar around Portland. Or leashed up Lickie to find his car . . .

My phone buzzes again, and I pick it up. A text from Harrison, to both me and Natalie.

Harrison: You'll hear the door open in a minute. Don't panic. And I'll be sure to lock up.

About a second later, my daughter puts a heart on the text.

From upstairs, I barely hear the front door open and close, but I do hear the jingle of Lickie's collar as she goes to investigate.

There's no barking—just the low sound of Harrison's voice as he greets the dog and probably the cat, too. They're both smitten.

I put my phone facedown on the bedside table and curl under the quilt. For a few minutes, I listen to Harrison moving around downstairs. Then all is quiet.

Closing my eyes, I relax against the sheet. My eyelids feel heavy.

It shouldn't be relaxing to have a man in the house. Especially an ex-con who once abandoned me.

It shouldn't be. But somehow it is.

40

In the morning, I hit the snooze button too many times and end up rushing to get ready for work. By the time I make it downstairs, it's after eight.

In the kitchen, I notice coffee's already been made. Harrison is quietly nursing a cup at the kitchen table, while watching Natalie buzz around the kitchen.

She's on a call, her earbuds jammed into her ears, buttering toast as she argues with a friend. Tessa, from the sounds of it. "We don't want to work at a gym. That place smells like feet." She jams a corner of the toast in her mouth. "Yeah, okay, the smoothie bar seems better. It's small, though? Do you think they need *two* people?"

I nudge her out of the way and put a piece of bread into the toaster for myself. Then I point at the crumbs on the counter.

She ignores me. "Yes! The gelato place. Good call. When do you think they open?"

With a sigh, I brush the crumbs into my palm and dust them into the sink.

"Okay. Sure. I'll be done with my bio exam at . . . eleven? Yeah, I can get the car."

I make a noise of disbelief.

Natty turns to me, as if suddenly realizing I'm alive. "Mom, can I use the car?"

"You *may* use the car, and thanks for asking. But you can't get a job that *requires* the car. For obvious reasons."

She frowns. "Okay, yeah, I can use the car."

Harrison gives a low chuckle from the corner.

"See you in a while?" She shoves another bite of toast in her mouth.

"I've got my test. And today's the last day to take my textbooks back to school before they fine me."

"Again?" I grab a mug and pour myself a cup of coffee.

She finally hangs up her call. "It's under control, Mom. I'll make it." She runs out of the kitchen.

My toast pops, and I butter it tidily. I'm self-conscious with Harrison sitting there at the table watching me. Maybe he senses it, because I hear his chair push back against the wood floor. "Rowan."

Without even thinking, I turn at the sound of his voice. The way I used to.

He's in the doorway, mug in hand. "I'm calling every room for rent in Portland today. I promise." He gives me a faint smile. "This was selfish of me. I could probably have conned Cal Baxter into letting me crash on his couch for a few nights. I know I don't deserve your generosity. But this right here . . ." He waves in the direction of the messy countertop. "Just a half hour watching her run in circles in your kitchen is the best gift anyone has given me in a long time. And I won't forget it."

Then he slips out of the room.

———

It's a busy day of meetings with the general contractor. But most of the time we're outside in the sunshine, walking the site and discussing the plans for the Orangerie.

As a bonus, I've successfully avoided Beatrice all day. I don't have the bandwidth to navigate her judgment of my new living situation.

Eventually I have to go inside, though. And when I enter the library, I can hear her voice in the inner office. "You *say* that, but I'm still the best man for the job."

I stop midstride, because she sounds upset.

"Hank, that's crap! I'd bring more energy to the job than anyone else. I care more, and that counts for a lot. You *know* it does."

Uh-oh.

"Fine. Yes. You can't talk me out of applying! You know what? We'll discuss this later. I have to go." A half second later I hear the smack of her phone on the desk blotter.

Shit.

"I'm off my call, Rowan. You don't have to lurk there."

I walk into the office. "I'm sorry. That sounded like a bad moment, and I wasn't sure I should stay."

She looks utterly shaken, and for once it's not me who's having a small breakdown at her desk. Beatrice rests her head in her hands and lets out a growl of rage.

I can pretty much guess what happened here. "Is this about the director's job?"

"He posted it today. A *national search*." She lifts her face, and it's red. "He told me I should apply to be the assistant to the director and work my way up. Which we all know is a *load of crap*."

"An actual load of crap," I agree. "If the director they hire ever leaves, they'd just . . ."

"Do another national search." Beatrice rolls her eyes to the ceiling, as if looking for guidance from the trompe l'oeil ceiling. "He says that the director's job is really a development job. That it has to go to someone with *influence*. He just means a white man with money and Ivy League connections."

"I'm so sorry." I sink down in my chair. "That's lazy thinking on his part. Nobody cares more about this job than you do."

"Nobody," she says firmly. "At least he's your problem tonight. Not mine."

"My problem?" I repeat.

An eyebrow lifts. "The Historical Commission dinner. Before he ruined my week, Hank told me to tell you he'd pick you up at six."

"Oh God. That's *tonight*?"

Her eyes widen and all of a sudden her mood shifts. "You forgot? Need me to find you a blowout? I'll call in a favor."

"No, no. It's fine," I backtrack. "I'm good. But what the hell am I going to wear? I can't even remember the last time I put on a dress."

She gives me a grin that's slightly feral. "I want pictures from this date."

"There will be no pictures," I say, checking my calendar just to make sure it's true. And, yup, it's right there. I've just been too overwhelmed to keep track of my life. "This is *not* a date. Hank just expects to be bombarded with questions about the renovation, and he wants my help answering them."

"I'm sure that's part of it." Her smile is bitter. "But you're also the kind of woman he wants at his side. The right degree. Old Maine family. Age appropriate, yet still good arm candy."

"He's definitely not my type. Honestly, I always thought he was more *your* type."

"Oh *hell* no." She laughs dryly. "Hank's like a brother to me. Even if he weren't on my shit list, I would *never* go there."

It's a pretty convincing reaction, but I still don't buy it. She seems downright obsessed with the whole Wincott family, and Hank especially.

"Besides, I'd never date anyone that high maintenance," she says. "His manicure is better than mine."

I laugh in spite of myself. "Good point."

"Should we get coffee? My turn to treat."

"I can't even do coffee. I've got an off-site meeting."

"Oh?" She sits back in her chair. "It's not on your calendar."

"What calendar? I'm a walking wreck. We covered this already." But of course, I left my meeting with Detective Riley off the schedule. I don't want to have to explain to Beatrice why I've volunteered to spend time with the cops.

Since I don't even know myself.

By four, I'm alone in the office, which makes it easy to pick up my bag and head outside. Riley is waiting at the curb, alone in an unmarked Subaru.

I slide into the front seat. Riley turns the car around and then navigates toward the north, away from the water.

"Do you need me to look up the address?"

She shakes her head.

"She probably won't even be home," I point out.

"I did a drive-by. And she works nights as a cocktail waitress. Thank you for doing this, by the way."

"I'm not doing it for you," I point out. "It's for Tim. And for my daughter, who will lose her mind if her father is arrested again."

"I heard about your new roommate."

"It's not illegal to house my daughter's father for a few days."

She's wise enough not to comment on that. "Let's discuss your conversation with Peebles. What are you going to ask her?"

"If she doesn't slam the door in my face? I'll tell her how sorry I am for her loss. And I'll ask her how long she'd been in touch with Tim. And then I'm just going to listen to whatever she's willing to share. And give her his watch."

"Not a bad strategy. I'd like the dates of when she and Tim made contact." She pulls up to a stop sign and plucks a device out of her purse. "Take this. It's a recording device . . ."

"*What?* That's not the plan. I'm not recording that woman without her permission."

"New plan," she says. Then she pulls over to the curb and turns to face me. "Take the mic, Rowan. You say you want Tim's killer caught. But you keep lying to me. You lied about knowing where Tim was on the night of his death—"

"Why do you think so?" I gulp.

But I already know what she's about to say, and her unyielding gaze misses nothing as she watches me panic. "A judge gave us your phone data, Rowan. We know you checked the FriendFinder app before you left your house. And you unfollowed him en route."

My whole body flashes hot and then cold. *Oh God.* "If I were Tim's killer, that would be a pretty stupid thing to do."

She gives half a shrug. Her poker face is better than mine. "You keep insisting there's a deep, complicated reason for Tim's death. But all I see are simple jealousies. You told me yourself you were angry that he dumped you. And then there's Harrison, who kept a photo of you in his bedroom. Now you're housing him for a nice little family reunion and probably paying for that new lawyer he has."

My brain is static, and it takes me a long beat to reply. "You can't make a murder case out of my family drama. Of *course* we need lawyers, so long as you're focused on the wrong things."

"That's why you're going to help me focus on the right things," she says crisply. "Record the conversation you have with Ms. Peebles. If something fishy happened to her and Tim when he was born, I need to know it sooner rather than later."

"I *am* cooperating."

"Then take this." She puts the recording device in my lap. "Put it in your bag, and leave your bag unzipped. There's a switch on the side."

The car starts again, but I barely register the neighborhoods we're passing over the pounding of my heart.

Now they *know* I lied. If I don't help her, it could be my face on the nightly news.

When we arrive at Peebles's address, Riley passes the house and parks down the street. "Don't forget to turn the device on," she says. "Good luck, Rowan. We need this."

Feeling shaky, I get out of the car and walk back toward the little one-story house where Laura Peebles lives. The homes on this street are in various states of repair. Little old houses on small lots. Most were built in the sixties. Many have been shined up, but some have cracked front walks and faded siding. And shingle roofs that have seen better days.

Ms. Peebles house is avocado-green, with a slightly overgrown lawn. The doors and windows are shut tightly, but there's an aging Ford truck in the driveway. I climb onto the peeling porch and knock.

Then, feeling like the worst kind of traitor, I reach into my bag and switch on the recording device. Unless I'm totally wrong about who she is, talking about Tim will be painful for her. Recording our conversation will be a betrayal.

And yet I knock again.

The door opens suddenly, and there she is, squinting at me, her expression wary. "Do I know you?"

"Not exactly," I say, faking a smile. "But we sat beside each other at the funeral last Monday."

Her eyes widen. "What funeral." It isn't a question. "You got the wrong lady."

It hadn't occurred to me that she'd deny it. When she turns away, I start talking faster. "I was dating him," I stammer. "Recently. And I brought you something of his that he left at my house."

She goes still, and her eyes drop to her slippers. "You were the girlfriend? The architect?"

Holding my breath, I nod.

"You'd better come inside."

Five minutes later I'm sitting at her kitchen table while she fills two mugs for tea.

"I'm truly sorry for just showing up on your doorstep," I say carefully. "But I'm confused about some things I've learned since Tim died, and I brought you something of his that you might want to keep."

She braces her hands on the counter and drops her head. "I don't know if I should thank you for coming or throw you right out that door. Tim and me . . . it's really fucking complicated."

"I can imagine."

She looks up, and I clock the dark circles beneath her eyes. "No, you can't. I'm sure you mean well, but you have no idea what I've gone through with him. Did he even tell you about me?"

For one ugly second, I consider lying. Then I shake my head.

She looks uneasy. "So how did you find me?"

"It was some guesswork, plus I found a list of birth dates and women's names from the Wincott home. I found Tim's birth date and matched it to your name with a little internet sleuthing."

"Jesus." She turns to put the mugs into the microwave. "Whatever I tell you doesn't leave this room."

God forgive me for what I am about to do. "Okay."

"Even my sister doesn't know the whole of it."

"You aren't in touch with Tim's fam—" I catch myself in time. "His adoptive family?"

She shakes her head. "They don't know about me. Tim showed up on my doorstep this February. I'd never met him before that."

February. I take a sharp breath. "That must have been a terrible shock."

She opens a box of Lipton tea and removes two tea bags. "You don't know the half of it. Last year my sister did one of those tests. For DNA?"

I nod.

"She gets a call almost right away. It's Tim, and he tells her he was adopted in 1979 from the Magdalene Home. And that a genetic test said she was his biological aunt." Laura retrieves the mugs from the microwave, putting a tea bag in each one.

I notice how bony her hands are. She gives the impression of someone who doesn't have a lot to spare. Not money, not energy, not flesh.

"I knew she was taking the test," she nearly whispers. "But I didn't expect her to find my child."

"I'll bet."

She looks up at me. "You don't understand. I didn't expect it, because they told me he died at birth."

Oh God. "Who told you that?" I whisper.

She takes a tiny sip of burning hot tea. Then she looks me dead in the eye. "Marcus Wincott said it to my face. May he burn in hell."

41

This terrible admission silences both of us for a moment. I listen to a clock ticking somewhere in her home, while she blinks away tears.

"Why would he . . . ?" I snap my mouth shut. Even through my rage, I might already know the answer. "I've heard of people paying for babies. Is that what happened?"

"Possibly." Her eyes are downcast. "That was Tim's theory. After we first met, he started digging into the Magdalene Home. He'd come over about once a week. He sat right there." She nods toward where I'm sitting. "And we'd just talk. He was trying to piece it together."

"He was investigating," I say slowly.

She nods, and another tear falls before she brushes it away.

"I'm so sorry," I say softly. "You'd just gotten him back."

She takes another sip of tea and takes a moment to compose herself. "For forty-five years I had so much guilt," she said. "They told me it was my fault that he wasn't born healthy and strong. They said it was God's will, and I believed them. Although it didn't take much persuasion. I already felt stupid for getting pregnant with a boy who didn't stick around."

"I did the same thing," I blurt out. *Not helpful, Gallagher.*

But maybe this was the right thing to say, because her gaze snaps back to mine. "Really? Did you give up a baby, too?"

I shake my head. "My family has some money, and I was stubborn. Everyone was *very* disappointed in me, but I got my own way. My daughter is sixteen now."

"Well, I was stubborn, too," she says slowly. "At the Magdalene Home, you weren't supposed to be stubborn. You were expected to sit down, shut up, and then give up your baby. All the girls did."

"*All* of them?"

She shrugs. "Basically. I was there in 1979, which was getting toward the end of that place. Birth control and abortion were both legal. But I was a ward of the state. An orphan. I lived in a Catholic group home. So the rules were different for me."

"Oh," I say softly.

"Yeah. It was a nun who figured out I was pregnant. I was seventeen. I barely understood how babies were made." She rubs her temples. "The father was also a resident of the group home. Almost eighteen. He ran away when they realized I was pregnant."

"Nice," I hiss.

"I don't even blame him." She gives me a tired smile. "He escaped while he could. Girls raised by the Catholic Church don't get abortions. They get married, or they give up the baby. They sent me off to the Magdalene Home to hide my shame. They treated pregnancy like a contagious disease, you know? Like I would ruin other girls with my sinful presence."

I wish I were more surprised. But I'm not. "What was it like? At the home?" It's a selfish question. I spend a lot of time wandering around the place, trying to picture it in years gone by.

She picks up her tea and takes a sip, her eyes unfocused, as if she's trying to recall. "Boring, mostly. With moments of humiliation. Like being in jail, I guess. And the jailers weren't very nice. They wanted us to feel very bad about the sins we'd committed. He *loved* talking about sin."

"Marcus Wincott?"

Her focus sharpens onto me. "He ran that place like a dictator. Everyone feared him—the girls, and the women who worked there, too. It was *all* young women, and a man in his midfifties. I don't think that would fly nowadays."

"I sure hope not."

She looks down into her mug. "Sometimes he hit us. Never on the face. Never where anyone would see. He liked the shock value, I think. There was one really mouthy girl. Debbie? Darcy?" She shakes her head. "That one had a death wish. She slapped him *back*. And as a punishment, he handcuffed her to a dining chair."

A dining chair. Holy Mary, mother of God. I know that dining chair.

"He also . . ." She rubs her eyes. "I think he got handsy with the girls sometimes. I heard a lot of rumors. And one night I got up for a drink of water, and I saw him disappear into another girl's room. The next morning she had a black eye. I asked her how she got it, she said she slipped in the shower." She shakes her head.

"That sounds . . ." Every word I can think of is inadequate to my horror. And now I *work* for these people. "It sounds barbaric. And terrifying."

She actually shrugs. "I can't be sure about everything that happened there. He never tried anything with me. Maybe I wasn't his type. Or maybe the girls exaggerated."

"Do you still talk to any of them?"

She shakes her head. "I never wanted to think about that place again. Besides, we didn't use our last names in there, which would have made it hard to find anyone I'd known. He said the name thing was for our privacy. But it was probably just another manipulation. If we didn't know how to reach each other, then we couldn't compare notes later."

"Right," I say softly.

"Now that I know the truth, I wish I knew what happened to the other girls. If they were molested. If they were told their babies died. That man's lie changed my life. I had plans to steal my baby away if I had to. He was mine."

The image makes my chest lurch—like the drop of a roller coaster. "He stole him from you. Because you wouldn't fall in line."

She nods slowly. "Tim wondered how he got away with it. The girls gave birth at the home. That probably helped. When I was in labor, they anesthetized me. I woke up and asked to see my baby. The nurse shook her head and sent Wincott in." She swallows hard. "The nurse had to be in on it. Maybe she was afraid of him, too." Her face crumples. "He came in and said that my baby died. *God's will.* I cried so hard. I howled. He told me to shut up."

My eyes get hot. "What did Tim say when you told him?"

"He didn't believe it. I could see it on his face. I wasn't sure I should tell him the rest. It's pretty shocking." She sighs. "But I'm not stupid, you know. When they told me he was dead, I screamed my head off and asked to see him anyway."

My heart trembles. "Of course you did."

"They brought me a dead baby."

"What?" I gasp. "Are you serious?"

She nods. "Poor little thing, all swaddled in a blanket and cold as ice. The blanket was cold, too. They said it was from the morgue."

"Oh God" is all I can manage.

"It sounds crazy, but I know what I saw," she says, lifting her chin. "Marcus Wincott looked me right in the eye and told me that God didn't let me keep my baby because I was a sinner." Her mouth pinches into a rough line. "After that, I wasn't careful with myself. Spent my life as a sinner. That man broke my spirit."

"I'm so sorry," I whisper. As if that could make it better.

"Tim thought they must have been selling babies. He said he was going to look for the money trail. He said he was good at that kind of thing."

I picture his Pulitzer nomination for investigative journalism, and I feel a chill. "I bet he *was* good at that kind of thing."

She nods. "And I was thrilled. Here was this smart, handsome boy, and I had something to do with it. I was so proud. And so happy I got the chance to tell him that I didn't really give up on him." She grabs a paper napkin and blots the corners of her eyes. "At least I got to say it. But maybe I should have lied, you know? Maybe if I'd slammed the door in his face, he'd still be alive."

The hair stands up on the back of my neck. "Why do you think that?"

"Because he died in front of the mansion. It can't be random." She blots her eyes again. "Tim made somebody angry. And now he's gone."

She's upset now, and it's my fault. "I'm so sorry. I shouldn't be asking so many questions."

"No, you shouldn't." She shakes her head. "It's dangerous. The police want to talk to me. But I don't really know a damn thing. Tim didn't tell me what he found. Maybe he knew it was dangerous. Someone threatened him a week or so before he died."

Another chill races down my spine. "Threatened him how?"

"He didn't tell me much." She rubs her temples. "He just said that he must be getting close to the truth, because someone put a note under his windshield wiper. Telling him to leave it alone."

I lean forward in my chair. "Did you see the note?" I wonder if it's the same black Sharpie bullshit that I got.

"No, I didn't." She sighs. "He said a note on the windshield seemed like a cowardly move. And that in his job, if he wasn't making someone angry, then he wasn't trying hard enough."

I take a sip of my tea and try to think. How do you go from a note under your windshield to dead in a week? "Did he have any idea who was mad?"

She spreads her hands. "I don't have a clue. He told me he was digging around for a list of people who worked for the home when he was born. Some of them are dead. It was slow work, he said. And even when he thought he had the right name, sometimes people hung up on him. If they knew what was going on back then, they probably didn't want to talk about it. And Marcus Wincott is long dead."

It sure puts a new spin on Tim's final months in Portland. I was buying new jeans and thinking about where we should go on our next date. He was building a relationship with his secret bio mom. "And he never discussed this with his adoptive parents?"

"No." A quick shake of her head. "He said he'd been asking a few questions, trying to figure out if there were irregularities about his adoption. His parents made a big donation to the Wincott's charity, but he didn't think they had the first idea about the ugly stuff."

"I guess they wouldn't," I say slowly. "Marcus wouldn't want to incriminate himself. And people who are desperate for a baby don't ask too many questions."

"They raised him up real good." She wipes her eyes again. "I don't blame them for what happened. Did he tell you any of this? About his investigation?"

If only. "Not a word. And when he died, we hadn't spoken in several days, because he'd broken up with me."

She blinks at me. "He broke it *off*?"

"Yes. I was still feeling pretty confused about it. But that doesn't seem very important now."

"But he really liked you. He *told* me."

"Maybe he met someone new," I say softly. "It happens."

"I have to ask." She fingers her mug. "Did you find him? Was it you the news was talking about?"

I only nod.

"Do you think he suffered?"

"No," I say immediately. "It's terrible what happened to him. But I don't think he suffered. I think he was gone really quickly. Listen," I fumble into my purse, pushing past the recording device for the little drawstring bag. "I had a couple things of his that he'd left at my house. I'd like to give them to you."

She watches solemnly as I extract the cuff links and the watch.

I lay them on the table. "I'm sure you know he collected watches. And he had an old-school style that I admired."

She lifts a cuff link and studies the monogram. "He dressed so nice," she whispers. "Like a gentleman."

"He did."

She picks up the watch. "This is beautiful. It looks vintage."

"Doesn't it? I don't know anything about watches, though."

She gazes at the watch's face before setting it down again. "You keep that. I'll keep the cuff links."

"What? No. He'd want you to have it."

Her eyes are red when she raises them again. "I know myself. It will only be a temptation."

"Sorry? I don't understand."

"You wouldn't. And that's a good thing." She lifts her chin again, almost defiantly. "I have a little problem with heroin. It's gotten worse since Tim passed."

Oh God. "Is there anything I can do to help?"

She gives her head a slow shake. "I don't see how. Just keep yourself safe. That's all we can do now." She picks up the watch and hands it to me.

"I'll keep this safe for you. Maybe you'll change your mind."

She gives me a tired smile. "Maybe."

I push my chair back. "I'll let you get on with your day. Thank you for talking to me."

She walks me to the door. "Rowan, wait. There is one thing. Do you have any pictures of him?"

I pause, one foot out the door. "I have two. They aren't great, but I'm happy to send them along. Do you have email?"

"Course I do. I'm old but not dead." She smiles faintly at her own joke.

"Sorry. Stupid question." I dig into the exterior pocket of my bag. "Here's my card. Email me, and I'll reply with those two pictures."

"Thank you, honey. I'll do that."

"I appreciate what you shared with me." My voice is a little unsteady, because I know I'm about to betray her confidence to a police detective.

She grabs one of my hands. "He was half in love with you. I could hear it in his voice when he talked about you. Please take care of yourself."

"Don't you worry about me," I assure her. "I'll be fine. I just wish they'd catch whoever did this, so you could get some peace."

She gives me another sad smile. "We don't always get what we want, do we?"

42

NATALIE

"Now do it again," her father says. "If you can get her to do it twice in a row, it's more likely to stick."

Natalie takes another crumb of cheese off the cutting board, and Lickie's tail wags immediately. "Speak."

Her tail thumps the kitchen floor, but she doesn't bark.

"Lickie, speak!"

The dog barks exactly once.

"Good girl!" Natalie says, feeding her the cheese.

"The soup is ready," her father says. "Can you cube the avocados? Just use a butter knife. In a grid pattern." Her dad draws invisible lines over the avocado. "Then turn it inside out over a bowl."

"Sure, okay." She washes her hands first.

He cracks open the oven door to peek at the progress of the crackers he's baking.

Cooking dinner together was his idea. He was waiting in the kitchen when she got home from her discouraging day of applying for jobs.

He didn't ask how the day went, and this somehow makes it easier to tell him about it as she dries her hands. "The bio exam was brutal. And then Tessa didn't like *any* of my job ideas. She only wants to apply to places that are too bougie to hire us. We filled out a bunch of applications, but I bet none of them call us back. That might actually be her plan."

"Hmm," he says, closing the oven door.

"She also doesn't want to work weekends because her parents have a place on Sebago Lake."

"Must be nice," he says.

The front door clatters open out in the living room. Then she hears her mom's computer bag hitting the floor.

"Mom?" She puts the butter knife down and trots over to the doorway. "We're making dinner! It's almost ready!"

Her mother is basically a blur, headed for the staircase. "I can't, baby. I have a work thing."

"What kind of a work thing?" Natalie tracks her movement as she jogs up the stairs. Why are her eyes red?

"The stupid kind." Her mom disappears from sight.

Natalie deflates. She thought her mom might appreciate her father's home-cooked meal. And that he's scraping the old paint in the den in his spare time, just like she's always intended to do. "I've got the time," he'd said when Natalie asked. "It's no trouble."

Her mother could just thaw out a *little*. Like, 10 percent.

She goes back to the kitchen and dices the avocado very carefully into a bowl, while her father pulls a baking tray of crackers out of the oven. Actually, it's one giant cracker until he grabs a fork and gently cracks it into rectangles along lines that he'd scored in the dough before baking it.

"That's a good trick," she says.

He plucks one off the tray and hands it to her.

It's warm and salty and basically perfect. "Where did you learn to make these?"

"The last restaurant where I worked had homemade crackers. Looked so easy I tried myself. Baking bread is a cheap hobby. All you need is a bag of flour and some yeast."

She watches her father's long hands as he moves the crackers to a cooling rack. "Maybe set the table?"

"Sure."

From the cutlery drawer, she pulls out three spoons. But then puts her mother's back. She's not going to beg.

While she's getting the napkins, her mother calls her name from the top of the stairs.

"*What?*" she yells back.

"Can you put my hair up? I've got ten minutes to get out of here."

She lays the spoons on the table and walks out into the living room. Her mother stands on the staircase in her bathrobe, looking agitated.

"So this is, like, fancy?" Natalie asks. "What's the occasion?"

"Historical Commission banquet."

Yawn city. "What are you wearing?"

"God only knows." Her mother looks truly flustered. "Will you do my hair?"

"Sure. You could wear that new dress. The one you bought for dinner with *the guy*."

"No can do." She waves a hairbrush. "It's too much."

"Too much . . . cleavage?"

Her mother gives a miserable shrug.

"Figure it out, because you can't put a dress on once your hair's done. I'll get my stuff." Natalie follows her mother up the stairs, turning into her own room for the styling products and the hair pins. She'll do a French twist. That's quick, and always a winner. She grabs her makeup kit on the way out. "Can I do your eyes?"

"Lightly?" her mother says from the bedroom. "I found a dress."

Natalie pokes her head into the room, where her mother is squinting at a navy-blue dress on a hanger. "That's nice. I mean, that color doesn't say much, but the fabric is pretty."

Her mother frowns. "I was going to get rid of this and now I don't remember why."

"Find me downstairs on the couch?"

Natalie sets up in the living room, all the pins lined up on the back of the sofa. Her mother hurries down two minutes later, carrying a clutch purse and a pair of navy heels so cheugy that Natalie has never bothered to borrow them.

"Can you finish the zipper and do the hook and eye?" her mother asks, dropping the shoes.

"Sure, but sit down." As soon as she lands on the sofa in front of her, Natalie pushes her hair out of the way and fiddles with the hook above the zipper. "There's no . . . thing? It's just the hook, but no loop."

"*Shit.* I knew there was something wrong with this dress. Maybe we can find a really small safety pin in the sewing box?"

"Where's the sewing box? Oh—wait." It's actually in her room. Natalie turns and jogs upstairs again. Luckily, the sewing box is easily located under a pair of dirty leggings and a hoodie.

Downstairs, she hands the box to her mother. Then she grabs the brush and stands behind the couch, taming her mother's hair. It feels misty from the shower.

"We don't have a tiny safety pin," she grumbles. "We don't even have a medium one. It's only these honkers." She holds up a fat safety pin. "I'll have to change. Or cancel. I'd rather cancel."

"Got a needle? I can tack it."

They both swivel to see her father standing in the kitchen doorway. "If this is a wardrobe emergency, I'll stitch it for you while Natalie does . . . whatever Natalie is doing."

Her mother blinks. "That's not necessary."

He actually rolls his eyes. "You want to get out the door in five minutes or what?"

She sighs. "Okay. Thank you. I'll thread a needle."

Natalie twists her mother's hair carefully into a roll at the back of her head and pins it liberally. "This isn't going to be very elaborate . . ."

"Good," her mother says. "I don't have time for elaborate."

"All right. Then hold your breath."

They take a gulp of air in tandem, and then Natalie mists the back of her mother's head with setting spray, while her father watches with an openly amused expression.

When they both exhale, Natalie hustles around to sit on the coffee table. She grabs her makeup kit and roots around for a gold eye shadow.

"Don't make it sexy," her mother says, pausing to snip a length of dark thread. "I don't want to send the wrong message."

"Fine. Be boring."

Her father's lips twitch. He reaches over and plucks the threaded needle from her mom's tense fingers.

"I didn't tie the knot yet."

"Yeah, I have eyes, Rowan." He takes Natalie's old spot behind the couch, licks his thumb, and expertly ties a knot at the end of the thread.

They both lean in toward her mother at the same moment, her father gathering the two halves of her mother's dress. Natalie has the strangest sensation. Like she's having a very lucid dream where she's swapped places with a girl whose parents aren't strangers.

"Close your eyes," Natalie demands.

Her mother closes her eyes.

Natalie strokes gold eyeshadow across her lids. But then her father puts a hand on her mother's bare shoulder, causing her to jump.

"Easy, Gallagher," her father drawls. "Let's not add 'stabbing' to my rap sheet."

"Sorry, sorry."

He gives her mother's shoulder a quick squeeze, and Natalie is fascinated. She's never been able to picture them as a couple, but suddenly she can. Her mother would be the high-strung one. Smart and ambitious and a little neurotic. Her father must have been the bassline—the calm, beating heart in the background.

He bends over his work, looping a tiny stitch between the two edges of the fabric with steady fingers.

Natalie puts the eye shadow away. "Mascara real quick," she says. "And then lipstick."

"I'll do lipstick in the car," she says. "Do you hear a car?"

"No," she and her father say at the same time.

"He said he's coming to get me at six."

Natalie tenses. "*He?*"

"Hank Wincott."

"Oh," Natalie sniffs. "The boss man."

Her father suddenly goes very still. Then he takes a visible breath. "Pass the snips?"

Her mother hands the scissors back over her shoulder.

He frowns over the back of the dress for another moment, like a surgeon finishing up with a patient. "Okay, problem solved." He hands back the scissors just as they hear a car approach. "I think he's here."

43

ROWAN

I shove my feet into the navy pumps and stand up. Hank Wincott is outside, and now I have to spend the next several hours pretending that I didn't just hear horrible stories about Hank's uncle and what went on in the Wincott Mansion.

"Thank you both." I grab my clutch. "Got to run."

Natalie shrugs moodily. "You're going to miss the tomato soup and homemade crackers. But whatever."

My gaze flies to Harrison. "You made the *soup*?"

He shrugs. "There will be leftovers."

Heading for the door, I grab a trench coat off the coat tree. A wave of garlic-scented air wafts in my direction, and I feel a pang of naked longing for Harrison's tomato soup. He used to make it all the time that first year in Ithaca. I'd walk into our little apartment and find him stirring the only pot we owned in our galley kitchen.

"Lipstick!" Natalie yells as I walk out the door.

"Love you," is all I reply.

Her answering smile is so conflicted.

Outside, the breeze shakes the new leaves on the trees, and I'm grateful for Natalie's heavy hand with the hair spritz. Hank's just climbing out of his Jag. "There she is," he says with his homecoming-king grin.

He's only half right, though, because I'm only half here. Even as I exchange pleasantries and slip into the passenger seat of his luxury car, my mind is on the spin cycle.

Handing over that recording to Detective Riley had gutted me. In fact, I threatened to erase it until she told me they wouldn't pursue Laura Peebles for any drug-related crimes.

"I already knew she was an addict," Riley told me. "She has a prior drug conviction."

"She's been through a lot," I'd said guiltily.

But ultimately, I'd handed the recording over. If someone killed Tim because of his investigation, I need the police to find him.

Now I'm sitting in a Jaguar beside the person with the most to lose if Laura's story becomes public. And I'm supposed to spend the evening smiling brightly and representing the good works of the Wincott Foundation. In a dress that Harrison stitched me into.

I pull a lipstick out of my bag and apply it, as Natalie would want me to.

"You look lovely tonight," Hank says as the car glides down another narrow West End street.

"Thank you," I say stiffly. "I'm ready to woo the historic preservationists of Portland."

He chuckles. "I appreciate that. I know you had a chaotic week."

You don't know the half of it, pal.

Or does he? Now that I've heard Laura's story, I realize how ugly things could get for the foundation. And he's the head of that organization. The records from all those adoptions are under his control.

I wonder if there were formal complaints against Marcus, or even financial settlements.

They brought me a dead baby.

I shiver.

"If the air is up too high, feel free to adjust it."

"I'm fine," I lie.

Luckily, the art museum is only a few minutes' drive away. Hank pulls up in front, where a valet opens my door.

Hank hands over the keys and looks up at the facade. "Okay, truth time. As an architect, how badly do you want to firebomb this place?"

The question takes me by surprise, and I snort out a laugh. "Pretty badly."

"Tragic, right?" He looks up and shakes his head at the awkward design. It's a big brick mass, with half-circle arches looping across the top and bottom. "I've never been sure if I'm supposed to see portholes or aqueducts."

"Bricks aren't cheap, so it's a pretty expensive eyesore. But it's still an important institution."

Hank chuckles. "You're always so careful with what you say."

Because I have to be. Unlike you. I turn my head and really study him for the first time tonight. As if a careful analysis of his strong jaw and close shave could tell me the truth about what I heard today.

It couldn't, and Hank, of course, is unaware of my turmoil. He's the same Hank I've always known—the gracious man guiding me through one of the arches and down toward the banquet hall. Tipping the coat-check woman and slipping my trench coat off my shoulders.

His hands are smooth. Not like a laborer's. Or a bass player's, for that matter.

But are they too smooth to fire a gun? Or to pass a bundle of cash to someone who'd pull the trigger for him?

I wonder what Hank's handwriting would look like in block letters with a black Sharpie.

"We need a drink," Hank says, oblivious to my riotous thoughts. "And then I need to track down the mayor and say hello."

Steering me toward one of the bars, he puts a hand lightly at the center of my back. I feel it like a brand and walk a little faster until he drops his hand. I just need to survive the next couple of hours with a smile pasted on my face. Then I can go home and hide under my quilt.

"Pick your poison," Hank says when we arrive at the bar.

"White wine," I blurt out. "Any kind."

This proves a mistake when he hands me an acidic Chardonnay that tastes like the inside of an oak barrel. Whatever. I'm not here to drink. I'm here because Hank holds my career in his hands, and I didn't feel I could say no.

Laura's words from only a couple of hours ago echo in my head. *You were expected to sit down and shut up.*

She was a scared girl of seventeen, and she didn't have a choice.

I do, though, and yet I'm still letting my good-girl complex rule me.

It's the only explanation for why I'm standing in this room, surrounded by the influential people of Portland when I'd rather be at home.

"There's the mayor," Hank says, cupping my elbow and angling me toward a cluster of people at the center of the room.

Somehow the good girl finds her plastic smile. I meet the mayor, a genial man in his fifties. He and Hank call each other by their first names. And Hank introduces me as "my brilliant architect, who's spearheading the restoration and construction of the Maritime Center."

"Terrible thing that happened on your property," the mayor says, a frown creasing his tanned forehead. "Terrible thing. I keep asking the chief of police when he's going to bring me some real news."

Hank nods, his expression troubled. "They'd better get this guy soon."

I take another sip of my oaky wine and try not to wince as I wonder whether Hank knew his uncle kept a dead baby in cold storage.

"How is the construction coming along?" the mayor asks.

I make small talk for a couple of minutes about the restoration and the West End neighborhood. And then Hank steers me onward to a business acquaintance. Another handshake. Another sip of wine. Hank's hand is at the small of my back, and it's a struggle not to squirm.

Anxiety begins to blur my senses. Hank introduces me to people who all look the same. I'm nodding along to the conversational patter of a man whose name I forgot the moment he pronounced it. His blue silk tie is peppered with white anchors. There's a lot of seafaring people in this room.

In fact, it's hard to say which had more influence on Portland, Maine—the Wincotts or the sea. I used to think that only one of those things was cold and terrifying. Tonight I'm not so sure.

Hank touches my arm to indicate who he wants to speak to next, and I grit my teeth. We come face-to-face with yet another couple, this one in their sixties. Rick and Caroline something. I paste on my professional smile.

Caroline has a surprisingly firm handshake, complete with a jingling charm bracelet. When I glance down at it, I freeze. Because I'm pretty sure one of those charms is of Saint Raymond.

Hank and Caroline launch into a discussion about somebody's new sailboat, while I sneak glances at Caroline's wrist. She talks with her hands, so the bracelet is always in motion. But I'm sure I saw the familiar image of the saint pressed in sterling.

They move off before I'm ready. I take a deep gulp of wine and track her silver-blond bob across the room. Hank's hand lands on the small of my back again, ready to steer me toward new conquests.

But I can't stand here and smile for one more minute. "Forgive me," I murmur, peeling away. He'll probably assume that I needed the ladies' room. I ditch my empty glass onto a tray and locate Caroline again. She and her husband are in line for the bar, so I beeline in that direction.

"Excuse me, Caroline?" I sidle next to her. "Can I ask you a question?"

Her eyes widen with curiosity. "Of course." She tells her husband which beer she wants, and steps out of the line with me.

"It's about your charm bracelet," I say apologetically. "I've seen one of the charms before, and I wonder if you can tell me what it means."

"Oh!" She lifts her wrist and spins the bracelet. "Of course! Which one? You know that's the whole point of charm bracelets, right?" She chuckles. "Explaining their significance to whoever will listen." She points at a charm shaped like a daisy, with a pearl in the middle. "My husband gave me this one after we named our daughter Daisy."

"That's beautiful. But it's this one that caught my eye." I lift Saint Raymond with a finger. "A friend of mine had the same one."

"Oh!" Her finger traces the oval shape in a way that suggests a lifetime of familiarity. "That's Saint Raymond, the patron saint of childbirth. I have it because I was born at the maternity home here in Portland. All the babies left with this charm."

"Oh." *Oh God.* "So it's a . . ." I hesitate. "Souvenir isn't the right word."

"Talisman." She smiles. "My mother always told me that it must be a very powerful luck charm, because she felt like the luckiest woman in the world when the lawyer called to tell her that I'd been born, and I was ready to come home." She smiles, but her eyes look suddenly wet. "I lost my mother last year."

"I'm so sorry for your loss," I say almost automatically. My mind is whirling. "That's quite a story. *All* the babies got a charm?"

"That's what she said. Although I met only one other person who had one. At a Christmas party once. She was just standing there by the punch bowl, and I gasped when I saw it on a chain around her neck. Is that how your friend wears theirs?"

"Yes," I lie. "But he's gone now, before I could ask him about it."

"Oh wow." She pats my hand, her bracelet jingling. "I'm sorry. I would have loved to meet him."

―――――――

"Hank, my man!" Someone steps behind my boss and slaps him on the back. A real slap. "Where you been? You missed my birthday."

He looks familiar, but I'm not sure if it's because I met him in high school or more recently.

"Deacon. Dude, I'm sorry." When Hank grins, he looks sixteen again. We could be standing in the courtyard of Chatham Prep after school. "I'm sure I missed a good time."

"Do a shot with me," the guy says without even a glance in my direction. "Come on, buddy. You owe me."

Hank has slightly better manners than his friend. "Deacon, I have to drive Rowan home later. Rowan, this is my irascible cousin, Deacon Wincott."

"Who knew there were so many Wincotts?" I say, extending my hand to shake.

"Oh, you have no idea." The guy laughs and shakes my hand without even making eye contact. "C'mon, call your driver, Hanky Panky. A couple of shots won't kill you."

Hanky Panky? *God.*

For a moment, I think Hank won't go for it. But then he pulls out his phone and sends a text. "All right. Bring a shot for Rowan, too."

"None for me," I say quickly. "I have work in the morning."

"He can drink yours, then," Hank's buffoon of a cousin says. "I already asked the bartender for a bottle of . . . oh, there he is." Deacon waves to a black-vested bartender, who hurries over with a bottle of vodka and a bunch of shot glasses.

When I decline a shot for the second time, Hank plucks a glass of wine for me off the full tray of a passing caterer.

I was only going to have one glass tonight, but suddenly that doesn't feel like enough, as Deacon Wincott launches into the story of a drunken night on Grandpa's boat.

I'm only half listening, until Deacon suddenly says, "Oh hell. Darth Vader on your six."

A hand clamps down on Hank's shoulder. And my boss gets a sour look on his face even before the newcomer speaks. "Shots, Henry? There comes a time when the drunken bachelor thing stops being cool and starts looking pathetic."

It's Hank's older brother, William Wincott the . . . fourth? Fifth? He's an inch taller than Hank, and slimmer, with darker hair and a hard mouth.

"Lucky for you," Hank says, "having that stick up your ass actually looks better with age, bro. You've finally grown into your dry personality."

Deacon honks out a laugh, but William looks stormy. For a half second I wonder if he'll haul off and punch his younger brother. But then a woman appears at William's side. She's a tall woman with the kind of complexion that could only be called "porcelain," in a gorgeous floor-length gown. His wife, I think. Cecilia Wincott.

"Ooh, vodka," she says. "Deal me in." Then she puts a hand on Hank's sleeve. "When am I getting a tour of the mansion renovation?"

"Absolutely," her husband snaps. "Maybe he'll throw an opening gala for his vanity project, and we'll do more shots in the parlor that costs a few million over budget."

"For fuck's sake," Hank says tightly.

"Should have sold the place and let some developer turn it into condos," says William with a bitter laugh.

"What an interesting take," I hear myself say. "Especially at an event for the Historical Commission." And when heads swivel, I hold my hand out to William. "Hi, we haven't properly met. I'm—"

"I know who you are," William says, turning to fix his chilly gaze on me. "The architect who has cheap taste in men and expensive taste in fixtures."

"Enough," Hank snaps, grabbing his brother's biceps and tugging him away.

The three of us are left standing awkwardly together, and Cecilia Wincott grasps my hand—still held out in greeting—and shakes it. "Sorry about that," she says. "They make Thanksgiving fun, too. I'm Cecilia."

"Rowan," I say, swallowing my shock. "I'm the architect at the mansion. You can stop by for a tour anytime."

"I'd love to," she says, even as Hank and William hiss at each other from a few feet away.

I take another gulp of wine, and realize the glass is half gone already. I don't even know how it happened.

44

ROWAN

Hank's mood never recovers. By ten p.m., I'm tipsy, but he's officially drunk. And as Natalie would say, I'm *so over* this party. At least they fed me dinner. I ate every bite, including the appetizer, the slightly over-cooked steak and sides, and a tiny cheesecake they served for dessert.

When Hank finally decides that it's time to leave, we fetch my coat and step outside, where it's now dark and rainy.

"I really can take an Uber," I offer as the wind whips the lapels of my jacket around. "It's no problem."

"That'll take forever," Hank says, pronouncing his words carefully. "And there's my guy already."

Hank's Jaguar glides into view and halts at the curb. An older gentle-man gets out. "Ready, sir?"

I march to the car, open the back door, and slide in.

To my dismay, Hank slides in beside me.

"Home, then?" the driver asks mildly.

"Two stops if you wouldn't mind," I say quickly. "I'm on Spruce Street, number fifty. Near Clark. It's just a few minutes from here."

"Of course, miss."

I sit back and try to relax. It's not that I'm afraid Hank will murder me in his Jag in front of a witness. I'm just exhausted, and I have so many questions without answers.

Without warning, Hank puts his hand on my bare knee. "Can I ask you a question?"

My skin crawls, and surprise makes me slow to reply. "Um, sure."

"How mad is Beatrice?"

"What?" I barely process the question, because his palm is still on my knee.

"I told her she wasn't a good candidate." He rests his head drunkenly against the seat's back.

"Oh, the director job." In what I hope is an unobtrusive maneuver, I cross my legs, and his hand slides off. "She's . . . not happy," I say brilliantly. "Because she knows she's got a lot of skills that the job needs."

"It's not a matter of skills," he says.

Tell me something I don't know. "That doesn't make her feel better," I point out, "when she clearly cares so much about the mission."

"She's very loyal to the family." His careful diction makes me wonder if he's had a lot of practice trying to sound sober. "But loyalty only goes so far. You've also got to have the connections. You have to make it rain money."

"Right," I agree. "But maybe you'll find something else for Beatrice. Director of Programming? You could lose her, you know."

"Lose her?" He laughs. "Never."

God, the arrogance in this family.

"I'm sorry my brother was a tool to you," Hank says, as if reading my mind. "He's like that to everyone, in case that helps."

"Can I ask what his issue is? Does he hate the mansion?"

Hank goes silent, and as the moment stretches out, I wonder if I should have kept my mouth closed. "He likes to play the martyr," he says eventually. "Any bad PR for the family makes him cranky."

Cranky is an understatement.

"He thinks it's bad taste to draw any kind of attention. That we shouldn't show off our family's two hundred years of history in Portland. It might make it harder to fly under the radar when he's laying off American factory workers or whatever he's up to this week."

"But you think it's worth it," I press. "To burnish the family name? Maybe for political reasons?" My pulse kicks into a higher gear as I wait to hear what he'll say. I'd really like to know which of the Wincotts thinks the family has the most to hide, especially where the mansion is concerned.

"Yeah, sometimes it's useful to remind the people of our fine state that Maine was built on the shipping industry, and that my family did a lot of the building." He chuckles to himself. "I'm saddled with my shitty family, so I might as well get a few perks of the legacy."

"Right," I say slowly. "The mansion is a jewel, and you wouldn't be the first Wincott to show it off."

"Did you know that Maine was a dry state when Amos built the house?" he asks. "And did you also notice the big wine cellar in the basement? There's a reason his parties were popular. The Wincotts have always been hypocrites."

"Have they?" I ask carefully. "Until Marcus Wincott painted over the wine-swilling gods on the walls. Did you know your uncle well?"

"My *great*-uncle," he corrects. "And no, I don't remember much about him. He was the bachelor uncle at the Thanksgiving table. Liked his scotch. As if I should talk, right?" He laughs.

"It's funny," I say, although nothing seems funny. "But your uncle really took the place in a new direction. Most old mansions don't have a birthing table. And an incubator and forceps and graffiti on the wall, saying, *Help me. I want out.*"

His head swings in my direction. "Graffiti? Where?"

"It's in a closet. The conservator found it."

"Weird." Hank shrugs but doesn't say anything more.

If Hank knows what happened at the Magdalene Home, he isn't going to confide in me.

The driver pulls up in front of my house and kills the engine. "Spruce Street," he announces.

"Thank you," I say, popping open the door before anyone can consider helping me out.

It doesn't work. Hank exits his side of the car at the same time I exit mine.

I really don't need him to walk me to the door, even if I might have welcomed the gesture a week ago, when I was still imagining a murderer in a ski mask hiding in the shrubberies.

Now I'm wondering whether the murderer owns a Jaguar.

The rain has turned to mist. I head up the walk, fishing out my key. Hank is right on my heels. "Cute house," he says, stepping up onto the porch. "Did you renovate it yourself?"

"Of course."

His grin is a little broader than necessary. "Hey—thanks for coming out with me tonight, Rowan. I appreciate it."

"My pleasure," I lie.

It's time for his smile to dim, but it doesn't. My wariness flares.

He says, "Tell me this—how come we never dated in high school?"

I try to laugh it off. "Because you were cool, and I wasn't?" *And please get off my porch.*

I lift my keys, but he's leaning against the doorframe, blocking my way.

"Rowan," he says slowly, and my stomach drops. "You are cool. You're one of the cool kids. Maybe we should see more of each other."

I don't answer right away because I'm trying to think of a nice way to say "That's the worst idea I've ever heard in my life." And the hesitation costs me. He lifts a hand to cup my face. And then he plants a wet kiss on my mouth.

I freeze, even though my mind screams *Run!*

The porch light flashes on. Blindingly.

Startled, Hank jerks back, lifting a hand to shield his eyes against the glare. "Jesus."

Inside the house, Lickie lets out a warning *woof.* And then, after a beat, another one.

I finally find my voice. "Hey! I have to call it a night. I need to get in there. Let the dog out. You know. And your driver is waiting." I'm babbling, but it works.

"Shit, okay." He's still wincing against the light, but he turns toward his Jaguar like he's forgotten it's even there. "Another time. You have a good night."

The moment he moves, I slip the key into the lock and disengage the deadbolt. I'm inside the house faster than you can say *worst night ever.*

I close the door, lock it behind me, and lean against it. And there's Harrison, feeding Lickie a piece of . . .

"Is that *cheese*? She's not supposed to get table food."

"But she's such a good girl," he says maddeningly.

I use my forearm to wipe off my mouth. "Was that you? Did you just flip on the porch light?"

"Sure. Awful dark out." He shrugs.

I squint at him while my heart does calisthenics in my chest. What did he see? "Is Natalie home?"

"Upstairs. Watching a movie with a friend. Some girl named Tessa who's sixteen going on thirty-six."

I've had the exact same thought about Tessa many times. But that isn't what we need to talk about. "Look, I learned something tonight. You know that silver saint medallion? The one that was your mother's?"

"Sure. Natalie has it now." He strokes Lickie's head absently. "She showed it to me. And she told me about the one they found in Kovak's car."

"Right. And that was a shock. But there was a woman at this event tonight who *also* had one. When I asked her about it, she told me it was a gift to babies born at the mansion."

He frowns. "That's weird?. But I wasn't born there. My birth certificate has the name of a hospital on it."

"Are you sure? Can I see?"

He studies me for a beat with solemn gray eyes. "Sure, Ro. Whatever you need." He turns around and heads for the den, Lickie on his heels, as if she's his dog. Traitor.

I take off my coat and follow them both into the room. The first thing I notice is a Shop-Vac—the one I usually keep in the basement. And the second thing I notice is that lots of old paint has been scraped and sanded off the woodwork. "Whoa. What are you doing?"

"Finding my birth certificate." He's sorting through an old shoebox that appears to hold his personal documents.

"No, I mean in here."

He looks up. "You said you were trying to remove the paint and wallpaper in here. If I rent a steamer, I could get the wallpaper off in a day."

I blink. "You don't have to do that."

"Least I can do," he mutters. "Now where the hell is . . . ah." He pulls a manila envelope out of the box and flips it open. "Here we go." He hands me a birth certificate.

George Harrison Jones. Born June 22, 1982, 10:25 a.m. at Mercy Hospital, Portland, Maine.

I read the details twice. His mother—who obviously loved the

Beatles—listed her own name. But on the line for the father, someone has typed UNKNOWN in capital letters. Harsh.

"Satisfied?" he asks.

"Sorry." I let out a sigh. "Nothing makes sense."

"Rowan?" he asks quietly. "Are you okay? You seem really stressed."

"Yeah. That was the longest night of my adult life. And I work for a man who may or may not be covering up a baby-selling scandal."

He takes the birth certificate out of my hand, puts it away, and sits on the futon. "I think you'd better explain." He pats the spot beside him.

———————

"So . . ." Harrison pinches the bridge of his nose. "You think it's possible that Hank Wincott is a killer? Because he wanted to shut Tim up?"

"Hank, or his asshole of a brother. Think about it—Hank runs the same foundation that his great-uncle used to run. And he's positioning himself to run for Senate. Meanwhile, somewhere in the books and records of his charity are all these adoptions . . ."

"And some of them were coerced."

"Right. There could be a dozen more women like Laura. The Wincotts ran that maternity home for, what? Thirty years? More, actually. It opened in the fifties, before closing in the late eighties or early nineties."

Harrison strokes his beard. He's always been the kind of person who thinks before he speaks, while I'm sitting here on the sofa in my dress, practically vibrating with anxiety. "It's not just the bad adoptions that are rotten in this story. Laura said he was cruel to those girls. He liked punishing them. He might have been molesting them. If Hank knows about *any* of it, then he's up to his neck in scandal."

"Okay, I can see it." He picks up a pair of scissors off the side table. "You want a cup of soup?"

"What?"

"If I snip the thread at the back of your dress, you can put on comfortable clothes and have a cup of tomato soup. Your call."

"Oh." Am I stubborn enough to refuse the best soup in the world? Apparently not. "Yes, please."

His smile is so quick that I almost miss it. "Then turn around."

His voice is low and steady, and I find myself doing exactly as he asks. I'm too tired to find that irritating.

"Hold still."

One of his roughened hands lands on my bare shoulder, and I try not to shiver. But he's so close I can feel the gentle exhale of his breath on my neck as the scissors snip the stitches he made. Goose bumps rise on my skin as he unzips my dress a couple of crucial inches. The sound of the zipper's teeth and the drag of his fingers against my bare skin make me close my eyes.

"All set," he whispers, the words vibrating inside my chest.

I pop off the futon without a word. Upstairs, I change into sweatpants and an old T-shirt, and head to the bathroom to wipe off my makeup. From behind Natty's closed door, I hear the shrieks of two teenage girls laughing.

I return downstairs to find Harrison standing in my kitchen, looking like he belongs in it. Maybe this is his strategy. To ingratiate himself with my daughter and lull me into submission with soup. And also by looking as hot at forty-two as he did at twenty-two.

Men. It's not fair.

"Here," he says, putting a bowl of soup onto the table. "We put a dent in the crackers, but I saved you a few." After I sit, he sets down a saucer with four toasty-looking crackers on it.

I pull the bowl toward me, dip in the spoon, and take a sip. "Wow. Good as ever."

"Glad you still like it." He's smart enough not to look smug, and this solidifies my belief that he's playing the long game.

"So tell me this—why do you think your mother had that medallion? You said she worked at the mansion when you were little. That's the early eighties. The maternity home was still open then."

"What if she just stole it? Maybe there was a stash of them in the office."

"Maybe," I concede. "You don't know what she did there?"

"No idea. But she was only nineteen when I was born. Whatever the job was, it had to be something pretty basic. Cleaning. Food prep. Laundry. Those were the kinds of jobs she always had."

"Do you remember ever going there with her?"

He shakes his head.

"She was so young," I say slowly. "What if *she* was born at the mansion?"

Another shake of his head. "She was born in Canada. Moved here when she was a toddler."

"Oh right. I wish we knew other people who worked there at the same time. Somebody might remember her."

"But Ro." Harrison pins me with a gray-eyed glare. "This isn't your mystery to solve. If you really think Hank Wincott is violent, and hell-bent on keeping this shit buried, then maybe you should let him. Can't forget that warning someone sent you."

"I mean, obviously, this is a job for the police. But I want them to have all the information." *So they leave you and me alone.*

He reaches across the table and covers my hand with his. "Just watch yourself. Would Hank have any reason to believe you're a threat—that you've already seen too many of his family skeletons?"

My heart thumps against my chest. Because not an hour ago I asked Hank about Marcus Wincott. "I'll be careful."

"Natalie needs you," he whispers.

"I know," I whisper back, getting trapped in the tractor beam of his serious gaze.

We're having a staring contest. And neither of us can figure out who's going to break first.

He does, as it turns out. He stands up and takes my now-empty soup bowl over to the sink, rinses it, and puts it in the dishwasher.

The cat slides her body between his ankles, and after he dries his hands, he scoops her up into a football hold.

"Thank you for the soup," I say as he turns to leave the kitchen.

He stops beside me, and I wait for him to say something. Instead, he bends down and kisses me gently on the forehead. It's a quick press of warmth and whiskers.

He's left the kitchen by the time I realize I'm holding my breath.

45

WEDNESDAY

My sleep is filled with confusing dreams—I can't figure out exactly where I am and I've lost the map. When I finally see another person, it's a man with his back to me. I want to ask directions, but I'm afraid of him.

Excuse me, sir?

He turns around, and it's Tim. His face is bloody and terrifying. And he's holding what looks like a swaddled baby. But it isn't moving.

He takes a staggering step toward me, and I wake in a sweaty panic.

I glance at the clock. Seven, and the house is quiet. I tiptoe downstairs and find Harrison seated in the kitchen, his chair sandwiched between the cat and dog.

"Natalie's still asleep?" he asks, looking up. "I don't think her friend left last night."

"You probably won't see them until noon." I find a coffee mug and pour myself a cup. "School's over. They're supposed to be looking for jobs."

"Not sure that's going well," he says. "What happens if she can't find one?"

"She'd *better* find one. It's that or volunteer work. This is a hill I'm willing to die on."

He looks amused. "Want an egg? I could whip something up."

"No time," I lie.

But I wish I never had to go back to the mansion.

———

With no meetings scheduled, I spend the morning at my desk. Today's task is a redesign for the third-floor railing. Replacing a large section of the banister—and all the balusters on the third floor—won't be cheap, but if I attempt a revamp of the existing pieces, the smooth line of the staircase will be ruined.

It's difficult to care and impossible to concentrate. Beatrice is on a call, chattering away with someone about furniture delivery times. Meanwhile, Hank is blowing up my phone with texts.

Hank: Hey, got a minute? I want to apologize for last night.

I don't respond, because I'm not in the mood for that phone call. Fifteen minutes later he tries again.

Hank: Rowan? Can I call you? I'm really sorry.

Am I supposed to be grateful that he's sorry? Wincott men seem prone to taking what they want without asking. The more I know about them, the more Poseidon seems like a worthy choice for the family mascot.

Now he wants to apologize, because I'm his architect and we have to maintain a professional relationship.

But the girls who once lived in this house weren't so lucky.

I ignore Hank's second message, too, but his next gambit is a little more straightforward.

Hank: Can we reschedule the budget meeting for tomorrow at one? I'll come to your office, or we can meet wherever makes you most comfortable. My deepest apologies for my behavior last night.

A response is necessary, because that damn meeting is essential to the next phase of my work.

Rowan: Don't worry about last night. No harm done. One p.m. works.

I hesitate on the location question. I don't really want to be alone with Hank. But if he's sober in the middle of the day, then I should have nothing to worry about, right? And I don't want to discuss a multimillion-dollar budget at the coffee shop.

Rowan: My office is fine. See you then.

That done, I put my head in my hands and let out a nearly silent groan. Stupid Hank. His drunken kiss isn't even in the top five of my biggest issues right now. I keep picturing Laura Peebles clutching her mug of tea, telling me that story of how Marcus Wincott handcuffed a girl to a chair.

I'm not stupid, you know. They brought me a dead baby. He was so cold.

That happened right here in this building. I believe her, but I don't think Detective Riley was convinced. "That's a wild story," Riley said after listening to the recording. "Is there a morgue in the mansion?"

I had to tell her no.

"Rowan?"

I look up to find Beatrice watching me. "I was just about to ask if you're okay, but then I remembered that you hate that." She gives a tired smile. Actually, it's a very tired smile. She looks more haggard than I've ever seen her. "How'd last night go at the thing with Hank?"

"Fine." I'm never telling her the truth. Not about the drunken kiss, and not about the way Hank asked me about her. "The speeches were too long. And I cut myself off after three glasses of wine to be a professional. But three felt insufficient."

She laughs. "Been there. Was this one at the art museum? Or in that design studio? That place feels like a basement dungeon."

"The art museum," I murmur. But my brain snags on *basement dungeon*. "Hey, Beatrice? Do you remember what was in the basement? Before we started the demo?"

She blinks at the non sequitur. "Bunch of old metal furniture. Why?"

That's what I remember, too—metal baby cribs and folding chairs. Plus, another creepy old birthing table with stirrups at the ready. I rub my eyes, forgetting how much concealer I'd applied. "I was just trying to remember what all was down there. Like"—I grasp for an excuse—"hopefully, an old section of the third-floor banister?" I push back from my desk. "Maybe I'll take a look and jog my memory."

Zombielike, I walk out of the room. I turn toward the back of the mansion and head for the door to the servants' quarters.

"Rowan, hold up." Beatrice is on my heels. "It's locked."

"Oh." I wait for her to catch up. "Thank you."

"No problem," she says, going ahead of me with her giant key ring.

In the stairwell, we head down to the left. The first turn of the stairs is well lit. But then we reach an old-looking arched door that predates all the mansion's nineteenth-century finery. It's a rare glimpse into the earliest section of the house.

Beatrice flips through her keys and locates the one that fits the old door. It swings open, and she takes a step down, feeling around in the dark for the light switch.

Even when she flips it on, the light is barely adequate. "Watch your step." I don't want her turning an ankle just because I had a wild hair.

The stairs were hammered together from plywood several decades ago after the original staircase rotted. We've got a dehumidification system running down here now.

It still has that scary-old-basement smell, though. And as I descend into the gloom, the air temperature drops.

"So . . . what are we looking for?" Beatrice asks as we reach the mottled concrete floor.

If I answer that question truthfully, she'll think I've lost my mind. "The first time we were down here, all the furniture was at this end." I point toward the front of the house. "Metal bed frames and baby cribs. Rusty folding chairs."

"And that big old incubator."

"Right. But that was on this side." I turn my body toward the back of the house, where the shadows are deepest. My memory is visual, which is why I need to stand here, taking in the space again.

Suddenly I'm sure I saw an old chest freezer down here. Gray. Boxy. I can picture its shape against the wall. Edging in that direction, I let my eyes adjust to the gloom. Freezers need electricity. And, yeah, there's an electrical conduit running along the wall, with an outlet about knee height.

There, on the wall a few feet away from the outlet, is a shadowy patch, freezer-shaped. My guess is that the freezer's coils had caused condensation on the wall behind it, encouraging mold to darken the surface.

I lean down and rub my finger against the wall's rocky surface. Dark, powdery mildew comes away on my finger.

"There's a reason this room isn't on the new floor plan," Beatrice points out. "What are you looking at?"

"Do you remember a freezer?" I ask slowly. "I think I do."

Beatrice squints at me a moment before shrugging.

"It was big," I say, indicating the size. "And yet there was another freezer upstairs in the galley. A walk-in. Why would they need two?"

"No idea." She shakes her head. "There were a lot of people living here during the sixties and seventies. You'd need a lot of food storage?"

They said they brought him from the morgue.

I turn once more in a slow circle, picturing the room as it was the first time I saw it, before everything was cleared out. The birthing table shoved up against the incubator. The old furniture crowded together.

Scrap metal fetches a nice price, so Beatrice gave the moving contract to a scrap company. Workmen came to carry everything out via a pair of bulkhead doors—like in *The Wizard of Oz.*

I inhale sharply.

"What?" Beatrice asks.

"The bill of sale. Can I see it? From the scrap company?"

Before she can answer, there's a loud *bang* at the top of the stairs.

We both jump practically out of our skins, because it's deafening. And then I realize that the door at the top of the stairs has slammed shut.

Beatrice glares up at it, rubbing her arms. "Don't even say it. I don't want to hear it."

"Fine." I let out a nervous laugh. "That was definitely just a breeze. Because ghosts aren't real."

"You don't think . . ."

I know what she's asking, and I don't want to say it aloud, either. *Are we locked in this basement?* My mind flashes to an image of my phone, which I'd stupidly left on my desk.

"I guess I'm finished down here," I say, ignoring the hum in my ears.

Beatrice climbs the stairs, with me on her heels. I hold my breath as she reaches for the doorknob. It turns in her hand, and she pushes the door open.

I am full of relief as I flip off the light switch and leave the basement.

Back in our office, I wait impatiently as Beatrice hunts through her files.

"Here," she says eventually.

She passes me two stapled sheets of paper, and I scan the contents. The scrap was weighed, the inventory detailed. My finger drags down the list until I find the heaviest object on the list: *Chest freezer, 200 lbs.*

I snap a picture of the list with my phone.

"Okay, what is the deal?" Beatrice asks. "Did something happen last night? Why are you interested in an old freezer? You're acting so strange. Did Hank do something?"

Shit. I wait a beat. "No. Hank was . . . no big deal."

Her eyes widen.

I drop the bill of sale on my desk and sink back into my chair, resting my head in my hands. "I understand how loyal you are to the Wincotts, and I admire that. So if I heard a freaky story about the mansion, I'm not sure you'd want to hear it. Let's just go get lunch and move on."

She's quiet for a second. Then she gets up and crosses to the door and closes it before sitting down across from me. "Rowan," she says, her voice almost a whisper. "My loyalty to the family is based on a lot of things. History. Gratitude. But also trust. I'm well aware that not every Wincott lives up to the family name. So if you know a reason why I shouldn't trust my boss, then I would like to know."

Discomfort hums through me. Beatrice knows more about the Wincotts than I ever will. I don't trust Hank at all, and I can't share Laura's story. Even if I could, there's no way I could prove it. That chest freezer might have only held extra hamburger meat.

"I've discovered a few things about what Tim was up to before he was murdered," I say quietly. "He was researching the maternity home. He was born here in this building, and his adoption seems to have been . . . irregular. Coerced."

"Jesus." She swallows audibly. "You're serious?"

"Very. And if that happened to Tim, then it probably happened to other people. The maternity home was open for more than thirty years. All those adoptions. And potentially a huge cover-up."

She takes a slow breath. "Can you prove it? The family would lose their minds."

"No, I can't. But it's troubling me a great deal. If Tim's death had anything to do with his investigation, I can't just sit at my desk and pretend everything is fine. Especially if the police are trying to pin it on my child's father." *Or me.*

"Well . . ." She fiddles with the bracelet she's wearing. "What if I could help? I might be able to access Tim's adoption record."

"*Oh*," I breathe. "That could be really helpful. But what about other records? It would be great to know more about whoever worked here in the eighties. And, uh, one employee in particular."

She frowns, twisting her bracelet and giving me a serious, blue-eyed frown. "I don't know how far back that stuff has been digitized. But I guess I can poke around and see." She grabs a pad of sticky notes. "Who's the employee?"

"Betsy Jones."

She tosses the pad aside. "Well, that's easy enough to remember. I'll try, okay? But if I found something—what would you do with it? How far are you willing to take this?"

"I'm not sure," I admit. "I'm just trying to make peace with the work we're doing here. I want to know if the Wincotts have a clue about the bad adoptions."

Beatrice blows out a breath. "I've basically given my life to this family. I've always felt that was a worthy investment. Really hope I wasn't wrong."

"I hope so, too."

"Yeah. But at the same time, Marcus Wincott is dead. You may never get your answers. And Hank would *not* appreciate us digging into this."

I think of Hank last night, looming over me on the front porch. His entitled smile. And this job suddenly feels a lot less valuable. "Let's just make sure he doesn't find out."

46

CORALIE

About one day after Coralie accepted her pregnancy as a thing that's really happening, her breasts tripled in size.

At least it felt that way.

Consequently, she did some bra shopping last night after work, and what's the point of a new bra if it's not a little sexy? And what's the point of sexy if nobody notices? She's paired the new, lacy bra with a pink blouse that's *slightly* see-through. And as she dressed this morning, she'd wondered how long it would take her boss to notice.

About two seconds, apparently. When he enters the office midmorning, his eyes go immediately to her bustline.

"Hello, Mr. Wincott," she says silkily. "How was your breakfast meeting?"

"Long," he says gruffly, his eyes lingering another moment on her chest, before he turns his gaze to the IT guy leaning over the tangle of cords in the corner.

Mr. Wincott makes a face, and Coralie smiles sweetly.

"Coffee ready?" he asks.

"Almost." It isn't even a lie.

"Bring me one in ten?"

"Of course."

She waits until the techie leaves and then fixes Mr. Wincott a cup of coffee. After carrying it into his office, she shuts the door behind herself.

He looks up. Smiles hotly.

The weird thing is that she sometimes enjoys moments like this, with his gaze focused like a laser on her body. She moves languidly toward him, hips swaying.

He's *so* much older than she is. She's not attracted to him in the traditional sense. Still. That hungry look in his eye makes her feel special. It's like a drug sometimes.

There must be something seriously wrong with her.

"Is he gone?" The boss waves in the general direction of the outer office.

"Gone," she says, and he smiles. "He was here to fix your broken fax machine."

"I think he was here to admire your tits."

"They are spectacular." She sets the Wedgwood cup and saucer on the desk. Then she circles the desk and slides into his lap.

"*Hello*," he says, reaching around to cup her breasts. They're tender, but she doesn't complain. "This blouse is sheer, you realize."

"Is it?"

He chuckles, sliding his hand to her belly and holding it there.

She stops breathing. Her pregnancy seems very real when he does this. There are three of them in this chair right now.

"Well? Have you chosen a name? It better be a good Christian name."

She frowns, because he can't see her face. "You mean like Mary?"

"That's only one of many. See that book? With the gold spine?" He points across the room at one of the built-in bookshelves. "Go fetch it. I want to show you something."

She obeys, giving him a look at her backside on her way to fetch the book. When she returns, he tucks her into his lap and opens the cover. It creaks with age.

There's a bookplate on the inside flap. *From the library of Marcus Wincott*, it reads.

"This is a hagiography," he says. "A book of saints. Borrow it, and you'll find all the names. There's Catherine. Clare. Even Rose is a saint's name."

"Okay." She flips the book open to a random page, and the first thing she sees is a dark woodcut image. *The Martyrdom of Saint Bartholomew*. A man is shown in the midst of being flayed alive. He's bound to a frame, his skin being peeled off by his executioners, who wear grim expressions of determination. But St. Bartholomew's face is turned upward, his eyes reflecting a mixture of pain and transcendent focus.

Such a dark place to search for baby names. And when she'd told Mr. Wincott they were more alike than different, it was really true.

He's already forgotten about the book, though. His fingers are stroking her tummy. She's noticed that he's stopped referring to her as his little sinner. His touch is still sexual, but it's more possessive, with a side of tenderness that surprises her.

Those fingers dip under her skirt.

"Stand up. Put your hands on the desk," he says quietly.

She hurries to comply.

"Good girl," he says. "Good girl."

47

NATALIE

"Which hours are you available to work?" asks Cal Baxter, the owner of Docksiders.

"Doesn't matter," she admits. Her summer vacation isn't exactly packed. "I mean, it's summer break. And I can bike here whenever."

After two days, Tessa has already bailed on their job hunt. She's going to take an online college course instead, so she'll still have something to brag about on college applications. Her parents don't care that much, and Natalie wishes her mother had the same attitude.

As if.

Mr. Baxter grins. "Working at Docksiders on summer break—it's practically a family tradition at this point, yeah?"

"Yeah," she agrees, even though she hasn't discussed this with her mother yet. Or her father. He's back in the kitchen right now, prepping for the lunch rush.

That's how she got this idea. Her dad is always saying how strapped for help Mr. Baxter is, especially in the summer. And the guy hasn't even asked her to fill out an application. They're just sitting at the deserted bar drinking seltzer with lemon and talking.

"All right, tell ya what," he says, smacking his lips. "You'll come in at four today and learn to be an expediter. Thursdays aren't as crazy as a weekend night. Then tomorrow, come in at eleven and we'll also train you to hostess. I'll look at next week's schedule and see where the gaps are, okay? And we'll either put you on the door, or you'll be running food out of the kitchen. I'm sure I can give you three or four shifts a week, no problem."

"That's great, Mr. Baxter," she says. "I'm in."

"Marilyn!" he yodels. "Bring me a W-4 and an I-9?"

"What?" a voice calls from somewhere nearby. "Your legs broken? Come and get it yourself. Or send your latest victim in here."

"I'll go," Natalie says, sliding off the stool. "Thank you for giving me a try."

"You're gonna do fine, honey. It's not rocket science. Ask Marilyn for a T-shirt. You got black shorts or a black skirt?"

"I'll figure something out," she says.

"Bet you will." He drains his soda. "How do you tell when you're old? It's when your employees' *kids* ask you for a job." He shakes his head. "See you at four, okay? Your dad can help train you."

"See you then."

———————

She bikes home with two Docksiders T-shirts over the handlebars.

"Are you sure about this? You're going to smell like fried fish," her father had warned her when she went back to the kitchen to tell him.

"It's only for the summer," she'd pointed out. Embarrassment set in about one second later, because this is his full-time job. But he'd only smiled at her.

Working with him will be nice. And now her mom can't nag her to find a job anymore, because she found one.

At home, she pulls the bike into the garage. She heads for the kitchen door and is surprised to find it standing open. "Mom?" she calls, nudging the door the rest of the way with her toe. Her mother must have stopped home for lunch.

No answer.

She goes inside and finds the kitchen empty. Something feels off. Her heart begins to pound.

But then Lickie comes through the doorway, tail wagging, and the cat is right on her heels.

"Hi," she says, sinking down to her knees. "Hi, girls." She opens her arms and Lickie invades her personal space, snuffling into her hairline and giving her forehead a brief, polite lick. Meanwhile, the cat makes a silent inspection of her knee before slinking away.

Her heart rate drops back into the normal range. After showing Lickie some love, she kicks off her sandals and carries the T-shirts into the living room, dropping them on the couch. "Mom?" she calls again.

Silence.

Okay, that's weird. So it must have been Natalie herself who left the door open? Big yikes. Luckily, her mom never has to know.

Natalie climbs over the back of the couch because it's faster than walking around. She plunks down and opens her phone to see what everyone is up to. As she props her feet on the coffee table, she notices something unfamiliar. A wallet in the center of the table. It's blue and orange and made out of some kind of shiny material like you'd find on a heavy-duty shopping tote.

It must belong to her dad, but it doesn't look like his style. She sits forward and flips the wallet open. The first thing she sees is a driver's license. From New York State. The name on the license is Timothy E. Kovak.

She sits back quickly, the wallet flopping closed. She tries to think of a reasonable explanation for why the hell it's sitting on the coffee table in her living room, but there just isn't one.

She picks up her phone and calls her mom.

"Natalie?" Her mother answers on the first ring. "Is something wrong?"

"I just got home, and the door was open. Then I found Tim's wallet on our coffee table."

"You . . . what?"

"Tim's wallet. It's blue and orange. And it's sitting on the coffee table. His ID is inside."

There's a brief, shocked silence. "Are you home alone?"

"Well, yeah. Dad's at work."

"Get out of that house. Leash up the dog, go outside. I'm on my way."

"Okay?" She's struggling to catch up. "There's nobody here."

Or is there? Natalie springs to her feet and turns around, glancing up the staircase and then into her father's room. She seems to be alone. But her heart is pounding again.

"Go outside," her mother repeats. "And hang up, because I have to call the police now."

"Right," she says, her voice wavering. Her phone beeps to tell her the call has ended. "Lickie! Let's go outside."

The dog is instantly on her feet. Natalie leashes her with shaking hands. And then she walks the dog out the front door so quickly she doesn't even stop to find her shoes.

48
ROWAN

"You said the door was open," Detective Riley says. "How far open? How many inches?"

My daughter tries again to describe what she saw, while I rub my tired eyes.

We're standing in the front yard. I'd made it home in under ten minutes, and the first police cruiser pulled up at the same time.

"Ma'am, can we take a look around inside?" a uniformed officer asked.

I waved him inside and it's now dawning on me that I've given the cops carte blanche to search my house.

But at this point, I don't care. I want this fucker caught. I can't believe someone broke into my home in broad daylight. It's terrifying.

"And you're sure you locked the door when you left?" Riley asks a nervous-looking Natalie.

"I'm ninety percent sure," she says, her gaze everywhere but on me. "I mean, I don't *think* I'd leave it open. We've been locking up really tight, and I knew I was the only one home."

"Okay. And your mom was at work. Anyone else in the home? Maybe Harrison came by while you were gone, and then left the door open?" Riley poises her pen above her notebook.

"No. He couldn't have. I was at Docksiders applying for a job. And he was in the kitchen while I met with Mr. Baxter."

"You got a job at Docksiders?" I demand. "You're too young to work there. It's a *bar*."

"It's a fish restaurant," she fires back. "And you *told* me to get a job!"

How I hate this idea. But I'm not going to argue about it in front of the detective. "So you saw Harrison," I prompt.

"Yeah, he was back in the kitchen the whole time," she says. "Besides—

even if he had the wallet, which he didn't, why would he leave it on our coffee table? That doesn't make any sense."

She isn't wrong. But, as usual, Detective Riley doesn't share her thoughts on the matter. "What time did you leave, and what time did you get home?"

"Not sure exactly when I left," Natalie says with a shrug. "I couldn't have been gone more than an hour and a half. And I got home about three minutes before I called Mom. That was at"—Natalie whips out her phone and checks it—"twelve twenty."

"Tell me again what you did when you got home," Riley says.

For the third time, Natalie describes her journey from the garage to the kitchen in excruciating detail.

"And how did the dog act when you called her?" Riley asks.

Natalie purses her lips. "Normal," she says after a second. "She was happy to see me."

"I've always said she makes a terrible guard dog," I grumble.

Riley turns to me. "And where were you when you took your daughter's call?"

"At my desk in the mansion."

"Anyone see you leave?" she asks.

Oh, for fuck's sake. "I doubt it." Beatrice is off-site at a museum to meet their programming director. And I didn't chat with the art-restoration team. "Can't you check video footage from across the street?" I point at the house with the doorbell camera—the one that filmed Harrison knocking on our door. "Won't it show you who was here?"

"Of course, we'll try that," she says. "But I still have to ask about everyone's movements."

"Sure you do. Someone is terrorizing my family, and you think maybe it's me."

She doesn't even react. "I'll need to get fingerprints from Natalie so we can exclude her prints on the wallet."

"Is that okay with you, Natalie?" I ask tiredly.

"Sure," she says with a shrug. "But if this person is really trying to scare us, he probably isn't dumb enough to leave his fingerprints on the wallet."

"We'll just have to be sure," Riley says. "Let me get my scanner."

She trots off, and I pull my ringing phone out of my shoulder bag. It's Beatrice.

"Where are you?" she asks. "It's time for the budget meeting. Hank is at the mansion alone."

"Oh shit." My heart sinks. I'd forgotten all about the meeting. "Can you tell him that someone broke into my house? Natalie called me in a panic. I'm here with the police."

"Oh God. I'm so sorry. I'll call him back right now."

"Thank you."

"Keep me posted!"

We hang up, and I check my texts. There are three from Hank. All politely checking to see if he got the time right.

God, could the timing be any worse? I took the high road, and now he thinks I'm blowing him off.

Then again, there's no good time to be stalked at home by a killer.

The older detective, Fry, emerges from my house, the wallet in a baggie dangling from his hand. "Can I speak to you a moment?" he asks.

"Of course." I take this to mean that he doesn't want Natalie to hear, so I move a few paces away.

"There's no one inside except for a very friendly cat," he says. "That was our first concern."

"Thank you," I say numbly.

"Aside from the wallet, we didn't spot anything else that seems out of place," he says. "But of course, you'll know better than me."

"Okay. I'll be sure to look." I won't be able to *stop* looking. The idea that someone was in our home makes my skin crawl.

He holds up the baggie. "So what's your take? What was the point of leaving this in your home?"

"To scare me. Or incriminate me. And I'm scared, so I guess it worked."

His nod reveals nothing. "Any thoughts on who'd want to do that?"

"Somebody who heard about my trip to Laura Peebles's house with Detective Riley. Someone who saw me go into her house. Someone who needs to confuse you guys about this case . . ."

"Hmm," he says. "No signs of forced entry, though. Unless the door was left open, someone had a key to your home. Or maybe you or Harrison wanted to make it appear like the killer is terrorizing you."

I close my eyes for a brief second, needing a break from looking at his face. Then I open them again and stare him right in the eyes. "I don't know if you have children. But terrifying them with a dead man's possessions isn't great parenting. No sane person would do that."

"Ms. Gallagher," he says, "you already lied to us about why you went to the mansion the night Tim died. I have to consider the idea that you or Harrison are lying to me now."

A bright burst of panic washes over me.

"So," he says, "if you're suggesting that you always do the calm and rational thing, pardon me if I don't quite buy it. You keep telling us that you don't know a thing about Tim's death. But every new development in this case brings us back to your door."

I'm so upset that it's difficult to speak. "I did *not* shoot anyone. And I don't know who did. I'm just an easy target." *Because I made myself a goddamn easy target.*

"A target for who, though?"

"One of the Wincotts. They'd be at the top of my list." I bet Hank gets updates from the police department. Maybe he even knows I've spoken to Laura Peebles. "Or what about Tim's ex-wife? She knows where I live."

"We're in touch with all those people," he says slowly. "We're very thorough, and we're moving as fast as we can."

"Not fast enough," I snarl. "Not when you're still standing here suggesting I'd terrorize my own family just to get a little more of your super-fun attention."

His expression hardens. "I see. Take care of yourself, Ms. Gallagher. And make sure you lock your doors."

He walks off, and I'm shaking too hard to do anything but try to breathe.

Riley and my daughter join me a moment later. "We're all set," Riley says. "If you see anything at all that doesn't seem right, will you take a picture of it and call me?"

"Yes," I say automatically. But the truth is I'd think twice before calling the police. I'm so tired of being treated like a suspect. Or a crazy person.

"I'll ask patrol to make frequent trips down your block. And I'll look for any neighborhood footage showing someone approaching your house. But if they came through the backyard, it might be tricky. Your back fence is easy to jump."

"Yeah. Okay." There's a door into our garage from the rear yard, too.

"Hang in there, Rowan." She squeezes my upper arm.

"You're looking into the Peebles thing, right?" I ask before she can walk away.

"What Peebles thing?" my daughter pipes up. "Wait—did you talk to her?"

Crap. "Yes. She told us a sad story and insisted on privacy."

Natalie's eyes widen. "But did she know what happened to Tim?"

I shake my head.

"Will you give us a minute?" Riley asks my daughter.

Natalie makes a grumpy face. "We're going back inside," she says, meaning her and the dog.

"If you see anything weird . . ." I start to say.

"Yeah, I know. Don't touch it."

Riley waits until she walks away. "I'm working on the adoption history," Riley says. "But older documents take time and another court order."

"By all means, take your time," I snip. "Meanwhile, is it even safe for us to stay in this house?"

"Probably. We'll step up our surveillance. But leaving the wallet on the table is a cowardly display," Riley says. "It's what you do when you don't want a confrontation."

"Right. I just hope he doesn't change his mind about that."

49

After the police leave, Natalie and I search the house and find nothing. Lickie follows us from room to room, wagging her tail.

"Why didn't you take a bite out of him?" I ask my dog, ruffling the fur between her ears.

"Maybe she did," Natalie says. "That's why she looks so pleased with herself."

I wish.

"Let's eat something. I'm starved," my daughter says.

We troop down to the kitchen, where she opens the fridge. I eye the contents with suspicion. Nothing feels safe anymore.

"I have to be at work at four," Natalie says. "I'm training to be an expediter."

"At Docksiders," I repeat, because it still doesn't sit right with me.

"Yup."

My head gives a throb. "Why did it have to be there?"

"Family tradition." She snickers. "No—it was just easy. Cal Baxter didn't even make me fill out an application. And I'll get to work with Dad." She pulls the leftover tomato soup out of the fridge.

"Was it his idea?"

She shakes her head. "I didn't ask him first, because Cal has done him so many favors lately. But he also said how bad they need help, so . . . ?" She pulls two bowls out of the cabinet. "You want soup, right? It's *so* good."

I'm too tired to argue, and too emotionally drained to think about the ways Harrison is worming into our lives. "And you're *sure* he wasn't here when you left today, right?"

She frowns over her shoulder. "Of course I'm sure. He was in the Docksiders kitchen washing lettuce and cutting fries."

"Okay. Sorry. I had to ask."

———————

After our late lunch, I don't go back to work.

Natalie heads to Docksiders in a black denim skirt and Docksiders T-shirt. It's eerie. Like I'm looking at my younger self.

I warn her several times to be careful. "We have to lock the doors, no matter what."

She pulls a hurt face and mumbles that she *knows*. Then she leaves, disgruntled, and I'm alone in the quiet house, lying on the sofa and feeling vulnerable.

Zoe the cat has perched in the center of Lickie's dog bed, possibly to assert her dominance. So Lickie chooses to plop herself near the couch, where we both listen to the gentle creak of the clapboards expanding in the afternoon sun.

Beatrice texts, asking where I am and what happened.

I don't answer. I don't want to explain the break-in. And I don't want her talking to Hank about this.

He knows where I live, and he also knew I'd be at work today.

I take another lap around the house, scrutinizing everything in it. It doesn't help, because my imagination works overtime. *Was my closet door ajar like that?* Probably. Or maybe the cops opened it making sure nobody was in there. *Were those curtains open this morning? Or did an intruder do that? Is that where I set down my toothbrush?*

And so on.

I make myself sit down on the sofa again, even though I'm restless. I open the FriendFinder app and see Natalie's dot at Docksiders. At least I don't have to worry about her for a few hours.

My phone chimes with a new text, and I expect Beatrice again. But it's Harrison.

Harrison: I'm about to unlock the door and come in.

Barely a second after I read this, I hear his footfalls on the front porch. The door swings open, and the animals go wild with excitement.

"Ro?" he calls over Lickie's barking. Then he spots me on the couch. "Hey, are you okay?"

"Why? Is something else wrong?"

"No, baby." He locks the door behind him, gives Lickie a pat on the head, and sits down beside me. "It's my break, and I just wanted to make sure you're not freaking out."

"Shouldn't I be?" I make an exaggerated shrug. "Someone left Tim's wallet right here." I point at the table. "The way a cat leaves a dead mouse on your bed. And the police wonder if I did it. Or maybe you. Did they visit you?"

He shakes his head. "All they had to do was check the data for this." He lifts one leg and pulls up his pant leg to reveal the black device strapped around his ankle.

"*Oh.*" I'd forgotten all about that thing.

"Yeah." He drops his cuff. "That'll be the only time I'm grateful to be tagged like cattle. But I'm pissed off I wasn't here when someone walked into your house with a dead guy's wallet."

"Seriously," I grumble. "Could really have made yourself useful."

He flashes me a sudden smile. "Aw, Rowan. You must be losing your mind."

Part of me wants to bristle, because I *am* losing my mind. "Do you really want Natty working at Docksiders?"

Harrison passes a hand over his beard and lets out an awkward chuckle. "I don't know. Kind of like the idea of keeping an eye on her. Especially now. But she's so young. Seems like I was never that young."

I have to grudgingly admit that I don't hate the idea of him looking out for her. "She's going to forget the tartar sauce and the garnish. Be gentle."

He smiles, but then he puts his head in his hands. "Can't believe she found that wallet. Did you see it? Was it really his?"

"Yeah. It was."

"Shit." He's quiet for a moment. "Obviously, someone is trying to scare you. Or point a finger at me."

"Or me," I point out.

"You need cameras to monitor the house."

"Yeah, I realize that."

"I'll order them tonight," he says, straightening up. "With express shipping."

"No." It comes out a little sharp. "I'll do it."

"Okay. And you'll keep the doors locked?"

"Of *course* I will."

His smile is quick, but fleeting. "I'll walk the kid home tonight. Told her not to leave before me."

"Thank you." My shoulders drop a tiny fraction. The truth is that I want the help, even if it's from him. The idea of her biking home alone at midnight gives me the cold sweats. "If her shifts don't match up with yours, I could pick her up some nights."

"Or I'll bike home with her," he says. "I would just have to remember to let my probation officer know when I do that."

I take a moment to process what he's said. A snort of laughter bursts from my mouth. But then it happens again, and I cover my face to try to stop laughing.

"Rowan?" he demands, possibly because I seem deranged.

"Aren't we just the c—" I hiccup. "The cutest little family? You have to tip off your probation officer before picking up the kid"—I try to take a deep breath, but I shudder instead—"so that a murderer can't follow her home."

"What, like that's weird?"

I howl. My throat tightens from laughing, and the sensation feels almost like the sting of tears.

Because it is.

"Oh, Ro. Ro. Hey."

My eyes are suddenly fountains. I guess there's only so much stress you can take before the dam bursts.

"Hey, hey. Shh." Harrison scoots closer and pulls me in.

My forehead clunks against his shoulder, and I can't help it. I just sort of slide onto his chest and push my face into his Docksiders T-shirt. He smells like fry oil and sunshine and my carefree youth.

He wraps his arms around me and rests his chin on top of my head. "It's okay. It will all be okay."

"You don't know that," I mumble wetly.

"No, it will." He kisses the top of my head. "They'll find a print on that wallet. Or something. And this will all be over."

I lift my face and almost beg. *Promise me.* But I stop myself just in time. I'm too old to ask for promises.

Although now I'm gazing up at him at point-blank range. Close enough to see the fine lines at the corners of his eyes. Close enough to discern darker flecks in his gray irises.

And it's odd how familiar this feels. It used to be normal for us to be so close that I could feel his breath on my face. This was us. And some part of my consciousness still remembers.

Which is probably why I kiss him. It's just too easy—he's *right* there. All I have to do is tilt forward and lift my chin to find the firm warmth of his mouth.

For a split second, he goes completely still. Before I even have time to panic, his broad hands gather me in, and his mouth invites mine closer.

His kiss is like sliding underwater. All the noise in my head is suddenly muffled. The peace is just what I need. So when the kiss ends, another begins, and then another. I lose myself, and I want to be lost. I want to grip his biceps with both hands and feel his heartbeat against my chest.

He's strong and solid when I slide my hands down his chest and then up under his T-shirt. I need more of his warmth.

He catches my hands in one of his rough ones. "Rowan," he breathes. "Hey."

I blink up at him, my mind full of static fuzz.

"Honey." His eyes get sad. "You're upset and not thinking clearly. And I have to go back to work. I was only on my break, and Natalie is there."

"Oh. Shit. Of c-course," I stammer, my sluggish mind playing catch-up. "God, I'm sorry."

"Probably not as sorry as I am," he says, sliding me off his lap and onto the couch. He stands up with a sigh, then leans over to place another kiss on the top of my head. "You'll text me if you hear anything, right?"

"Yes," I say, dropping my face into my hands. I can't believe I just pawed him like a cat in heat. Hell, his *actual* cat is much more polite.

One broad hand lands on the back of my neck and squeezes. "Hang in there, baby. Just a little longer. I'm locking the door behind me."

"Thank you." It comes out muffled.

I don't even watch him leave. I listen for the sound of the deadbolt sliding back into place before I lift my head. I need to get a grip. I need to get my life back on track. Yet my heart is still racing, and my lips still chafing from beard burn.

People say you never forget your first love, but those people are liars. I'd forgotten all about how I turn into a drooling hormone whenever Harrison gets close to me.

And I'd *lunged* at him. Who does that? Someone whose house has just been broken into by a killer.

This has to stop. I need to figure out who's so angry at me. Hank? Hank's family?

Jules Kovak?

I grab my phone off the coffee table and scroll to my message thread with Jules. Where was *she* when all this went down? I tap on her avatar and initiate a call. No—that's not good enough. I stop and initiate a video call instead.

She actually answers, her face winking onto my screen a moment later. "Rowan? Hi. To what do I owe this pleasure?"

"Where are you?" I demand. All I can see behind her is a dim room. A home office, maybe.

"I'm in New York? Why?"

"Prove it. Show me the view out the window." I don't care if I sound crazy. I need to know who I can trust.

Jules doesn't argue. She carries her phone through a small apartment. The screen momentarily flashes white as she points it toward a window. Then the image stabilizes, and the bricks of a building across the street come into view. "I'm on the seventh floor. And—here—can you see the traffic on Ninth Avenue?"

She angles the phone down, and I see an oblique slice of a busy urban street. There's traffic, including an iconic yellow taxi.

"All right. Thank you." I sag against the sofa, because Jules really *is* in New York. And she probably didn't murder her ex-husband.

"Rowan, what's this about?"

"Someone broke into my house today and left Tim's wallet on the coffee table. With his license inside."

Her startled face comes back into view. "You're shitting me."

"I wish. Someone wants to scare me. Or make the police believe I have access to Tim's stolen things. Or prove Harrison does. I actually don't know what they wanted, but if they wanted to rattle me, it worked great."

"Wow. You must have really stepped in a steaming pile of shit. Who'd you piss off?"

"That's what I'm trying to figure out."

Her expression turns thoughtful. "By any chance have you been poking around in Tim's adoption?"

"Yes," I admit. "I have the birth mother's name, and I met her."

"Whoa." Her apartment becomes a dizzying blur as she trots back to her desk. "Who is she?"

"Not so fast. You told me that if I gave you the name, you'd give me everything you had."

Her gaze sharpens. "Fine. It's a deal. What's her name?"

"In a second. This is what I need from you—every name Tim asked you to search for. And anything you found about Harrison's mother. No holding back."

"Okay. But you met her? What was that like?"

I try to think what I can say without violating Laura's privacy. "She's in a lot of pain. If you try to talk to her, be gentle. She's fragile. And it's possible that the police are already talking to her."

"Interesting," Jules says almost gleefully. "If you've got the detectives' attention, maybe that's how you managed to piss someone off."

"Maybe." I rub my gritty eyes. "But how would the killer know?"

"The department has a lot of manpower on this murder. They do their best to keep everything quiet, but all you need is one guy who's willing to talk."

To Hank? I wonder.

"What's the birth mother like?" Jules asks. "What did she tell you?"

"Well . . ." *Poor Laura.* "She's had a rough time with Tim's death. They were only recently acquainted. They first met in February."

Rowan lets out a low whistle. "How'd that happen? Genetic test?"

"Yes. There was some trauma surrounding the adoption, and it sounds like the maternity home was a horrible place. Lots of shaming and mistreatment. You'll have to ask her yourself. She won't want to be interrogated, but she'd probably like to meet Tim's ex-wife."

"Sure. I can be gentle," Jules says with a shrug.

I'm not sure I believe her. She wears her relentless curiosity like perfume. "It sounded *bad*. And even if you can get her to talk to you, it will be hard work corroborating her story. Unless you got a whole bunch of those women in a room together."

"Well. That's what I do for a living. Track people down and get them to talk."

"She said they didn't use each other's last names. That's why I need everything Tim gave you. Right now, please."

She gives me an appraising glance before putting down her phone. All I can see is her ceiling, but I hear her clacking away on a keyboard. "What's your email, Rowan?"

I give her the address, and then there's more typing.

"Okay, sent."

Not willing to take her word for it, I find my laptop and open it on the coffee table. Sure enough, I have a new email from Jules Kovak with a lengthy list of names, some with more information than others. "How are these sorted?"

"That's part of the puzzle," she says. "Tim held his cards close. He told me almost nothing more than what you see here. But I've been searching the shit out of this list since he died, and I have some theories."

"Let's hear them."

"Okay—the first six names? They all come up in old news articles if you google the Magdalene Home for Wayward Girls. The date that's listed after their names? That's the date of the article."

I squint at these names. Each woman's name—and they're all women—is followed by a date. Like *Mary Donagen, March 17, 1978.*

"I'm pretty sure he found those first six names just by googling the maternity home."

"Only six names, huh?"

"From news articles, yes. And I've located only two of these women so far. They're bolded on the list. The first one is in jail, and the other one won't talk to me."

"Hell." It's not a lot to go on. "What about all these other names?"

"That's where you come in. I think the next part of the list is from that ledger you found."

"The pictures he stole from my phone?"

"He didn't say where he got them, but you gave me that clue yourself."

"How nice of me," I mutter. And when I scan the list, I can see that she's right. The first name is from 1951, and it's the same pattern: first initial, last name, and a complete date. Then there are names from the late eighties—which reflects the jump I'd made when photographing the ledger. "Yeah, okay. I think you're right."

"There's something curious about the last four names. A first initial, followed by a last name. No dates at all."

I scroll down to read the names. "These were from my phone, too. There was a separate page at the end of the ledger." One of the names stands out. *Vespertini.* It's unusual enough that I remember it without consulting that photo on my phone.

"Well, Tim wanted me to focus on those. The weekend before he died, I came up to Portland to see him. And he said something like—'I know it's not much to go on, but those last four matter the most.'"

"But he didn't say why?"

She shakes her head. "I wish. But I have a copy of his hard drive. His mom shared it with me. I've been looking at any files he downloaded this spring, but there are a lot of them. He was really good at tracing financial stuff."

"You mentioned that."

"He's got a trove of quarterly reports from the Wincott Foundation. Those are public documents. There's always a section at the back where they disclose payments over twenty grand. But there are hundreds of them over the years. The foundation gives out a lot of grants."

"And . . ."

"Tim also saved a flyer from a 2011 choir concert at the University of Maine. The name Vespertini was underlined on it. I cross-checked, and in 2011, the Wincott Foundation paid the University of Maine $22,700, which was exactly the in-state cost of tuition, plus room and board."

"I'm not following," I say slowly. "2011 wasn't very long ago."

"Exactly," she says, propping her face into her hand. "I think the foundation was still paying off some of the people who lived or worked at the maternity home. And that's what Tim was chasing."

"And you think they were paying off—specifically—the four names at the end of the list?"

"That's my theory," she says. "I'll bet you a stiff drink that he had a special obligation to these four. Riddle me this—whose college tuition do you trouble yourself to pay even after your death?"

"Your child's," I say slowly.

"Ding-ding! I'm wondering if Marcus Wincott had four children. Or some other deep, personal commitment to those people—a connection strong enough to involve payments for things like tuition. And remember—he died in 1997, and someone is still paying tuition in 2011. The Wincott family had to know about Marcus's indiscretions."

That shouldn't surprise me, but it does anyway. "And who took over the foundation after Marcus died?"

"Well, another Wincott took over for several years, but he died on the job."

"Died on the *job*?" I picture a man collapsing in the mansion.

"No, I mean he dropped dead of a heart attack at sixty. Then the foundation was leaderless for a couple of years before Hank took over in his twenties."

"Oh."

"You can see it all in the annual reports. I've been plowing through them, looking for any other connections. I'll send you the PDFs. Tim must have found *something* in here, or he wouldn't have gotten himself killed. I wish I had his notebooks."

"Yeah." I sigh.

"Now it's your turn to share, Rowan. What's the name of Tim's birth mom?"

I close my eyes and say a tiny prayer. *Laura, please forgive me.* "It's Laura Peebles." I spell it for her. "She lives in Westbrook. I don't have a phone number."

And, come to think of it, Laura never emailed me for those photos of Tim.

"Peebles." On the screen, Jules scribbles it down. "I'll run a background check."

"Is the name familiar to you?"

"Nope. But I bet it's in his notebooks. He was such a throwback." Her brown eyes get sad. "And someone used it against him."

"I'm sorry," I whisper. It's clear to me that while Tim Kovak didn't actually break my heart, he broke Jules's for real.

After we hang up, I realize that I forgot to ask one more crucial question. I text her immediately.

> Rowan: Hey wait! You said you'd give me everything you have on Harrison's mom. Betsy Jones.
>
> Jules: I did. But all I had was her name. There's a Jones on the list. Maybe it's the right person.

"You sneaky bitch," I mutter. But there is, in fact, a *B. Jones* on the list. She's one of the four names at the bottom—the special ones.

And when I look at the damn list again, I notice that it's right next to C. Vespertini.

50

NATALIE

It's midnight and her feet are aching. But she's still doing side work—wiping down serving trays and rolling silverware into napkins for tomorrow's lunch shift.

In better news, she's making fifteen dollars an hour for expediting, and the waitstaff "tipped out" thirty bucks to her on top of that. She didn't even know that tipping out was a thing.

Her father is patiently waiting for her. He's sitting at the bar, sipping a Coke and chatting with the bartender. He's not going to let her bike home alone, even though it would be easier for both of them if he just left without her.

"Okay, that's good for now," the head waitress finally says, pulling off her apron. "You're on tomorrow for the lunch shift?"

"Yeah," she says, even though the idea exhausts her. "See you then." She puts her apron in the dirty-linens bag and walks to the front of the house to find her dad.

"I'd better go," he says to the bartender. "Thanks for the soda."

"Anytime, dude. Can't believe you have a kid. Where you been hiding her?"

He gives Natalie a wry smile. "She's been busy. Right, Natty?"

"So busy," Natalie agrees.

"How was it?" he asks as soon as they get outside.

She unlocks her bike. "Hard. I don't have the table numbers memorized yet. And all the fried food looks the same."

He laughs. "I don't have a lot of life lessons to offer, except for one. Every new job you ever have will include a few days of thinking—what the fuck did I just do?"

She lets out a startled laugh, and they set off down Commercial Street toward home. "Good to know."

"I mean it. Every single job. You're not allowed to panic until the second week."

"Fair. But I don't want to screw up someone's dinner."

He grins. "You won't. And they'll eat again tomorrow, anyway. It's not rocket science, it's just labor."

"I think this is part of Mom's big strategy. She made me get a job just so I'd be stoked to apply to college."

"I thought the point was making money?"

"That, too. Although Tessa is mad at me for taking a job without her."

"Fine. Let's get Tessa an application. See how long she'd last as an expediter."

She smiles. "Not long, I bet."

It's a gentle uphill walk toward home, but it's just dawning on her that she's going to have to sleep tonight in a house where someone—possibly a murderer—recently broke in.

Her father is here, though, pacing quietly along beside her. It's a comfort.

"Do you still love Mom?" she blurts out.

"Oh, Natty," he says, and she already regrets asking.

But it's late and it's dark and it's been a really weird day.

"God, just don't ask your mom the same question."

"I won't," she mumbles. "It's none of my business."

"Well, no. You have a right to wonder what happened. And it's an easy answer for me—I'll always love your mother. I never stopped. But things aren't the same for her. I promised her we'd be together forever, and then I left her to raise you alone. I don't think that's something you ever get over."

"Maybe not," she agrees.

But it's hard not to hope.

———————

They get home fifteen minutes later. She locks her bike in the garage while her father sends a text to what is now their family group chat.

Harrison: We're back. Coming inside in a second.

Lickie goes into a greeting frenzy, and the cat swings by to let her dad know she noticed his absence. "That cat really likes you."

"Eh. I think it's just that I smell like food."

When they cross into the living room, they discover her mother is still awake. She's cross-legged on the couch, a half-eaten bowl of popcorn on the coffee table, and sheets of paper in various sizes covering every available surface.

"Mom? What are you doing?"

She glances up, clearly exhausted. "I got some new information. Tim asked a friend to run some background checks before he died. She's good at that. Today she gave me the names he wanted her to check, so I'm doing some research."

The mess makes more sense now. Natalie's own bed looked the same way during finals. "Did you learn anything?"

"Yes and no. There are a lot of names, and they're mostly partials. But I have some ideas." She lifts a sheet of paper from the coffee table. "Tim didn't reveal where all these names came from. But his friend cracked the code. These at the top"—she points to a section of names that she's circled in pink highlighter—"were found in news stories via regular Google searches. And the names below are from the birth ledger I found at the mansion—the ones Tim took off my phone."

Natalie scans the list of mothers' names, noting the gap between the early years and the eighties. "But I thought you'd found Tim's birth? In 1979?"

"I did—but later," her mom says with a wave of her hand. "Tim only saw the sample pages—plus four names in back." Her mom hands Natalie her phone so she can look at the photo. It's a picture of four names: M. McNamara, T. O'Neil, B. Jones, and C. Vespertini.

The four names are printed at the bottom of the paper list, as well.

"Wait, do you think B. Jones . . ." Natalie glances at her father.

"Is my mother?" her dad finishes the question. His elbows are propped on the back of the sofa as he leans over to listen.

"Possibly." Her mother takes the phone back, squinting at the photo like it might reveal more details. "The first time I saw this, it didn't occur to me."

"Why would it?" he asks, perching on the back of the sofa. "Jones is, what, one of the top hundred most common names?"

"It's the *fifth* most common surname in America," Mom says. "And you weren't exactly top of mind when I found the ledger." She picks up her list of names again and stares at it. "I'm trying not to see things that aren't there."

"Hey." He puts his hands on her mother's shoulders and digs his thumbs into the muscles there. Her mother visibly tenses. But he doesn't let go. And after a second, she relaxes. "I know you're doing good work here, and that this is important. But what if you and Natty drive over to your dad's house, so you could forget about this for a few hours, and get a good night's sleep?"

She squints up at him. "You think I'm losing it."

"I think you're tired," he says carefully.

"My life has been taken hostage by a freak who wants . . . vengeance? I don't even know what he wants. Of course I'm tired."

He digs his thumbs into her shoulders again. "Do you feel safe in this house?"

"I don't feel safe anywhere right now," her mother says. "We could wake my father up and sleep there. But for how many nights? The wallet was meant to scare me, and it did. But it's not the only thing I'm scared of. I can't let yet another man control my life."

Natalie's dad winces. Like he knows he's at the top of her mother's short list of men who make things difficult.

"Look," her mother says, casting the papers off her lap and onto the mess on the table. "Quick family meeting. Harrison, you're looming. Move somewhere that isn't there."

Her father walks around the couch, shoves the papers aside, and perches on the corner of the coffee table. "Talk," he says. "How can we get you out of this mess?"

"All we can do is be careful. Natalie"—her mother places a hand on her knee—"there's a cop driving by our house every fifteen minutes. But do you want to sleep at Grandpa's?"

"No," she says immediately. "I want to stay here with you."

"I bought you some pepper spray," her mother says. "It's up on your bedside table. I need you to carry it, and keep your phone on and handy at *all* times. If you don't, swear to God I'll microchip you like Lickie until they catch this guy."

"Gross, Mom." She's pretty sure that isn't even legal.

"And if your father isn't working the same hours, I'll pick you up. No exceptions."

"Or Dad can get me on his motorcycle," she says.

"No," her mom says immediately.

"We'll walk," her father says.

"Or I'll pick you up in the car," her mother counters. "I just don't want you on your own at night until this is done."

"All right," Natalie agrees. Then a yawn practically cracks her jaw in half.

"We'll try to sleep," her mother announces. "If I look at that list anymore, my eyes will cross." She starts gathering her papers into a pile.

"Night." Natalie gets up off the couch and heads for the stairs. At the top, she looks back down at her mom, who's bent over, trying to scoop sticky notes off the floor.

Her dad is helping, a fond expression on his face.

But her mother doesn't even seem to notice.

51

ROWAN

"I'm going to drag that futon mattress out here," Harrison says as he hands me the last of my printouts. "I'll sleep right in front of the stairs."

I want to tell him that's not necessary. And that playing the role of a martyr won't get him back into my good graces. Except I don't think I could deliver that speech convincingly when I'm scared out of my mind.

Should I have taken Natalie to my father's house tonight? Or even out of town?

"Ro," he whispers. "Are you okay?"

I'm so tired, but I refuse to cry on him again. "I'm fine," I murmur. "I'm sorry about earlier. That was stupid."

"Stupid?" He takes one of my hands in his and begins massaging it, pinching the flesh between each of my fingers in turn. He used to do this when my hand cramped from drafting. I'd forgotten. "Stupid is a strong word."

"Impulsive, then. I wasn't thinking," I whisper.

"You say that like it's a bad thing."

He trades hands, massaging the other one as thoroughly as the first. Then he lifts my hand to his mouth and kisses it softly, his beard tickling my palm.

"Harrison . . ." If our daughter decides to come downstairs, she'll get the wrong idea. "Not here."

"All right." He stands and tugs me off the couch.

It takes my sluggish brain a moment to realize he's pulling me into the den and closing the door. "What are . . . ?"

"You said not here, so we're somewhere else."

My back hits the door, and he steps into my personal space, gray eyes blazing. He runs one rough thumb over my cheekbone and then tilts his head to kiss me.

It's not a polite kiss. It's the stuff of my passionate, twenty-year-old daydreams. All tongue and hands and hunger.

I take two seconds to wonder if I'm making yet another mistake as my hands grip his T-shirt for the second time today. But Harrison's kisses are still capable of making me forget myself. As one of his hands tangles in my hair and the other makes a naughty trip down the back of my sweatpants, the only thing on my mind is a fervent wish that he'd yank off my bra and suck on my nipples until the point of pain.

Then he scoops me up off the floor with one clever arm and pins me against the door, and I wrap my legs around his hips. My kisses are urgent, because I know I can't stop and think. That way lies the abyss.

Harrison doesn't give me a chance to reconsider, either. He rocks his hips forward, showing me exactly how much he wants this.

Until he gets carried away and bangs my ass against the old door. Loudly. And Lickie, on the other side, chooses this of all moments to bark out a warning.

We both freeze, mid-kiss, instantly transformed back into exactly who we really are—two strangers, old enough to know better, in a compromised position. In the midst of a crisis, too, in a house where the dog's bark at zero dark thirty is enough to bring our nervous teenager out of her bedroom.

"Mom?" comes Natalie's distant shout. "Why is Lickie barking?"

Harrison quickly releases me, and my feet connect with the chilly floor. He opens the door a crack and calls out, "I'm moving the futon around, and I bumped the door. Go to bed, hon."

"Is Mom coming up?"

"In a sec. She's just helping me."

What I'm really doing is finger combing my hair and trying to find my misplaced dignity.

Harrison moves calmly toward the futon couch and rolls the mattress burrito-style before lifting it.

"What are you doing?"

"Moving this. Just like I said."

I step out of the way so he can carry it awkwardly to the wood floor between the stairs and the back of the couch.

When he returns, I'm still standing in the den's doorway, red-faced, wondering what's wrong with me.

Harrison picks up his pillow off the floor and gives me a grin. "To be continued."

"Not a chance," I whisper. "And why am I the only one who looks contrite?"

"Because I don't have anything to be contrite about," he says in a low voice. "I've loved you as hard as I can since the first time you let me talk you into a beer after work. I love you still. It's not a crime to care."

My jaw slams shut as I scan his features. His gaze is steady, and his well-kissed mouth is drawn in a serious line. He means what he's just said.

"I realize that not everything that happened in the past was really your fault. But you can't just walk back in and expect me to pick up where we left off. It's not fair to me. And it's *really* not fair to Natalie. She's wanted a normal family for her whole life. Do not toy with her emotions."

"I would never," he whispers. "And I love her, too, which is also not something you can control. Now go up to bed before you'll have to step over me to do it. Or I might just grab you when you pass by. Like a troll under a bridge."

I stalk by him without a word, because I believe that he might actually try it.

And the stupid thing is that I'd probably let him.

52

NATALIE

Her second day on the job, Natalie works the lunch shift as a hostess in training. She wears her Docksiders T-shirt knotted at the waist to turn it into a crop top and the Saint Raymond medallion as a good luck charm.

Hostessing, it turns out, is easier than expediting. There's a laminated map of the table numbers, and seating people is simpler than remembering their orders.

And even a monkey could keep a waiting list straight.

She makes another million silverware rolls while waiting for her father to finish up in the kitchen. Tonight he's playing with his band onstage instead of working in the kitchen. And there's no dinner shift for Natalie. So when they walk out into the sunshine at three, she's done for the day.

"Where's your bike?" he asks, looking at the empty rack. The only thing here on two wheels is his motorcycle.

"I don't have it. Tessa dropped me off after brunch."

He swears under his breath. "Okay, I guess we're walkin'."

"You could just ride me home on that." She points at the Honda Rebel tucked against the building.

He looks uneasy. "Your mom didn't want you on my bike."

"But it's, like, a mile or two, right? Besides—tonight you'll have your bass and your amp, right?"

He closes his eyes briefly. "Okay. But it will be just this once unless you can get your mom to agree to letting you ride with me."

"All right. Let's go."

He hands her his helmet. "You're not riding without this."

She has her first wave of guilt when she puts on the helmet. It hadn't occurred to her that she was asking him to be unsafe or break the law. But they'll be home in five minutes. Tops.

He shows her where to put her feet and where to hold on. They head off at a speed she estimates to be, like, fifteen miles an hour. He's driving more slowly than she even thought a motorcycle could go.

It's still fun, though. Like flying.

When they get home, her mom's car is in the garage, which is a little weird. Natalie thought she needed it for work today.

The kitchen door is locked up tight, as it should be, and her father is right on her heels. *Everything is fine*, she assures herself, turning the key in the lock.

The dog trots to greet them, wagging her tail.

The cat does not, and when Natalie crosses into the living room, she finds her mother lying on the sofa, the cat in her lap, reading one of the printouts the journalist gave her.

"Mom? Don't you have to be at work?"

"Theoretically," she says, sitting up. Her voice is strangely cool. "And I was at work, but I left because Hank is after me to have a meeting, to convince himself that I'm still a loyal member of the team. And I cannot look that man in the eye today. So I came home. How was day two on the job?"

"Easier," Natalie says, but she's still studying her mother, who has wild hair and tired eyes. "Are you okay?"

Her dad approaches, wearing an expression of concern that probably matches Natalie's. Because her mom looks rough.

"I'm just sitting here, digging through these annual reports. Trying to find what Tim found. Trying to work out how to keep everyone safe." Her expression hardens. "Speaking of safety—I thought we agreed you wouldn't be a passenger on that motorcycle."

Uh-oh. "It was my idea," Natalie says quickly.

Her mother stands, unseating the cat and tossing papers onto the coffee table. "Harrison, I need to speak to you for a second."

His face falls. "Of course."

"Your place or mine? Oh wait, it's *all* my place."

Oh shit. Natalie has the unfamiliar urge to put her hands over her ears. It's just dawning on her that one of the few upsides of not having a dad is never having to listen to her parents fight.

He follows her into his room, where her mother closes the door with an angry click. Natalie is left outside, helpless and feeling sick. Knowing this is all her fault.

For maybe ten seconds she can't make out their low voices. But then it escalates quickly.

"I said no motorcycle!"

"I'm *sorry*. It was only supposed to be once!"

"But you don't get to do this!" her mother shrieks. "You don't get to parachute in here and be the cool dad when it suits you. It's not fair to the child you abandoned. And it sure isn't fair to me."

"I made a mistake!"

"You make too many of them. This isn't working. Find somewhere else to stay."

Lickie lets out a whine of distress, and Natalie knows just how she feels. This is a disaster. She's chasing him away again, even though he still loves her.

I'll always love her, he'd said, and it's so obvious. Can her mother not see it? Or worse, does she really not care?

Natalie sinks down on the sofa, noting the half-empty coffee cups and balled-up sticky notes. She starts gathering up the debris just to have something to do with her hands.

While she's throwing the trash away in the kitchen, she hears the den door fly open and her mom's quick footsteps on the stairs.

Her father doesn't emerge from the den. But when she sits back down on the sofa, she can see an oblique view of Lickie's tail wagging from inside that room. The dog needs everyone to be happy and calm.

So does Natalie.

Her mother reappears a few minutes later wearing running clothes. "Lickie, let's go for a run."

The dog spasms with joy, racing out to join her. And a minute later her mother is on her way out the door. "Lock this behind me," she tells Natalie, not meeting her eyes.

Natalie locks the damn door. Then she sinks down on the couch, feeling shaky. She wonders if her father is already packing.

This is a disaster.

The coffee table is a little tidier now, with her mother's work sorted into piles that Natalie hasn't touched. Two fat piles are annual reports from the Wincott Foundation.

Her mother has also written four names in big letters on a legal pad:

M. McNamara

T. O'Neil

B. Jones

C. Vespertini

Beside the names are questions: Child support payments? College tuition?

And underneath that, her mom wrote: *MW's 4 children?*

Marcus Wincott was a busy guy.

Natalie picks up one of the annual reports off the stack. It's from 1992. The cover shows the Wincott trident centered inside a heart. Underneath, there's a photo of a dozen smiling children at a school lunchroom table.

Natalie turns the pages, picking up where her mother left off. It's hard to concentrate, though, especially when she hears her father make a call.

"Hey, Cal. Just wanted to catch you before the dinner rush. I gotta ask a favor. Will you check out an apartment for me tomorrow? Yeah. It's not available until next month, but I gotta sign a lease soon. Ro has had all she can take."

Natalie's heart tumbles.

"Thanks, man. I will never be able to repay . . ." He sighs. "Yeah, okay. Thanks. I'll send you the deets."

53

CORALIE

"Two cheeseburgers. Fries are coming up in just a second." The guy behind the counter gives her a wink. He's cute, with a piercing in one ear and artfully shaved hair. A little punk rock.

He was the kind of guy she would've flirted with at a bar not too long ago, hoping he'd buy her a drink. Hoping he'd take her home.

But now she's standing here in an elastic-waist skirt, waiting for their lunch. Hoping they don't skip the pickles, because cravings are real. She uses her thumb to jiggle the fake wedding band on her ring finger.

The radio is playing "I Will Always Love You," by Whitney Houston. That song is everywhere lately, and she's starting to hate it.

Too unrealistic.

"Here you go!" the pierced hottie says, tucking the fries into her bag. "You have a nice day now."

"Thanks." She allows herself a single flirtatious smile before leaving a dollar in the tip jar and tucking her boss's change into her pocket.

She heads back to the office quickly, so the fries won't get cold.

They never have lunch together. He always goes out, and she eats a sandwich at her desk. But today his lunch meeting was postponed and then finally canceled, and he said, "Let's get some burgers. I'll buy, you fly."

By the time she strides back into the office suite, she's been gone twenty minutes. She opens her mouth to call out that lunch is here, but his door is partway closed, and she catches herself, in case he's on a call.

A glance at the phones says he's not. She puts the bag down on her desk and hears an unwelcome sound from the office. A *giggle*.

She freezes. A woman's laughter erupts a second time.

Her heart banging hard inside her chest, she edges closer to the partially open door, the carpet swallowing the sounds of her footsteps. She eases into a position that allows her to see inside. Her stomach drops.

There's another woman sitting on the edge of Mr. Wincott's desk. Coralie can't see the woman's face, but her bare legs dangle from a skirt that's frankly too short.

Mr. Wincott's smile is downright lecherous.

A hot cloud of shocked rage envelops her. She steps away and goes back to her desk, her heart thumping with anger.

And shame, honestly. She's surprised that she's surprised. Tigers don't change their stripes, as her mother used to say.

YOU'RE A STUPID BITCH, CORALIE, yells the voice inside her head. WHAT DID YOU THINK WOULD HAPPEN?

She sits down at her desk and removes one of the burgers from the bag. She unfolds the foil wrapper and takes a bite.

It grows quiet in the office. Too quiet.

Fuck him. Fuck him sideways. In the ear.

Her anger feels good for a minute or two, but then it feels lonely. And all of a sudden she understands how *very* lonely she'll be when the baby comes.

She dumps out her fries and eats them while they're still crisp. His loss if the rest of them get cold.

It's another twenty minutes before the other woman comes out. She walks past Coralie's desk without a glance.

Coralie is full of greasy food and really fucking depressed. She doesn't walk his lunch into his office, like he probably expects. She waits for him to come out. A petty rebellion.

When he finally emerges, she hands him the bag without making eye contact. "You should have eaten when it was hot."

"Hey," he says in a cheerful voice that fails to notice her coolness. "Make some coffee? Bring me a cup when it's done. And bring yourself a cup of something, too. I haven't seen you all day."

She pushes back her chair and crosses to the coffeepot, her shoulders back and her spine as straight as a poker. The bag crinkles as he retreats to the inner office.

She knows she needs to calm down. She can't cop an attitude. He'll never let her get away with it. The worst part is that he *wanted* her to catch him flirting. She'd bet money on it. It's his way of making sure that she knows her place.

Maybe she needed the reminder.

The coffee takes a good ten minutes. She makes herself a peppermint tea and arranges both drinks on a tray. Then she musters up a waxen smile and carries it into the office.

"*There* she is!" It's a greeting he's given before, but there's a new edge to it. *You'd better keep smiling.*

Sticking to her role, she closes the door behind her. And when she places the tray on his desk, she leans over to give him a good look at her cleavage.

He makes a noise of appreciation, a sound she's grown to enjoy. It usually feels powerful, but today it's crystal clear that he'll make that noise for anyone. The second she's left this office to care for her child, a new girl will replace her. She won't even be here a year.

No more Wedgwood. No more gifts from Tiffany or the Coach store. She'll be back to ramen noodles and fights outside the windows of her awful little apartment.

With a baby to care for.

The thought causes her to set his cup down with slightly more force than necessary.

"Come over here," he says, rolling his desk chair back and tossing the wadded-up take-out wrappers into the wastebasket. "How are you feeling today?"

"Lovely," she lies. She can hardly bear the idea of his hands on her body, but it's too late to disagree, isn't it? She circles the desk with tanta-lizing slowness—or procrastination, depending on your point of view—and then slides her rounded body onto his knee.

His hand is under her blouse and onto her stomach immediately. He makes a strangled growl that causes her to roll her eyes at the bookshelf across the room.

"You're going to have to hire a new girl," she says softly. "Eventually."

"I suppose. Unless you want to stay on."

"How could I?" she wonders aloud. "Is there a company daycare somewhere I haven't noticed?"

"You know," he says as his fingertips creep across her skin, "the family has arranged a great many adoptions."

Her heart drops. "I don't want that."

It's not like she never considered adoption, but she grew up in and out of foster care, and some of it was pretty bad. No child should suffer that if there's a rich man on the hook for its well-being. And the well-being of the mother.

Mr. Wincott is going to pay *twice* as much as usual, or she'll go to his brother and threaten to tell the papers.

His fingertips reach up to cup her breast. "Have you picked out some good Christian names?" he asks.

Her eyes slide toward the thick book of saints, wondering how carefully he's read it. "Why, yes, I have. A girl name, anyway. I think I'm having a girl."

"Do you now?" he asks in a voice that's clearly humoring her. "And what are we calling her?"

The name was on the first page she opened to. Her gaze snagged on a particular phrase about the saint: *an illegitimate daughter.* It will be her little secret. And—bonus—the saint's name is lovely, too.

She turns around, straddling one of his thighs and resting her hands on his chest in a suggestive way.

"Marcus." She cups his chin, so he'll look at her face and not her tits. "I'm going to call her Beatrice."

54

ROWAN

I'm trying to outrun my anger, but it isn't working all that well. After several miles, I'm viciously thirsty, and the dog is shooting me worried looks. Like maybe she deserves a drink and a treat for all this exercise.

When I reach the busy part of the waterfront, I slow to a walk and catch my breath. It's a Friday evening in June, so the sidewalk is packed with tourists and couples holding hands. Clouds are brewing overhead, and the wind is kicking up, and I predict within the next few minutes everyone will scurry into the nearby bars and restaurants.

In the distance I hear a band playing a Jimmy Buffett cover. It might even be Harrison's band. For fifteen years I didn't see his face. And now I can't seem to get away from that man.

I can't believe he put Natalie on the back of that motorcycle. Sure, he gave her the only helmet. But that was *so stupid*. If he'd gotten pulled over, he'd end up in court *again*.

And I can't *believe* I threw myself at him last night. I'm so angry at both of us. He has to go.

I stop walking and check the time. Maybe I can find some take-out food to split with Natalie. Lickie and I can have a drink at one of the restaurants' outdoor areas while I wait for the food.

While I'm weighing tacos versus fried fish, I pull my phone from my fanny pack and glance at it. Beatrice has called me. Twice. But she didn't leave a message.

It's odd to get a call from her on a Friday evening, so I call her back.

"Hey!" she answers a little breathlessly. "God, do you have a second? I'm freaking out a little."

My skin prickles. "Why?"

"I was doing a little work on our extra project . . ."

"Yeah?"

"Don't get too excited. I found something a little confusing. I have a little theory, and I want to run it by you. But . . ." She laughs, and it sounds nervous. "You know how I hate it when people talk about ghosts?"

"Yeah?"

"I'm not a believer. But I keep hearing a weird sound here . . ."

"You're at the mansion?" I ask.

"Yeah. And I swear to God, I keep hearing a baby crying. It's so creepy. Would you, uh, come and listen? I feel like I'm losing my mind."

What the hell? "Okay. And you'll share your theory with me? I've been doing some digging of my own."

"Of course I'll share."

"All right. Give me thirty minutes to get there."

"Thanks. You'll appreciate what I've found."

55

NATALIE

Annual reports, sadly, make for some very dull reading. Although the Wincott Foundation does a great job of making itself sound indispensable. By the third report, Natalie is well versed in their efforts to improve lives all over Maine as well as in Haiti and Africa.

Interspersed with numbers and accolades, there are lots of photographs. Sometimes the names of employees and volunteers show up in captions. Natalie reads each one diligently, because it would be fun to be a hero and spot one of the women her mom is searching for.

But Natalie really only cares about one name. *Jones*. She's never seen a photo of her grandmother and she'd like to know more about her father.

Her father was born in 1982, so she started her search with the 1981 report and has moved slowly forward in time. Her mom is still out on an epic run, and her father has gone upstairs for a shower.

When he returns, he sits beside her on the sofa. "I've got to get to work. Cal wants me to help him inventory the bar before we play. But what are you going to do about dinner if you're on your own?"

She looks up. He's dressed for the gig in dark jeans and a black button-down shirt. He's trimmed his beard carefully, and he looks like a hipster. "I dunno. I'll eat something. Or order something. It's not like I'll starve." His question triggers a traitorous thought. *But where were you when I was too young to take care of myself?*

"All right," he says lightly, his gaze sliding away. Her mother had called out his part-time concern. Natalie doesn't want to agree. But a tendril of doubt has curled itself around her consciousness. He clears his throat. "Hey, your mom was right. We should have left the bike at work."

"Yeah, I know. But she'll get over it." *Maybe.*

He sighs. Then he taps the report on her lap. "What are you looking for?"

She tosses the shiny brochure onto the coffee table. "I got sucked into a rabbit hole trying to find Betsy Jones."

"Ah," he says wearily. "The elusive Betsy Jones. She wasn't an easy person to know, even when she was alive."

"Why?"

"She was usually depressed." He shrugs. "But I didn't realize that when I was a kid. And then, when I was in middle school, she started doing drugs. And in high school, it got really bad. There was a lot of crack around back then. I'd come home from school, and . . ." He glances at her and then shakes his head. "It wasn't a great scene. I'm old enough now to realize how much it affected me. So many decisions I made were because of the things she did."

"Like what?"

"For starters, I told myself I'd never do hard drugs. And that's why I chose pot." He lets out a sharp laugh. "We all know how that turned out."

Natalie knows, because her mother explained it to her the other night. "But that was just unlucky."

"Yeah, but I didn't really see it that way." He leans back against the couch and crosses his arms. "I grew up in chaos. Then I met your mom, and for a minute there, my life made more sense."

Natalie holds her breath, because she knows this will be difficult to hear.

"But then I caused the same amount of chaos in your mother's life that my family caused in mine. That's why I stayed away, Natty. Because I knew your mom would raise you like this." He spreads his hands wide in a gesture that manages to indicate Natalie's whole existence. The little renovated house, with its refinished wainscoting and shiny wood floors. Books on the shelves, organic milk. Private school. "And I thought I couldn't be what you needed."

"Okay," she says softly.

"The problem is that when you're told your whole life that you're trash, you end up believing it. I was dyslexic, but none of my teachers tried to figure out why I couldn't read. They just told me I was stupid. I didn't have a mom like yours to help me navigate the world. She probably grew up in chaos, too."

"When was the last time you saw her?"

He has to think. "I guess it was December—right before I moved to Ithaca to be with your mother," he says. "I went to say goodbye, and she asked me for money. I didn't have any to spare, and she called me an ungrateful bastard."

Ouch. "What about your father?" she asks. "Where was he?"

"Who knows?" he shrugs. "He paid child support for a while. Then he stopped. That's when my mom kind of went off the deep end."

Something tickles the back of Natalie's brain. "What year was that, do you think?"

"Um . . . Mid-nineties? Somewhere in there."

"Back when dinosaurs roamed the earth."

He laughs suddenly. "This dinosaur has to go play some covers." He stands up. Then he leans over and kisses the top of her head. "Lock the door behind me?"

"All right." She rises to follow him.

"Kind of surprised your mother went out when she knows you'll be here alone."

Natalie shrugs. She's kind of surprised, too. But she doesn't want to say anything disloyal.

"I'm leaving my phone on vibrate. Call for any reason."

"Will do."

He slings his bass on his back and picks up his amp.

Natalie locks the door behind him and makes a bag of popcorn. She opens the next annual report. Her eyes skim the captions of the photos, on the hunt for *Jones.*

She finds a lot of big hair, and some *really* high-waisted jeans. But if Betsy Jones attended the foundation picnic in the eighties, she never posed for the group photo.

And now she's running out of years. Natalie knows the maternity home closed for good in 1989. So she pulls the 1990 report into her lap halfheartedly. She peeks at the masthead. Marcus Wincott was still running the foundation. His headshot smiles confidently out from the first page, his smile smarmy.

His "Letter from the CEO" says something about new directions for the foundation. Yada yada yada.

Natalie flips the page to a photo of four young people, linking arms and smiling. They're all unfamiliar, and mostly unremarkable, except for one detail—two of the women are wearing silver oval medallions.

Natalie stops breathing and reads the caption. It's a reunion! The Wincott Foundation hosted a tea for grown adoptees who were born at the maternity home. *Our guests enjoyed a tour of their birth place, plus cake and conversation. We hope to make it an annual event!*

The names under the photo are unfamiliar; they must have been born in the sixties. But Natalie flags the page with a Post-it to show her mother. And then she flips through more of the later issues, looking for medallions of Saint Raymond.

It takes most of an hour before she spots another one, in the report from 2001. But when she does, it makes her gasp.

The caption: *Shenanigans at the Wincott Foundation Family Picnic.* The photo shows a few children waiting in line for a dunking booth, while one of them aims a softball in a cocked hand.

There's a very attractive little girl in the photo, maybe nine or ten. She's wearing what looks to be a Saint Raymond medallion around her neck. But that's not what's so shocking.

First there's her face, which is unmistakably familiar to Natalie. Even as a child, she was already beautiful. And stuck to her shirt she's wearing a paper name tag that reads, *Hello my name is* . . . BEATRICE VESPERTINI.

56

ROWAN

I buy a bottle of water to split with Lickie in preparation for the walk back to the mansion. But then I'm so curious that I grab an Uber instead.

Beatrice sounded rattled.

A few minutes later, Lickie and I climb the mansion's steps. "No chewing any hand-carved masterpieces, m'kay?" I scratch her between the ears before punching the code in the front door's keypad.

Inside, it's dim and quiet, as it should be. The lights are off and workers have gone home for the day. Still, the mansion feels extra desolate.

"Beatrice?" I call as I walk through the empty atrium. Aside from the clicking of Lickie's nails on the bare floors, there's only silence.

I head to the library, but find the same quiet darkness.

Confused, I retrace my steps. "Beatrice?"

Then I hear a sound upstairs. Footsteps.

Lickie freezes midstride and flattens her ears.

"Come on, girl," I say, shortening the leash and leading her toward the staircase. We start the climb, and as the stairs curve, I see light shining from above. It's coming from the third-floor gallery. "Bea?"

"I'm up here," she calls, her voice strained. "But that baby won't stop crying. Don't you hear it?"

I pause on the steps and listen, trying to hear anything besides Lickie's panting.

Then it comes. A thin wail. And the hair on my neck stands up.

57

NATALIE

Natalie stares at the photo of Beatrice for so long that she forgets to breathe.

She can't make sense of what she's seeing. In the first place, Beatrice's last name is Chambers. Not Vespertini. But more importantly, what is Beatrice—the Beatrice she and her mom know so well—doing in this report?

What the hell does this mean?

Natalie literally runs to get her laptop. She's typing *Beatrice Vespertini* into a search bar almost before her bottom hits the couch again.

The search turns up nothing.

Okay. That's frustrating. Maybe she changed her name a long time ago? But why? And how does any of this fit together?

She searches *Beatrice Chambers Portland Maine* with predictable results. She finds a few pictures of Beatrice at various charity events around Portland and a profile on LinkedIn that reveals nothing.

Natalie grabs her phone and opens Instagram, where she's already following Beatrice's private account, and where Beatrice follows Natalie, too. But Beatrice's list of followers is unremarkable. No Vespertinis.

She sorts through everything she knows about Beatrice, and it doesn't amount to a lot:

She's younger than Rowan, so she was born in the early nineties. This was after the maternity home was closed, but in the photo, she wears a Saint Raymond medallion.

Beatrice said her mother died when she was a little girl—probably before this picture was taken.

Her father was somebody who thought he was "too good" for her.

And Vespertini appears on that list of four names. Why?

She grabs her mother's notes and sifts through them again. The only other Vespertini her mother found was a name on a University of Maine flyer for a choral production. There was a Vespertini in the alto section.

Natalie looks at Beatrice's LinkedIn profile. She graduated from the University of Maine.

Her mother needs to see this.

She types a text.

Natalie: Hey, where are you? I found something.

She hits send, and then decides the text doesn't properly convey the situation.

Natalie: I found something WILD.

Because it really is. Natalie clearly remembers the first time she wore her Saint Raymond medallion to yoga class. It was a bad wardrobe choice—every time she leaned into a forward fold, the medallion smacked her in the chin.

But after class, Beatrice took note of it. "I like your necklace," she'd said. "Where did you get it?"

"From my father," Natalie had replied.

But then Beatrice didn't say: I have one just like it.

She only said: "It's so unique. And so beautiful."

58

ROWAN

The sound of a baby's cry rises and then falls into silence. I forget to breathe.

Beside me, Lickie whimpers.

I force air into my lungs. God, where is that noise coming from?

"Beatrice? We're coming up."

"We?" she asks in a strained voice.

"I have the dog with me."

"Good," she says. "I could use a cuddle right now."

I can hear her clearly, but I can't see her even as I reach the second floor and ease my way around the curved gallery toward the next flight of stairs.

It's gloomy here. There are no lights on in any of the rooms. And cloud cover outside means there's barely any light filtering through the stained glass above.

Every open doorway that we pass gives me the heebie-jeebies. But the glow from the top floor gets brighter as I begin the final climb to the third floor.

Lickie suddenly overcomes her hesitation, and her tail begins to wag. Maybe she's caught the scent of Beatrice. So I let go of the leash and let her proceed ahead of me. She vaults up the stairs, toenails clicking on the polished wood. Then she disappears from view.

"Hello, girl," Beatrice says in a low voice. "Hi. You just sit right here, okay? Who's a good girl?"

My phone chimes with two texts as I reach the top of the stairs. I reach for it automatically, but I don't look at the screen. I'm distracted by a mess on the floor—torn pages strewn around.

Lifting my gaze, I'm about to ask why, when I finally spot Beatrice. She's reaching behind an old metal radiator on the gallery wall.

And drawing out a gun.

By the time my brain makes sense of this, she's pointing it at me. "Hands where I can see them," she says. "Drop the phone."

I freeze. "What the hell are you doing?"

"*Drop the phone!*" she shouts.

My fingers loosen their grip on the phone, and it crashes to the wood floor. "Beatrice," I say, my voice tense. "Please. Tell me what's going on. You need to put down the gun before someone gets hurt." Even as I say it, my stomach drops into my shoes.

Because I think she intends to hurt me. And I'm realizing that she probably killed Tim, too. She must have. All these papers on the floor? They're the right size and shape to have come from his Moleskine notebooks. I think I recognize his slanting script.

"*Why?*" I demand.

But she isn't listening. "Look at me," she says. "Catch."

She lobs something at me, and I grab it so it doesn't hit me. It's a pair of handcuffs, unlocked.

"Put one of those around your wrist." She squares her body with mine and aims the gun straight at me. "*Now.*"

I fumble with the handcuffs, managing to close one of them around my left wrist. My mind is whirling. What the hell is she doing?

"I want to hear the cuff click," she orders.

It does. But my mind is still churning. If Beatrice killed Tim, then she's the one who threw his gun in the dumpster. "Did . . . did you try to pin Tim's murder on Harrison? How'd you even know who he was?" I can't look her in the eye, because my gaze is trapped on the gun's barrel. It's still aimed squarely at my chest.

"Harrison was my only mistake. He was the wrong choice anyway. Wincotts always land on their feet."

None of that makes sense to me. But she doesn't seem inclined to explain herself.

"Walk over to the railing and sit down. *Move.*"

Lickie whines, and I cast a glance in her direction. Beatrice has looped her leash around the cast-iron radiator, trapping Lickie by the wall.

My dog can tell that something is wrong, but she can't help me.

I move toward the banister on shaky legs, because I don't think I have a choice. I step over Tim's papers, wondering what Beatrice learned. And why she cares.

Beside the railing, I lower myself carefully to the floor.

"Face away from me. Spread your arms on the spindles as wide as they can go."

Balusters, not spindles, my architect brain suggests. I know buildings, but people confuse me. And whatever is wrong with Beatrice is way above my pay grade.

Trying to stay alive, I do exactly as Beatrice commands. I spread my arms wide, gripping the balusters with my hands. The gesture reminds me eerily of a crucifix.

Beatrice is *insane*. I really am the worst judge of character in the world.

"Don't move a muscle," she demands.

"*Why?*" I repeat, my cheek resting against a baluster. "What did I ever do to you?"

"Not to me," she says in a low voice. "To my family."

"Your family," I repeat slowly, her words sloshing around in my terrified mind. "You're . . . a *Wincott?*"

She doesn't answer. Instead, she quickly yanks the free end of the handcuffs and locks it to a baluster. Having cuffed me, I can hear Beatrice backing away again.

But I'm so confused. She could have shot me already if that was her plan.

So what *is* the plan? My heart is racing and my head is muzzy with fear. It's hard to think.

Then my phone chimes again from its facedown spot on the floor. We both turn our heads toward the sound.

And I don't think at all. I lunge for the phone with my free hand, my body flailing awkwardly as the cuff clanks against the balustrade.

My fingertip grazes the phone. And then Beatrice slams her foot down on my hand. I actually hear bones snap.

I howl as pain streaks up my arm, instant and shocking.

Lickie loses her mind, snarling and barking. And she's straining so hard on her collar that I hear choking sounds.

My hand is screaming, my dog can't help me, and my eyes are flooding with tears. On a silent sob, I curl myself around my broken hand.

"Stupid bitch." Beatrice kicks me in the ribs and then in the kidney. Two quick jabs. "Sit up before I kick you in the head. And *you* shut up!" This last order is directed at Lickie.

Lickie quiets, but probably only because Beatrice backs away from me.

Nausea wells in my throat as I look over my shoulder at her. She's still aiming the gun at me.

"So now you know I'm serious," she says in a low voice as I struggle onto my ass, my broken hand cradled in my lap, tears streaming.

I don't understand why this is happening. But I know I could die here tonight.

Beatrice—still aiming that gun—grabs my phone up off the floor with a gloved hand.

Oh God, gloves. She planned this. She lured me here to kill me. Panic claws at my insides. "Who's the text from?" I gasp.

"Doesn't matter," she says, powering down the phone. "Nothing matters anymore. This ends tonight."

"What ends?" I need to keep her talking.

"You're going to kill yourself, Rowan. You poor thing. Because you feel *awful* about killing Tim, and the guilt is eating you alive." She nudges a notebook toward me. "After all, Tim used you. His notes are very confessional. Now you know that he never loved you. It was just too devastating, so you cracked."

You're the one who's cracked. It's the first clear thought I've had since she broke my hand. Blood pounds in my ears, but I need to concentrate. "If you shoot me, you'll get caught. Why take that risk? We spoke on the phone just a half hour ago."

"That was by design. Actually, I learned this from you—watch your location data. My phone is at home in my apartment right now, pinging away. I called you on my iPad. Later tonight I'll throw it off the pier."

"But the new surveillance cameras," I choke out. "You'll be on the footage."

"They're switched off. In fact, they've been flickering on and off for two days," she says. "Maybe the ghost did it!" She laughs.

"Nobody would believe that."

"I'm *very* believable, Rowan. You bought into a *ghost baby*, for fuck's sake."

Pain throbs through my arm like a wave. But I keep arguing. "It still won't work. Too many people know what I was working on. I dug up a lot of information," I lie. "And Tim's birth mother has decided to talk to the police."

"That junkie? She's dead, Rowan. It was so easy. All I had to do was gift her some high-quality fentanyl. She OD'd this morning."

My chest seizes. *Oh Laura.* If it's true, then it's partly my fault. My digging set her off. *Oh God.* "But why cover up for Marcus Wincott? Why do you care if the whole world knows he was a creep?"

She grabs a broom that's leaning against the wall and swings at me. My hands are useless, so I yank up my knees defensively. The broom handle slams into my head, and I gasp.

"That creep was my father, you idiot. And I won't let you take down the family. Not over one dead man's bad choices."

I'm trying to process this bombshell as she steps up to the railing. My phone is still in her hand. She throws it over the railing, and it seems to take forever until I hear it smash two stories below.

59

NATALIE

Her mother isn't answering her texts, and Natalie is about to explode. Because if Tim had these reports, he probably found Beatrice's picture, too.

And he would have wanted to ask her some questions. About the medallion around her neck. And the name tag.

Natalie also has questions. Beatrice said her father was "too good for us." Did she mean Marcus Wincott?

And if she did—and Wincott also had a child with Betsy Jones—then it leads to an even wilder possibility. It means Natalie could be Marcus's grandchild.

And also Beatrice's *niece*?

It's too crazy to say out loud.

She grabs up her phone and sends another text to her mother.

Natalie: Where are you?

She checks the time and sees that it's past seven o'clock. Her mom has literally been gone for hours. And with the dog?

A prickle of fear climbs down her spine. This isn't ordinary behavior. Especially not now, when her mother has become the queen of locked doors and checking in with Natalie every half hour.

But hang on. She can use her mom's favorite trick. She opens the FriendFinder app and looks for her mom. No avatar pops up. She waits, but there's nothing. Her mom isn't on the map.

Okay, that's super weird.

Natalie puts her phone down and gets up off the couch. She walks away from the stacks of reports and the list of names they'd been searching for.

Suddenly it doesn't feel like a fun little game anymore. She puts several paces between herself and the pile of research. As if that would make the whole thing less eerie.

Zoe the cat wanders into the room and brushes her sleek body against Natalie's ankles. "Where is she?" Natalie wonders.

The cat meows.

Natalie scoops her up and carries her back to the sofa. She picks up her phone and finds her father's number. He's probably playing the bass right this minute.

Call for any reason, he'd said.

So she does.

60

ROWAN

Beatrice paces around me, a grim, thoughtful expression on her face. "I have a couple of questions. You're going to answer them. Did you speak to Hank today?"

"Um . . ." I hesitate. Should I say yes or no?

In my peripheral vision, Lickie is chewing on her leash. She used to gnaw through leashes often as a puppy, which is why I upgraded to indestructible leashes. Damn.

"*Hey.*" Beatrice aims a kick at my ankle. I'm ready for her, though, and I kick back.

She aims the gun right at my head. "Don't fucking move. Did you speak to him or not?"

"*Yes,*" I gasp. "But I don't remember when. He wanted to reschedule the budget meeting again. If you hadn't destroyed my phone, you could check for yourself."

"A voice call?"

"Yes," I lie. It was actually just a series of texts.

"Who else?" she demands.

Think, Gallagher.

"I spoke to Tim's ex-wife." Another lie. "She's a journalist writing a story about the Wincott family. If you hurt me, she'll be first in line to ask questions. She gave me a big file of names she's working on. People who knew Marcus Wincott and worked with him. People he paid off for years."

And now I realize that Beatrice must be one of those people. "Did he pay you, too?" I ask. "Were you supposed to keep quiet? That would sting." Even as I say it, I get the chills. "So you're a Wincott, but you can't tell anyone? But Hank knows, right? He made you a *secretary* instead of a cousin."

Beatrice makes a face of pure rage. "Shut up or I really will shoot you."

My heart skips a beat. There's something funny about the way she put that. Like she'd prefer not to. "You don't really want to shoot me, right? Too messy. You won't get away with it again."

She shakes her head. "I have a better plan this time."

61

NATALIE

"And what does Beatrice look like?" her father asks.

He'd answered the phone right away. He'd jumped off the stage and gone outside to take Natalie's call.

"She's . . . blonde. Very pretty. A little younger than mom." Her voice trembles a little. The fact that her father is taking this so seriously makes it more scary, not less.

"Straight hair? Kind of a ski slope nose? Like . . . Sorority Barbie?"

"Yes," Natalie gasps. "Why?"

"I met her. She seemed to know who I am. Doesn't matter. We have to find your mom. Where does she usually run?"

Natalie has to admit that she doesn't know.

"Could she be at work after hours?"

"With the dog?" That doesn't make sense.

"Got a better idea?"

"No," she admits. She pictures her mom with the dog on a leash and that skinny fanny pack she wears. Her earbuds in her ears.

Oh! The earbuds!

"Wait—hold on one second."

"Okay. Why?"

"Because . . ." She navigates to the menu of apps on her phone and opens the FriendFinder app again. Her mother still doesn't appear on the "friends" menu, but the app actually has two jobs. It keeps track of people and helps to find lost devices. Natalie flips to the devices menu and scrolls past her own stuff to her mother's section. She taps on the icon for her mother's earbuds.

And there they are—a cheery little picture of wireless earbuds right on Bond Street.

"Omigod, she's at the mansion!" Natalie springs off the couch and grabs her shoes.

"Hey, don't just run over there," her dad says. "Let me check it out."

"But I'm so much closer," she argues. "Like, five minutes on my bike."

"Wait—"

Natalie is already shoving her phone in her pocket.

"So where'd you leave things with Hank?" Beatrice has a lot of questions about who I've spoken to and what I've said.

Stalling, I've alternated between self-aggrandizing lies and outright refusals to answer.

"Why do you care?" I yell back this time.

Lickie barks. She's stress-drooling and chewing the shit out of her leash. But every time she gives it a yank with her strong neck, it holds.

"I have to know what to write in your suicide note," she says. "Hank is really embarrassed about trying to maul you the other night." She snorts. "Then you blew off a meeting and took most of two work days off. This morning I told him you seemed distraught."

Suicide note. "But nobody will believe that I shot myself. Not after you broke my dominant hand."

"Doesn't matter," she says. "Kick off your shoes and your socks."

"What?"

"Now."

Buying time, I toe out of one of them, moving slowly. "You don't have to do this. We could just walk out of here. You probably didn't mean to kill Tim, right? You two had a disagreement."

"He was an idiot," she hisses. "He thought I'd spill the tea on the Wincott family. He said he was going to write the damn article no matter what."

"So you thought shooting him would fix it? You have to know you'll get caught eventually."

"He got angry at me when I was grabbing his notebooks out of the back seat. Then I opened his glove box to see if there were more. I picked up the gun to shut him up."

My heart feels like it might explode. "And you just pulled the trigger."

"He tried to grab it!" She aims the gun at me again. "Stop talking. Maybe I didn't go to Cornell, but I'm not stupid. Give me your other shoe before I break something else of yours."

I wedge the other running shoe off my foot. Beatrice kicks both shoes away from me. She aims the gun at my head. "Roll over. Onto your stomach. The best you can." Her finger massages the side of the gun, and I'm afraid to look away. But I make myself do it.

God God God. I know I should keep talking. Arguing. But my mind is white noise. I curl my body toward the railing, my hand useless, throbbing.

It's a shock when Beatrice's weight comes down on my hips, flattening me to the floor, pinning my feet with what must be her forearm.

I wriggle on instinct, but she's got leverage on her side. Then I hear the sound of ripping tape, and two seconds later she's binding my ankles together. I try to bounce her off me, but she's a heavy weight on the backs of my knees.

My dog howls.

"All right," she says. "Now we're ready."

Ready for what?

She grabs my thighs, and I suddenly understand. "You're going to throw me over."

"Yes." She loops an arm around my lower legs and hoists them off the floor. "You're not even the first person to die this way. If it's good enough for her, it's good enough for you."

The words barely penetrate. I'm struggling with all my might. If she manages to wrestle me over the railing, I'm dead for sure.

Beatrice is smart. She's pulling me away from the balustrade where my hand is cuffed, limiting my leverage. I try to curl inward, using my abs to jerk out of her grasp. But her grip is too tight on my ankles.

Still fighting, I close my eyes and picture Natalie's perfect face. *I'm sorry, baby. I'm trying.* But Beatrice hoists me farther off the floor, and I think: *At least she has her father.*

Harrison. I screamed at him today. That *cannot* be the last conversation we ever have. I let my body go suddenly slack. It's the only trick I have left.

Beatrice is forced to adjust her grip, and it slows her down. So when I suddenly yank my knees in toward my core and flail my broken hand toward her head, I take her by surprise. I get a handful of her hair and tug as hard as I can.

She makes a noise of rage and I feed off it. I use the advantage to twist my bony knees into her face. And I discover there's more fight left in me. So much more.

I hear pounding. A fist on a distant door. And maybe the squeak of the mail slot.

"*Mom?*" Natalie shouts.

Lickie goes berserk.

"*Call 911!*" I scream.

"Shut up!" Beatrice hisses, fumbling for the gun. Her face is red and sweaty. "And shut your mouth." She turns and points the gun at Lickie, who's straining at the leash.

Then it snaps.

I see the dog fly forward.

Beatrice takes a sudden step backward and trips, one arm windmilling as she starts to go down.

Lickie's body arches toward Beatrice, who screams.

There's a deafening bang as the gun goes off. The sound is followed immediately by the piercing crash of breaking glass.

A scream lodges in my throat. Lickie lands on Beatrice with all four paws and clamps her jaws onto Beatrice's arm with a growl that would frighten the devil.

Beatrice screams, the gun dangling from her fingers.

I do one more ab curl and use my bound feet to awkwardly kick her hand. I hear the satisfying sound of the gun sliding across the wood floor, out of reach.

Beatrice screams again, this time in agony. Lickie makes another terrifying sound, while I suck in the sudden breeze. Above me, there's a gray, cloudy sky where there should be a century-old, stained-glass window.

I'm trying to make sense of that when I hear more glass breaking somewhere else in the house. "Rowan?" yells Harrison's voice. "Are you there?"

"YES!" I shout back.

I am. I'm still here.

63

NATALIE

Natalie is pretty fast, but her father *flies* up those stairs.

Broken glass crunches under their feet as she tears upward toward the sound of someone screaming. And the dog is making unholy noises, like a creature from a horror film.

Her father clears the stairs first. "Lickie, OFF!" he shouts.

Then her mother's voice says something unintelligible.

Natalie is so scared that her legs almost give out. She makes it to the third floor a few seconds after Harrison.

There's blood everywhere. It's literally flowing toward her shoes, and soaking Beatrice's hair. And there's a smell. Like wet pennies.

Her mother is lying haphazardly on the floor, one arm chained to the balusters, the other hand bent in a sickening way that hands shouldn't bend. Her eyes are closed, but her chest rises and falls in great gasps.

Natalie hears sirens.

Her father's voice breaks through her terror. "Natalie, look at me."

She turns her head toward the steadiness of his voice, finding his gray-eyed gaze and holding it.

"Go downstairs and let the cops in. Tell them to call an ambulance and that there's a gun here on the third floor. Go now."

She looks once again at her mom, who's obviously in pain. But her chest rises reassuringly with each new breath.

Then she turns and runs to do what her father asked.

64

SUNDAY

ROWAN

I open my eyes, but the room swims, and I let them fall closed again. Everything is heavy.

"Hey, Gallagher," says a voice nearby. "Feel like waking up? I'll buy you a beer."

Harrison.

With great effort, I open my eyes. All these years later I still feel the pull. It's strong enough to motivate me to roll my eyes toward his voice.

I find him sitting close to my hospital bed, stroking my left hand. My right one feels immobile, and it takes me a moment to remember why. "How'd it go?" I croak, meaning the surgery I just had.

"Pretty good," he says, a furrow in his handsome forehead. "They got all the bones lined up where they want them. No surprises."

"Okay." I relax against the pillow. "Let the healing begin. Where is Natalie?"

"Doing donuts on my motorcycle in the parking lot."

"Harrison."

He gives me a sly grin. "Tessa brought a pizza. They're eating it in the hospital cafeteria. I told her I'd text her when you woke up. So hang on . . ." He lets go of my hand and pulls out his phone.

"You can let her eat."

"Yeah, but she made me promise."

It's been two days since Beatrice attacked me. I spent yesterday having my hand scanned and waiting for the hand surgeon to decide on his course of action. Between medical exams, Detective Fry asked me questions until I was so exhausted that I literally fell asleep in the middle of a conversation with him.

I'm not sure how useful I was. My memory of what happened after Natalie came pounding up the staircase is pretty shaky. I'm told that I managed to convey two things clearly: that the gun was loaded, and that Beatrice had been trying to kill me.

I have only vague memories of Harrison struggling—and finally succeeding—to pull Lickie off Beatrice.

Beatrice lost a lot of blood after Lickie nicked an artery, but somehow survived. She'll be charged in Tim's death and my attempted murder. And she'll be undergoing a psychiatric evaluation.

In the meantime, I'll be spending the next several months rehabbing my hand and trying to regain my grip strength and range of motion. That crazy bitch stomped on my drafting hand.

Thinking about it makes me burn. *Another* person I trusted.

The recovery-room nurse comes buzzing by to check on me. She makes some notes on my chart and encourages me to sit up a few degrees as the anesthetic wears off. Her energy exhausts me. "Can I have some water, please?"

"Here." Harrison produces a cup with a straw from a table on wheels. He brings the straw close to my face.

I still have one good hand, so I take the cup and help myself. But when I'm done, he gently puts the cup back. Then he takes my hand in his and kisses the back of it, his beard tickling my skin.

It's so confusing to realize that the man who gave me all my trust issues is the one I can most rely on right now. He's taking good care of me, and of our daughter. I'm basically staring at him in wonder as Natalie comes prancing through the door.

"Mom! How does it feel?"

Astonishing is my first thought, as Harrison gently squeezes my hand in his. But Natalie is talking about my hand. "Ask me in a couple weeks, baby. But right now, I'm fine."

Her smile is tired, because it's been a terrifying week.

But it's a little less terrifying now.

———————

They move me to a regular hospital room a little later, and I spend the afternoon napping. My father comes by to see how I'm doing.

I hadn't told him that Harrison was staying with us, and apparently he got a little testy when Harrison called him to tell him that I'd been hospitalized. I heard Natalie take the phone and more or less tell her grandpa to knock it off.

He's behaved himself ever since. And after spending a few minutes asking questions about my surgical outcome, he makes an announcement. "I've come to steal Natalie away for dinner and a movie marathon."

"That sounds like a great idea," I agree.

"Maybe she'll want to stay with you tonight," Harrison suggests in a quiet voice. "If so, I'd stay here with Rowan."

You don't have to do that. The words are on the tip of my tongue, but I fall asleep before I can say them.

———————————

The next time I resurface, it's because of the urgent tone in Harrison's voice. He's having a whispered argument with a hospital worker.

"Sir, I can't give you any information about another hospital patient. It's against privacy laws."

"I'm not asking you for her social security number," he grinds out. "I just need to know if she's still a patient in this hospital. Because if she is, I'm not leaving this room."

Oh.

It hadn't occurred to me to worry about Beatrice climbing out of bed to finish the job she started.

The nurse lets out a heavy sigh. "There's a patient on another floor of the hospital with restraints and a policeman stationed outside her door."

"Thank you," he says stiffly.

"I can find you an ottoman. You'll be more comfortable overnight."

"Much obliged."

When I wake up again, Harrison asks me what I want for dinner. "Maybe I can get somebody to deliver to the hospital."

We're just reviewing our choices when there's a knock on the door. Officer Riley pokes her head into the room. "Hi, guys. Can I come in?"

Harrison gets a sour look on his face. "Only if you keep your handcuffs to yourself this time."

She flinches. "Yeah, I'm sorry about that. It's what I came to tell you both." She walks all the way in and takes a deep breath. "I just wanted to say that I'm sorry you had to live through that. We didn't look closely enough at Beatrice. And I regret it."

"I didn't exactly catch on, either," I admit. "Makes me feel like a fool."

She shakes her head. "That woman is a gifted liar."

"Not to mention straight-up crazy," Harrison mutters.

"It will be a while until we piece together a full picture of what she did," Riley says. "She's given us a partial confession—before she halted the interview and asked for a lawyer. But I feel confident that she won't be a free woman anytime soon."

"Thank you," I say quietly.

"Now, regarding Tim . . ." She gives me a slightly nervous glance. "It seems that Beatrice destroyed most of his notes. But she kept the pages where he wrote about you. They were supposed to, uh . . ."

"Make my suicide look like heartbreak," I supply. "She mentioned that."

Harrison makes a noise of dismay.

"Well . . ." Riley clears her throat. Then she looks pointedly at Harrison. "Is there any way that Rowan and I could have a private conversation? I want to share something with her, and it's sensitive."

To my surprise, he gets right up. "Do me a favor and stay here until I get back, detective? I'm going to get us some dinner."

"I could do that," she says.

"Good." He snaps his fingers. "You're on duty, officer. Stay sharp." Then he takes his leave.

Riley waits until the door closes before giving me a funny little smile. "Ex-cons aren't usually my thing, but he seems like more of a catch than I expected."

"I noticed that, too," I say. "We seem to be an evolving story. Now what did you want to tell me?"

She purses her lips. Then she sits down in Harrison's chair and speaks to me in a hushed voice. "Listen, I took some photos of Tim's notes," she says quietly. "They're not the kind of notes I would expect from a journalist writing a story. They're more like full-fledged journal entries."

"Like . . . dear diary?"

"Almost." She spares a glance toward the door, as if to make sure it's still closed. "I could get fired for sharing them with you."

"But you're going to anyway?" I guess. "I won't tell a soul."

"I feel like I owe you." She pulls her iPad out of her shoulder bag and flips open the cover. "Read this. Just this page. It says a lot."

June 3rd—

Made a decision today. Not an easy one. But R's daughter called me out. Was at Black Cow with J . . .

I blink at the page. This is about Natalie? Black Cow is a burger joint with excellent fries. She goes there with her friends.

Didn't notice N until I paid the bill and J went to the ladies. N comes up to me @ the bar, red face, so angry. Accuses me of cheating on her mom. Says I should be ashamed, and she saw me going through R's phone.

Didn't even defend myself, because she's right. Not about cheating. But she's right on the basic facts. I met R for research purposes. She's spectacular. Maybe even perfect. But I can't think of a way to come clean that doesn't make me sound like an ass & a thief. Which I guess I am. Plus, my job is in NY.

Will do the right thing and let her go.

"Oh shit."

"Yeah," Riley says quietly.

"My daughter didn't mention to me that she'd told him off. Maybe she thinks I'd be mad." I feel a rush of love for my girl and her righteous anger on my behalf.

Riley takes the iPad back. "I just thought you needed to know. He thought you were spectacular. Maybe even perfect."

"Nobody is perfect."

But poor Tim. He made me feel unlucky. Then he turned out to be the unluckiest of all.

"You described your relationship to me, and now that I've read this, I know you were telling me the whole truth." She taps the iPad and then puts it away. "My job is brutal sometimes. I have to look at everyone like a would-be criminal."

I lean back against the pillow and think that over for a minute. "For fifteen years, I've been looking at the men in my life as would-be criminals. And, unlike you, it's not because of my job."

"It's your hobby," she says. And we both laugh.

65

NATALIE

When she hears the car pull into the garage, she's in the kitchen putting groceries away with her grandfather.

"They're back!" her grandpa says. "I'll put the coffee on. You open the door and then hold the dog. Can't let 'er jostle your mom's hand, okay?"

"Yeah, I got it." Natalie pulls the door open and then intercepts Lickie when she comes flying through the kitchen to investigate. "Sit," she says.

Lickie sits.

"Good girl," Natalie whispers. She's been told to monitor Lickie carefully and to be both firm and calm with her. They have to watch closely for any signs of doggie PTSD. There's a risk that Lickie could become quicker to violence after her justified attack of She Who Must Not Be Named.

Natalie won't let that happen.

It takes a minute for her parents to appear in the doorway, her mother first, carefully cradling her hand in a fiberglass cast. Her father appears just behind her, grasping her elbow as if to help her into the kitchen.

"I've got it, Harrison. No need to hover."

Her father steps back, contrite, and then follows her into the kitchen when he can.

"How's the hand?" her grandpa asks, folding up the last grocery bag.

"Painful," her mother sighs. "But I'm pretty happy to be out of that hospital. Natalie, would you put a plastic bag on my cast for me in a few minutes? I'm desperate for a shower."

"Sure."

Natalie ends up sitting on the toilet seat while her mom showers, assisting with the shampoo bottle and the conditioner.

"What a pain in the ass this is," her mother grumbles. "Can you hand me a towel in a sec?"

"Yup."

Together, they do the clumsy work of shutting off the water and wrapping her mother in terry cloth. "What if I brushed out your hair?" Natalie asks.

"Maybe just this once."

"What clothes will be easiest to put on?"

"Good question. I don't really want you to button my jeans."

Natalie laughs. "Let me find you some sweats. Let's be quick, because I'm supposed to go to work at noon."

"Is your dad working, too?" her mother asks.

"Nope. We're alternating for a little while. Just until you can, you know, get dressed without help."

"This is a disaster," her mother complains.

"No, it's really not," Natalie insists.

It was close. But she knows the difference.

66

From: Zoya Anastos
To: Rowan Gallagher

OMG Rowan! We are all appalled. I wish I'd had half a clue about Beatrice, but she totally had me fooled.

I *liked* that bitch. That pisses me off.

Anyway, you might not care about the mansion, and I wouldn't blame you. But in case you were worrying about the rain getting in through the skylight opening and soaking all the woodwork and paintings you had restored, don't worry. It wasn't that bad. They boarded that sucker up pretty fast.

Today I heard the contractors discussing the window. Stained glass that size is super spendy, so Hank is probably going to have plain glass installed up there for now instead. As a conservator, I'm not supposed to say this, but I'm not that sorry the old triple penis is gone. Sue me.

Seems like the Orangerie you had planned is on hold? They took all the earth movers away, and the tool trailer, too.

You know what else is gone? The ghost. No lie. Maybe she escaped out of the gaping hole in the ceiling. I just don't sense her anymore. The aura around here is shiny and bright.

Please take care of yourself. Maybe this is just workplace gossip, but I heard your dog attacked Beatrice, and also that you have a punk-rock boyfriend who had to pull her off. I hope all that is true.:)

Let me know when I can come and visit and show you photos of the last Poseidon painting. He's menacing another water sprite. But the colors are great.

Thinking of you,
—Z

67

ROWAN

The next few days are rough. I spend too much time sitting on the couch, waiting for my next dose of Advil.

Harrison putters around the house, trying to make me comfortable. He feeds me inventive sandwiches, a delicious gazpacho, and more of those homemade crackers. And does an admirable job ignoring my terrible mood.

I know I'm supposed to be grateful to be alive, and I am. But my hand is often throbbing, and I feel clumsy and helpless.

And there's an endless stream of visitors. Detective Fry interviews me again. The police are finally digging into the history of the Wincott Foundation and Tim's adoption scandal. They want to build an airtight case against Beatrice. "What did she know, and how did she know it," he explains.

I help where I can.

But then, on Sunday, someone else knocks on the door. And when Harrison goes to answer it, I see his shoulders tense up.

"Hi," says a voice from the front stoop. "Can I come in for a second?"

"I guess," Harrison grumbles.

He opens the door, and Hank Wincott strides in, dressed like an ad for Ralph Lauren weekend wear. He comes to an awkward stop in front of the coffee table, folding and then unfolding his arms as if he can't decide where to put them. "Hey, Rowan."

It's the most uncomfortable I've ever seen Hank.

"Have a seat." I indicate the nearby slipper chair.

"Thanks. So . . ." He sits down with a wince. "I just came to say how sorry I am and how badly I feel about everything that happened. As soon as the lawyers can draft it, the foundation will be offering you a settlement. It'll be a generous package for your medical and recovery costs, plus lost income. And a buyout of your contract, so you don't ever have to set foot in the mansion again. Unless you want to, of course."

"Not fucking likely," Harrison mutters. "Would *you* want to go back to work where someone tried to kill you?"

Hank winces again. "Probably not, no. But I just want to say that we're cooperating with all requests from law enforcement. And when the lawyers are ready, you can take a look at the settlement and tell me what you think. No rush." He rubs his neck awkwardly. "I'm just really sorry. I didn't know Beatrice was unraveling like that."

Something about the way he says it makes me ask a follow-up question. "Has she been mentally ill *before*?"

"She's had . . . manic episodes," he says, clearing his throat. "As a teenager. But none recently. The thing is, though, anyone could hire an employee who might suddenly exhibit a grave mental illness. What I feel bad about is not realizing how she felt about the family. The Wincotts."

"So you knew she was your cousin?" That's the big question burning inside me.

"My first cousin once removed," he corrects. "But, yeah, I knew she was Marcus's daughter. My family paid for her education and gave her a job." His ears are turning a shade of red that I've never seen on Hank before. "And I knew she had big ambitions. She wanted that director's position, even though I'd always told her that it was out of the question."

"But that's not all she wanted, right? She was your family's dirty little secret," I clarify. "For her, it wasn't just about a job."

He sighs. "You could put it like that."

"She wanted to be a bigger part of your family," I press. "She wanted to be a Wincott."

"I guess." He shrugs. "My family has a long history, and some of it is godawful. So I didn't truly understand her burning desire to join the clan."

Harrison snorts.

Hank turns his attention to Harrison. "Sorry, I don't believe we've officially met. I'm Hank Wincott. And according to some journalist who's been hounding me this week . . ." He clears his throat again. "You and I might be related, too."

Harrison goes still. Then his eyes flick up to Hank's, before he looks away again. "That theory has come up," he says. "But I don't know."

"You, uh, could find out," Hank says. "Marcus Wincott obviously never anticipated DNA testing. But I'm sure I'll be swabbing my cheek any day now when this story breaks and people wonder if Portland is full of unknown Wincotts."

"I'll bear that in mind," Harrison says stiffly.

Hank nods. "Meanwhile, I'll be spending the foreseeable future in rooms full of lawyers, untangling all the messes the foundation is in," he says. "But I want you both to know that we'll take full responsibility for whatever happened in the past."

A girl could almost feel sorry for him. Almost. "And what about Beatrice?"

He sighs again. "The police will build their case against her—for murder, attempted murder, and some kind of drug charge."

"Because of Laura Peebles?" I ask.

He nods. "I don't know much about that part. But Beatrice's lawyer will argue that she's incompetent to stand trial, by reason of insanity."

"A lawyer that you're paying for?" Harrison asks.

"Well, probably. I know I'm not supposed to feel sorry for her, but somebody has to. And it's such a waste of potential. Beatrice is smart and talented."

"And deeply disturbed," Harrison adds.

"True." Hank does that thing where he rubs his neck again. "I believe her mother was mentally ill. Maybe you've heard the rumors, but she took her own life in the mansion."

"Wait, did she . . ." My throat goes suddenly dry. "Did she go over the railing?"

Hank spreads his hands. "I can't confirm or deny. But when I was a kid, that was the story I heard."

"Is that why the house stood empty for so many years after Marcus died?"

"Probably. But I was thirteen when he died. Not exactly brought in on all the big family decisions."

"You are now, though," I point out. "And some of those family decisions are going to be examined if Beatrice goes to trial."

"And even if she doesn't," Hank says, sounding resigned. He stands up. "There's a lot to be done. You know where to find me, Rowan. I'll have some paperwork to you in the next few days. And please don't worry about anything job related. I've asked the new girl to call every contractor and let them know that we've hit pause on the site."

"The new girl," I echo, rising to walk him to the door. "What's her *name*?"

He winces. "Yeah, I've got to stop calling her that. Her name is Lisette. She's still not as efficient as Beatrice used to be. But on the positive side, I don't think she's a murderer."

"Hang on to her, then," I say.

When we get to the door, Hank pauses. "Let me just say one more time that I'm sorry I embarrassed you after the dinner, too. That was very bad behavior."

"I've forgotten it already." It's true—if only because I've been very busy trying not to die.

We shake hands very awkwardly, because my right hand is out of commission. And then he leaves.

Returning to the sofa, I sit down beside Harrison. He's got his feet propped up on the coffee table and a distant look in his eye.

I take his hand in mine, which is a thing that I seem to do now. He's basically worn me down with homemade soup and soft glances. Propping my feet up on the coffee table beside his, I ask what's on his mind.

He strokes his thumb across my palm and doesn't answer for a moment. "Nothing much," he says. And it sounds a little evasive.

"Look, I know I'm the neurotic one, and you're Mr. Cool and Collected. But a billionaire just sat here and wondered if maybe he's your cousin. You barely blinked. And you never even said whether you thought the B. Jones on that list was your mom. Aren't you curious? There could be a settlement for you."

He goes quiet beside me.

"Harrison? What aren't you saying?"

He tilts his head back and stares up at my antique tin ceiling. "Maybe I'm not curious, because I already had a hunch."

"What? Why am I hearing about this only now?"

He reaches across the sofa and tips me carefully over, so my head is in his lap. And then he smooths my hair away from my face and starts talking. "I definitely heard the name Wincott a few times when I was growing up. Whispered conversations. Didn't think much about it."

"And . . . ?"

He shrugs. "And some guy sent us checks every month for most of my childhood. But then the checks stopped. And my mother got pretty desperate. That's when I heard the name Wincott one more time—one night when she was on the phone. 'That asshole died,' she said. 'Wincott died and I can't make the rent.'"

I remember to exhale.

"So, yeah, I had a hunch that I finally knew my father's name. But it didn't matter, Ro. He was just a name and a check. He never once met me. Never showed up to a Little League game. Some kids are just trained not to ask, you know? You're nobody. No father will claim you. And it's better not to ask, because the truth won't sound very good."

It's hard to swallow, because I realize I did this to Natalie, too. My silence made the topic shameful, whether I meant it to or not.

"So, yeah, I don't feel a lot of sympathy for Beatrice. But at least I understand her deep well of crazy. She spent her life kissing up to the Wincotts, waiting for the moment they'd claim her for real. Somehow, she convinced herself that if she was a really good little soldier, they'd make her a copy of the key to the castle."

"Ouch."

"Yeah, ouch. And then Kovak follows his own trail of breadcrumbs, tries to interview her, and says he's going to blow her father's reputation sky high." He snaps his fingers. "And just like that, she breaks."

"That sounds plausible."

He smooths my hair away from my face. "It's just my take. But I know what mistakes you can make when someone tells you that you don't matter. It's an ugly cycle. I did the same thing to you and Natalie. And I'll always regret it. But I don't need any of Hank's money. I'm getting my life back together without his help."

My eyes feel hot, because I believe him. I'm still mad that he wrote us off. But I can understand how it happened. "Seems like you're campaigning pretty hard for Father of the Year. I think you'll get Natalie's vote."

"Yours counts, too," he says softly. "Actually, there's something I need to show you, and I haven't found the right moment. Can I show you now?"

"Sure, as long as it isn't a piano concerto you want me to play." I sit up, taking care not to bump my cast.

"Yeah, Lefty. I know." He leaves the sofa for a minute, fetching something out of his room.

Is it weird that I've come to think of it as his?

He returns a moment later, holding a passport. No, it's an old-style bankbook. But he doesn't hand it to me. "Fifteen years ago, I did a thing, and at the time it felt like an inevitable decision. But I don't know anymore." He sits down and flops the booklet into my lap. "I'm not sure you heard, but your parents offered me money to sign away any parental relationship with Natalie."

Oh. "I did know that. My mother told me."

He rubs his forehead. "Okay, well. Your mother said it was the right thing to do."

"The right thing to do," I repeat slowly.

"She said it would be easier on you if I broke off contact and just disappeared. That you could start over. I didn't want her blood money, so I put it in Natalie's name. For college. And I've been adding to it with my gig money, which is peanuts. But there's, like, seven grand in there now. It's in her name."

I press my hands against my mouth and taste bile in the back of my throat.

He frowns. "You don't have to give it to her now. You could wait until she's older."

I swallow hard and flip open the booklet with my good hand. It's a passbook savings account from Fore River Savings Bank. The balance is around seven grand, like he said. And the most recent deposit was just last month. One hundred dollars.

The account's owner is my daughter, with Harrison listed as the custodian.

"She told me you took the money," I whisper. "Didn't even put up a fight."

"Well, I didn't," he says quietly. "She said that Natalie deserved a father who wasn't behind bars. And that if you two had a real chance at happiness, it was selfish of me to stand in your way. I believed her, honey."

"Shit." I drop the bankbook onto the coffee table just as an inconvenient tear rolls down my face. "I loved you so much. All I needed was for you to love me back."

"Yeah." His voice is rough. "But I had a voice in my head telling me I was never good enough for you. And, uh, your mother's actual voice saying the same thing. She's not here to defend herself, Ro, so I feel bad saying all this. But she told me I was a terrible father."

It's not very hard to picture. My mother was so angry when Harrison got arrested. She raged, and said it only confirmed what she already knew about him.

"She said the right thing to do was give Natalie up. And I believed her."

God, they said the same thing to Laura Peebles at the Magdalene Home. "I'm so sorry. I hate that she did that."

He reaches over, puts his hands under me like a forklift, and pulls me into his lap. "She probably thought she was doing the right thing for Natalie."

"And yet Natalie wouldn't agree." I tuck my head against his shoulder and relax into his arms.

He drops his head and kisses my jaw. And then my neck.

I forget what we were talking about, because he cups my chin and tastes my lips slowly. The way a vintner takes a contemplative taste of a new blend.

I wrap my good arm around him. "Harrison?"

"Mmm?" He kisses me again.

"Would you ever want to move upstairs?"

"Yeah, right now," he says, kissing the corner of my mouth. "While the kid is at work."

"No, I meant for real."

"How about . . ." He kisses my throat. "Right now, and then also later."

"Okay. Sure."

He stands up suddenly, keeping me tightly in his arms. "Hold on, Gallagher. Watch that hand, m'kay?"

I let him carry me toward the stairs. Both animals follow us. "Your cat sure made herself at home," I point out as he begins the climb.

"Yeah, I still owe her fifty bucks for that," he says.

I laugh so hard that he has trouble carrying me.

68

CORALIE

She walks slowly up the stairs, the same way she has every day for twenty-five years. When she reaches the top, she'll do a slow tour of the third floor and gaze out her favorite window.

Her baby girl isn't here at the mansion today. She wasn't here yesterday, either. But this doesn't bother Coralie much, as she has only a vague sense of time.

Maybe her girl will come back tomorrow. She isn't worried, because her girl is strong, and she loves this house almost as much as Coralie does.

She'll be back.

On the third floor, she discovers some men standing on a scaffolding, taking careful measurements of the window opening. They're wearing hard hats and work boots and pencils behind their ears.

She drifts past them without so much as a glance. There's no need to pester them anymore. She won't flicker the lights or drop their tools, because she's in a peaceful mood these days.

This is *her* house. It will always be hers now. She won it the hard way. And now that they've removed the tool trailer, things are back the way they should be.

Moving leisurely, she sweeps into her favorite third-floor room. Unlike most visitors to the house, she favors a view of the back of the property. She stops at her favorite window and sees that the grass is growing back in, now that the hideous tool trailer is gone.

This is the unobstructed view that makes her happy—the one of Mr. Wincott's headstone. This is her favorite spot in the whole house, because she can see the crisp granite monument rising from the grass. With the baby angels carved into its surface.

Every day she visits him. It's a ritual. Now she leans through the glass in the window and feels the breath of the wind rush through her.

Then, as she always does, she spits—three stories—right down onto Marcus Wincott's grave.

ACKNOWLEDGMENTS

To the incredible team that turned this book from a wild dream into reality—you're all rock stars!

Sarah Stein at HarperCollins, thanks for seeing the potential in this story and helping me polish it until it shined. Megan Looney, your marketing magic is unmatched. And Heather Drucker, publicist extraordinaire, thank you for getting this book into readers' hands.

To my dream team at CAA—Mollie Glick and Olivia Romano, your enthusiasm and support mean the world to me.

Melissa Frain, Edie Danford, Claudia Fosca Stahl, and KJ Dell'Antonia—my literary lifesavers! Each of you swooped in at different moments to rescue this book from the brink. I owe you all a lifetime supply of chocolate and/or wine.

Pi Smith, thank you for letting me pick your brain for architecture wisdom! Your insights were invaluable in bringing authenticity to the story.

And a big thank-you to Lt. Tim Cotton (Ret.) of the Bangor Police Department. Your expertise on Maine murder investigations added that crucial touch of realism. Don't worry, I promise I'm not planning any real-life crimes.

As always, all mistakes are my own.

Love,
Sarina

ABOUT THE AUTHOR

Sarina Bowen is a twenty-four-time *USA Today* bestselling author, and a *Wall Street Journal* bestselling author of contemporary romance novels. Formerly a derivatives trader on Wall Street, Sarina holds a BA in economics from Yale University.

DON'T MISS SARINA BOWEN'S
DEBUT THRILLER

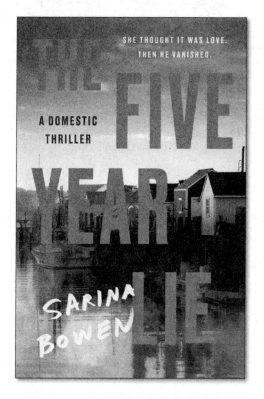

"More than just a twisty thriller. . . . explores themes of loyalty and family, motherhood, and the tragedy of having to say goodbye too soon. I devoured this book in one day, and I guarantee you will too."

— JULIE CLARK,

New York Times bestselling author of *The Last Flight and The Lies I Tell*